THE NAIVE DARING

VOLUME 1

OF

OUTSIDERS

A NOVEL

Ryan E. Long

TABLE OF CONTENTS

PREFACE

Some have been protecting devilish priests through the years. At times, they are transferred to different jurisdictions to avoid prosecution.

Throughout history, however, an invisible hand has assisted others in the Vatican in fighting such tyranny. During World War II, for example, heroic Catholic priests in Italy stealthily and quietly saved Jewish and Allied escapees from Adolf Hitler's talons – often using very mysterious means.

In the following pages, consider whether some of America's dodgiest pitch-black outlaws are guiltless decoys for a powerful unforeseen force.

Enjoy your read,

Ryan E. Long

CHAPTER ONE

PASSED AROUND

"How long have you been sinning?" I asked 45-year old Father Luther Wolf over the long country table this morning, June 30, 1876, in the church mess hall.

"Since I was 12," he said as his Viking blue right eye just stared at me. His other eye had a black leather patch on it. Found out about why he had that patch on it later, you'll see.

"I thought things would have changed," the 45 year old said with his eye looking down on his six foot four frame, "after I joined the church. But I feel like the sinning has only gotten worse."

These were surprising words from a man who'd been a priest for twenty-six years in San Francisco's Mission Dolores Parish. As for me, I joined the priesthood in the start of this month.

Wolf and I had talked a few times about Church politics, the Mission's flock, and other things about California. He seemed to like me, and feel comfortable with me. Maybe it's because cause nobody else talked to him much except for Father Shane Egan and Sister Emerald Beem, who I always saw with Father Wolf.

Cold medieval walls surrounded Father Wolf and I as we sat at the table. As always, we were wearing our priestly uniforms — black suits, white priestly collars, well manicured, and freshly shaven. It was Sunday morning, about 8:00, and our Churchly duties were about to begin for the day.

"When did the sinning start?" I asked carefully asked Father Wolf as I sipped my cowboy coffee.

Wolf put down his mug of coffee. His hair was real long, like he never been to cut it. He slowly answered my:

"Reckon it done started right after they killed my Injun parents," he at me with his calm blue right eye. "Injun," just in case you didn't know, means Native American. I just stared at Wolf's chiseled chin and his claw like hands, which looked like they had choked a lot of animals before he ate them for supper.

"Who killed your parents?" I asked as I put my spoon down. I wanted to make sure I gave him my full attention.

"The U.S. government," Wolf answered without waiting.

"And why did they kill your Injun parents?"

"Done reckon cause they had the wrong color skin, and was in the wrong place at the wrong time with that skin, in the way of them manifest destiny folks who wanted to go West."

I leaned back in the stiff wooden chair. I had never felt a stiffer chair, even though I was born Jasper Amos in Rocky Mount, which is in Franklin County, Virginia, to be exact, on September 4, 1846. Damn strict authoritarian home, cause my parents was real anal Episcopalians, you know, straight down the line and all.

"So that means you are Injun?" I asked wolf.

"That's a damn good question," Wolf said as he looked around almost like he wanted to make sure nobody listened. He went over to the door leading to the back garden and closed it, stopping the fresh air from backyard visiting itself upon our priestly faces.

"My poppa and momma from Mother Nature done died when I was 10. Some nasty shit plague hit Vandalia, Illinois, which is where I was raised, and killed 9 of out 10 people in my town, and my parents one of them 9," he said as he walked slowly back to the table.

"Did you know your parents well?"

"Yes," he said as he sat down. "I loved them very much. They was some Quakers, I done never seen people like them since. Never went to church cause they thinking that the church in the home, no need for no father to do the deal between you and your maker, you see," he looked back at me as he put his hand into his jacket, and came out with a small silver box. When he opened the box up, I took a whiff, and I don't think I had smelled such a smell before in my life.

"Smoke?" He put the silver box in front of my face.

Put my hand up.

"I quit smoking some time ago, but thank you," I said, my inner demons wanting to join him, but my outer angel telling them no.

"Suit yourself," Wolf said as he took out what looked like a fancy hand rolled cigar with his long calloused hands, which had seen too much sun, rain, wind, and snow to look like they cared anymore if they were on the inside or the outside of some gloves.

He pulled the cigar up his mouth, lit it, and started inhaling in and out as he remembered back to his parents:

"They was some of the most loving people done ever met in my life, cause momma was a teacher and she having all the kids from my school over to play, and poppa was the town doctor,

3

so people looking to him to make them feeling better," he said with emotion in his eyes.

"And so what did you do after they died? I mean, how did you survive?"

"Taken in by an Injun family that was gone to school with me."

"By an Injun family?"

Wolf nodded as he smoked.

"They made me remember what poppa always told me, that we all have a guardian angel or angels by our sides in our lives, might be someone from our past that we thinks is dead, or a spirit from the past or the future who is there to watch over us, and it up to us to listen to that there angel to make us safe, to make sure we have the pure intentions."

I guess he didn't care about the fact that we weren't supposed to smoke inside the Church because Poncho, the Mexican janitor, sometimes bent the rules on Sundays with his own smoking.

"My father was a doctor for them local Injun families and their kids, and momma taught at the local school, where them Injun families sent their little ones."

I could tell the subject made Wolf sentimental.

"Them Injuns loved me like I was their own," Wolf remembered softly and sadly as he looked at the wooden table, a short pause, as he played with the cigar case, "cause they loved momma and poppa like they was Injun."

"Until when did they raise you," I asked as my stout fingers played with the napkin next to my coffee mug.

"Until about 12, which is when them feds came into town and started making the Injun disappear," he said with slightly camouflaged anger. "I woke up one morning and they were gone," Wolf snapped his fingers, "just like that."

"So what did you do then?"

"Government put me in a foster home, but them parents was some mean fucks, not going to be my family, so I ran away when I was about 12, and started running those streets out there," Wolf's

4

head motioned towards the street outside the church. "And it's about that time, Father Jasper, when I done became a sinner," Wolf said as he watched the cigar smoke crawl up towards the stone roof above

"And how did you sin?" I asked.

"You really want to know?" He asked as though he wanted to spare my ears.

"Yes," I nodded.

"In more ways than I can cover this here morning," Wolf looked outside the window for a moment as he thought back, smoking slow like, and then staring back at me as he said: "started living the street wolf life, real rough bunch, but, you know Father Jasper, we ran together and it was alright — cause I was good at picking pockets, doing some hits for hire." Wolf looked at me.

I looked back at him in disbelief.

"What do you mean by hits for hire?"

"What do you mean what do I mean?" He asked.

"What are hits?"

Wolf leaned slightly closer to me over the table, and said in a more quiet voice:

"I done killing me some people for money, don't you see, Father Jasper?"

He leaned back into his chair and behind his Lucifer smoke.

I looked at my soup, I looked at the coffee mug, I looked up at the ceiling, I looked down at my feet, and I looked outside the door, which had God's glorious sun shining just beyond. I wanted to be anywhere else but here looking into Wolf's eye. But I asked for it, and they say that when you ask God for what you need, you shall receive. And I suppose I needed this.

"How many you kill?" I asked after my brief moment of nervous silence.

"Too many to remember," Wolf said. "I only remember their faces," he flicked some ash into a black oyster ashtray.

5

"So, Jesus Christ oh Lord," I said with concern, "what else did you do, Father Wolf?" I said with worry in my face.

"Cause I was so damn good at killing, I did me some bank robbing, too, which has some more moving parts, I reckon. First it was small time stuff, like the local banks, in Southern Illinois. Me and the crew got bored with the easy prey, so I we got more up the ladder and started hitting them big banks in Chicago."

"How many banks?"

"About 19, I think it was 19," Wolf said with a satisfied smile as he looked at his cigar.

"Christ," I said as I looked below the bench at my boots. "Is that why you fled Illinois?" I asked looking back up at Wolf.

"Shit, Father Jasper, I knew I wouldn't have a future in Illinois much long, so, when I learned that we were going to war with the Mexicans, I joined the U.S. Army to get out of the state, done reckon it would have been the perfect escape."

"Was it?"

"Was in the start," he said as he sipped more coffee and passed it through his tobacco-stained teeth. "Cause I escaped from the cold damp winters of Southern Illinois, and landed here in the warm plump breasts of California."

"But?" I asked.

Wolf leaned over the wooden table and confided:

"I ended up going with him."

"With who?" I asked.

"Riley . . . name was . . . John Riley. He was a wily Irishman who formed a battalion called St. Patrick's Battalion to fight for — not against — the Mexicans."

"Really?" I asked with surprise. I had never heard of American soldiers fighting against their own.

"Really," Wolf nodded. "Not many soldiers sticking around in that war, cause they wanting to desert, one of the highest desertion rates ever. A lot of soldiers didn't want to die when they could go to California and find gold. Others didn't much like what we were doing to the Mexicans and, with promises of gold and land from the Mexican government. An Irishman named John Riley formed the battalion."

"So why you came back here, not stay down there?" I asked point blank.

"Right," he nodded as he licked his cigar, "I thought it would been stupid to stay down there when I could get rich up here."

"But there would have been a warrant out for your arrest for fighting with them?" I asked.

"Yes. Most of the men from the Battalion were killed. But some of my Mexican brothers helped me escape. Some up through the wilderness west of Texas."

"So you should be dead?"

"But I not dead," Wolf smiled devilishly as he puffed his cigar. "And so once I made it into that there wilderness, I took what money I had from Mexico and bought some clothes and enough supplies to last me until I am came here."

"And then?"

"Traveled around the backwoods of Texas as much as I could to stay away from the city sheriff posses patrolling for people like me. I huffed it under blue skies, dark skies full of stars, and dark skies full of clouds and rain."

Wolf just stared at his burning cigar for a moment, deep in thought.

"Remember running into this drifter, he a mysterious look-ing drifter with long sideburns," he slowly blew the smoke out while he looked at the cigar. "He got me into smoking these here cigars," he said staring at me. And then, as he looked back at the cigar thinking back: "done remember when I seen the man, cause it was one of them weird ass nights you having in life, you ever have one of those?"

"Like when you wake up in your vomit, or wake up next to a farm animal in bed?"

7

"Well, that's weird," Wolf chuckled, "but this was more spooky." Wolf sat and smoked more.

Had not had many spooky meetings with drifters in my life since I moved to this place they call the city by the bay, or San Francisco, after I graduated from William & Mary in Virginia. I wanted to get away from all that home stiffness I felt in back home, and I reckoned that San Francisco would let me open up to the world more than I could back home. Funny cause, I often find myself missing my innocent childhood there.

"Why you say that night was spooky, Father Wolf?"

"Shit, cause I was in my little camp and Trigger, my horse, was just standing, you know, relaxing, and there was no moon out, just them stars, so it one of them dark nights. Laying there, trying to get my eyes shut, and then I done seen these two shadows of people far off on their horses. One of the shadows had a lit something in their mouth, which stuck out cause there not nothing around but that shadow's lit smoke and the big fire in front of me," Wolf blew some more smoke out, looking at his cigar.

"So these two shadows is coming towards me, and I pull out my rifle, cock it, with ammo at my side, pistol, too. I aim my sniper rifle at the them shadow heads, done tell them I'm going to blow their heads off, but then one of them, a man, saying some shit like they coming in peace. They just needed some warm times on the cold Texas night, so I is letting them come closer, tell them to put their hands up, and when they coming closer, I done see his woman next to him, dark looking eyes, tall, real strong looking, and he just looking, well, um."

"What?" I asked.

"He was downright nice looking, on his face, but there was this secret wicked look to him, like he could get real, what the word, sinister and all, cause he got these real dark hairs on his head, big old graying sideburns, but them eyebrows making him not look human, like he from somewhere else, and those eyes, they was dark, so I couldn't tell, but reckon they was blue, or green, some light things like that. My horse Trigger making the noises like he like these two strangers, and I seeing they got no guns on them, so they coming around the fire, we talking, me saying I going to San Francisco, but they never done tell me where they from — or where they going."

"So what was so spooky about that night?" I took a long swig of my coffee as I heard the mission cook make more breakfast in the kitchen.

"Well," Wolf exhaled a bunch of smoke, "they was an older couple, and they got no guns on them, out in the middle of the desert wilderness. Made me wonder how they was surviving. She making some beans, with some bacon, and he pulling these here cigars out, a shit load," Wolf looked at the cigar he was smoking again, "offering me one up, me smoking the damn thing, and he saying he got them cigars from, where the fuck he say, um, somewhere that not America."

"Cuba?" I asked.

"Don't remember, Father Jasper, just know he got me into these things here," he said as he looked at the cigar. "Never done seen this type of cigar before meeting that there drifter," he looked up as the smoke drifted upwards to the ceiling, "or since." Wolf looked at me, "but maybe I just never done pay attention cause I always liked my cigarettes," he blew the cigar smoke out real slow.

"So we smoking these here cigars in the desert, and this drifter man pulling out the best moonshine I ever done tasting, and I tasting the best that is out there, from wherever you want to say, Virginia, Kentucky, you name it. And we just getting downright fucked up, then I done going to bed, passed out, then waking up in middle of morning twilight, and they is gone, done leaving nothing but a big stack of these here cigars, and a fire that big and bright."

"To keep you warm?" I asked.

"Yea, it was like they was thinking of me like that, just pretty much weirdest night, cause, I reckon, they reminded me of my damn parents, man's old lady looking like, reminding me of mamma, and the man, well, shit, if I done didn't have so much moonshine in me, he like the mirror of my poppa's soul, even though poppa wasn't so wicked looking, but they was like cousins or something, two sides of them coins in our pockets," Wolf just scratched his head, in a way you do when you think you see something, but you are not sure, so you just say you must be dreaming, or some shit. It was one of those scratches.

"That there couple remind me of what I done told you before about them guardian angels and all, cause they felt like that for me, felt like that for sure, cause momma and poppa showed me one time what it mean to have them angels."

"How?"

"One morning momma and poppa acting like they wasn't home, cause they told me they was going out, to the store or something, and I done thinking I was in the house alone, you know, but I kept hearing them things up in the attic, and then I done heard some things down in the basement, but I didn't touch them cookies in the kitchen, the ones that momma told me not to eat, and I didn't touch no money that was in the open safe, cause poppa told me not to touch them things, and I thought about them in my old head when my stomach looking at the cookies and telling me to eat them, or that there money hunger in me, the one that we all got, said take some money, poppa not going to notice."

"But you didn't take the cookies, or the money?"

"No, sir, no sir, I didn't. I just playing with my kid toys and shit, and feeling like I not fearing no Lucifer, cause momma and poppa saying you don't fearing Lucifer when you not doing Lucifer things."

"So you didn't take the cookies or the money," I wanted to draw Wolf out so I probed, "and?"

"Momma and poppa was there the whole licking time! They some tricky beasts like that. She was in the attic, and poppa was in the basement, they was just seeing if I was going to be a good boy, watching down on me through little holes in the ceiling and floor. When she come down, and he come up, I says, 'I thought y'all was gone?' And poppa says to me, 'sometimes people you love leave your side to see how you going to do your life, if you going to be a good boy, it a test, you see, to see if you listening to your angels, the ones we told you would be by your side, and you listened son, you listened, and you passed the test, son,' poppa said."

"Tricky parents, eh?" I said.

"They was tricky in more ways than you know, just real smart, and you thinking they is gone, but they not, and them people in that desert reminded me of them, but . . ."

"But?" I asked.

"Shit," Wolf dipped some of his cigar into the black oyster ashtray, "I knew that they couldn't be no parents of mine, but sure did feel like it, and that what so spooky, the feeling that someone is there, next to you, loving you, even though you knowing all along they below the ground."

"Or above watching down on you from above," I said.

"You got that right, Father Jasper," Wolf held his cigar up to me. He took another long pull on it, not city slicker rushing, this Wolf.

"And, with their help," he looked above, "I made it over," he motioned over to the mountains surrounding San Francisco, "from the wilderness outside Texas to this here city on Trigger."

"Trigger?"

"Yup. My black horse parked out there," Wolf motioned towards the stable outside with a smirk. "Once he and I arrived in San Francisco sometime in May of 1850, I got a place at some shitty hotel, went downstairs for a cup of coffee, stat down to read some local newspaper called the *Californian*, and saw in an advertisement that this here Church was recruiting priests."

He let the cigar ash drip into the ashtray.

"And that's when it hit me," he said with a smile and snapping of his fingers. "I'd escape my sins, past, and them police chasing me by becoming a man of the cloth!"

"When all else fails, when you are down on the luck, join the church?" I asked.

He took a long drag and nodded sarcastically.

"I shaved away my heathen beard, took a long bath so I smelled pure, and went in for that there initial interview."

"It must have went well, huh Wolf? I mean, you are still sitting here, wearing the cloth, and doing your priestly duties."

"You can done say that," Wolf said in his sinister tone, the tone that you would use when you doing something you are not supposed to be doing, like taking your momma's laundry money and gambling with it. "Must admit, now, Father Jasper, that the God's honest truth is," Wolf put his right hand over his heart, "working with these kids here, these families," he looked down to the dirty ground to think, "is making me feel the most home I've found in a long time, since I was with my momma and poppa, even. If you told me before that I'd be a priest, I'd say you was a plum fool, but I reckon that this is the most peace, most free, that I've felt in my dark soul since I was that little boy with my parents back in Illinois, see?"

Wolf slowly took his right hand off his heart.

His right eye gouged out towards me, reaching out like he had put his hand out to touch my shoulder to see if I understood, but his eye did the touching.

"I do, Father Wolf, I do understand," I said, not really seeing what he was saying, seeing only the side of him that I wanted to see at the time, and not the touching side of him that I'd later see, but which I was blind to that day. I had my secret agenda, my secret job to do, and that secret agenda, that secret job, didn't want me to think. While I could tell from our conversation that day that Wolf had many layers that I wanted to understand,

12

I couldn't, because I wasn't supposed to. It wasn't part of my job. I felt like I was in a mental and spiritual straightjacket, feeling trapped, about understanding Wolf's past, so I did what any of you would have done to escape.

I changed the subject.

"See the article this morning in the *Chronicle*?" I asked.

"You mean the one about the priest getting the cat down from the tree for those little kids in North Beach?" Wolf smiled a smart-ass smile.

He knew exactly which article I was asking him about, the opinion piece called *Church Chickens Come Home To Roost*, by Dr. Liza Anscombe, a philosophy professor at the University of California, Berkeley. Dr. Anscombe's article was a commentary on the fifteen Catholic priests murdered in San Francisco so far that year.

As I paused for Wolf's answer, the church cook came out and put our breakfasts on the table.

"Yes," Wolf finally said as he looked at his breakfast — eggs, bacon, biscuit, "I saw Liza Anscombe's article."

"I can't believe they haven't caught the killer yet," I said and then took a big fork full of my own eggs.

"Maybe **they** some killers," Wolf said. "I reckon one killer couldn't do all that killing," he ate some biscuit.

"Anyway," he wiped his face with the napkin, "maybe them priests who got it deserved it, like that Liza professor says in her article. Cause sometimes there is wolves in sheep clothing . . . or I reckon I should say in priest clothing," he smiled at me.

Wolf wasn't the only one thinking this way.

There had been allegations of child abuse by priests in the Church all around the world. San Francisco was no exception. The *Chronicle* had several articles about cases brought against the Church. Wolf and I had talked about the articles a few times since I had arrived at the Mission earlier this month, Wolf always

13

sharing Professor Anscombe's view: that the murders were church chickens coming home to roost. Many Church members, who I'll call the "true believers," didn't share Wolf's — or Professor Anscombe's — opinion. According to a April 19th *Chronicle* article from that year, *5 Priests Hung On Easter Sunday*, about the murders on April 16:

> *All members of the Archdiocese interviewed about these gruesome killings were very upset. Cardinal Maciel Degollado, one of the oldest priests in the Archdiocese, and who is said to have strong connections with the Vatican and current pope, Alberto Scrivener, explained: "Fathers Ricardo Aube, Roger MacRae, Gordon Fortier, Zachery Connor, and Jerry Paralta were well cherished members of this parish. Our flock loved them. Their brothers and sisters in the Church did, too. These men have been serving the poor and other desperate people of the community for years. They will be missed.*

Still, there had been some *Chronicle* articles in which some more radical members of the Archdiocese, who I'll call "true realists," echoed Wolf's — and Professor Anscombe's opinion — about the murders. In one article, *The Underbelly of the Church*, which came out on January 8, 1876, the Chronicle reported that a shadow group of vigilantes called the "crows" or "ravens" leaked sensitive interior Vatican documents to the press on December 25, 1875, showing that the Vatican had a policy of protecting abusive priests.

Some who I have spoken to around the Mission Dolores think the raven are church insiders — priests or nuns — who are opposed the covering up of child abuse by priests, and want to avenge God and Jesus for the Vatican's sins. Others say that the raven are heathen outsiders of the church, members of an old order of witchcraft worshippers in Italy who the Catholic church hunted and killed when it was founded in order to get new converts. These people say the killings were these heathens' revenge against the Church, and also a slap in Church's face, as if to say: "if you are so righteous, so good, then why is that we, us sinners, us outsiders, need to clean up your house — not you?"

One of the leaked documents mentioned in *The Underbelly of the Church* article, called "From the Supreme and Holy Congregation of the Holy Office" and with the "Instruction" on "The Manner of Proceedings in Cases of Solicitation," orders priests to keep "toward impure and obscene matters," such as passing around children, secret. Lawyers who sued the Church on behalf of supposed abused children claim that this document shows that the Vatican was covering up known abuses by either keeping them secret, or transferring the abusive priests to other Archdiocese so that they could avoid prosecution.

For the *Underbelly of the Church* article, a *San Francisco Chronicle* reporter interviewed Father Canon de Vivaldi, an Italian priest in the Vatican, about the hangings of the five priests on April 16 of that year. This Father Vivaldi wasn't so upset about these killings, as you can see from what he says below in the article:

> *It is a sad, cause, um, these killings do not surprising me. Seventeen boys saying in a lawsuit that Father Aube took, how you say, a road trip with them to the Yosemite for four to six weeks, and these boys saying the trip was a 'rape fest' — this cause Father Aube doing the sex contact, against God, with one boy after next in the same 'session.' Another 39 boys saying, eh, in these lawsuits, you now understanding, that Father MacRae photographing the sexual with his victims, and even sharing these photos with Father Aube and Fortier. These two, uh, ecco, eh,*

> *been how you say, i-n-d-i-c-t-e-d on 16 counts of*
> *the sex assaulting, one of these boys saying he was*
> *forced into the fellatio one to three times per month*
> *for a year. As if this not enough, another boy said*
> *that, at an age of 10 years old, he was raped orally*
> *by one of the priests who was murdered, Father*
> *Connor, "passed around," to the another murdered*
> *priest, Father Paralta, who also orally and anally*
> *raped this poor boy.*

If I recall right, this priest, Vivaldi, was excommunicated — or fired — from the Catholic Church by Pope Scrivener not long after the article above came out. The Pope actually resigned sometime in early February of 1876, and a new pope claiming to be a reformist, got sworn in sometime later in February. The new pope's name was Pope Giovanni Iustus, his last name meaning "just."

"Maybe you right," I agreed with Wolf.

"Right about what?"

"That maybe it wasn't a killer — maybe it was a bunch of killers."

"Maybe," he said.

"Regardless if it was one or many, if they aren't sinners, then what are they?"

He paused.

"Angels of death sent from Gabriel," he answered real slow.

I looked at him with wonder.

"Gabriel?" I asked.

"Shit, son, you don't done know? He is," Wolf pushed his breakfast plate away, pulled out another cigar from his silver tin, lit it up, and said as he admired his cigar: "Gabriel an archangel, one of the good Watchers who dwell in Fifth Heaven, what with them others, Uriel . . . Raphael . . . Michael. Gabriel, shit, this

Gabriel, he a slayer . . . slayer of unrighteous kings, you done don't know that?"

"Nope," I waved some of the cigar smoke from my eyes.

He looked at me with his right blue eye to see if I was on his page.

"So, what you are saying is that, to get rid of darkness, Gabriel goes deeper into the darkness than even Lucifer?" I asked with my eyebrows raised.

He nodded:

"Sometimes, God and what we think of as Lucifer riding on the same buggy," he blew out some cigar smoke. "But maybe it not no Lucifer in that buggy. Maybe he more like one of them Watchers in the fifth heaven that God has do his dirty work. So he sending stuff out to the outhouse, outside the house, to the Fifth Heaven, for the works of Gabriel to be done there instead of inside God's house, but it still on God's property!"

Wolf stopped for a moment to look at the rays of sun coming into the room with a small-satisfied smile.

"And so you see, Father Shane, Gabriel needs to be close to Lucifer, and make him his best friend. Otherwise, Gabriel is never going to get to where he needs to go, and that's getting Lucifer to shove his knife right into those that be following him, and he is happy to be unfaithful to his children, cause that is what Lucifer does."

Wolf moved his six foot four frame into a more comfortable position.

"Them Lucifer followers is like that rich, fat, gambler who does a deal with Lucifer in the middle of Nevada, thinking this going to get him more wins, and it does. He shakes Lucifer's hand, and the gambler thinks he has got it made when he wins the poker game. But then, then, when the gambler is leaving town, with all of his money, fat from meals, booze, and women, he gets robbed of everything that he just won."

17

"Let me see if I get it," I said through the cigar smoke. "As that fat sweaty . . ."

"Didn't say he was sweaty," Wolf said with a smile.

"Reckon he must be if he is fat and in the desert."

"Right, that's right," he said.

"So the gambler sits in the middle of the desert with nothing to his name, without a horse, with a deadly stab wound to his stomach from the bandits, and without even his clothes because the bandits took them, he looks down to the ground, cries, and yells as he dies to Lucifer: 'I thought you were my friend?'"

Wolf took a long smoke off his cigar.

"Old Gabriel sitting underneath that there ground, right below Lucifer, close enough to whisper in Lucifer's ear, looking upward, and Gabriel says back to the gambler, 'oh, my child, I so wanted you to think Lucifer was your friend. I wanted you to trust him, and for you to think you had his power, that he was weak, and lost without your belief in him,'" Wolf said, "'but I was only using Lucifer to get to you,'" Wolf said with a evil grin.

"So it was all a hoax? It was all a lie? It was all made up?" I said to Wolf, as I though I was the too fat to fall sweaty gambler.

"Just like you are a hoax, my son," Wolf said, responding as though he was Gabriel to the gambler. "You see, I am a spirit who has been around since the first sun come upon this here earth and, sometimes, I appear to people through Lucifer as though he is the answer when, in fact, he is the opposite. And so I just learned your weaknesses, mister gambler, your lust for money, power, and glory at all costs, and used your system against you."

As Wolf said this, he held his right hand over the table holding an imaginary knife towards my stomach.

"And those bandits who just visited themselves upon you," Wolf went on, "were my messengers. I send some of my messages through outlaws like them bandits, cause Lucifer done get a kick out of it."

Wolf then lunged the knife as if he were sticking it into my stomach — the gambler's imaginary stomach — and twisted. As he did, I saw the right side of his mouth open in a murderous sneer that I had never seen before from him. His eye looked into mine as though mine were the only two that existed in the world at that moment, at that time. I listened to his eye.

It said: "I, too, am an outlaw."

He pulled his right hand back after making his murderous gesture with his imaginary knife, and kept smoking his cigar. I had to stop eating to catch my breath. I just looked at him. I had seen a far off foreign land in this local island of Father Wolf that I thought I knew pretty damn well after spending almost every day around him for a month.

"What is it?" Wolf asked me.

I just sat there.

"You look like you seen the Holy Spirit himself," he said.

I took a long gulp of what remained of my coffee.

"You . . . are . . . a . . . sinister . . . man," I said point blank as my eyes were blinking with surprise.

He slowly put his napkin on his lap and leaned forward to me over the table. He looked around again, just like he did earlier before telling me about his dead parents and smoking his cigar. He then said in a quiet inside the church tone:

"I am," he nodded, closed his right eye, and then opened it again.

Wolf went back to smoking his cigar like nothing just happened, like he didn't just take back, with those two words — "I am" — all of the vows that he undertook when he became a man of the cloth.

"Fathers," Sister Barbara, one of the older nuns popped her head into mess hall we was sitting in, "it is getting late and

19

preparation for the flock needs to be made," she said with a worried tone. She sniffed around. "What is that smell?"

"Mr. Sanchez has been smoking again while he works," I said about Poncho Sanchez, the Mexican church janitor.

"Dang it, I thought we told him not to?" Sister Barbara, the seventy year old or so short Viking looking nun, said with frustration.

"You can lead a horse to water," I started saying.

"I know where you are going with this," Sister Barbara said. "I don't care if you have to shove his face in the water, you need to make Mr. Sanchez stop smoking on Church grounds."

"I will do my best, sister," I said with sincere eyes to her.

She looked at Wolf, who just sat there without saying a word. He had put the black oyster full of cigar ash on his knee under the table.

"Good day, Sister Barbara," Wolf calmly said as she walked out of the mess hall, a cool black cat that can't be bothered with reacting to a gun shot in the background when it isn't directed his way.

"Good day, Father Wolf," the stout nun.

"Close call," I said to Wolf after Sister Barbara had left.

"Closer than I liking them calls," Wolf responded. "I owe you one," he said as he took the black oyster ashtray back up from his knee under the table.

"Anytime," I said with a thick as thieves smile.

"Well, Father, I think it is time for us to get going," I nervously said to Wolf. I wanted to get out of there in the worse way possible. I pointed up to the clock above the table to emphasize the point.

"You right, brother," he nodded. "We must get to our Godly duties, right?" He smiled as he started collecting his things. I did the same.

"See you at lunch, Wolf?"

"See you at lunch, brother," he said.

I gathered up my things. I brought them to the kitchen. Instead of going to prepare for mass, I asked Father Shane to cover for me, and I immediately walked over to local police precinct.

"Father Jasper!" the local precinct captain, Captain Sullivan, said to me with a big friendly grin on his face as I walked in. "Top of the morning to you."

"Top of the morning, Captain Sullivan. May I go up and see Commissioner Boyle, please?"

"Nothing I can't help you with?" He asked.

"No, Captain, thank you, just some fundraising issues I need to discuss with him.

"Yes, of course, he is right up the stairs, father."

After I walked into the open door of the Commissioner's office, and closed it, I looked at the green-eyed Commissioner Boyle, and he said:

"Sergeant Amos! What brings you back home so soon?" He said as he held his thick cigar in his right hand, with a pencil in the left.

You see, my real title is Sergeant Jasper Amos and I joined the San Francisco police force on October 26, 1853. I have been serving continuously in the force since that time. As a criminal officer, I traveled once to Scotland Yard to learn how to be a secret mole in organized crime. Armed with that know how, I was one of the officers they charged with investigating the three sets of priest killings I told you about, and which were written about in the *San Francisco Chronicle*. To do that, I joined the priesthood, and went undercover at the Mission Dolores on June 8, 1876, which is not long after the third set of priests were found tortured in the basement of a fancy San Francisco hotel on May 21, 1876.

You might ask: why Mission Dolores?

On May 24, 1876, which is but few days after those smelly priest bodies were found, someone left an anonymous note with the police precinct, with the following written in very messy handwriting:

> <u>Dolores</u> *is her name, and she kills with no shame,*
> *cause she thinks she is on a <u>Mission</u>, but she is just*
> *a killer, and you had better get her.*

Since that June day I went undercover, I have been a priest to everyone. The only people that know my real identity are: the special attorney appointed by the District Attorney's office to investigate the murders, and prosecute the culprits, John Jarboe, Esq.; Cardinal Marciel Degollado; and Police Commissioner Edward Boyle.

"I think I know whose been doing these Goddamn priest murders," I said to the Commissioner with shivers going down my body.

"Well, then, let's hear all about it, lad," the Police Commissioner winked his green Irish right eye at me as I sat down to write the following names into the report he took out of his drawer: Father Luther Wolf, Father Shane Egan, and Sister Emerald Beem.

While I didn't know it then, my report would open up can of worms. I knew the inside of the can was going to be dark. But I never knew how dark it would be. I also didn't know how big the can would be, how many people would be in on it, and how I would get out. Father Wolf may have been right about getting deeper into darkness to do what is right. The thing is, sometimes you get so deep you forget whose side you are fighting on. But, then again, sometimes, you have to do wrong to do right.

I just didn't know how wrong I would do in order to get things right.

CHAPTER TWO

WINDOW DRESSING

"**D**o you believe in God?" John Jarboe, the special prosecutor, asked standing in front of they jury on the first day of the trial.

As I sat in the audience right behind the prosecutor's table in the crowded Mariposa County, California, courthouse on that cold but sunny morning on December 4, 1876, I took a quick glance behind me. Everybody in the audience stared at one another. The jury members did, too. Maybe Jarboe's question had made everybody in the courthouse question their faith?

Except for me.

I was too busy staring at the lovely legs of this beauty on the jury when Jarboe asked the question. I didn't know her name. I didn't know her religion. I did know that she had the prettiest legs I'd seen in a long time. They say the eyes are the soul's windows, but, for me, a woman's legs are windows to her body and lifestyle.

Opening statements in a trial are a lot like a woman's legs. When the statement is good, you know the rest of the trial will be good. When the statement is bad, you know the rest of the trial is going to be a long, slow, torture. I should know. I've been through more trials as a witness for the district attorney's office in San Francisco than I can remember.

"Of course I know you all believe in God. We are, after all, God fearing people," Jarboe continued with his polished smile. "Ladies and gentlemen of the jury, my name is John R. Jarboe. I am the special prosecutor appointed by the District Attorney of San Francisco to prosecute this case on behalf of the People of the State of California against the defendants sitting at that table over there," Jarboe turned around and pointed to the defense table. "The names of the three defendants are Amber Francis a/k/a Sister Emerald Beem, Shane Egan, and Blue Hardin a/k/a Father Luther Wolf a/k/a Eden Taylor," Jarboe then looked back at the jury.

The man who I had called "Father Wolf," but whose real name is Blue Hardin, sat at the old wooden defense table along with Father Shane, the fair-haired 22-year-old Irish priest from the Mission Dolores. They both were wearing their black priestly suits. Sister Emerald Beem, real name Amber Francis, the 34-year-old turquoise-eyed nun from Mission Dolores, was wearing her Sunday's best nun outfit.

"In summary, ladies and gentlemen, this case, *The People of the State of California versus Egan, Francis, and Hardin,* is about murder. And we aren't only talking about murder on a small, isolated scale, but a serial murder of the likes this county has never seen before, and the state will make sure that you never see again," Jarboe shook his head and looked down onto the floor in disgust.

"The evidence will show," Jarboe continued now looking at the jury, "that these three defendants sitting over there invaded the Church. To do that, they impersonated God's servants to escape their sins and the authorities. But once they got into the church, their mission became to murder 19 fine and well-respected men of the cloth over the course of the past year. And why did they do that? The answer is a five-letter word . . . money. All of the murdered priests were corruption fighting, and against dirty gold rush money coming into the house of the Lord. These three thieves sitting over there were using the Mission Dolores as a front to line their own pockets with this filthy sin money. Talk about outlaws dressed in sheep's clothing!"

Jarboe swung his head back and forth again in disgust.

"Now, who are these 19 fine dead men of the cloth? I will tell you — Father Ricardo Aube, Father Roger MacRae, Father Gordon Fortier, Father Zachery Connor, Father Jerry Peralta, Father Ricky Vasquez, Father Timothy Cruces, Father Felix Trupia, Father Lou Tugade, Father Doug Teta, Father Chris Murphy, Father Gary Keisle, Father Jose Maciel, Father Jerry Hargadon, Father Steve Hahn, Cardinal John Krol, Cardinal Justin Bevilacqua, Bishop Eugene O'Sullivan, and Archbishop John Pilarczyk."

At the time of my first sin talk with Blue Hardin that one smoky day in the church canteen, on, what was it, June 30, of that year, 1876, only fifteen lower level members of the cloth above had been killed. Afterwards, on the weekend of September 3 earlier that year, Cardinal John Krol, Cardinal Justin Bevilacqua, Bishop Eugene O'Sullivan, and Archbishop John Pilarczyk, all higher ups in the church, disappeared without a trace, except for their crosses and necklaces.

After Jarboe read off the names of the dead priests, he paused to let the names sink in. As members of the jury made slight noises of disgust, sixty four year old Benny Hyman, a famous Russian Jewish defense attorney from New York's Lower East Side, shook his head in the way you would if someone told you gravity didn't exist.

Benny wasn't only Amber, Shane's, and Blue's defense lawyer.

He was also, according to some *Chronicle* articles I read about him, highly connected in San Francisco's — and the nation's — criminal syndicate circles. According to the articles, he has defended made men in New Orleans, New York, and Chicago. Part of me hated him for how many guilty I am sure he got off the hook. But part of me admired what must be his certain artistry.

Standing in front of the jury, calm, cool, and collected, Jarboe continued:

"And yet you know, and I know, there are some among us who do not believe in God. These heathens," Jarboe pointed to Amber, Shane, and Blue, "don't care about what the afterlife looks like, because they don't believe God has an after life for them."

He started walking back and forth in front of the transfixed jury of seven men and five women. They were the caged animals and he was their tamer. He prowled to his right, and pointed his Englishman looking eyes towards the right side of the twelve jurors. He then slowly made his small green eyes walk their way over to the left side of the jury box. Once he made sure that he made eye contact with everyone in the jury, he continued.

"And so these heathens live in the here and now."

Jarboe paused.

Even though I am sure Hyman was a weasel with words, I had faith in Jarboe. He knew how to put on a show. He was a smart fellow who graduated from Yale in 1855. He had been bred his whole life to play this part. Born to an upper crust family in Maryland in about 1836, the man came west and joined the top shelf firm of Shattuck, Spencer, and Reichert. In 1863, he was named general counsel of First Interstate Bank of California. In 1864, after Judge D.O. Shattuck bailed out of his firm, and it became Spencer & Jarboe.

"Of course, I know such a life is foreign to your God fearing hearts, ladies and gentlemen of the jury."

He paused again.

"But this is the life that they, and many like them in our midst, lead. You know this. I know this. And so I want to explain in my opening statement, which I will make as brief as possible, *who* these heathens are, *how* they killed, and *why* they killed."

Jarboe patted his sweaty clean WASP forehead. He had the window dressing of a fine lawyer. According to the some chronicle articles I read about him, he wore bespoke English suits that were tailored just for him in London's Savile Row. He wore the finest boots, the finest linens. The part on the right side of his head was the neatest one I had ever seen in my life — it was like he would wake up in the morning, look in the mirror, and part his hair on the right just like his poppa had done, just like his grand poppa had done, and so on. They was all from an old blue blood line of Americans that came over from England, or was it Scotland, something like 1700 or so.

"Now, who are these heathens sitting over there?" Jarboe asked the jury.

Nobody heard it but me. Right when Jarboe ended his sentence, there was a small sound that sounded like a little kid in elementary school back in Virginia quietly passing gases. I knew cause that little kid back in Virginia was none other than me. Shit, Jasper hearing things, I thought to myself. I looked over to the old people on my right, and to the young lady on my left, and they didn't even flinch. It was like I was the only person in the whole courtroom who heard what I think I heard.

Maybe there wasn't any smell because the windows were open, and the ceilings were so high, but I am darn sure it was what I think it was. I'd find out later I was right, and you'll see who the gassing pirate was, but let's stick to this part of the story for now.

"I'll tell you who these heathens are, ladies and gentlemen," Jarboe started walking back and forth in front of the jury, a pace that a snake charmer makes so that the snake is the one who thinks he — or she — is the boss, the one who makes the decisions, when, in fact, it is the charmer — Jarboe.

"Let's start with Defendant Amber Maggie Francis. That nice little missy sitting over there in her black Victorian nun garb, up to her neck in it, with her hair nicely resting softly on her shoulders. She looks like she is going to go to church, now doesn't she, my fine jury members, right? You could see here just sitting there, listening to the word of God, and you feeling good that she is next to you in mass cause she a good Christian woman, a child of God, just like you and me, right? She plays with the children of the Mission Dolores, she smiles while she does, and she tends to all the needs of the church, like she is just your run of the mill good sister of the lord."

Jarboe was just staring over at Amber. Most women look away when a man like this looks at them. But Amber just stared back. She was no deer frozen in front of rifle fire. Maybe he was the deer? He looked back to the jury.

"But this woman with the far away eyes is a ruthless killer who likes her prey hung from trees. You'll hear testimony from a former lover of hers how she grew up with a gypsy family that traveled all through California playing circuses, tending to their herd of cattle that they brought everywhere they went to feed themselves and trade with, in addition to being part of the Underground Railroad — helping escaped slaves — private property — leave their southern owners. And what was her role in this dirty circus family?"

Jarboe did a survey of the jury with his green snake eyes.

"She was an expert marksman and knife thrower. She was so good with the gun that she could shoot an apple off a man's head from half a mile away."

He started back over to Amber as he walked in front of the jury, "but that's not all, ladies and gentlemen, that she did. No, you're going to hear testimony from this former lover of hers from the circus that she was one of the circus enforces, even at a young age, who was responsible for hanging bounty hunters who came to retrieve these escaped convict slaves that have been running loose through this great Republic of ours for some time now."

Looking back at the jury, Jarboe said with anger: "and how did she do her nooses? Well, she did her noose the standard way, like anybody else would when they hang someone, but she had an extra touch that was her trademark in these open parts of the land. That trademark was to always cut the man's hands off before he was hung, and leave them under the hung body, just to let people know that if they was going to mess with her circus family, they were going to not only have their hands cut off, but they was also going to hang for it."

Jarboe paused.

"This, ladies and gentlemen, is precisely how the following first five priests found their maker on the morning of April 16 earlier this year, Fathers: Ricardo Aube, Roger MacRae, Gordon Fortier, Zachery Connor, and Jerry Paralta. Below their hung bodies, the police found these men's hands on the ground, and some smoked cigar butts in and about."

Jarboe looked at his notes.

"On that Sunday morning this past April, the first witness, Mrs. Patsy Burton, and the second witness, Mr. Nicky Williams, will testify that they found these five poor souls hung from several trees, two in front of Mrs. Burton's St. Mary's Church, and the other three in front of Mr. Williams' St. Teresa of Avila Church. These vicious defendants," Jarboe looked over towards the direction of the defendants, "were able to wake these fine priests up from their deep slumber, and walked them out to the trees in their sleeping attires."

"Now," Jarboe patted his forehead with his now almost drenched handkerchief, "you might ask, why did they do these hangings in the wee hours of the morning? Well, as you know, around that part of town, there aren't many lights, especially around the church grounds. While there are many neighbors, doing the murders early in the morning would ensure that there would be no witnesses."

The jurors will all fixated on Jarboe's voice and his presence as he walked back and forth in front of them.

"These savages," Jarboe looked over to the defendants' table, "didn't even have the decency to keep the bodies clothed. You'll hear Mrs. Burton and Mr. Williams testify that the bodies of the five priests were naked when they were discovered, and that their priestly collars were stuck in their mouths, so as keep the men from screaming as they were forced out into the cold morning air."

Jarboe looked disapprovingly at the defendants' table.

Joining Jarboe, I looked over at the same table and I couldn't believe my eyes. There, sitting, was Amber. And what did I see but a small, pleasurable, smirk on her face as Jarboe stared at her. It's like she had just eaten a piece of Jarboe's cake, and was enjoying the taste of it as it went down to the bottom of her dark stomach.

"Ah," I could picture her thinking when Jarboe was describing the murder, "that is my piece of art, look at the beauty of those bodies, the open discolored eyes on their faces, and, look at that, the urine on that one body, like a strawberry on top of the ice cream, isn't it so?"

A shiver came over my body. I looked back at Jarboe, who, at this point, was fuming with rage. His hands became fists. He loosened them as he looked back at the jury.

"Below these priestly bodies were their cut hands, and smoked cigars, which indicates that the killers, or at least one of them, was a smoker."

The jurors all started talking to one another. The people around me were making sounds of disgust under their breaths. The old man next to me, with his Sunday's best on, whispered to his wife, who was sitting to his right, "and this woman is a nun? What a joke. They should do the same to her that she did to these poor men of the cloth."

"Order in the court, order in the court," Judge Isaac Parker said forcefully as he slammed the gavel on the counter. Judge Parker was a burly looking man with a white goatee and white hair, thick hands like his bailiff. He was known as the "hanging judge" for how many criminal defendants he had sent to the noose.

"Next," Jarboe continued, now looking at Defendant Shane Egan, "we have this quiet storm of a man, Shane Egan. He is reported to be a very well liked member of the church among the children, and a quiet man at that, sitting here with his priest outfit, with his nicely combed hair, fancy looking wire rimmed professorial glasses that make you think of the most timid church mouse that you could ever find in your life, that little one that the church can never find or catch because the mouse is so quiet when he takes the cheese, that you can't ever know where he is. Too smart to get caught by some mouse trap, so he keeps taking that cheese without ever getting caught."

Looking back at the jury, Jarboe continued.

"Plus, this man has done a great deal of work studying the words of the Lord. A few years after graduating from Yale University, he attended the divinity school at Harvard University in Cambridge. What did he do between Yale and Harvard? Well, you are going to hear from a former Chinese cook of this man's fine Pacific Heights family, the Egan family, who will give you that answer."

"You see," Jarboe looked at Shane, "the Egans are an old Irish family from back east, South Boston to be precise, and have made their money the old fashioned way in America — they killed for it. You name the black market, and they have their hands in it — booze, gambling, arms dealing. They have a hand in it all, and they expanded their enterprise from back east to California in 1866, their former cook will tell you."

"But the most interesting part of this story," Jarboe looked at the jurors, "isn't Shane Egan's crime family, but how they punished their opponents in these dark markets that they operate in, the markets that cockroaches partake in every day. You will hear from this former Egan cook that the family is famous — or infamous — for cutting their opponents bodies up into little pieces, and hanging the pieces, including feet, arms, fingers, toes, around their enemies' homes or neighborhoods, or putting them into rivers, for one simple reason."

Jarboe looked at Shane, who was whispering to Hyman, and then back to the jury.

"To terrorize whomever challenges the Egan family's power!" Jarboe said with intensity.

"And who did this Lucifer's work for the Egan family?" Jarboe quickly looked over again towards Shane, then to the jury.

"The family cook will testify that it was Defendant Egan who dismembered the bodies and got the pieces ready for hanging wherever the family sought fit, all taught to young Shane by his father and the family's nasty Siberian enforcer."

"As you will see on April 23, of this year, which was Easter Sunday, ladies and gentlemen, we discovered the dismembered bodies of Fathers Ricky Vasquez, Timothy Cruces, Felix Trupia, Lou Tugade, and Doug Teta."

Jarboe closed his eyes to gather his thoughts, and then opened them up:

"These men were slaughtered the same way the Egan family slaughtered dozens of Chinese in New York City before, through the hands of that quiet church mouse, Shane Egan, sitting in our midst. After the priests' throats were cut, parts of their bodies, God bless them, like their fingers, toes, eyes, and ears, were cut up and hung on the trees outside their churches, and their torsos were found floating in the San Francisco bay. You will hear testimony that dozens of Chinese in New York City were killed exactly the same way by Defendant Egan and his black Irish hoodlum family."

And then Jarboe just couldn't get out the words.

He paused.

A broken machine, unable to work, he just stood there. I wasn't sure, sitting there in the audience, whether this was the man's act, like the little child who hides behind the door as though playing hide and go seek with you, or whether this was the always cool, always calm, never emotional, always all business, Jarboe having a moment.

"I'm sorry, ladies and gentlemen," he said as he wiped his forehead in disgust, "I just couldn't even spit out the words."

I had seen this before with prosecutors. They try and get the jury to feel rather than think. They describe the crimes in such horrible detail that they jury will convict whomever you put in front of their eyes — even if they were innocent. It appears that Jarboe graduated from this school of thought — the one where you get people to make wrong decisions for seemingly the right reason and with the right spirit in mind.

But they end up being wrong in the end.

"Hung from all different parts of trees," he finally blurted it out, "their body parts were hanging in trees all around their churches, ladies and gentlemen," and at this point Jarboe pointed up to the court's ceiling as though he were actually pointing at the trees. "Just think of the horror," Jarboe continued, "of seeing these priests' bodies close to the church, or should I say their carcasses, and then, as you head father and farther away from the church, we found smaller pieces of their body parts, also all hung high up in trees for all to look at, in horror."

He paused.

"You will hear from Otto Hale, a beer distributor, who was the first to see the dismembered bodies hanging in front of Star of the Sear church, and then you'll hear from Chip Lantz, who is runs a coffee shop not far from St. Peter's and Paul church, who saw the bodies hanging from the trees in front of that church as he was setting up shop in the morning."

The jurors at this point were covering their mouths in disbelief. I doubt any of them have heard of such horrors before. Many people in the audience watching the trial were also gasping for breath, it seemed, the more that Jarboe went into the discoveries.

"The sick part of it all was that, tied to the parts, were, police later discovered and determined, little pieces of rope."

Some of the jurors looked away when they heard this.

"Picture the evil, ladies and gentlemen, of these men's parts being hung up and then, tied around them like they were pieces of meat from the butcher, were pieces of rope. To think of the evil of the defendants is really . . . impossible."

Jarboe looked over at the defendant's table. I looked over, too. It seemed like the whole world was looking at that table. Amber, the nun, whispered in Hyman's ear ever so briefly, and then she caught me looking over at her. Like Shane before her, she smiled a knowing smile at me, like she knew something, I knew the same thing, and we both knew we couldn't talk about that thing in public — except for with a wink.

What was that thing she knew? Maybe she thought I was one of them?

But they were in for a rude awakening. That's because, later on in the trial, I was going to be the government's star witness.

Amber then turned to look back at Jarboe, who had his green snake eye on her, and she did something I will never forget for the rest of my life. As though she didn't care, as though it was all a game, she winked, ever so slightly at Jarboe.

He just stood there, and then he slammed his foot on the ground. I remember Hyman look around and smirking at the play he was producing. He looked back at me with a confidence in his eyes. It wasn't in his mouth, or in the way he dresses, but in those eyes. Jarboe couldn't stand the daring in Amber's wink, so he turned back around to look at the jury.

"Ladies and gentlemen, as you can see from the wink that the defendant just gave me, neither she nor anybody on that table takes any of this all too seriously. Let us see how they feel about it when they are hanging from a noose in the town's square."

Some of the jury members made small nods of agreement to one another. Jarboe then walked back and forth, the pitcher getting ready for his next pitch.

"Defendant Egan's murdering occurred in the early morning hours, just like Defendant Francis's hanging. You'll hear from Gerald Campionoti, a fisherman, who found these priests torsos in the San Francisco bay, which means that their bodies were put in the ocean in the morning."

Jarboe paused.

"Finally, you'll hear from the Mission Dolores janitor who says he saw a large saw, like the one which was used to cut these poor men up, underneath Defendant Shane Egan's bed," Jarboe stared over at the defendants' table.

The conservative looking defense attorney stopped as though to catch his breath. As he did, I looked over at the defense table. Shane whispered to Blue as though they were passing a note in elementary school that made fun of the teacher.

Members of the jury again started talking, and the young blond lady sitting next to me, a mother I thought to myself, whispered to herself, "disgusting, how disgusting, these brutes," she said as she looked down toward her knees.

"Order in the court, order in the court," Judge Parker said loudly in his bass voice.

Jurors and the folks in the audience quieted down.

Jarboe then said to the jury as his right index finger pointed over to the defendant's table without looking, like he knew exactly where Blue was sitting by memory, "this next character in our all star cast of sinners sitting there at the defense table, is Defendant Blue Hardin, who snuck into the church under the assumed name Luther Wolf, and previously snuck into the U.S. Army under the assumed name Eden Taylor"

"Now, who is this man of aliases, ladies and gentlemen?" Jarboe asked out loud like he didn't know the answer as his index finger kept pointing over the defendant's table.

"A well respected man of the cloth, who does the God's work in the Mission Dolores, as his oath would seem to tell you?" Jarboe asked the jury like they might know the answer to this question.

Jarboe paused.

"No. This was all sinister outlaw camouflage," he put his index finger down next to his side. "The real Blue Hardin is a murderer from Illinois," Jarboe's eyes bulged towards the jury like they were going to come out of his head. "Unlike the others, this man wasn't just a killer — he was a killer for hire who enjoyed killing so much that he would sometimes only charge two dollars for his hits!"

Jarboe raised his voice for emphasis, the jurors reacted with aghast.

"Oh, and I forgot to mention that Defendant Hardin," and now Jarboe pointed over his shoulder with his right thumb towards Blue, "also robbed banks throughout the state, including in Chicago," he dropped his hand back down to his side.

The jurors made noises of horror.

"Quiet, quiet," Judge Parker said with force.

"We will hear testimony from the Mayor of Vandalia, Illinois, the town where Defendant Hardin is from that, in order for him to carry out his reign of terror over the State of Illinois," Jarboe said as he walked back and forth in front of the jury as he almost seemed to think out loud, "Mr. Hardin tortured and killed nineteen bank presidents."

And now Jarboe looked directly in the jurors' eyes.

"You will hear the good Mayor testify that Mr. Hardin was known to knock his victims out in their own homes while they were sleeping, just hit them with something across their head. While the person was unconscious, Hardin would strap them down on their bed, put something in their mouth so that they couldn't yell, and then he would slice the person's stomach open so that all of the guts would come out onto the body and bed. He did the same thing to his other bank president victims, but

36

only after abducting them off the streets and bringing them to his preferred location of torture, which were usually high end brothels."

The old man said to his wife sitting next to me, "this man is worse than Lucifer."

Now Jarboe looked over to Blue sitting at the defendant's table then looked back at the disgusted jury, "but it wouldn't end there, ladies and gentlemen. This sick man, this sick, sick, man, would sit there watching the person, smoking his cigars, waiting for the person to wake up in their own blood. Defendant Hardin would then sit there watching the person's face react in horror at what their eyes were seeing."

Jarboe paused to let the effect settle in of what he just said. I could tell that the jurors were that Blue seemed to get some special joy, and almost dark pleasure, at seeing his victims' suffering.

"We will see shortly, ladies and gentlemen, that this is precisely how this agent of Lucifer killed the following five men of cloth on May 20–21 of this year, Fathers: Chris Murphy, Gary Keisle, Jose Maciel, Jerry Hargadon, and Steve Hahn."

"Four witnesses will testify to seeing this third set of victims abducted right off the streets of San Francisco over the weekend of May 20–21 by masked bandits, and then you'll hear from one Ms. Fanny Porter who will testify that she found these servants of God dead on beds in the basement rooms of her fine hotel."

The jury made noises of aghast.

"But these men of God weren't only found dead in those beds, ladies and gentlemen of the jury," and now Jarboe was looking at the jury with his arms crossed, "no. Ms. Porter will explain that she found the men with their arms and legs strapped with chains to the bed, naked, and with small cuts to their stomachs.

He will explain that she found the beds soaked with blood, and that several cigars were found next to the chairs adjacent to the bed, which indicates that the at least one of the killers, if there were more than one, was a smoker."

37

As Jarboe made his case, I could see the older man next to me, the one sitting with his wife, pulling out his stash of tobacco and confirming that it wasn't the same.

"The very same methods that made Defendant Hardin infamous for the way that he killed and slaughtered in the state of Illinois, ladies and gentlemen, have now made the same man so very infamous in our fine Republic of California by the killing of these five men in the hotel managed by Ms. Porter."

All of a sudden, someone from the back of the courtroom started yelling, "Hang him! Hang him!"

"Order, order, order in the court!" Judge Parker yelled to the crowded, sweaty, Mariposa County courtroom. Several courtroom sheriffs went over to the back and escorted the yeller, an old man with long sideburns, outside of the courtroom.

Jarboe waited for the old gentleman to be escorted out.

"Ladies and gentlemen, I would like to direct your attention to the fourth and final set of murders. Over the weekend of September 2 and 3 this year of our Lord, 1876, Cardinal John Krol, Cardinal Justin Bevilacqua, Bishop Eugene O'Sullivan, Archbishop John Pilarczyk disappeared without a trace, and did not come back to their parish, as you will hear Father Donald Bronstein, the Archdiocese accountant, testify to shortly."

Jarboe wiped small beads of sweat from his brow with his now soaked fancy white sea-island cotton handkerchief, one that only a blue-blood man like Jarboe would wear.

"After a few days with no word from these four holy men, Father Bronstien reported them missing. The police posted posters throughout the city asking people to report anything they had seen about these priests."

Jarboe walked back and forth.

"During the evening of September 13, earlier this year, Mrs. Lila Khan, came into the precinct and reported that she heard screaming from different people on September 13th," Jarboe at this point stopped walking back and forth, looked into the eyes of the jury members, "coming from the butcher shop across the street. Th is screaming was so loud, so intense, ladies and gentlemen, that Mrs. Khan was woken from her deep slumber to listen in horror to what was happening."

Th e jurors started whispering, people in the courtroom were all mumbling, and then a tall, elegant looking, grey haired lady yelled out from the back of the courtroom, "murderers, murderers, cold blooded murderers!"

"Order, order, order in this court," Judge Parker screamed as he slammed his gavel. "Any more outbursts, ladies and gentlemen, and I warn you that I will close this courtroom to you all." Regaining his composure, the red faced judge looked back over to Jarboe, who was standing with a small smile, knowing that his opening statement was getting the jurors in a mood to do justice — preciscly what he wanted.

"Police Commissioner Boyle will testify that, aft e r t hey received the report from Mr. Khan on September 13th, they investigated the butcher shop, which is called Lenny's Fine Cuts. And what did they find?"

The circus leader paused for effect.
"Parts of the gold necklaces and crosses of these four missing holy men, ladies and gentlemen, on the floor of the butcher shop."

The jurors made quiet sounds of horror.

"The rest of the necklaces and crosses were discovered by the intake boy at the office of the Archdiocese in boxes of beef that this butcher shop had shipped."
Shit, I thought to myself when I heard this, those pieces of metal must have been rough on the teeth when eating that meat.

"Now, how did these crosses get in those boxes from the Lenny's Fine Cuts butcher shop to the archdiocese?" Jarboe asked out loud.

"I'll spell it out for you," Jarboe reviewed his notes. "Mr. Bronstein will testify that a beef salesman purporting to be from the Lenny's Fine Cuts butcher shop got the Archdiocese as a client on August 11th of this year, that the first shipment of beef came in on August 18th, and that the same sales person lured these four men of the cloth to the Lenny's Fine Cuts butcher shop, which is located across the street from Mrs. Khan's apart-ment, on Sunday, September 3, as though there was a customer appreciation party."

Jarboe paused.

"The Lenny's Fine Cuts butcher shop owner, Mr. Tommy Kelly, will testify that on the evening of Saturday, September 2, his shop's locks were picked, and that his shop is always closed on Sundays."

Jarboe did his next dramatic pause.

"The evidence will show that Defendant Hardin used

the same break in skill set he used to break into the homes of his bank president murder victims in his home state of Illinois to pick the locks of the Lenny's Fine Cuts butcher shop on the evening of September 2nd, that these poor servants of God were tortured in that butcher shop on September 3rd, their bodies were skinned and cut, put into boxes, and shipped out along with the other meat, by these Lucifer worshippers sitting over there," Jarboe glared at the defendants. "The only thing that remained of these four holy men were their gold crosses, and that is how we know what happened to them."

Many of the jurors just had their hands over their eyes or mouths at this point, disgusted at the very thought of what the Jarboe was telling them, some men even tearing up.

I didn't.

"Ding, ding, ding!" I heard in my head as I remember back to poppa calling us to the table for supper back in Rocky Mount, Virginia, as he rang the bell in the kitchen. He'd often cook up what he said was black bear meat he got in from some friends.

Rumors went around our small Rocky Mount town that one of the local Catholic priests was doing what some of the papers said these 19 Catholic priests was doing — crimes against Mother

Nature with children. Oddly, that local priest supposedly left town around the same time as our bear supper.

Guess it didn't matter cause that meat was the tastiest I had in my life.

Jarboe, head sweating, with his black linen suit now visibly soaked with some of his sweat, walked back over to his table to take a long swig off of his water. As he did, Blue started looking around the courtroom. He looked behind to his right, and over to me. I had a small smirk on my face as he did. That's because, as I sat there in my priestly outfit, which Jarboe demanded I wear for dramatic effect, I kept thinking of poppa's "ding, ding, ding!"

But that's also because Blue didn't yet know who I was, undercover cop, rat, mole. He would soon find out when I testified. In a way, I wondered if I even knew who I was. Yes, they were expecting me to testify, the right way, the truthful way about everything that I had seen, heard, and thought during my times with Blue, Amber, and Shane. And I was prepared to do that. No, I wasn't so sure of myself that I would in fact do that. And I think that Blue's looking over at me was, in a way, his checking in on me, as though to ask with his eyes, "you still with us, boy?"

And I suppose my smirk was a way of saying yes to his ancient Viking like blue right eye, which just stared at me as would a wolf would his prey, but I wasn't his prey. I think Blue sincerely thought I was, like him, a wolf, one of the pack. Perhaps that's why when he looked over, and after I smirked, he did what any wolf would do with another wolf in the pack, he licked me. But he didn't actually lick me.

He just smirked.

Jarboe finished drinking his water and took off his jacket. I could tell he was close to finishing his opening statement. His black linen vest and black tie remained, but he rolled up his sleeves, a fighter who is about to finish the other fighter, in the final round, tired, but ready to make the kill. And I was going to be part of the kill, a tool that they would use against these naïve daring outsiders on trial, to hang them, and to see all the people feel good about themselves that the 19 fine men of the cloth were avenged.

"Now, our undercover police officer, who you will hear testify later on, the one we planted with these heathens sitting over there, in their beloved Mission Dolores church, overheard Defendant Egan, after the final set of murders occurred at the butcher shop on September 3, saying to Defendant Francis 'sister, they are minced meat, and they never coming back again.'"

The jurors looked at one another.

"And what was heathen bearded Defendant Blue Hardin response, ladies and gentlemen?"

Blue started growing his beard back when the indictment came down on about the last date of October earlier this year. I didn't think it was a smart move. I thought it made him look like a dirt bag. But maybe he did it as sign of rebellion against the trial. Or, maybe, it was a smart move. In some ways the gruff beard, when coupled with his big dark blue right eye, made me think of a Jesus who came back with pirate protection.

"The undercover sergeant," Jarboe continued with his statement, "will testify that the bearded devil sitting over there at the defendant's table responded: 'Shane is right, sister, they is minced meat, good riddance.' The sergeant will testify that Defendant Hardin spit on the ground and, get this, ladies and gentlemen, urged Defendant Francis to do the same, saying it would 'make her feel better.'"

Jarboe stared with this mad dog intensity at the jurors.

"The good sergeant will further testify that this sorry excuse for a woman of God, Defendant Francis, didn't then not only spit on the ground, but also pushed her shoe on the spit as though to smother the spit even further, as she screamed, screamed a scream like you never heard in your life and then started laughing,

laughing so hard that the rest of the defendants started laughing with her."

The audience members made sounds of disgust.

"Just in case this screw showing the defendants' guilt weren't tight enough for you, ladies and gentlemen, our undercover police sergeant will testify that Defendant Hardin took out a bottle of moonshine, a bunch of glasses, and filled them all up, and that they all drank that moonshine, together, with Defendant Francis making the following toast: 'no more suffering.' At which point they drank Lucifer's potion."

Shane and Amber looked over in my direction. They must have known now it was me who was the police sergeant in their midst. Shane's look was of a serious preacher, with his eyes focused on my brow, about to explain the dangers of playing with Lucifer, who would be the police, the 19 dead priests, the Church. Amber's look was of sorrow, like she had just found out her brother wasn't her brother, but an imposter, someone who was standing in for her real brother, who the fake brother had killed, just to take over the position of the real brother, and act like he loved her — when, in fact, he didn't.

As I sat there, though, thinking back to when I first heard Blue confide in me that one day in June of this year about his thuggish past, I still wondered if they knew who I was. Maybe they said nothing because they wanted to plant ideas with me, ideas that they knew would be untrue or misleading, just to throw the sniffing dog — which is me — off the right scent, and onto the wrong one.

Or maybe they gave me power of choice and wanted to see what I'd do with it.

"Those devils, those devils, burn them, hang them, get them out of here, get them out of here!" A loud Injun man's voice came from the back of the courtroom and interrupted the relative silence. The court officer and his men went to take the Injun man outside the courtroom as he continued to yell, "heathens, heathens, heathens!"

After Jarboe stared at the Injun man being taken away, he turned back towards the jury: "I understand how he feels, ladies and gentlemen, at hearing these horrible events that I am now recounting. And that is why we are here: to bring these heathens to justice! So that Injun man's heart is in the right place."

"Ding, ding, ding!" I heard poppa yelling in my head for momma and I to come down for supper. Maybe the meat in those archdiocese boxes wasn't all cow meat? Maybe it was from some Virginia black bear?

"Now, ladies and gentlemen," Jarboe continued, "I told you I would not only explain **who** these heathens are, and **how** they killed, which I just went over, but **why** these heathens did it."

"We read about it in the daily papers. By the end of last year, 1875, the population of San Francisco increased by more than 80,000 because of greedy Gold Rushers who have been flooding that peaceful God fearing city with their brothels, gambling, and sinful living."

Jarboe paused to wipe his forehead clean of sweat. The temperature in the small country courtroom, which had puny windows that overlooked the vast northern California landscape outside was blistering.

"That's why the good citizens of San Francisco have organized vigilante committees to take care of these sinful souls. Many of these filthy philistines attend Defendants' mass at Mission Dolores. I have no doubt in my mind the Defendants' parish has profited handsomely from their flock's outlaw deeds. And that's all the more why we need good men of the cloth to take care of the flock in San Francisco — and in Northern California, in general."

He then placed his left hand softly in the vest pocket of his fancy three-piece suit, which he could well afford. Since joining the Shattuck firm, Jarboe's biggest and most lucrative client has been the Catholic Church. Over the past few years, he has defended the Church against all of the civil suits, which have ranged from simple slips and falls to the sex abuse cases I have read about in the *San Francisco Chronicle*.

And so Jarboe didn't only have the window dressing of a fine lawyer, but he delivered on the dressing, too. The inside of his law office, which I frequented many times before the trial to prepare, was full of jury verdicts dismissing complaints brought by various lawyers, who have sued the Church throughout the years for all of the alleged abuses that the greedy lawyers have, in my view, been just making up, and taking advantage of their clients pain, to get more money to line their pockets.

One of the first cases I read about, and which got Jarboe's name in the papers, was *Michael Smith v. The Archdiocese of San Francisco*. The plaintiff, an older man now in his 50s, alleged that he was abused by Cardinal John Krol and was suing the church for $100,000.00 in pain and suffering. Jarboe was able to get the case dismissed because he found some dirt on the plaintiff. Evidently he had a record of theft when he was younger, and was a drinker and thief when he got older. His attorney said that plaintiff Smith did all of this only after his abuse at the hands of Krol.

Jarboe got the jury to not believe that explanation.

Now Jarboe was seeking to use his cunning and skills for offense — not defense.

"The lawless background in which we are living leads me to these nasty criminals sitting there. They don't want your community to have the priests it needs to keep light in the times of darkness, hope in desperate times, and faith in God when Lucifer seems to have won."

He paused to look at all of the jurors in their eyes.

"All of the 19 priests who were killed, ladies and gentlemen, were corruption fighting men of the cloth who wanted to protect you, their flock, from the sinning money that was being rushed into the dirty Mission Dolores, and lining the pockets of the killers over there," Jarboe looked over at the defendants' table, "who were all to happy to take this dirty quiet money."

The jurors made sounds of disgust.

"These dead men of the cloth had started a commission on February 18 of this year, 1876, to investigate the dirty quiet money being put into the church, particularly Mission Dolores. Only when the commission was getting wind under its wings, gathering the evidence, were the feathers of those wings clipped, one by one, by these murdering children of Lucifer," Jarboe looked at the jury with a warm Christmas smile your momma or poppa would use when you seeing your presents in the morning.

"Cardinal Marcial Degollado, a senior member of the San Francisco Archdiocese, will testify that Amber, Shane, and Blue knowingly took money from parish members in contravention of the Church's rules regarding, in essence, the laundering of gold rush money, and that he was forced to leave the Mission Dolores parish at the threat of force by the three defendants."

Jarboe stopped to review his notes.

"Why Mission Dolores? You might ask as you sit there in the jury," Jarboe surveyed the members of the jury. "Well, for the last few years, Mission Dolores, which is in one of the poorest neighborhoods of San Francisco, has been the most lucrative parish in the city, even more than the wealthy and well heeled Pacific Heights church, where I attend mass. Now, how did the Mission Dolores parish get so rich?"

The jury members made small glances at one another.

"I'll tell you why. Because they accepted gambling, prostitution, and God only knows what other type of monies from their faithless flock!"

Jurors sighed in disgust, as did some of the members of the audience watching the trial, at the thought of two priests and a nun running a black market racket in the middle of San Francisco, all under the banner of Jesus Christ. The depth of the alleged fraud on the good will of the people, and on the Church, could be seen in the juror's eyes, as they winced in anger at the defendants. Jarboe continued:

"The dead were the ones who drafted resolution Stop 666! regarding the illegal collection of unattributed flock money. So the motive of the defendants here is clear: they didn't want their true identities to be shown to the outside world, or else their golden calf, which is all of this Lucifer money they were skimming from the church, would be done forever."

Jarboe took one last sip of his water.

"And their method of keeping people from the truth?" He asked out loud.

"Very simple, ladies and gentlemen," Jarboe said quietly as he leaned over the banner in front of the jury.

"Terror," he said quietly, "terror," he said louder, and then he yelled "terror!" This time his hands went up like he, himself, was a preacher. "They wanted to breed terror into all of you, into me, into the good judge, into all of these people sitting in the audience out there, into anybody who would challenge their reign of corruption," he looked out into the audience and then back at the jury.

"And it is your duty to not give into to their terror. To not let them get away with making a mockery of the Church, of our culture, of me and you, and, most importantly, of God," Jarboe pointed above to the ceiling, "and his son, Jesus Christ."

"That is why, ladies and gentlemen, I ask you to return a verdict of guilty on all counts for which we have brought against these defendants, and have them hung, so that no child, no man of faith, will ever have anything to fear again from such evil doers!"

Jarboe went slowly went back to his chair at the prosecutor's table.

"Ladies and gentlemen of the jury," Judge Parker Said, "we shall now have a recess for lunch, and, when you return, we shall hear the defense counsel's opening statement. I ask that you not discuss this matter while on your recess, and that you come back at 1:00." It was about 12:00 p.m.

We all left the courtroom. I walked out into the light of the warm California sun spreading its rays on my face. The warm sun made me remember back to a Sunday I spent with Blue, Amber, and Shane in July earlier that year.

Just couldn't get the kids' screaming out of my head from that day.

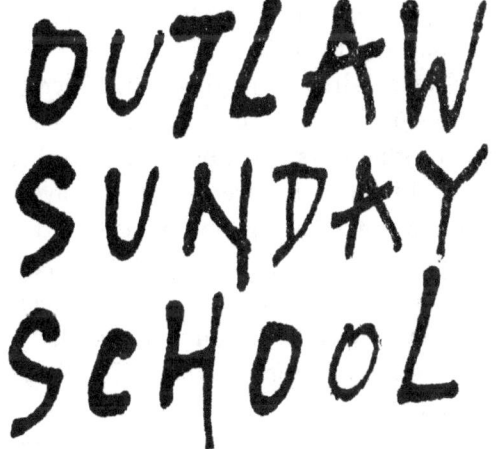

CHAPTER THREE

OUTLAW SUNDAY SCHOOL

"Stop it . . . stop it . . . stop it!"

As I walked towards the bench far into the back country brush behind the courtroom to eat my lunch, the screaming of "stop it" from inside the walls of Mission Dolores that Sunday morning on July 2 earlier that year ringed in my memory.

When I sat down on the long wooden bench, which was unprotected from the warm California sun, I opened up my paper bag of lunch. It was food of cops, construction workers, janitors, or any other laborers on break — sandwich, fruit, and a canister of water. As expected, there was nobody else sitting at the table with me at the time.

Eating into my apple on that first day of the trial, which was December 4, 1876, I thought back to that warm July Sunday. The

December sun reminded me of the July sun. But maybe it was my nerves that were making me sweat through my shirt and jacket, which is why I took it off when I sat down.

Chewing on an apple piece, I remembered back to how I had gone to a children's shelter that Sunday morning, as I did on every Sunday. Usually, I'd be at the shelter all day, and even into the evening, before I'd go back to the Mission.

That Sunday was different.

Many of the children at the shelter had been placed with families in and about the Bay Area, so there wasn't as much need for me there as other days. Plus, priests from other churches were there, and I figured they were enough. Traveling around for the Mission was exhausting, not to mention the fact that I had to often go back to the Precinct and make reports to the Police Commissioner about things that I had seen — or not seen — during my days. So a day off was needed.

To get to the Church from the shelter, I walked up on 16th Street to the corner of 16th and Mission Streets, where the Mission Dolores is located. As the wind went through the trees, and as I slowly walked towards the Mission, I heard horrible screams over the old brick walls that protected the backyard of the Church, where there is a cemetery, a garden, and where the kids to played.

My veins started rushing with blood as my heart pumped.

I remembered back to how I started running towards the entrance of the backyard. It was about three or so blocks that I ran, so the screams were loud. When I got to the entrance of the yard, which is protected by a large iron door that has medieval bolts on it, I pushed it open with all of my might, as you would do, I am sure, as if kids were stuck inside a burning building.

Suddenly, I saw total anarchy.

It was one of the most beautiful things I had ever seen.

Blue was running along with a bunch of the children from the local orphanage — little boys with yellow, black, brown, red faces. Faces with grit, with sorrow, with pain, feelings of abandonment, feelings of inferiority, feelings of being nothing, messy haired boys, torn clothes, shoes with holes in them, some even without shoes.

And they were running with Blue.

And they were smiling with Blue.

And their pain was gone for that brief passing moment of time.

Sitting at that bench in the brush outside the courtroom, I opened up the peanut butter and jelly sandwich I had made in the morning. As I chewed my first bite, I thought back to how the target of Blue and his heathen group of children were another smaller group of heathen looking girls, many with ratty hair down to their wastes, who were running with Amber. These girls were like the boys, with the same faces, the only difference being that they were girls — not boys.

Instead of keeping these kids in class Sunday school all day, as they were supposed to under Church rules, Blue and Amber were playing hooky with them, and water fighting on top of it all.

Amber and some of her girls were drenched with water.

Blue and his boys were drenched, too.

The boys chased the girls around the yard, until Amber yelled:

"Enough is enough, now we kill them!"

Suddenly, I remember staring with my mouth slightly open as a slew of girls came out of the church, joined Amber's crew, and started to chase the boys as the girls yelled "kill!" Sister Amber's sleeves were off, as I reckon she had a special outfit she made for herself, and I could see her tight arm muscles and bushy armpits. Not fancy and shaved like I seen some of the city women doing. She was more like the wild and pretty country girls I grew up with in Rocky Mount.

"We going to get you! We going to get you!" Amber's girls said in a chorus. The little blond girl with a filthy coal miner face looked with eyes ablaze as she chased a little red headed boy, and yelled: "going to get you, going to get you!"

Now, the predators, which were Blue and his boys, were the hunted.

"Let's get the hell out of here!" Blue yelled.

The boys, now outnumbered by the girls, spread all over the grounds of the Church. They were running this way and that, going into hiding so that the girls, with their water and demonic — and yet fun! — eyes chased them. Amber tossed a whole pale of water on Blue, whose priestly suit was now drenched, his right cool blue eye smiling as his mouth made what sounded liked a pirate laugh.

Taking in the scene, I couldn't believe my eyes. I looked to my right and there was Shane, sitting there on a bench, next to the brick wall, in the shade. His shirt cloth was angelic white, not a smudge on it, and was finely pressed. It was almost like he was orchestrating it all, sitting there, with a small smile of enjoyment. He didn't say a word, but just stared into the organized fun anarchy that was taking place before his eyes.

Sitting on that long bench behind the courthouse remembering back to that Sunday water fight, a priest suddenly came out from nowhere. Never met him before. Never seen him before. He had dark features, long hair that was put in a ponytail behind his head, large black hat that kept his face form the sun, and a thick dark mustache that had little strains of gray in it.

"Good day, my son," he said with what sounded like a foreign accent. "May I join you?" He asked before he sat down across from me.

"Of course, father, please sit," I said as I pointed down to the space across the way from me.

"Thank you," he said and sat down.

I couldn't see his eyes. The father was wearing silver wire rimmed sunglasses. The lenses were so dark that they were a black Virginia night without stars or moon.

"My name is Jasper, father, pleasure to meet you," I said as I reached my hand over to shake his.

"The pleasure is mine," the five foot five or so father said as he reached his dark colored hand over to shake mine. As we shook hands, he said, with a thick accent as he looked into my eyes, "I was born Canon Carlos Francisco Alberto Julio Lorenzo de Vivaldi, but this name will taking you the all day to say, so most people calling me Father Canon de Vivaldi, or, if you like, just Viva," he smiled a very humorous smile.

I smiled.

"I'll just call you Father Vivaldi, father," I took my hand out of his.

"As you wishing, my son, just trying to make things the big easy."

"Where you from, father?"

"Ah, from Austin, Texas, you cannot telling from my accent?" He pointed to his mouth.

I just sat there. Austin?

"Son, I playing, no, I wishing I were from Texas. But, is too bad," he wiped some dust off his knee, "I from Sardinia, Italy."

"Not close," I said, "to Texas."

"The world is becoming the small place," he said. "Look at, what is that thing called, the telegraph!" He snapped his fingers.

"Good point, father," I nodded.

I paused to think for a moment, and remembered that there was a Father Vivaldi from Italy quoted in the *Underbelly of the Church* article that came out after the leaked documents. I remembered that this Father Vivaldi, according to another article I read, was excommunicated not long after being quoted in the article by the pope at the time, Pope Scrivener.

"Say, father, aren't you are the Father Vivaldi, the one that is quoted in the San Francisco Chronicle article, *Underbelly of the Church*, about the leaked documents?"

"Yes, I am this Father Vivaldi, unless they have the other that they is making up to talk to the papers," he smiled.

He took out his little lunch from his satchel — a piece of bread, some salami, and a knife to cut it all.

"Care for this?" He asked as he pointed to his food on the table.

"No thank you," I waived my hand.

"Suiting yourself," he shrugged.

"What brings you here, Father? Just wanted to check out the trial?"

He ate his food and, as he did, pulled out what looked like a small silver flask and poured some of its contents into a little cup. He finished his bite, held out the little glass with wine in it, "care for the splash?"

"No thanks, Father."

He took a long sip of the wine, closed his eyes, and then said in Italian:

"Ah, eh buon vino."

He opened his eyes.

"This means the good in Italian," he smiled.

He was wearing the priest suit, but it was more fitted and tailored than the other priests I had seen. Before he sat down, I checked out his pants, and they looked super fancy, his jacket was form fitting around his waste, bigger at the shoulder, and his shoes didn't look the standard style that all of the priests wore. They looked like an Italian version of a cowboy boot, if you can imagine that — dark, embroidered, black stallion like. Father Vivaldi had style and a certain debonair that I had never really seen before, except for some blue bloods — like Jarboe — I'd seen around town in their fancy things.

Maybe this Father was from some Medici family money?

He sat calmly, and, before he took another bite of his sandwich, he said softly:

"I am the witness for the defendants," he then took a big bite out of his sandwich.

I just stared at him as he ate. Should I be talking to him? I am a witness for the prosecution, after all. What if people see us talking? Not likely since not many folks know about this backwoods bench. How did this father know about it?

"How'd you know about this bench?" I asked.

"Ah, my son, I know many benches, it is, how you say, one of my favorite things to do, take the a bench, take a the wine, and have the good time, we say it is the art of doing the nothing."

"But I thought they say that Lucifer loves idle doing nothing hands?" I took a long swig of my water.

"God does too," he smiled again and then took a big swig of his wine. "And you, my son, what brings you to this trial on this day?"

He asked like he didn't know.

"Well, father," I looked down at my dirty brown cowboy boots. "I am actually going to be testifying for the prosecution," I said.

"Ah, why you say this in low voice, you should, how you say, be proud, no? I mean, we here to find the truth, and you, my son, a messenger from God," he stared at my priest collar, "is helping, is not true?" Father Vivaldi didn't seem to care about my answer to his question, cause he took a bite of his sausage and started spinning his wine around in the mug as he sniffed it. He didn't give a rat's ass, I thought, and was just making bullshit talk, like any old-timer would.

"Uh, let me think about that one for a second, father," I said and just sat there.

"Ok, son, you think about why you speak in the low voice and I going to take, how you say, the shit and small walk, cause my stomach is being, the terrible," he said with crass words uncharacteristic of a priest as he walked into the brush. Father Vivaldi's question about my low voice caused me to think back to my conversation with Shane on that water fight Sunday in July earlier that year, where I found Shane sitting and staring at all of the kids chasing one another along with Blue and Amber.

"What's going on here Shane?" I asked standing next to him.

"Fun . . . in . . . the . . . sun," he said with a quiet voice as he kept staring into the distance.

"Right, but I thought all of these kids were supposed to be taking their Sunday school lessons about the father, the son, and the Holy Spirit."

"Yes," he looked at me with his green Irish eyes, "but sometimes the father, the son, and the Holy Spirit can wait," and then looked back at the kids playing.

Shane seemed to be troubled, deep in thought, when I came upon him. The scene of the kids playing with the water and the dirt under the sun seemed to take his mind off whatever was troubling him.

Then, suddenly, I remember hearing, "Oh my god, my leg," crying and screaming from one of the little children, a little five year old Chinese boy, rang out. He had a bowl haircut, dirt on his cheeks, socks that were next to his ankles, shoes with holes in the them, and a scratch on his right knew that had some blood coming out.

Before Shane or I could do anything about it, Blue had come running over, soaked in water, with his boots making that sound your boots make when they are drenched with water.

"What's wrong here little monster?" He said in a sort of sympathetic tone, but also not so much that the little Chinese boy got scared, like something was horribly wrong.

"My knee, my knee, my knee!" The boy pointed to his knee, and then threw some dirt at the tree where he fell. "That tree, that tree!" He said in anger and then just cried.

Blue kneeled down among the rest of the chaos in the backyard, with kids doing the water fighting, and took his long index finger with the long dirty fingernail on it, the one I had seen up close and personal in the Mission's mess hall, and licked it.

"There, there, now, son," Blue wiped his index finger over the wound on the boy's knee to take the blood way. Then he pulled out what looked like an old black bandana from his pocket, and put it over the wound. To make it secure, he pulled out a thin piece of rope that was in his pocket, the thin type of rope you might use to curl up a napkin, and put it around the boy's knee so that the handkerchief stayed in place.

When the Chinese boy couldn't see his blood any more, his crying died down. As Blue finished his primitive bandage job, he looked in a caring away at the small boy. Then, suddenly, without expectation, Blue started making some of the funniest faces I had even seen. Was he a guardian angel in Lucifer clothing?

"Look here, mate," he said with an old English pirate accent, like one from the Barbary coast I had read about in college, with his tongue out like he was a splattered face, "you think you have it bad, but look at me face, looks like we both in the bad straights, eh mate?"

He slapped the little Chinese boy playfully, and the boy's crying went down more. Blue tried to get up, but then fell back down, like he was a drunk man, tried to get back up, and then fell back down.

"Looks like that hurt you had there, mate, was hurting me, and now that you feeling better, seems like I have that hurt you just have, but, ahoy mate, I don't want this on my body, hear me mate? Can't make me legs walk now!"

Blue then got up and started walking, but walking like he was a horribly drunk man, swaying here, swaying there. As he did, the kids started surrounding him, but not all of them, just the ones that were in the area. They all started laughing and pointing at Blue. The small Chinese boy saw all of the commotion, and just couldn't help but laughing at the drunken man walk that Blue was pulling off.

"You funny, you funny, Father," the small Chinese boy said as he pointed, along with the rest of the children, at the tall, blue eyed, tight muscled, look like he could choke you with his bare hands, pirate patched priest. Blue came back, helped the boy to his feet, and then patted him on his head.

I remember standing there with Shane sitting to my right on the bench and looking over to him to ask:

"Why did you join the priest hood?"

"Because there isn't anything else," he said in his soft under-stated voice, "I'd rather be doing in the world other than sitting here and watching what I am watching," he looked over to me and said as his eyes glared at me through his scholastic round wire rimmed eye glasses. "My family didn't need me to work, they have what they need, so I felt like I wanted to help those less fortunate, like these little ones here," he nodded over to the yard, "rather than just helping myself more."

He stared back to the courtyard where the kids were playing, looking at Blue like a loving younger brother would.

"Are you happy with your decision?" I asked as I stood with my arms crossed.

"At first, when I joined the church in August of last year, 1875," Shane started playing with some dirt that was below his boot, "I was so happy and elated. It was one of the best times of my life when I was ordained. I felt like my life finally had meaning," he threw a little piece of dirt that was in his hand onto the dirt ground below, "like the training I did at the Divinity School wasn't just for my own self-betterment."

"Divinity School?"

"Harvard Divinity School," he said as he looked over the children playing. "I went there a few years after graduating from Yale, and after working with my family's business," he threw another little rock onto the dirt floor below, a bored farmer waiting for the autumn harvest.

"I see," I remember nodding, still with my arms crossed.

"Come sit, come sit, some sit, Father Jasper," Shane said to me in a warm welcoming voice. I found Shane to normally be the quietest of all the three, never talking much. But on that warm Sunday in 1876, he had warmed up to me. Shane's right hand offered up the spot next to him on the bench.

"Much obliged," I said as I took off my big black hat and went to sit down next to him. We sometimes called each other by our first names, and at others by the more formal "father" and then the first name. I took the black worn satchel that was around my shoulder and put it on the dirt floor under the bench. We were sitting below a large tree above that covered our heads from the powerful California sun.

We sat in silence for a minute or so as a small breeze came in off the Pacific and brushed our faces with the cool air that had traveled all around the world to end up there, on our laps, in our eyes, and bringing refreshment on that summer day.

Then, suddenly, without me asking or saying anything, Father Shane continued:

"But, more recently," he looked over at me, "I have been troubled by certain dark events I have become aware of in the church," he said with his intense green eyes looking into mine, a plea for help, almost, from a drowning swimmer who has given up hope.

"I have even sent several letters to the Archdiocese about these events, these dark things, but the Archdiocese hasn't lifted a forceful finger so far to fix the problems. Supposedly," he looked back to the kids playing, "the new pope is going to be better at getting rid of this darkness cause he is supposed to be a reformer."

I joined Shane in overlooking, in a good shepherd way, the playing children.

"I must admit," he said with a sad hopeless tone, "these events have challenged my faith, my belief in whether there is a God."

He paused.

"And in the church in general," he said slowly, like you would say something you don't want to admit. He then looked over in Amber's direction in a caring way, the way you would look while

59

you are trying to escape from something, like when an alcoholic church going father finally admits his history of abuse."

"Days like this," he continued, "renew my faith and make me feel like all will end well, like my life isn't just a waste, and that my faith will have a positive impact, like it is having today," he said with some relief as he looked over at me with a soft smile and then just stared upon the scene.

The smile matched the way Shane spoke.

He had an understated almost whispering voice, the type you might hear when you are at a library and people are speaking the background, but they don't want to disturb anybody. It was a deep whisper.

We sat there for a minute or so before I inched up to asking him about just why he was troubled about the church, just why he had lost his faith, and I hoped that it would get me farther in my police investigation.

"Can I ask you something, Father Shane," I cautiously looked over to him.

"Of course, anything," he looked back over at me and patted me on the shoulder. I could tell he wanted to share, and hadn't been able to share, what had been troubling him.

"You said earlier, let me see," I looked up into the tree above us with the sun shining through and the wind slowly running through the leaves, sand in the hand that slips through your fingers, "you said earlier something like," I closed my eyes, "that you were 'troubled by certain dark events' that you 'become aware of in the church,' something like that?"

I looked over to him.

"Yes," he nodded and looked out in the distance.

"What dark events in the church have been making you question your faith in the God almighty?"

He looked over at me.

"Maybe he is not so almighty," he said point blank. "I'll tell you, as I haven't really had a chance to tell anybody before," he quietly said as he looked around to see if anybody was listening. "It started that day," he looked off blankly into the distance towards the yard of playing kids, "that day when I walked in on him, when I found him doing it."

"Who?" I remember asking.

"Father Ricardo Aube," he said with a troubled tone to his voice. "He was visiting our Mission for the weekend from his parish."

"And what was he doing, what did you find him doing?" I eagerly asked, like I was about to kiss the girl — his answer — that I been looking for, trying to reach, for oh so long.

Father Shane just kept blankly staring into the distance, like he was in a trance. A tear started coming down his left eye, then one started forming in his right, which I saw when he looked over back to me and said, with a tremble in his voice:

"The most unspeakable thing, Father, the most unspeakable thing," Shane then put his head into his hands, covered his eyes, and sobbed in a very understated way so that nobody could hear — but me.

"It's alright, Father, it's alright," I said in a comforting tone as I put my hand on his back, a way to get his trust so that he felt comfortable opening up to me more.

He looked back up at me.

"What is this unspeakable thing?" I stared into his eyes.

I thought to myself:

Maybe Father Aube was in on the gambling money that was being investigated by the "Stop 666" corruption commission, and was closing in on the circle of corruption that had supposedly enveloped the church?

"Aube was with," Shane started to say but then a little 5 year old or so leprechaun looking Irish boy with rotten teeth from the neighborhood came up to us and started crying.

"Father, Father, Father!" The boy said with pain in his voice, tears coming down onto his freckled face, sweat or maybe water in his bright red hair, as he tugged on Shane's jacket.

"What is it my son? What is it?" Shane asked.

"She hit me, she hit me, she hit me here," and then the Irish boy pointed to his arm where a tomboy girl who reminded me of Amber, perhaps, when she was younger, had bruised the boy's arm.

Suddenly, my memories of that July water fight Sunday talk with Shane were interrupted by Father Vivaldi, who came back from his take a shit digestion walk and said, as he sat down, "Eh, you miss me?"

He took a big bite out of his sandwich.

I just sat there watching Father Vivaldi eat, realizing I never found out what really troubled Father Shane that day in July.

"Sorry there, Father, I just was thinking about something that happened this past July."

"Is okay, is okay, my son," he nodded as he took a long sip off of his wine, and subtly wiped his mouth in the classy way that was becoming of his fancy clothes.

"What did you ask me about again before you took your walk?" I took a bite off of my sandwich. There was a rustling of the brush behind us, maybe some coyotes, maybe some crows, maybe something that wanted us to hear the rustling.

"What I ask you before I take the walk, let me see, I remember now, I was saying, let me see," Father Vivaldi said to himself as he looked into the distance behind me and, when he did, I could smell cologne.

"You smell that, Father?" I asked him.

"What, my son, the smell of the Mother Nature?" He smiled sarcastically.

"No, it's a smell of, a smell of . . . oranges, or something fresh like that, but there's no oranges around here," I looked around.

"Ah, my son, ah, this my cologne, is good, non?" He pulled up his collar to smell it.

"Cologne?" I asked.

"Yes, cologne. I travel much during my time when I was in Europe, and I pick up this scent in Paris, is made by, what is

62

name of this . . . Guerlain! Guerlain is the name of the maker of this, is good, no?"

"Never seen a man of the cloth wearing anything like that before."

"Eh," he shrugged and took a big bite off his salami, chewed it, wiped his mouth, "there no reason God not wanting his agents to smell the good smell, eh?" He smiled a sort of mischievous smile that let me know there was a lot more to this Italian priest that I didn't know, and perhaps would never know.

"So," he poured some more of his wine into his little silver cup that this "holy man" had in his jacket pocket while sitting in court — and through mass, too, I wondered? Was this his version of communion on the go?

Another reason why Vivaldi was excommunicated?

"The thing I asking you is, let me see," he looked down to his fancy boots, "ah! Is this: why you not the proud one for being the witness for the prosecution? I mean, I thinking, we here to find the truth, non? And you going to help this in the process, right?"

He looked at me through his dark Transylvania in winter-tinted sunglasses.

I just stared back at him, in a trance, thinking to myself why, deep down, I felt sort of ashamed, not proud, not at peace with myself, for doing what I was about to do. I thought back to the July water fight, thought back to my feeling that there was something horrible that Father Shane saw, and how it perhaps didn't have to do with gold rush money in the church. Instead, I wondered if it was something that was even more disturbing, something that was briefly covered in the *Underbelly of the Church* article in which Father Vivaldi is quoted, and which I — and likely Jarboe — have doubted all along until the leaks.

"Guess, Father," I shrugged as I played with a piece of grass on the table with my right hand, "that I was thinking back to when I seen them defendants doing great things for the church, taking care of the flock, and making the kids who didn't smile much smile a lot."

"And," Father Vivaldi nodded to me as he took another bite of his sandwich, "what did you think about these defendants when you seeing them doing these great things?" He chewed calmly and I got the feeling, maybe I am nuts or something, that maybe the Father was planted here, and that he was kind of playing some type of poker game with me.

Couldn't help but shrugging again, and just looking off into the shrubs behind the Father, where we heard some sounds earlier. Growing up in Virginia, I was always told by poppa and momma to tell the truth.

But remembering back to my July talk with Shane made me more comfortable, at the time, for not telling Jarboe everything I knew, and had seen. That's cause Shane got me thinking that maybe I had been wrong about all these families using their youngsters just to get money from the Church.

When Shane said "The most unspeakable thing, Father, the most unspeakable thing," and put his head into his hands and covered his eyes, he made me think there was something deeper, deeper in the Church, which was hurting his heart. Plus, seeing Blue and Amber playing, smiling, loving, and being so content with the children of the Mission got me questioning whether I had convinced myself to only see one side of the church story.

While it was Blue, Shane, and Amber on trial, I wondered if they were one shell in a three shell game that the hustler plays on the San Francisco street. He puts one shell out in front, wanting you to pick that one as having the quarter under it, when he knows that the quarter is under a shell closer to him. Something told me that there was more to the story, someone behind these three defendants, that was having them do them killings, or was doing the killings themselves — with Blue, Shane, and Amber being, what they call it, the red herring? Or maybe it was a little bit of both? Maybe they all in it together, whoever "they" is?

"I guess, Father," I said looking back at Vivaldi as he seemed to wait, so calmly, for my answer, "that I have some doubts about what the truth really is."

"Eh, son, we all have doubts about the many things, but what you have the doubts in," he leaned over slightly over the table, his fresh smelling scent now even more powerful in my nose, "what is the things you doubting?"

"Just can't," I looked down at my cowboy boots again, "just can't," looked over to the side of the table where a squirrel was fetching a nut with his mouth, "just can't believe that that those defendants would do such things," I said finally, quietly, like I was confessing to something I wasn't supposed to say.

And I wasn't, for God's sake!

I was supposed to be on their church's side, the right side, the proper side, the side of God, the true believer, the side of Jesus, the side of following the rules set out for me, and the picture that was given to me of what is real — and what is not. But I was beginning to feel, just a little, like you do when you feel that chill when it going to get to winter, but it only fall, and you feel it come, but it isn't there yet — you just feel that little chill in the air of the coming winter, but it is only fall.

"Eh, eh, my son," Vivaldi put down his little wine glass, which he was swigging all the long I was talking, "this is the normal, don't you thinking? This man, the nice looking gentleman of the prosecution, he going to tell you the things, going to tell you that the winter is not coming, even when you feel it, down in the, how you say, in the heart, in the bones, that it coming."

Vivaldi started putting his things away into his little satchel. He put the cap on top of his little flask, put the scraps of food back into the little Japanese looking wooden box he had the food in, and put all of the stuff into what was little his black doctor's case.

"Maybe, my son, just maybe," Vivaldi said as he started to get up from the bench, "they trying to make you see only the one side of the coin, only the one side of the moon, when there is the whole other side, that side you know is there, maybe only because you feel it in your heart, your bones, don't know for sure is there, because maybe you never been there, but," he paused to take his pocket watch out from his fancy suit vest to look at the time, "ah, my son, we must go back to the courthouse, cause it is time, but you go first, and I come long after, cause, as you saying, we can't be seeing with another, right?"

He looked over at me as though he knew it was wrong all along that we were speaking. But, perhaps just as Amber, Shane, and Blue, did right by doing wrong that day with the water fight, Father Vivaldi did right — or was trying to do so — by sitting with me that day during the first day of the trial.

"You are right, father, you are right," I started to get my things together. As I did, I didn't want to leave without knowing what he was going to say.

"Father?" I asked.

"Yes, my son,"

"You started to say before, but didn't say cause you looked at your watch, what were you going to say, please finish what you saying."

"Ah, yes," he said looking away for just a second at the black crow chirping behind me, patting his black doctor bag. "I saying that sometimes only the heart can know what your mind cannot see," he said to me then stopped rubbing his black bag. "And maybe that day your heart feeling something that your mind never seeing before, cause it never been told to see it, but your heart feel it is there, how you say?"

"How you say what?"

"Uh, that there is the other side of . . . uh, what they say now," he rubbed his forehead.

"The other side of the story?" I asked.

"Eh, yes, my son, yes," he said with a warm smile as I closed my eyes to take in what he was saying. When I opened my eyes,

Vivaldi had started walking back towards the white courthouse in the distance.

I also started walking towards the courthouse. Suddenly, I heard some rustling in the heavy brush next to me.

Got scared. I briefly looked up towards the clear sky wondering what to do as I walked. I stopped walking through the dusty path. The rustling stopped.

"Who's there?" I asked out loud. "I got a piece, you know," I put my hand in my jacket on my .45 Colt revolver, which was tucked neatly in my shoulder holster.

Stood there for a moment as a small breeze brushed up against my face. I shrugged my shoulders, thinking that the rustling was, perhaps, a coyote. I kept walking, with the dusty cloud coming off the ground as my cowboy boots dug up all the dirt that had been stuck in the ground for God knows how long. Northern California was going through a heavy drought, and so this land hadn't seen rain in months.

As I approached the clearing of the brush, and saw the top of courthouse in the, I heard more rustling. This time, I thought I heard some talking, maybe in a foreign language. But it was impossible to understand the whispering.

I stopped again but didn't say a word. I pictured the breeze that was rubbing itself against my face saying, in an ancient voice that had seen storms, wars, death, birth, autumn nights, and fires most of its days on the earth: "stop trying to figure it out so much, boy, and trust in the process."

While I kept walking through the brush, a deep voice from within asked: maybe those whispers in the brush were from insiders who caused the gruesome priest killings?

The answer would come, but not I until did some soul searching.

CHAPTER FOUR

BIRDWATCHER

"Fuck you and your bullshit timetable."

That's what I pictured Mr. Hyman's empty seat at the defendants' table yelling out to the judge while it held up a big middle finger. His empty seat stared everyone in the eye even though it was already about ten minutes after the bailiff had yelled out loud in the small courtroom, "all rise, all rise, all rise, this honorable court, the Superior Court of Mariposa County is now in session, Judge Parker presiding."

By then, everyone, including the defendants, had taken their rightful places — except for Hyman. Looking over at the jurors, Judge Parker looked pleased. I could tell he liked running a tight ship, and didn't play games with the people in his courtroom. Word has it that he has sanctioned witnesses and attorneys for being late.

He looked downright pleased until he glared at Hyman's empty seat.

"Bailiff," he looked over a the brawny sheriff with a thick beard, barrel chest, and who stood about five foot nine, "where the hell is that Hyman?"

"Uh, sir, I don't . . ." The bailiff started saying.

"I don't care," Judge Parker snarled at the bailiff, "get Hyman!"

Didn't let anybody see it, but I put my head down, looking towards my dusty cowboy boots and, yes, well, I admit it. I smirked.

That's when I heard the door to the courtroom open. I looked back towards the door with everyone else. Hyman walked in. He had his ratty looking black leather satchel with him.

Oh, that satchel was a Hyman satchel.

Looked like it had been underwater, then burnt by the sun for days on end, then pissed on it some by Hyman. He pissed on because he couldn't be smoking cigars with his clients, playing cards with them, spending time with his family — anything other than "being in this fucking boring courtroom" — and that satchel stood for courtroom drama.

Couldn't blame Hyman — I hated this courtroom, too.

He slowly walked down the right aisle next to the windows. I just stared at him. Everybody did. His faded black crappy suit was too big for him. It looked like he got it from a charity. One of his unpolished black dress shoes was untied, with the ragged shoelaces dragging on the ground.

Then there were his pants, which were too short. He made up for it by sagging them slightly below his waste, with his little belly hanging over his belt, which was on the last hole.

His "white" shirt was no better. Wrinkles upon wrinkles were on it, plus a smudge of a pencil or pen mark here and there, with his black knit tie loosely hanging from his neck.

In a whiney, or should I say weasel voice, he said, with an oblivious tone as he finished stuffing what looked like the last piece of a pastrami sandwich into his mouth surrounded by a face of overgrown whiskers:

"Apologies, your honor," he said as he licked some of the sandwich off his right index finger, "but I had to head home, problem with the little one throwing up all over things, and then I had this to finish," he held up the last piece of sandwich before he quickly put it into his mouth.

Judge Parker just stared disapprovingly at Hyman.

The sloth lawyer kept walking up the right aisle, towards the front of the courtroom, and then I could see him more closely. His skin looked like it hadn't seen the sun for days, or maybe even weeks, with little potholes here and there of, perhaps, pimples that had come and gone and left their bruises. Like his pants, his jacket was way too big for him, a little boy who wears his daddy's clothes trying to look grown up.

But the little boy still looks five years old even with those old man clothes.

As Hyman took his seat at the defendants' table, I could see Jarboe's face, the face of the establishment in San Francisco, the proper face, the face of the man with the hair parted on the right, the face of the man with the old American family that has a trust fund established for him, his kids, and his grand kids. A lucky sperm, some would say, for being born into the family he was born into. People like Jarboe hated people like Hyman, new comers, challengers, and outsiders to the power structure. But, for some reason, outsiders like Hyman were crafty enough to get power, respect, and money, even though, unlike Jarboe the proper WASP, Hyman was different.

He was Jewish.

There was a sneer on Jarboe's mouth, they way you would see one dog look at another and show it's fangs. Except that Jarboe's mouth didn't show his teeth. The right side of his lips just inched up, like he was grinding his teeth underneath, but not wanting to show it.

Judge Parker also had a sneer on his mouth as he glared at Hyman, not saying a word, as Hyman took out his items from the satchel and put them on the defendant' table.

Maybe the judge has that sneer because Hyman was late, or maybe its because Jarboe was everything that Hyman wasn't. Spoke to a reporter from the *San Francisco Chronicle* who wrote a feature article on Hyman, entitled *Legal Magician from New*

York, and I found out that Hyman was born on the Lower East Side of New York City on April 3, 1836.

That already makes him an outsider cause, like me, he isn't from these parts.

According to some of Hyman's fellow Jews from his temple, his family had to scrape and scratch for all they had, and, when they felt like life in New York City wouldn't do them any good, they came out to San Francisco. Suppose he was part of the wave of pioneering Jews like Levi Strauss, who has recently made some press with his jeans that all of the gold rush men wear to work.

Eager to show his patriotism, Hyman served in the U.S. Army during the Civil War — which lasted between 1861–1865 — for the Yankees.

Wouldn't have mattered to Judge Parker, even if he knew, cause he barked:

"If you are late one more time to my courtroom, Mr. Hyman, I shall sanction you $50.00." The judge pointed his thin authoritarian index finger at Hyman.

After the war, I found out, Hyman attended New York University Law School in that hodgepodge city of hoodlums from all around the world, not Jarboe's more prestigious Harvard Law School.

"Got it, your honor, my son is going to owe me a lot of money when he grows up if he gets any sicker," Hyman said with a wry sense of humor as kept pulling more of his crumpled notes out of his pissed on satchel, with little flakes of pigeon shit looking dandruff spewing on the table from his dark brown Jewish bouffant of hair.

Some of the people in the audience chuckled a bit at Hyman's comment. I sure did. I wonder if people in the audience knew that Hyman's five-year-old son had been diagnosed with a rare cancer not long ago.

"Order in the court, order in the court," the judge banged his gavel to quiet down people's giggling.

Judge Parker, like Jarboe, was of WASP background and had attended Yale Law School in New Haven, Connecticut, the place where, other than Harvard, most blue bloods go. And word had it that the judge's family, like Jarboe's was, old school, having arrived in the United States with the Mayflower.

During law school, I could have seen the judge, as professor, at Hyman's law school, warning him: "if you dress like that, and keep your hair like that, nobody will take you seriously, young man. You'll be a joke, a laughing stock of the Bar, and you'll wish you never went to law school, cause nobody will ever want to hire you cause you'll be a black sheep among white ones."

I could picture Hyman sitting calmly among the students, all laughing at him, smiling, and nodding in agreement with the judge. "You are right professor, you are right," he would say to the judge, "I got to get my act together, got to straighten up," as he would look down disapprovingly at himself and his notes on the table.

But, secretly, under his table, I could imagine Hyman flipping off the Connecticut proper professor off, and thinking to himself, as he did, "I'd run circles around you in front of a jury, you cracker fuck, cause I'd get my hands filthy — and you'd not want to ruin your fancy suit and manicure — to win."

"Is defense counsel ready to make his statement?" Judge Parker finally barked, looking down towards Hyman.

"Yes, your honor, I am ready," Hyman said softly and calmly as he sat with Blue on his right, Amber to Blue's right, and Shane at the end.

"Please proceed, counsel," Judge Parker said.

"Thank you, your honor," Hyman took a swig of his water on the table, put his crappy jacket on his chair, looked through some of his notes, and then slowly got up. The man wasn't drunk, or maybe he was, given how slowly he moved toward the front of the jury. It was like watching molasses drip off a piece of wood for days.

72

Remember Hyman standing in front of the jury. His hands were clasped together in front of him, as a priest might stand before his flock, with his shoelace lounging comfortably on the floor, and his left lace tied tight and nice, as he said:

"Counsel for the prosecution began his opening statement by asking you whether you believed in God."

Hyman's eyes stared sharply at the jury, a swordsman about to wield his sword on his victim — Jarboe.

"I will ask you a different question, ladies and gentlemen."

You wouldn't have believed from looking at him that Hyman was filthy rich. How'd he get that filth? Since starting to practice, he had tried 123 — you read the number right — jury trials, and won 80% of them, putting him in the top 5% of trial lawyers in the United States. Sure, Hyman was in the army, but I found out he never fought with his hands cause he was an intelligence officer.

"Do you believe that there is a dark side of the moon?" Hyman asked the jury.

The jurors all looked at one another.

"That's right, ladies and gentlemen, you can look at one another, speak, and wonder, but the question is very simple — do you believe that there is a dark side of the moon?"

Hyman now had a smirk on his face, a cat toying with the mouse — or maybe he was the mouse toying with the cat.

"I sure do. And, to be more specific," he nodded his head, "I **know** there is a dark side to the moon, just as I know that the number two follows the number one," he pointed to the imaginary numbers in the sky in front of him.

Oh, I am sure Hyman personally knew that dark side. From what the *Chronicle* reporter told me, Hyman got much of his start in The Five Points section of New York City, where he lived during law school. Reporters told me this section of New York had, at one point, the highest murder rate in the world, with one tenement, the Old Brewery, having a murder a night for 15 years until it was demolished in 1852. As you'll see later on from his extensive client list, the reporter told me living there was his introduction to another world that he may not have been privy to if it weren't for his neighbors, many of whom, if they aren't dead by now, have grown empires around the country, including here in San Francisco.

"You must all know there is a dark side of the moon because you have seen it. Of course, on some nights," he conceded in his speech to the jury, "there is only a full moon," and for this he moved slightly to the right, indicating the full moon. "But, on other nights," and now he moved to the left side of where he previously stood, "there is a dark part of the moon or, in the case of an eclipse, a completely dark moon."

Then he moved back to the middle, still with his hands clasped in front of him.

"In fact, you know and I know that, for most nights, the moon is slightly white, slightly black. But, regardless, there is a dark side."

He paused for a moment.

"And yet counsel for the prosecution wants to convince you that there is only a white moon."

He moved back to the right a little bit.

"'How's that?' You might ask yourself. Well, Mr. Jarboe has painted a picture of the Church, and of the victims of these heinous crimes, which makes it all sound so white and innocent. According to his view of the facts, these dead men were angels, investigating corruption in the Church, trying to save the white moon from becoming black, and that, as a result of their efforts, they were killed."

He looked up at the ceiling, as a young boy would when planning something sort of mischievous, and paused for a short moment.

"But I am going to show you that this is all untrue. You may be a child who has only seen the white moon, only seen a full moon, but I am going to show you that there is a dark side of the Catholic Church, and to these 19 dead priests."

Hyman walked back to his table and took a long sip of water. Unlike Jarboe's papers, which were all neatly put together in folders and labeled, Hyman's trial notes were, like playing cards, spread all around defendants' table, with some of them even falling on the ground.

This is the brainy brawler from New York? I asked myself.

I then looked closer at the sheets of paper. There weren't scribbles or chicken scratch on them. No. The writing was precise, an engineer type of writing, a blue print for a house, or a large building, but this was no house, and it wasn't a building, it was a criminal trial for murder. And yet I suppose they are, in some ways, the same.

And then Hyman did something that I hadn't seen any lawyer do during a trial. He plopped himself up on the table and sat on the edge, with his legs dangling and his loose shoelace touching the ground.

"If you recall," Hyman said still with his eyes focused intensely on the jurors, "the prosecutor split up his opening statement into who, what, and why," the banana slug moving attorney said smoothly as he summarized Jarboe's speech with those three words. "*Who* are these defendants sitting next to me, *what* does the evidence supposedly show what they did, and *why* did they allegedly do such horrible things to these 19 people of the cloth?"

He looked down to the ground and looked back up:

"Let's take a look at the dark side. Let's take the 'who' subject and flip it, ever so slightly, so that we ask: who are these dead men and are they as good as Mr. Jarboe makes them seem? And who are the defendants sitting next to me and are they as bad as Mr. Jarboe makes them seem?"

Hyman smiled knowingly like he had playing cards Jarboe didn't know about.

"The answers to these questions, ladies and gentlemen, are no."

He paused.

"And for the what question, does the evidence, all of the evidence, not just the pieces that the prosecutor wants to selectively tell you about, show that these defendants tortured or killed 19 priests?"

He looked up at the ceiling like he didn't know the answer.

"The answer to these questions, too, is no." He stared directly at the jurors.

"Finally, the why. Why were these 19 priests killed? The government's answer is they were killed because they were corruption fighting priests, and that these defendants were bad people."

He cocked his head slightly to the side, a man about to make an initial thrust with is knife, "as I will show you throughout the trial, these men were killed because they were evil, and there are many potential culprits who would have had the motive, means, and opportunity to do the killings, including, but not limited to, the parents of the children these men violated repeatedly throughout the years."

He straightened his head back.

"So let us begin with the who question, and ask: who were these 19 victims?

Hyman paused, took his hands from his lap, where they were intertwined, and put them on the desk next to his legs.

"These men," he then continued, "were not men of God, and they were not men of honor. No," he nodded his head, "these dead men were all rotten to the core, and they died in four sets of murders. I am going to take each set one by one to give you a glimpse of who these men really were."

The jurors all started to whisper. The people in the audience started to whisper, too, grasshoppers rubbing their legs together and making a background noise in the field on a warm summer night.

Judge Parker:

"Silence, I will have silence in my courtroom," he slammed his gavel down.

Hyman looked over his back on his left, and then over his right, back at me, to see what the audience was doing. When he saw me, he made a look of being fed up with the judge's antics, which I could tell for Hyman were too strong handed.

The whispering stopped.

"I really appreciate the noise control, your honor," Hyman sarcastically said to Judge Parker. "As I was saying, ladies and gentlemen of the jury, while these men died horrible deaths, and I am disgusted at the savagery of the murders, I think you need to know that these men weren't the upstanding members of the church like the prosecution would like you to think."

He paused.

"The first five who were killed," he kept his right hand up with the five fingers in front of him, "were: Fathers Ricardo Aube, Roger MacRae, Gordon Fortier, Zachery Connor, and Jerry Paralta. Now," he lowered his right hand, "who were these men? They were all men who came here to California from elsewhere in the United States, from far off places like Boston, Chicago, New Orleans, Milwaukee, and St. Louis. And why did they come to San Francisco from far off places? For money, for fame?"

He surveyed the jury with his dark beady olive colored eyes.

"No. The Vatican transferred these men to the San Francisco Archdiocese. Now, the Vatican is the headquarters of the Catholic Church and is based in Vatican City, Rome, Italy."

Hyman briefly looked out the window.

"Under the Vatican, there are each of the Dioceses in these United States, who act as the local headquarters for each of their cities, and then down the ladder. The Vatican is the umbrella, and under that umbrella are the Dioceses, and each city has one. On top of this ladder in the local Diocese are the Cardinals," he put his palm parallel to the floor to indicate the top level, "then there are the Bishops on the level below that," he held his palm parallel to the ground just below where he previously had it, "and then you have the Priests down here," he held his palm parallel to the ground even lower below the other two levels.

He took a sip of his water. The jury members were just staring at him at this point, and there wasn't a sound in the courtroom, making the chirping of the birds on the trees outside even more prominent.

"And why did the Vatican transfer these five men to the San Francisco archdiocese? They were transferred because in each of these cities from which these men came, they were being investigated by the district attorney for, indicted for, or convicted of violating laws prohibiting sexual relations with children, otherwise known as crimes against Mother Nature, cause it is against the natural order."

Some members of the jury were now covering their mouths, whereas others were shaking their heads, although I wasn't clear if they were doing this because they were in disbelief, or because they were disgusted, or a little bit of both.

"And what about the second set of five priests who were killed?" Hyman put his left hand up and flashed the number five. "Their names: Fathers Ricky Vasquez, Timothy Cruces, Felix Trupia, Lou Tugade, and Doug Teta. These men, too, were all from other cities outside of San Francisco, some coming from as far away as Lima, Peru."

He paused as he put his hand down.

"During my case in chief, which happens after Mr. Jarboe sitting over there is done presenting his witnesses and evidence, I will present witnesses on behalf of the defendants to show that these men, like the first set, were all," he stared at the jury for a moment, "rotten."

One of the ladies in the front of the jury just put her hand on her head and she shook it, disgusted, in disbelief, with sadness, depressed, I thought.

"Father Canon de Vivaldi, whew, I need to take a break after getting that name out of my mouth," Hyman smiled at the jurors, "is a priest from the Vatican. He will testify about the leaked documents showing the Vatican's policy of transferring priests known to be abusive in order to keep up their window dressing."

Hyman moved around his wrinkled notes.

"After Father Vivaldi, I'll have various district attorneys from other jurisdictions from where these priests were transferred from testify about the their bad acts, indictments, or convictions."

While I had read about these things in the papers, I always thought they were just planted information to get more money out of the church. I think Jarboe believed the same thing. Put a child up on the stand, and a jury will believe whatever he or she has to say. I always felt like the media was in on it, cause they sold more papers that way.

"The third set of dead priests? Their names: Fathers Chris Murphy, Gary Keisle, Jose Maciel, Jerry Hargadon, and Steve Hahn."

Hyman looked down at his shoe, noticing the shoelace wasn't tied, and put his shoe up next to his knee to tie it. As he did, he started to speak:

"The common tie between this set of five priests, and the previous priests I mentioned? I bet you can guess the answer now, ladies and gentlemen of the jury. These men, like the previous ones, all had either been in the process of being investigated for molestation charges, or had been convicted, in the cities from which they came. Not long after these investigations began, or after the convictions, these men were transferred to the San Francisco diocese."

Hyman put his leg down and let it hang. To add gusto to the final set, Hyman the showman got up off the desk, and walked closer to the jury, this time with his arms crossed. He stood just a few feet from the jury box now, looking at each of the jurors in their eyes.

"And the final set, the final four," he held out his right hand and put up four fingers. "These men were more powerful. Remember the church power structure I mentioned before, the Cardinals at top, then Bishops, and then the priests down below?"

Most of the jurors just nodded their heads at him in agreement.

"Two of these final four were cardinals, and two of them were bishops. Their names: Cardinal John Krol, Cardinal Justin Bevilacqua, Bishop Eugene O'Sullivan, Archbishop John Pilarczyk."

Hyman put his palm up as high as he could and faced it towards the ground.

"These men were way up here. And yet, from their conduct, they should have been down here," he made his palm go down to close to his shoe and then got back up after crouching down. "Like the lowly priests before them, these men, too, were either investigated or convicted for either directly committing crimes against Mother Nature, or overseeing and allowing such crimes to occur under their oversight knowing, all along, it what was going on," he said with a somber tone. "One of the worst being Cardinal John Krol, who is reported to have personally molested, or oversaw and allowed the molestation, of 21 children."

Other jurors, who seemed to be listening with disbelief, like they wanted to waive their hand and make it all go away, seemed to be paying attention now. One man, a more traditional looking one, who I could have seen saying "this is all made up bullshit for money," was now listening intently.

"Father Vivaldi will testify about how Archbishop John Pilarczyk worked with Pope Scrivener, the former pope, in getting abusive priests transferred from other jurisdictions to the Archdiocese of San Francisco."

I looked around and the courtroom's eyes were transfixed on Hyman.

"Father Raul Jimenez even reported Cardinal Krol's criminal acts to the Vatican, who at the time was being run by the old pope. What did the Vatican do?"

Hyman looked over all of the jurors with his hands clasped in front of him.

"They did worse than nothing. The old pope, Pope Alberto Scrivener, held an event in the Cardinal Krol's honor. And why?"

He now paused to let this one stick in.

"Because Cardinal Krol was one of the biggest fundraisers for the church."

The jurors were making subtle sounds of disgust under their breaths.

Hyman got me thinking, more and more, about what I believed — and didn't — as I sat there. Got me thinking back to the water fight I had seen that July in the church courtyard.

"So, just to be clear, we are still in the who section of the presentation, and we are still focused on who were these dead men. We'll get to these people sitting right there," Hyman turned around to look at Blue, Amber, and Shane, "shortly."

He then sat back up on the defendants' table. He was the folksy lawyer with the folksy presentation — and it seemed to be working. The jurors, some looking somewhat skeptically on him before, were now in a trance.

"If you recall," Hyman crossed his hands in front him, "the prosecution claimed that all of these men were members of a commission formed in January of this year, 1876, and that this commission was formed to investigate the infusion of dirty gambling and gold rush money into the church, the biggest offender of which was Mission Dolores."

Hyman stopped to look over the jurors to make sure they nodded.

"It is true there was a commission, as you will hear from the government's witness, Father Degollado. It is also true that the **stated**, and I'll say that again, the **stated** purpose of this commission was to investigate this supposed sin money coming into the Mission. But what the prosecution didn't tell you was that there was a major leak of sensitive Vatican documents to the press on Christmas day of last year, 1875."

The audience members started whispering in the background, but not loud enough for the judge to take notice.

"What was in these leaked documents, you may ask? Enough to show that there has been a practice of knowing priest shifting by the Vatican for years now, and that the San Francisco Archdiocese was one of the locations where priests — or cardinals and bishops — from other locations could be sent to find safe haven from prosecution."

An older man with a long white beard, sitting in the back, started yelling:

"Devils in priest clothing! Devils in priest clothing! And the Vatican protected them! They are the real criminals! The real criminals!"

"Order, order in the court," Judge Parker yelled. "Bailiff!" The husky bailiff went to the back of the sunny courtroom to remove the old man. Hyman had turned around to see the man being kicked out of the courtroom, and then turned back to the jury when the man was outside.

As the crowd quieted down and turned their attention back towards the front of the courtroom, Hyman, picked up where he left off.

"Ladies and gentlemen, great minds think alike," he said as he cracked a small smirk on his face, in reference to what the old man was saying. "And what the evidence will show you is that this commission was formed by these poor dead souls for no reason other than finding out who was responsible for the leaked documents from the local San Francisco Archdiocese, and in an attempt to discredit whoever made the leak by making them look like **they** were criminals themselves, thus taking the focus off the content of the leaked documents — and putting it on the supposed sin money coming into Church coffers."

"Now," Hyman went back to the table where his water was, he took a long sip, like he was ready to start on another part of his long distance race.

He put the glass down on the table. He walked towards the jury. He slowly looked them in their eyes. There wasn't a noise in the room.

"I have an admission to make, ladies and gentlemen," he said slowly as he looked down onto his shoes like he was ashamed.

He looked up.

"I am a heathen."

He stared at the jury for a minute or so.

"Do you know what that means? Do you know what it means to be a heathen?"

He surveyed the jury's eyes.

"It means someone who doesn't recognize the God of the Bible," he nodded over to the Bible that was sitting on the table next to the judge.

"Does that shock you? Does it shock you that I am a heathen?"

He paused.

"It shouldn't. If being a believer in the God of the Bible means being associated with a Church that allows its members to abuse helpless children, without any recourse, except for transferring them from one Archdiocese to another, then, I must admit, I'd only want to be a heathen."

He smiled as I imagined Lucifer would in criticizing the kingdom that God has created — "if you are so perfect, so pretty, so loving, then why is this world that you created so imperfect, so ugly, and full of hate?"

"Yes, ladies and gentlemen, the prosecutor, Mr. Jarboe came up here and said during his opening statement that my clients sitting over there," Hyman nodded to the three defendants sitting at the table, "are heathens. He asked the question, let me see what it was," Hyman looked up to the ceiling, "something like 'who are these heathens sitting over there?'"

Hyman paused.

"I'll tell you who these heathens are, and why I am proud to say that they are heathens if being with God means doing what these dead men were doing, as the evidence will show you."

"Mr. Jarboe says Defendant Amber Maggie Francis sitting over here: is a ruthless killer who enjoys hanging her prey from trees, grew up with a gypsy family, and is an expert marksman and knife thrower."

Hyman looked at Amber with affection.

"And Mr. Jarboe's proof?" Hyman then asked looking at the jury.

"A former lover of hers."

He smiled a smile like he had something that Jarboe didn't.

"Well," he shrugged, "some of this is true. You will hear from Mr. Theo Adams, the son of Mr. John "Grizzly" Adams, the man who ran the circus Ms. Francis and her family worked at. Mr. Adams will testify that Ms. Francis *is* from a gypsy circus family that has been running the open country of California for many years now with their caravan, attending and running country circuses from the south to the north of the state."

The jurors started rumbling to one another. The old man next to me leaned over and said quietly to his wife, "I knew this woman was bad news."

"Mr. Adams will testify that Ms. Francis *is* an expert knife thrower, marksman, and rope handler."

The jury started talking again amongst themselves. The old man said to his wife, "she an evil woman, I knew it when I seen her."

"But there are a few things that Mr. Jarboe didn't tell you about Ms. Francis' family, and about his scorned lover witness, maybe because Mr. Jarboe didn't know. You see, her family wasn't only a bunch of gypsies, but they were also members of what they called the California Underground Railroad, responsible for helping slaves escape from the south to freedom in California."

He paused.

"Not only that. But Mr. Adams will testify that this scorned lover of my client's was rejected by Ms. Francis, and, afterwards, Mr. Adams overheard this scorned lover say he would do anything to make her life miserable for rejecting his hand in love."

Hyman smirked.

"They say hell have no wrath like a woman scorned, but hell never seen a man scorned!"

The jury members chuckled, and so did many folks in the court.

"Order, order!" Judge Parker slammed his gavel.

"And the reason I mention the freed slaves? Well, you'll hear testimony from Mr. Adams that waves of southern bounty hunters had come to retrieve their clients' property — that is the escaped slaves — and that these black folks hung these bounty hunters and cut their hands off — just like how the first set of priests were killed. I'll introduce news articles into evidence reporting that these hangings were widely known to be done by these freed slaves — *not* Amber Francis."

Hyman stared intently at the jurors with sweat beading ever so slightly on his forehead. He calmly wiped the sweat away.

"The message, ladies and gentlemen, to the bounty hunters' employers was you might send them, but they not coming back alive. And so y'all better keep your hands to yourself."

Hyman surveyed the jury.

"Cut off hands to send a message of keeping your hands to yourself. Doesn't that sound familiar?"

A woman in the jury was visibly upset at what Hyman was saying. I wondered to myself as I sat there in the audience, waiting to testify, whether Hyman's strategy was a good one. Many folks in California, while they maybe didn't approve of slavery, nonetheless had a need for cheap labor, which was why many of the Chinamen was out here working on the railroads and such. Many folks also didn't like the Negro much, although many wouldn't admit it out in the open.

But maybe Hyman had a bigger plan under his sleeve.

"Finally, Sister Barbara Johnson will testify about the wonderful and joyous things that Ms. Francis did for the church, and how cherished she was not only by the children in her flock for following the example of the Virgin Mary, but also by other nuns and priests in the Mission of Dolores. Why would a woman who was so beloved by her community commit such heinous sins, and risk being excommunicated? And will you believe that she did do such things merely because an ex-lover of hers, someone who is willing to do anything to get back at her, says so? Does the fact that these horrible hangings were committed the way they were tie Ms. Francis to them beyond a reasonable doubt?"

He stared knowingly at the jury.

"You know the answer, deep in your hearts, to these questions, ladies and gentlemen, is no."

Hyman walked slowly back to the table, and took another long swig of the water, and reviewed the notes he made during Jarboe's opening statement.

"Quiet storm," Hyman then suddenly said out loud as he reviewed his notes, almost like he was taking roll in school for a boy named "Quiet Storm."

He turned around to the jury.

"Isn't that what Mr. Jarboe called Defendant Shane Egan?" Hyman looked warmly back at Shane, who was sitting there in his priestly outfit, looking intensely up at Hyman and the jury with snake green eyes.

"A quiet storm of a man, Mr. Jarboe called him," if my notes are right. "A storm that you don't hear coming, or even when it hits. It is silent but deadly."

Hyman looked over his shoulder in my direction, and made a small smirk. Whatever one could say about this man, him not having a sense of humor isn't one of them.

"And why does Mr. Jarboe," Hyman turned back around to face the jury as he walked in their direction, a tamer trying to get a hold of a wild animal that will bite if you move too fast, or in an untrusting way, "choose to tarnish Mr. Egan's character in this way?"

This was another rhetorical question that Hyman was about to answer for himself.

"For two reasons. The first is that the Mission Dolores janitor, Poncho M. Sanchez, supposedly saw a bloody saw underneath Mr. Egan's bed shortly after the first set of murders, the idea being that the saw was used to hack the priest's hands off."

Looking back at Shane, Hyman started his second point.

"The second reason is a Chinese cook, one Mr. Sun Tzu, who used to work at the Egan compound in Pacific Heights," Hyman looked over at Jarboe with an irreverent look, "this Chinese cook supposedly has the inside scoop on the Egan family's murderous methods, knows all of their gory details, and is going to tell you about them later today in this trial so as to link Mr. Egan to the second set of murders."

Hyman then cracked a small smile on his face and started doing a pace in front of the jury. But when Hyman did it, it wasn't so serious, like it was with Jarboe. Hyman waddled, like a comedian, whereas Jarboe paced, like a military man.

"But who is this Mr. Sanchez, the janitor at the Mission Dolores church? Our witness, the gardener at Mission Dolores, whose name is Mr. Katsumi Yamamoto, will testify that he saw Mr. Sanchez taking money from a representative of the San Francisco archdiocese before the trial started."

Some of the jurors whispered to one another.

"And who is this Chinese cook Mr. Sun Tzu?" Hyman asked the jury as he slowly walked with this right shoelace coming undone, and his pants looking like they would rather be floating in the river instead of hanging from his unhealthy body.

"Genghis Wu, a private investigator that my office uses, will testify that Mr. Tzu, the former Egan cook, is a Triad," he said as he stopped in front of the jury and looked at them with the eyes I imagine Amber would use when she was shooting the apple on top of the man's head from 440 yards away.

Hyman cocked his head.

"And what is a Triad? You might ask."

He smiled. About to push the knife in the cook's stomach.

"Mr. Wu will explain that Triads are a criminal organization, and that the Wo Hop To faction based out of Hong Kong have made inroads into the San Francisco market."

The jurors whispered to one another.

The old man next to me whispered to his wife, ever so quietly, "damn chink is going to ruin the man's case," he said, referring to Jarboe's case.

"What do the Triad's do in San Francisco? They ship in opium, sex slaves, illegal immigrants from China, in addition to intimidating the local Chinese population into paying protection money, or else they get their stores blown up," Hyman leaned over the little fence separating him from the jury to emphasize the point.

"Blown up, all of your life savings, your whole life, just because you don't pay protection money."

He leaned back away from the jury and crossed his arms.

"Mr. Wu will further testify that, shortly before the indictment against my clients, he saw this former cook from Defendant Egan's family meeting with high ranking members of the Triad clan, and taking money from them in dark alleys and other places in that city over there," Hyman nodded his head towards San Francisco, "where you wouldn't want to walk."

Hyman started walking back to the table where his water was. Unlike Jarboe, whose movements seemed more tense, more governed by a ruler, Hyman's movements were loose, more governed by scales that weigh right one time, and then left on others. Jarboe was the clean polished knife, Hyman was the rusty dull looking one that cuts you deep and wide anyway. Hyman lifted himself up onto the table, and, as he did, he asked:

"Why would the Triads want to have a plant in Defendant Egan's family, and why would they want to have this plant — the cook, Mr. Tzu — make up lies about my client, Shane Egan, and his family in general?"

"Simple. The Egan family is very wealthy. They are the perfect extortion target for the Triads. They say to the Egan family, 'you give us money to protect your businesses, or we not only will kill you like we have killed others, but we will ruin your son's reputation.'"

Hyman's legs were going back and forth underneath the table now.

"If you recall, Mr. Jarboe said that, in the second set of priest killings, priests were dismembered, their body parts put on church tress, and the priests' torsos were left in the bay," Hyman looked over the jury. "But I'll introduce convictions of Triad members to show, ladies and gentlemen, that the Triads — *not* the Egan family — killed their enemies in the exact same way."

Hyman made a fuck you look over at Jarboe.

And then I got to thinking. Was the whole trial a farce? Were Hyman, Jarboe, and these Triads somehow in on this thing? I've always had a vivid imagination, but, being a detective, I always think about the unthinkable. I started giggling even more when I thought about this. Nobody else seemed to notice, perhaps, or care. Except for the old man sitting next to me.

"Sorry, sir," I said quietly.

"This is no laughing matter, son," he said somberly.

"I understand, I'm sorry."

Hyman continued:

"Sister Johnson will testify that Mr. Egan, like Ms. Francis, has been one of the most trusted and respected scholars of the Catholic Church since he joined on August 14, 1875, after graduating from Harvard's Divinity School, and has been beloved by not only the priests and nuns that work with him, but his own flock, as one of the parish members of Mission Dolores will testify."

The jurors seemed confused. They didn't know which way to go.

"Finally, ladies and gentlemen, Dr. Ephram Emerson, chair of the Harvard Divinity School, will testify about the torture of children Mr. Egan saw at the hands of San Francisco Archdiocese priests, his written protestations to the Archdiocese insisting that something be done, the comforting he gave to parents whose children suffered this way, and the amount of praying that Mr. Egan did, hoping the new pope would do something about it, as relayed in several letters Dr. Emerson received from Mr. Egan."

Hyman took his hands out from under his secret passing gas ass.

"So you see," he put his hands out in a pleading way in front of him, "the fact that the second set of the these horrendous murders were done in this cutting fashion doesn't show that young Shane Egan perpetrated them."

Hyman smiled a sly smile. The smile, which said there was something that this man was hiding underneath, reminded me of an old Chinaman that I heard about a few years ago when a Chinese laundry woman came into the precinct to report a horrible fight between the old Chinaman and five men who jumped him.

The Chinaman was about 85. The laundry woman said he could barely walk, that he wobbled side to side, and that he had a foo man mustache — like the handle bar sported by so many around these parts, but longer at the edges, trailing down to the top of his chest. She said he would normally walk around with his hands clasped in front of him, so that you couldn't see them, sagging his pants, and ***seemed*** to not know where he was going most of the time.

He broke that illusion one night so many winters ago.

The laundry lady reported that the Chinaman was walking next to a dark alley when, suddenly, five young rough men jumped the Chinaman — she said that three of the men were massive, with tree trunk forearms, and that the two remaining smaller men had knives. She told us that the five men thought the Chinaman would be easy prey.

According to the laundry lady, as the five men started to attack the old man Chinamen, he suddenly farted as he:

1. Busted big man #1's nose with a ferocious agile kick;

2. Snapped #2 man's neck, who charged the old man from behind, in a head lock;

3. Spun over #2 man's back to do a knockout roundhouse kick on men #3–#4; and

4. Used his claw hands to fetch the eyes out of remaining man #5.

Like the Chinaman, Hyman looked like he had been out all night long drinking, like he didn't know where he was half the time, and sagged his pants. And so, as I just stared at Hyman's sly smile, I thought back to the Chinaman story, and how it was just a big head fake, a bunch of bullshit.

But it worked.

"And now we have the 'outlaw from the land of Illinois,' a phrase that Mr. Jarboe used to refer to my client," Hyman said as he looked down onto his notes next to him as he sat on the table as though he was leisurely picnicking on a Sunday.

Hyman got up and started walking towards the jury.

"Before I address opposing counsel's statement about Mr. Hardin, I wanted to first offer you a definition of a crucial term that Mr. Jarboe used," Hyman looked over, with smart ass affection over at Jarboe. "That word, ladies and gentlemen," Hyman looked back at the jury with a self-satisfied smirk, "is outlaw."

The old man next to me mumbled to his wife, ever so softly, "why the hell is this man telling us what we damn already know?" He shook his head in frustration.

"Murderer, murderer, Blue Hardin is a God damn murderer!" A witch white skinned lady said from the back of the courtroom, this time with her fist in the air.

Judge Parker:

"Order in the court," he slammed his gavel hard. "Bailiff!"

As the craziness died down, Judge Parker:

"Mr. Hyman, please finish with your opening statement, so that we can get out of here on time," the judge said as he took out his pocket watch to check the time.

"Thank you, your honor," Hyman said then walked back to the front of the jury.

"So, where were we, ah, outlaw, right?" He said to the jurors as he rubbed his teenager boy beard. "We all think of an outlaw as someone who has broken the law, but another part of the definition is someone who is still at large, that is, someone who hasn't paid for their crimes," he surveyed their eyes and faces.

He looked back at Blue.

"Is this man, Mr. Blue Hardin, an outlaw?" He asked out loud.

Looking back at the jury.

"Yes," Hyman said as he nodded his head in agreement.

The jurors all stared at one another.

"Mr. Hardin *is* an outlaw. He *has* done bad things in the past he hadn't paid for," Hyman looked back at Blue, who was sitting with his quiet blue eyes staring straight ahead, looking at Hyman.

Hyman turned to look back at the jury.

"But that doesn't mean that Blue Hardin committed these crimes."

He paused.

"Yes, Mr. Hardin was indicted by a grand jury for robbing 19 banks in the state of Illinois, including ten large banks in the City of Chicago. In fact," Hyman made a grand smile, "he was one of the most prolific bank robbers in the history of Illinois."

Hyman looked down to swipe some dirt off his knee.

"But the man never did time — always escaped the grips of the law, somehow. So, in this respect," Hyman nodded, "he is an outlaw. He remains at large for these crimes."

He paused again.

"And yet we aren't here to convict Mr. Hardin for any of his past bad acts, which are irrelevant to this jury trial, unless any of those bad acts are relevant to showing that he was using some common design or plan to commit the murders he is charged with today."

Hyman pulled up his sagging pants.

"Of course, Mr. Jarboe will have the Mayor of Vandalia, Illinois, the town where Mr. Hardin is from, testify not about the bank robberies, but that Mr. Hardin committed several gruesome murders of bank presidents back in Illinois, and that these murders resemble the third set of priest murders in San Francisco, because the bank presidents were either abducted off the streets or caught in their homes at night, knocked out, strapped down to beds, and their stomachs were cut open, all the while the murderer — or murderers," Hyman smiled at his twist from the singular to the plural, "just sat there smoking his cigar, or they sat there smoking their cigars," another small smile.

Hyman looked back behind the prosecutor's table at the Vandalia mayor.

"But Mr. Hardin was never indicted — or convicted — for the murders of the 19 bank presidents that the Vandalia mayor will testify to," he looked back at the jury.

"Don't get me wrong. The government wanted to get Mr. Hardin indicted for these murders, but he never was."

He walked to get some more water and then calmly leaned against the defense counsel's table.

"You might ask why?" Hyman looked to the jurors.

"Retired Judge Richard Neal of the Cook County Criminal Court, who oversaw the indictments of Defendant Hardin, will testify that it was well known among Chicagoans — including members of the grand jury — that these presidents' banks were members of a holding company that embezzled funds from various unions, including the retired teachers' union, under the guise that the money was being invested in the stock market . . ."

Hyman stood there for a moment, moved his untied right shoe to the right, and stared at each of the jurors, some type of mental telepathy, I thought. Or maybe he was checking out some of the female jurors cause he hated being there.

"In fact, ladies and gentlemen, the money was invested with the bank presidents' investment brokers, who lost the money in risky investments while, in the meantime, these bankers made handsome fees from the investments and the bank presidents compensation packages, get this," Hyman smiled to himself, "went through the roof!"

He clapped his hands at the cronyism he was outlining to the jurors.

"And which banks is Mr. Hardin alleged to have robbed? Judge Neal will testify that it was only banks that had such fraudulent holdings."

The jurors whispered.

"This explains why the jurors hearing this back in Illinois felt that there was enough reasonable doubt to think it was Hardin that did these murders — but the people whose lives were ruined by this white collar crime."

Hyman smiled at this next punch.

"And they were right to do so, because I have convictions to show you of some professors at the schools embezzled from, in addition to some union leaders, that were indicted for committing some of these murders," Hyman wiped his forehead free of the sweat.

"What a crock of shit," the old man said to his wife sitting next to me. "I can't believe they are letting this Jew piece of shit make a mockery of this fine establishment. I looked over at the old man, who asked me: "you got something to say, partner?"

"No sir," I said to back to him.

As though Hyman heard the old man:

"In any event, ladies and gentlemen, Judge Neal's testimony will show that Mr. Hardin wasn't convicted of these Illinois murders and that they don't show a common plan because only hand rolled cigarettes were found at these Illinois murder scenes, not cigars."

Hyman looked back at the old man's direction. He was surprised that the seeming lackluster Hyman heard the "piece of shit" comment. Hyman looked back in the direction of the jury.

"Finally, Sister Johnson will testify that Blue Hardin has been a cherished member of the Mission since joining it on November 21, 1851, that all of the flock love him dearly, especially the children," Hyman put his hand down close to the ground, "and that he has done much in the community to improve the reputation of the church," Hyman put his hand out as though he was offering seeds to some birds that would come and eat out of his hand.

He also smirked as his eyes squinted towards the jury and said: "don't you know that some of the best sinners are some of the best saints?"

In addition to that old Chinaman from the alley, I remember then also realizing who Hyman reminded me of. During police force training, we had a man who did intelligence during the Civil War. They called men like him "birdwatchers," or a "birdwatcher." They would walk around most days, looking like they were doing nothing, other than spotting, identifying, and checking out birds in the sky with their binoculars.

Meanwhile, in truth, every little movement, hand twitch, taking off the hat, or putting it back on a certain way, was a signal to those watching of the intelligence gathered by the man. There was no way to infiltrate the messaging, unless you knew the code. This allowed the birdwatcher to go into dangerous territory behind enemy lines, and give messages to their associates.

The birdwatcher doing the police training had the same subtle smirk as Hyman. Little gestures subliminally indicating certain messages that, while the jurors aren't conscious of them, get them thinking the way that Hyman wants them to think.

"Now, let us turn to the what question — what does the evidence prove that the Defendants' did?" Hyman asked.

He looked with annoyance outside the window — like he wanted to take a shit, go bird watching, cook dinner for his family, or go skinny-dipping with his wife. Then he glanced back at the jury.

"Mr. Jarboe's proof that these defendants did the crimes, these four sets of murders? He acts like his canoe had no holes in it, that it is perfectly safe. But as I have previewed to you so far, and I will show you throughout the trial, each of his witnesses for the first three sets of murders are stuck in quick sand."

Hyman briefly looked over to his notes, then back at the jury.

"That leaves the final set of murders. What is the government's evidence linking the defendants to these murders?"

He smiled.

"Their secret weapon is an undercover cop planted in the Mission Dolores who supposedly heard Defendant Egan, saying 'sister, the lads are minced meat, and they never coming back again,' on September 9, 1876, the date of the *Chronicle* article entitled *Four Church Higher Ups Reported Missing*, about the disappearances of Cardinal Krol, Cardinal, Bevilacqua, Bishop O'Sullivan, and Archbishop Pilarczyk on Sunday, September 3."

He said as he looked at his notes.

"This cop will also testify how the Defendants, on September 9th, celebrated the murders, drinking moonshine, and dancing in the Mission Dolores courtyard as this cop read the *Four Church Higher Ups Reported Missing* article out loud."

"Does this mean," Hyman looked up, "that the defendants actually caused the disappearances of these four missing priests, *or* that the defendants merely approved of their disappearances?"

He paused.

"There is a difference. If my clients merely approved of, or even celebrated, these disappearances, then they are not guilty of first degree murder."

"And what of," Hyman looked down at his notes, "Mr. Hardin's alleged response to Mr. Egan's comment which was, according to my notes, 'Shane is right, sister, they is minced meat, good riddance,' and then Mr. Hardin supposedly spit on the ground. What of that?"

Hyman just stood there for a second waiting for the train that would never come.

"Even if it's true," he looked up from his notes of paper, "this doesn't mean Mr. Hardin is guilty of murder. It merely means," this time he put his head down to stare at the jury, "that he is a good man who celebrated when he heard divine justice being served."

The jurors whispered, touched each other in their arms, as did the audience.

Hyman walked slowly back to the juror's box, leaned over so that he was as close as he could be to the jurors without violating protocol.

"Is there any doubt, ladies and gentlemen of the jury, as to why persons other than the ones sitting at the table over there would do such crimes?"

He closed his eyes.

He opened them then said:

"Others who would and could have done these crimes include: the parents of the kids, the priests who are angered that their crosses have been dragged through the mud, outlaws who think what these men did is worse than anything they could imagine, siblings of the children who couldn't stand another trial where the guilty evade prosecution, or, perhaps, just perhaps, maybe a few great cops who have had enough of the rule of law being floundered to the point where innocent children are tortured — and nobody listens."

Hyman put his head down.

"And why hasn't anybody listened, why hasn't anybody lifted a finger, why hasn't the Vatican been more interested in changing course?"

He then stared at the jury and answered his own question:

"Money. There is no money in saving the innocent smile, no illegal contraband for the state to seize and sell, no business lobbying the lawmakers in Washington D.C. or Sacramento to take action."

He stood back up straight.

"But you'll hear from a couple who did take action, and got themselves locked up as a result."

He crossed his arms and closed his eyes, seemingly in pain.

"Gustav and Carla Gianni," he started to say while his eyes were closed, "were some of the finest and most beloved members of the San Francisco community, the husband having founded Sutro & Co., San Francisco's oldest investment bank, in 1858. For years, this man's firm, you will hear, provided much needed capital to San Francisco entrepreneurs ranging from fishing companies to restaurants."

He opened his eyes and they had a sad intensity about them.

"That all stopped in 1869, which is when Mr. Gianni and his wife were convicted of conspiracy to murder — via poison. And who were Mr. and Mrs. Gianni conspiring to kill? Fathers

Aube and MacRae, the ones who were hung in front of St. Mary's church, along with the Archbishop, who was killed on September 3 earlier this year."

The jurors and the people around me whispered. Judge Parker just stared at the jurors, schoolchildren who stopped being naughty when they saw his disapproving eyes.

"Why, you might ask yourself, would such beloved and respected members of the San Francisco banking establishment throw it all away? Their parties, their house, their reputations, their friends, and the list goes on?"

Hyman's eyes were in ruthless Machiavelli mode.

"Mr. and Mrs. Gianni, both of whom I represented in their criminal trial, will testify that the Archbishop knew about the crimes of Fathers Aube and MacRae but covered them up, told nobody, and kept going about his business like nothing was happening at the St. Mary's church where these two priests presided."

But there was also a bitter sweetness in his eyes, too, at having to be ruthless.

"Meanwhile, Mr. and Mrs. Gianni's sons — Roberto and Luca — were touched repeatedly by Fathers Aube and MacRae when they sang as choir boys at the St. Mary's church. The boys, you will hear, didn't say a word to their parents because the priests told them they would go to hell if they said anything."

A few women in the jury had storming tears in their eyes.

"Where are these boys now? In an asylum for the mentally ill, cause they attempted to kill themselves on too many occasions to be left alone."

Some of the men in the jury briefly covered their eyes with their hands.

"As the boys kept trying to kill themselves, either by slicing their wrists in the bathtub, or trying to get a hold of their father's gun, Mr. and Mrs. Gianni hatched their plot to poison these priests. You'll understand when you hear testimony from this fine couple, who were recently released from prison, why

99

there are many people in this universe other than my clients," Hyman slowly looked back at the defendants' table, "who would find enjoyment in committing these killings."

Hyman then loved the jury with his open arms.

"Ladies and gentlemen of the jury, these fine people, Mr. and Mrs. Gianni, tried to take action and do what was right, but were punished by the government. Now you have the power to take action," he kept his arms up as though he was waiting to hug them, "you, the jurors, the backbone of our judicial system," he finally put his arms down, "can say to the Vatican: enough is enough!" Hyman raised his voice.

I don't think it was theatrics.

He sounded fed up, upset, disgusted that he even had to be there, rather than eating his pastrami sandwich while losing pennies and quarters — his wife wouldn't let him bet any more — playing poker with his high roller clients.

"To do that, you return a verdict of not guilty, because, at the end of this trial, you'll have reasonable doubt that these three people sitting behind me, these outsiders, were the ones that did these nineteen murders."

He shook his head.

"That's because, ladies and gentlemen, we, the fine people of this community, were the indirect perpetrators of these acts. We secretly prayed for this cleansing. And our prayers were answered via the hands of the men, women, dark spirits who nobly dared what we greatly thought and prayed for."

He put his hands out in an offering way, with his palms up.

"I urge you to make the right decision," he then clasped his hands together as though he were some usher at a theatre or a deacon at a church and closed his eyes in front of him, "I thank you for your time and attention," Hyman said softly and then turned to walk back to his table.

"Thank you, Mr. Hyman," Judge Parker said with a smile of admiration that he made against his will.

"Please do not discuss this case among yourselves between now and tomorrow morning, and especially not with anybody from the outside," he judge looked with authority down on the jurors. "We shall convene at 10:00 in the morning, ladies and gentlemen, nice and sharp," he said with intensity, "to hear the government's first witness."

The next day's testimony made me ponder whether those whispers in the brush outside the courtroom were from Jesus's lips to Lucifer's ears, or vice versa.

CHAPTER FIVE

NAKED IN THE WIND

After she was sworn in, Patsy Burton covered up her baby blue eyes and cried.

Her hands had callouses. They had done some planting, farming, watering, and other things with the plot of land that her and her husband had in the middle of the city, not far from St. Mary's Cathedral.

"A tissue, Mrs. Burton?" Jarboe held one up.

"Thank you," she took the tissue and slowly dried her eyes.

Jarboe patiently waited for the 29-year-old mother of three to gain her composure.

"I'm ready," Burton said as she sat there wearing her embroiled Victorian blouse, her hair put up in a bun, and small Quaker looking glasses resting firmly on the end of her nose.

"Are you sure?" Jarboe confirmed softly.

"Yes," she nodded.

"Now, Mrs. Burton," Jarboe leaned away and looked calmly into her eyes.

"Why are you crying this morning?" He looked at her with concern.

Jarboe had a hard exterior in court but I discovered a softer side when preparing with him for the trial. I saw it in his eyes when his two young children would come in and bug him in his law office.

"Their bodies, their bodies just flowing in the wind from those trees they were hanging from, I can't get them out of my head," she shook her head in subdued horror.

"What bodies, Mrs. Burton?" Jarboe asked.

"Those bodies, they were just swinging in the wind when we saw them," she looked into Jarboe's eyes in a confiding way.

"You say 'we,' Mrs. Burton. Whom are you referring to?" Jarboe looked back at the jury, all of whom were intensely focused on Burton, and then made his soft gaze again on her.

"Me, my two daughters, and son," she said.

"And their ages?"

"Three, five, and eight," she said. I could see and hear that this disturbed the jurors, the thought of those kids seeing such a gruesome sight.

"And their names, Mrs. Burton?" Jarboe said as he leaned over the little wooden fence separating him from her. I expected Hyman to make an objection, on relevance grounds, as I didn't see why the names mattered.

But Hyman didn't. He just sat there. He was an old man taking his afternoon summer stroll in the park, birds chirping, wind going through the trees, and sun shining. I wondered to myself, as I saw him looking calmly onto the witness stand with his dark beady eyes, whiskers a few days old, whether he was building up his case by keeping quiet so that, when he hit, the jury would know it. The boy who doesn't cry wolf type of thing — Hyman wasn't going to cry unless it mattered.

"Poppy, Delilah, and Billy," Burton said with a protective tone, not sure where Jarboe was headed with the question. I could tell where he was going when I looked over to the jury, and saw them whispering some to one another.

Knowing the kids' names made the image of the dead priests more personal.

"Thank you, Mrs. Burton," Jarboe nodded in thanks to her direction. "Now," he clasped his hands, "how many bodies were there?"

She closed her eyes, as I could tell this was hard for her, and then she blurted out after a short pause: "Three."

"And, if you can tell me, on about what date did you see these three bodies?"

This was something that she and Jarboe went over before the trial, no doubt.

"Let's see, I think it was April 16, 1876," she said.

"That's Easter Sunday of this year, right?"

"Yes, it was," she said softly.

"When during the day did you see the bodies?"

"I was during the morning," she said.

"Around what time?"

"It was about 8:00 in the morning."

"And what were you doing when you saw the bodies?"

"I was walking my children to school, which is just around the corner from St. Mary's Church."

Jarboe was asking the questions in a very delicate way. He was wearing his three-piece suit, and his hair was parted on the right, and he looked perfect. But I could tell that this was hard questioning for him, as his children went to school with Mrs. Burton's, and I could see on his face that the killings so close to home troubled him. His face sort of squirmed when Mrs. Burton answered his question.

"They were, they were," she looked down onto her shoes. She took a second to think and get her composure.

"Do you care for some water, Mrs. Burton?" Jarboe softly asked.

"No, no, no thank you," she said.

"I know this is uncomfortable for you, Mrs. Burton, but, if you can tell me and the jury sitting there," Jarboe said and looked back at the jury, "where you saw those bodies, it will help us find out who was responsible."

"They were hanging," she looked up from her shoes, "they were hanging on the trees just outside of St. Mary's Cathedral."

"Thank you. Now, was the sun up when you saw these bodies, I mean was there enough light to see what you were looking at?"

"Yes, the sun had just risen. It was that time when you see the sun coming over the ridge, and the night gives way to the day."

"I see," Jarboe said as he took his pen and put it up by his lips, "so could you see what clothing, if any, were on the bodies?"

She nodded her head with her eyes closed and then said:

"There wasn't any clothing on those bodies. They were completely . . . naked, swinging in the wind that came off the bay."

The jurors started talking among themselves. So did the old man next to me to his wife, who whispered: "damn murders, these damn murderers, I can't wait to see them hung."

"You said earlier," Jarboe continued, "that they were hanging and, in your previous answer, that they were swinging, right?"

"Right," said Burton.

"What, if anything, were they swinging from?"

"The nooses around their necks."

"You saw those nooses?"

"Yes," she nodded.

"What, if anything else, were on their bodies, Mrs. Burton?"

"Well," she put a finger up on her chin, "I remember seeing that their mouths were open, but that they were full of something, like cloth or something."

"So as to keep them quiet?" Jarboe asked.

"Objection, your honor," Hyman said as he sat, in his lazy crouched down posture, on his chair, seeming like he wasn't paying attention. But he was. "Calls for speculation," he said as he played with his pen in his fingers. Unlike Jarboe, who was wearing a whole new outfit, Hyman looked like he was wearing the same suit from yesterday, albeit a slightly different tint of black.

"Sustained," Judge Parker said calmly. "Mr. Jarboe, please rephrase the question."

Jarboe, looking up at the judge, "of course, your honor."

"Mrs. Burton, why do you think that their mouths were stuffed?"

"Same objection, your honor," Hyman said sitting crouched down at his table.

"I'll allow it, counsel," Judge Parker said over towards Hyman, "please answer the question, Mrs. Burton."

"Well," she said after looking in Judge Parker's direction and shrugged her shoulders, "I reckon that those things was put in their mouths to keep them quiet."

"Thank you, Mrs. Burton," Jarboe said with a self-satisfied smile. "Now, three more final questions. Did you see anything odd about the bodies, I mean, was there anything peculiar about them — were they mutilated in any way?"

She closed her eyes again — the closed eyes you get when you have a sick stomach after you eat fish or meat that isn't cooked right. She opened them.

"Yes. Their hands were missing."

A few of the female jurors started making gasps, and so did some of the women in the audience.

"Silence, silence," Judge Parker said forcefully. "I'll have no antics in my court room. This isn't a circus, for God's sake."

I thought to myself, when he said that, tell Hyman that.

Jarboe surveyed the audience, and looked over to me in confidence, we were on the same team, the eyes said, and we were going to get the bad guys.

"When you say their hands were missing, Mrs. Burton, do you mean from the wrist down?"

106

"Yes," she said with confidence, "that's exactly what I mean."

"Thank you," Jarboe said, "did you see where the hands were?"

"No, no, no," she shook her head. "Right when I saw the bodies hanging, my children looked over and they started screaming, at which point I told them to look away and scurried them to school as fast as I could."

"So you didn't have time to see?"

"No," she said.

"Thank you, Mrs. Burton," Jarboe said and then calmly walked back to his table. He started reviewing his notes to make sure he got everything. "Oh, Mrs. Burton," Jarboe said as he reviewed his notes, his right hand between pages, "there is one question I didn't ask you, and which will be my last," he said with a sound of emphasis to it.

"Yes?" she said.

"Did you know who these men hanging in the trees were?"

"Why, yes, of course," she said.

"Please tell the jury who they were."

"They were Fathers Ricardo Aube, Roger MacRae, and Gordon Fortier of St. Mary's Church," she said with a sad tone to her voice at what had been done.

"Thank you, Mrs. Burton. Your honor, no more questions for this witness.

"Sons of bitches," the old man said next to me to his wife. "They will be hung just like those poor servants of God." He looked over at me. The eyes asked me to agree, and, without even thinking, I agreed by nodding my head.

"Mr. Hyman," Judge Parker said in his direction, "any cross?"

"Thank you, your honor," Hyman said in his thick New York accent. He got up from his chair, pulled up his pants over his belly, took a sip of water, and walked over to Mrs. Burton. The stout and ant-elegant Hyman leaned over the wooden fence, but with a sweet voice, said:

"I know this testimony was hard for you, Mrs. Burton, and I appreciate you coming here today to give it."

She nodded.

"I only have one question for you."

She nodded again.

"Did you see who hung these three men?"

"What do you mean?" She asked back.

"You said earlier," he looked at his notes, "that you saw these priests swaying in the wind from the trees outside the church, right?"

"Yes," she said.

"And that you quickly got your young children together and scurried them to school so that they wouldn't see what was in the trees, right?"

"Yes," she said.

"But you didn't see who hung those priests up in the trees, did you?"

"No," she said.

"So would you say that the hanging occurred before you saw the priests in those trees around 8:00 in the morning on Easter Sunday of this year?" Hyman tapped his pen on his notes.

"Yes," she nodded.

"But you don't know what time that happened, I mean the hanging?"

"No," she said.

Hyman smiled a sweet smile. I was the same smile I saw Jarboe give his children when I was in his office preparing for trial.

"Thank you kindly, Mrs. Burton," Hyman said as he closed his pad and walked back to his desk. Not many questions, but he didn't need to ask many. That was the point — she didn't see who did it, only bodies.

As Hyman walked back, I thought about Jarboe. He defended the church against numerous tort suits for slips and falls, and for various other matters. But I wondered if Jarboe had ever come up against a wily attorney like Hyman before, the stand on one leg, play with a plate on the other, all the while shooting at you with his sharp shooter left hand.

"Thank you, Mrs. Burton, you may leave the stand now," Judge Parker said in her direction. As she slowly exited the courtroom, Judge Parker looked at Jarboe's direction. "Your next witness, Mr. Jarboe?"

"Thank you, your honor," Jarboe said as he stood next to his table, still looking over his notes. "I'd like to call Mr. Nicky Williams to the stand."

Suddenly, a burly looking man got up from the benches. After taking the oath, Mr. Williams sat ready in the witness stand, with his tightly wound brown bolo tie and white shirt, and cleanly shaven face.

"Mr. Williams, thank you for coming down here today," Jarboe said as he reviewed his notes and then, when he was ready, started calmly waking over to the witness stand. "Please state your occupation, full name for the record, Mr. Williams."

"Nicky R. Williams," he said.

"And what is your occupation, Mr. Williams?"

"Mail carrier, United States Postal Service," he said calmly.

"And what is your regular route for the postal service, Mr. Williams?"

"I usually carry the mail in and around the neighborhood surrounding St. Teresa of Avila Church."

"And where is that church located?"

"It is at 1490 19th Street in San Francisco."

"What is the cross street?"

"Connecticut Street."

"Thank you, Mr. Williams."

Mr. Williams seemed like a man's man. His hulking hands rested on the sides of the jury box in which he sat. His deeply set eyes were of a Cro-Magnon type. His cheekbones were high, and his chin protruded outwards, daring any man to take a punch.

But there appeared to be a softer side to him. Mr. Williams often shyly looked down at his hands, which he appeared to be nervously playing with out of sight of the rest of the courtroom.

"On April 16 of this year, you made a report to the local police precinct around the St. Teresa or Avila church, right?"

"Yes," Williams calmly nodded.

"I have the police report here," Jarboe put the piece of paper up in front of him so that Mr. Williams could see, "and I'd like to draw the testimony out from you as to what happened that day."

"Alight," Mr. Williams nodded.

"About what time do you usually pass the Avila church every day during your routes, Mr. Williams?"

He looked up to the ceiling in thought.

"I'm an early riser and I work the morning shift, so I get going around 7:00 in the morning or so."

"Right, but about what time every day do you pass the church?"

"About 7:30 a.m., since I live only a few blocks from it, and so its one of the first streets I hit during my route."

"And where is it that you live?"

"On Connecticut Street."

"And how many blocks is that from the church?"

"One block away."

"So, on the date in question, that is April 16, 1876, you were walking by the church in the morning, and what, if anything, did you see?"

Mr. Williams paused. I could tell he was troubled.

"Mr. Williams?" Jarboe made his face come closer so as to get Mr. Williams' attention.

"Yes, sorry," Williams came out of the temporary trance. "That morning I saw, I saw, I saw bodies, two bodies, hanging, blowing, moving, blowing in the wind from creaking trees outside the church."

"Thank you. And can you tell the jury, was there any clothing on the bodies?"

"No," he shook his head, like he didn't want to remember what he was remembering. "The bodies were completely naked, heads down, lifeless, staring at the ground below."

"Okay, now, what, if anything, did you see in the mouths of the bodies?"

Mr. Williams looked off again into the empty space in front of his eyes, towards the worn wooden courtroom floor whose paint had flaked after so many years of use. Maybe in that space, he saw the dead bodies, hung up in the tress, their dark eyes looking lifelessly at the crowded courtroom below, with the nooses around their necks, the bruises from being hung, their discoloration from being left out in the elements overnight, for hours, for minutes, nobody knew quite yet how long.

"Mr. Williams? Are you okay?" Jarboe asked.

"Yes, yes, I'm sorry," he said. "I saw, I saw pieces of cloth, pieces of white cloth, shoved in their mouths."

"Thank you, Mr. Williams."

"What did you do when you saw the two bodies?"

"I walked a little closer, and, after I did, that's when I went to the local precinct."

"What did you see when you walked closer to those hanging bodies?"

As Mr. Williams thought about how to answer the question, his lips quivered as he remembered back to that morning.

"I know this must be hard, so please take your time," Jarboe said softly.

"Thank you," Mr. Williams said as he kept his eyes closed and head down.

He slowly looked up, and his eyes opened.

"When I walked closer, I stood there and stared in sadness for a few seconds. And then I looked down. That's when I saw

111

the cut off hands on the ground. They were bloody. There was also some loose rope. In the general area was also what looked like some cigar or cigars that had been smoked and left there?"

"When you say cut off hands, just to be clear, you mean the hands form the bodies that were hanging in the trees?"

"Yes," he nodded.

"And how do you know? How do you know that these were the hands from those bodies?"

"When I looked up, I could see that the two bodies' had their hands cut off."

"Where were their hands cut off, I mean was it from the elbow down?"

"No, from the wrist down," Mr. Williams did an example with his own arm, pointing down from his right wrist to the tip of his fingers.

"And were the cuts clean? Did it look like they were cut with a sharp knife, or were there little pieces of skin hanging from the wrist?"

Big pieces of skin, little pieces of skin, I thought, what's the difference? What is this, a housewife convention where they compare cutting chicken techniques?

"From what I can remember, the wrists were cleanly cut, almost like they were butchered meat, with a saw or some type of cleaver."

"So it didn't appear that they, that is the hands, were torn off, say by a horse?"

"Objection, your honor, calls for speculation," Hyman, sitting in his crouched almost turtle like position, said suddenly. A brush of cold wind you get when the summer is turning into fall.

"Sustained," Judge Parker said. "Please rephrase the question, Mr. Jarboe," the judge looked down at Jarboe.

"Of course, your honor." Jarboe paused to gather his thoughts. "Mr. Williams, did you look down at the ground when you walked up to the trees where the bodies were hanging?"

"Yes."

"And what did, if anything, you see on the ground?"

"Cut off hands, what looked like a smoked cigar or cigars."

"Right, did the wrist part of the hand have loose parts of flesh hanging off it, like little pieces of skin hanging or dangling?"

"No."

"So, would you say, the hands were more cleanly cut, like they were cut by a cutting device, like a knife or saw, maybe like a hand saw?"

"Same objection," Hyman said with his knee resting against the defense counsel table as he played with his pen in his right hand.

"Overruled, please proceed, Mr. Jarboe," Judge Parker said.

Hyman shook his head in disagreement and made a note in his book. I had heard about his strategy of making a string of objections during trial, and then connecting them at the end like a necklace so as to tell his story to the appellate court on appeal.

"The guy is a master at making a record for appeal," Jarboe said about his opponent, Hyman, when I was prepping for trial at Jarboe's law office. "He makes little objections here, and then there, and then, before you know it, he has made so many little objections that, when you add them up, you have a constellation of objections that he will use to strangle his opponent on appeal, from what some of my prosecutor friends told me," I remember Jarboe telling me over scotch one night.

"The hands were cleanly cut," Williams continued, "kind of like I had seen beef cut by the butcher at the local butcher shop, no dangling skin, no veins, just straight through," Mr. Williams made a cutting motion with his right hand.

"Thank you, Mr. Williams," Jarboe nodded approvingly of the testimony. "You said you saw a cigar or cigars below the bodies. Do you remember how many there were?"

"No," Mr. Williams shook his head. "Once I saw what I saw, I hightailed it out of there and headed straight to the police station to make my report, the one you have in your hand there," Mr. Williams nodded to Jarboe's right hand.

"Do you remember what the cigar looked like?"

"Objection, mischaracterizes the testimony," Hyman shot out.

"Counsel?" Judge Parker asked in Hyman's direction.

"Mr. Williams said he didn't know how many cigars there were. There might have been one, there might have been more than one," Hyman said.

"Right," Judge Parker said. "Sustained. Please rephrase the question, Mr. Jarboe."

"Was there more than one cigar, Mr. Williams?"

"I don't remember, I just remember seeing what I thought looked like left over cigar paper and ash, but it could have been from one, or maybe more than one."

"I see. So, without commenting on how many cigars you thought you saw, could you tell me what that cigar carcass looked like?"

Mr. Williams rubbed his head trying to remember back.

"Dark cover, dark tobacco, but that's all I could tell you."

"Thank you, Mr. Williams," Jarboe said as he looked over to Hyman. Hyman, I could see, had his face down in his notes.

"There is one more question, Mr. Williams, before we end."

"Sure," he nodded.

"Did you know who the two dead men hanging in those trees were?"

"Yes," Mr. Williams said.

"Who were they?"

"They were Fathers Zachery Connor, and Jerry Paralta of the St. Theresa Avila Church."

"And how do you know that?"

"Because I personally delivered their mail for over 20 years. So I would see them on an almost daily basis."

"Thank you, Mr. Williams," Jarboe nodded with approval and appreciation.

"Your honor, I don't have any more questions."

"You are up, Mr. Hyman. Any questions?"

Hyman was busy writing in his notepad. He didn't even hear the judge ask him the question.

"Mr. Hyman, I expect an answer from you when you are spoken to."

"Yes, your honor, apologies. I am a slow writer," he said as he looked up. "Maybe it's the steal cut oatmeal that my wife made me this morning, but I am seem to have a limp hand settling in, maybe it's the steal going into my veins," he said dryly.

The people in the courtroom chuckled. Even the wife of the grey haired man next to me chuckled. He didn't.

"Get on with it, counselor," Judge Parker said with unappreciative eyes.

"Yes, of course your honor," Hyman slowly got up from his chair and waddled over with his limp leg, perhaps he had hurt it in the Civil War, I don't know, to Mr. Williams.

Or maybe his leg limp was just an act. Hyman was a spook during the war, after all, not a foot soldier.

"Mr. Williams," Hyman leaned over the wooden witness fence, "thank you for coming down here today. I know you're a busy family man," Hyman said with sensitivity. I wondered why Hyman thanked Jarboe's witnesses. But I guess there was some strategy to it.

"So I only have one question for you."

"Yes," Mr. Williams nodded.

"You didn't see who did the hanging, did you, of these two priests?"

"No," Mr. Williams shook his head.

"So it's safe to say that the hanging took place before 7:30 in the morning, the day you discovered those bodies?" Hyman asked.

"Yes," Mr. Williams responded.

"Thank you, Mr. Williams. That will be all of my questions for this witness, your honor."

"Alright, counsel," Judge Parker said, "Mr. Williams, thank you for your testimony."

As Mr. Williams left the witness chair, Judge Parker looked over to Jarboe.

"How many more witnesses do you have for today?"

Jarboe looked down onto his notes and then looked up.

"I have three more, your honor, Police Commissioner Edward Boyle of the San Francisco Police Department, Cardinal Marcial Maciel Degollado, and Abel Russell."

"Very well," Judge Parker nodded is head. "I suggest we break for lunch now, and then you we'll finish with these witnesses this afternoon. Court is adjourned."

Judge Parker slammed his gavel and all of the people in the courtroom exited out into the strong California sun.

As I sat down at the same table where I had met Father Vivaldi the day before, it hit me.

"You know why you didn't tell Jarboe, when you were doing the preparation for the trial, about seeing Blue smoke that cigar that one day in June," a little 12-year old boy voice said in my head. It was the little me, the former me, the little boy from Episcopal elementary school that liked hanging with the misfits, the oddball types that didn't fit in, the ones who the others called "outsiders," "bad," "oddballs," even "heathens" like they were going to go Lucifer's way.

And maybe we were. Hyman's opening statement got me thinking. If God's way, or the way of Jesus, is what Hyman said about these dead men had done elsewhere in the country, being shifted to this Diocese by the Vatican to evade prosecution, then is that the right way, God's way? If being an infidel, or a heathen, means a being hold out against what these men had done, and what the leaked documents say about the Vatican cover up, then is that the wrong way? Maybe that's why my parents raised me Episcopalian — Protestant — in Virginia, cause they protested the centralized power which allowed such evil to exist for so many years in the Catholic church?

"Don't Blue, Amber, and Shane remind you of your friends, the ones you had when you were my age, remember those?" The little 12-year old Jasper voice inside me with chubby cheeks, messy hair, ripped pants and shirt, slight freckles, and with some filth on his face from playing in the dirt all day, said to me.

He was right. As I ate my sandwich, I remembered my four friends from elementary school: Nicky Sparks, a skinny black boy who everybody wanted to pick on, maybe because he was skinny and could solve puzzles within a blink of an eye; Jerry Moses, a fat blond boy whose stomach jumped over his belt and who'd almost crawl to class, but who could figure out any math equation faster than anybody in the school, which made the athletic boys hate him and call him names like "fatso," "fat fuck," "lard ass"; David Sticks, a tall awkward boy who didn't know how to walk with his height, but, who, in class, would be the first, even before the teacher, to point out historical trends in history; and Cody Diamond, one of the darn near smartest people I ever met in my life, and she had the darn near prettiest green blue brown eyes I ever seen, but I reckon the boys didn't like her cause she was tougher/smarter than them, and girls hated her cause she was prettier.

The little Jasper, I imagined, was sitting across from me on the bench.

"Everybody in the school, even many of the teachers, didn't like you and your friends, remember? They even blamed you for the bad things that happened in the school, like the math teacher's missing purse, the stolen food from the kitchen, and the broken window in the principal's office," the little Jasper smirked.

He was right, partially. After the school administration blamed us for the stolen things, we did, throw a rock through the principal's window one night.

117

"But you knew," the little Jasper, I pictured, threw a rock down on the dirt, "that we were good, even when **nobody** thought we were good, when **everybody** thought we were bad, remember?"

As I chewed my sandwich, I thought back to being in Jarboe's law office before the trial. He had a big mahogany desk in front of him. There was an ashtray that was full of ash.

"Did you notice if any of them smoked cigars, Jasper?" Jarboe asked me as he smoked a fancy hand rolled cigarette. Most of them he didn't smoke all the way. Instead, he'd let them sit on his crystal ashtray on his desk.

If I had told Jarboe about seeing Blue smoke that cigar that one day, this would have created a stronger link in his case between Blue and the hung priests — in addition to the killings. But there was a voice inside me that said not to tell Jarboe, and to tell him later on in the trial if I needed to. For now, the voice said, let things pass for now and see how they turn out.

The advice was hard for me to stomach. I was the police officer, the one who was supposed to be the mole that infiltrated this circle of criminals, and who else but them could have done these murders? This little Jarboe from elementary school mysteriously affected my decision that day in Jarboe's office before trial.

"I seen Blue take a puff or two once or twice of a hand rolled cigarette, but I don't think I'd seen him smoke a cigar, nothing like that," I remember saying to Jarboe.

Not to say I didn't tell the truth about all of the other things I seen Amber, Shane, and Blue do and say. But I felt like, for this one, I'd let slide — for now.

After I finished my sandwich and put all of my items into my satchel, I started walking back to the courthouse through the brush, dirt, and shrubbery. A Pacific breeze cooled my face. It made me feel like I had made the right decision, for some reason.

"Order, order in the court," Judge Parker said loudly as all of the folks in the audience started taking their seats.

"Counselor," the gray haired Judge Parker looked over towards Jarboe after the jurors were seated, "your next witness. Let's get this thing going so we can get these people out of here on time," he motioned over to the jury.

"Yes, your honor," Jarboe said standing behind his table. "I'd like to call my first witness for the afternoon, Police Commissioner Edward Boyle, to the witness stand."

Police Commissioner Boyle was a stout Irishman with dark hair, a "black Irish" type, originally born in County Cork, Ireland, but who made his way to New York City and, then, with word of the gold discovery in California, moved to San Francisco to do business initially. But then merchants asked him to take the helm of the police department in 1849, which at the time was more of an idea than a reality. After the Commissioner was sworn in and Jarboe verified his current employment, he started to get into the meat of the matter.

"Commissioner Boyle," Jarboe said standing with his arms cross in front of Boyle. "Do you usually play a direct role in murder investigations? I mean, are you usually on the ground getting your hands dirty with the evidence?"

"Not normally," he shook his head, "but this isn't a normal case. In high profile ones like this, where the mayor is adamant about things being done right, I get directly involved," the Commissioner looked into the jurors' eyes to instill confidence in them.

"I see," Jarboe started pacing ever so slightly, "so did you go to the scene of the hangings at St. Mary's church?"

"Yes," the Commissioner nodded.

"When?"

"The day it was reported," the Commissioner said.

"And what about the hangings at St. Teresa of Avila Church? Did you go to the scene of those hangings?"

"Yes," the Commissioner nodded again.

119

"The day that the murders were reported?"

"Yes, that day," the Commissioner nodded.

Jarboe walked closer to the witness stand. He calmly leaned over the fence separating him and the Commissioner.

"Commission Boyle, did you inspect the nooses that were around those men's necks?"

"Yes."

"Did you inspect the knots on those nooses?"

"Yes."

"And, from your inspection, Commissioner Boyle, were the knots done professionally?" Jarboe asked.

"Objection, your honor, vague and ambiguous," Hyman said as he sat low on his chair playing with the paper on the desk.

"Do you understand the question, Commissioner?" Judge Parker asked.

"Yes, your honor," the Commissioner calmly responded.

"Overruled," Judge Parker said. "Please proceed, counsel," he said in Jarboe's direction.

"Let me ask you this, Mr. Commissioner, have you seen nooses before?" Jarboe asked.

"Yes, on many occasions. It is our preferred method of capital punishment for desperados and bandits in San Francisco, you see," the Commissioner said confidently, "all of which I oversee."

"How many hangings have you overseen?" Jarboe asked.

"Too many to count on a finger and my toes," the Commissioner chuckled. The audience didn't laugh at this dark humor. When he noticed nobody was laughing, he became more serious. "I'd say several dozen or so."

"And you would oversee the noose making for these executions, make sure that things were done properly?" Jarboe asked.

"Yes," the Commissioner nodded.

"Could you explain to the jury the complexity of the process, how it needs to be done, that is, the making of the noose?"

"Well, let's see," the Commissioner adjusted himself in the witness seat, "the length of the rope must be carefully measured in proportion to the person's weight. If the rope is too short, not enough velocity is generated to break the person's neck and he — or she — is painfully strangled to death. If the rope is too long, too much velocity is generated and beheading results. Even if the rope is of exactly the right length, a victim with an exceptionally large or strong neck may suffer strangulation rather than immediate death."

"In your professional opinion, reviewing the ropes that were around the three priests' necks at St. Mary's, were they tied by an amateur?"

"No," the Commissioner shook his head. "Whomever tied those nooses at St. Mary's had done it before, since the length of the ropes was exactly right, and, from my impression, was done with precision."

"And what about the nooses around the two priests' necks at St. Teresa of Avila Church? Were they done professionally, too?"

"Yes," the Commissioner nodded. "Whoever did both sets knew what they were doing, in my professional opinion," he said.

Jarboe nodded with contentment.

"Commissioner, I'd just like to ask you some brief questions about the bodies you found at the churches before I let you go."

"Alright," he nodded.

"Let's first focus on the ones at St. Mary's. Did your office come to a conclusion as to when those men were taken out to the trees?" Jarboe asked.

"Yes," the Commissioner nodded, "I personally investigated the bodies after we took them down from the trees, and concluded that the time of death was sometime early in the morning, say 4:20 a.m. or thereabouts."

Jarboe walked back to his table, took a long sip of his water, and then:

"How do you know that?" He asked.

"Well, the blood temperature, for one thing, and the discoloration on the bodies. You can tell how long the heart hasn't been pumping by looking at items like that, which is what we do for any homicide."

"And what about the two bodies found at St. Teresa of Avila Church? When was the time of death for those?"

"About an hour or two before or after 4:20 a.m., I'd say," the Commissioner said.

"The previous witnesses testified about seeing items stuffed in the victims' mouths, Mr. Commissioner," Jarboe said. "Can you tell the jury what were these items in their mouths?"

"Yes," the Commissioner adjusted himself in his seat. "We pulled the items out and, well, um," the Commissioner got visibly uncomfortable, "we discovered that the items were," he paused, "the fathers' collars."

"Heathens! God damn heathens, that's what they is!" A voice came from the back of the courtroom from a New York accented man wearing a proper three piece suit, monocle, and clean shaven, with a big banner that read, "End Gold Rush Sin in Northern California!"

"Order, order, remove that man!" Judge Parker yelled.

Everyone in the courtroom looked back at the New York accented man, who the bailiff quickly escorted outside. I took a peak towards the front of the courtroom. Jarboe was reviewing his notes and Hyman, instead of picking something off the floor, was picking some food out of his teeth with his index finger. Then he sucked the food off once he had it in his sights. He did this a few times. He saw me catch him eating what maybe was his lunch off his finger. Hid didn't look away. He didn't look down.

He cracked a small proud smile.

"Disgusting!" I whispered to myself.

After the fancy dressed man protesting the sinful gold rush money was removed, everyone turned their attention back to the front of the courtroom.

"Please proceed, Mr. Jarboe," Judge Parker said.

"Yes, your honor," Jarboe said as he stood in front of the Commissioner.

"Mr. Commissioner, you said that the dead priests had their collars stuck in their mouths. How did you know that these collars were theirs?"

I thought to myself, yeah, maybe they were on loan to the killer from the local Halloween store?

"Well, we pulled the items out of their mouths when we pulled the bodies down, and then went to see if there were any collars missing from their rooms in the churches."

"And what did you find?"

"That there was one set missing," the Commissioner said deadpan, "in each of their rooms."

"I see," Jarboe said.

"Mr. Commissioner, were the priests' beds made at both churches?"

"No. The covers for all five of the priests were mussed up, like they had been sleeping in their beds."

"So, would you say," Jarboe looked back towards the jury, "that these men were involuntarily taken by force from their beds in the middle morning?"

"Objection, calls for speculation," Hyman said lazily.

"Counsel?" Judge Parker said to Hyman.

"Well, your honor," Hyman said with a camouflaged smirk, "the priests could have gone voluntarily."

"Overruled, counsel," Parker looked at Hyman with disgust. "Proceed, Mr. Jarboe."

"Yes," the Commissioner said, "we believe they were taken by force."

"Which is why they had their mouths stuffed and hands tied, right?" Jarboe asked.

"Correct," the Commissioner agreed.

"Did you discover any bruises or marks on the bodies?" Jarboe asked.

"No, the only bruises were around their cut wrists, and, of course, the discoloration around their necks from the rope," the Commissioner said.

Jarboe started walking back and forth in front of the jury. He stopped and looked straight at the Commissioner.

"Mr. Commissioner, did you check the locks on the church doors from which these priests were taken?"

"Yes," the Commissioner nodded.

"Were they locked that night, according to your investigation?"

"Yes," the Commissioner nodded.

"Did you discover any forced entry? Were the locks violated at all? Broken?"

"No sir," he said.

"Any broken windows?"

"No sir," the Commissioner said.

"And who, according to your investigation, has keys to St. Mary's church?"

"Well," he said as he thought, "the priests and nuns of the church, but other members of the Diocese also have access to the keys, too, if they request them."

"The same is true with the Avila Church?"

"Yes."

Jarboe walked closer to the Commissioner.

"Mr. Commissioner," Jarboe said as he got closer, "I only have one more question for you."

The Commissioner nodded.

"Does the Police department suspect this as being an inside job then?"

"Objection, calls for speculation," Hyman said calmly from his perch. I had seen other attorneys jump to their feet when they heard questions they didn't like. Hyman just sat there. He didn't show any reaction — didn't raise his voice, didn't throw his pen on the table. Nothing. Maybe his strategy was to not show if he thought the question was injurious, and the only way to do that was to just keep mellow and in his seat.

"Overruled, counselor," Judge Parker said and looked back towards Jarboe. "Please answer the question, Commissioner."

"Given that there as no forced entry into the two Churches," the Commissioner explained, "and that the locks were locked that evening, I would say yes to that question. Someone in those Churches, or someone who had access to the keys within the Diocese, I mean, likely gained entry into the churches that morning."

"Thank you, Mr. Commissioner," Jarboe said. "I have no more questions for this witness, your honor."

"Very well," Judge Parker looked down onto the Commissioner and then over to Hyman, who was reviewing his notes, "do you have a cross, counselor?"

"Yea, yea, your honor, coming right up," Hyman made some final notes and then slowly walked over to the Commissioner, and, for a few seconds or so, didn't say a word. And then:

"Mr. Commissioner, have you ever lost yours keys to anything?"

The Commissioner looked around, unsure of how to answer.

"Well, yes, I guess I have."

"And what was normally the first thing you would do when you couldn't find your keys?"

"Objection, relevance," Jarboe objected to the question. He stood up in a very formal way as he made the objection. "Where is Mr. Hyman going with this, your honor?"

"Overruled, I'd like to see where he is going with this," the judge said with a curious tone.

Jarboe sat back down.

"Well, um, hum, I supposed I'd see if someone else I knew had an extra copy."

"Alright," Hyman nodded, "have you ever had copies of your keys made?"

"Yes, I suppose I have," the Commissioner said.

"Earlier, you testified," Hyman looked into the direction of the audience and then looked back, "that the police department believed this was an inside job, right?"

"Yes, that's correct," the Commissioner nodded.

"Is it possible that someone who wasn't a member of the church or diocese had copies of the keys for those two churches?"

"Objection, your honor," Jarboe stood up. "Calls for speculation," he said with a somewhat annoyed tone.

"Overruled," the judge said. Jarboe shook his head and sat back down.

"I don't know," the Commissioner said.

"Let me put it differently, Mr. Commissioner," Hyman straightened up ever so slightly as he said this, a sort of cock in the gun. "If someone who wasn't a priest or a nun, but, say, a janitor or a groundskeeper, had access to those keys, they could have made a copy, right?"

"Well, I suppose so."

"Did you know that, according to Sister Johnson, each church keeps an extra copy of their keys accessible to all priests, nuns, and, in addition, to grounds keepers, janitors, and others who service the church?"

"No, I didn't know that," the Commissioner said.

"And did you know that, according to Sister Johnson, the extra keys are normally kept in the drawer next to the sink in each church kitchen?"

"No," the Commissioner shook his head.

"Well, I knew you didn't know these things, Mr. Commissioner. That's why I am bringing them to your attention," Hyman smiled.

Jarboe shook his head in disgust.

"So, given those facts, it is possible, is it not, that someone with access to those keys could have either made an extra copy of them, or even used them to access each church?"

"I suppose so, yes," he shrugged.

"And is it not possible that this someone may not have either been a priest or a nun, but someone else who works at, or knows someone who works at, these two churches?"

The Commissioner paused.

"From what you have told me today, Mr. Hyman, I suppose it is possible that the killer or killers were outsiders."

I could see it. It was that little smirk. Those little smirks on your face when you get your way for little things, like a few cents off an item at the general store. But this was no little item. And yet Hyman had it on his face like it was a little discount — 5% off retail — that he got.

And that little item was reasonable doubt.

"Thank you, Mr. Commissioner," Hyman nodded to the Commissioner and then looked up to the judge. "No more questions for this witness, your honor," Hyman said calmly to the judge.

"Very well, counselor," Judge Parker said to Hyman. "Mr. Commissioner, thank you for your testimony today."

As the Commissioner started to exit the witness pew, I asked myself: could three people, especially if those three people are made up of one woman, hang five men in one morning? My imagination took over after I asked myself the question. For the first three victims, I pictured one of the three, probably Blue, putting a hand over the victim's mouth in his bedroom — they had separate ones, I knew — as the point of a sharp knife was thrust into either the victim's throat or his eye, along with a threat: "quiet father, or you'll lose your throat, or your eye."

Then, after the priest nodded and cloth was stuffed into his mouth, Amber would come, the man would be turned on his belly, and his hands would be bound along with his ankles. Shane would be either look out, or he would go to the next room and prep the next victim for the same procedure. Once the priests were subdued, they would be escorted out in the cold morning air, at which point Amber would skillfully prepare the nooses.

At that point, either the men's hands were cut off, perhaps by Shane, whose knife skills, as you will see, were top shelf, or after their bodies had been hung up by Blue and Shane, who would pull the priests up to their deaths, then tie the ropes to the tree so that the whole world could see the priests dangling in front of the churches. After the first three were put up to hang, the three culprits went to the next destination, where they rinsed and repeated with the final two priests.

Suddenly, Judge Parker interrupted my thoughts. With some delay after reviewing his notes, Parker blurted out: "alright, Mr. Jarboe, you have two more witnesses, right?"

Jarboe got up.

"Yes, your honor."

"Well, I'm not sitting here for my health, counselor, let's get on with it.

"Sure, of course your honor," Jarboe said.

"I'd like to call Cardinal Marcial Maciel Degollado to the stand."

There was whispering in the audience and among the jurors as the Cardinal made his way to the witness stand. I knew he was a widely respected member of the Catholic community, not because I knew first hand. I had heard others in the community talk about the greatness of this man, and all of the money he raised for the Church, which is why there were so many photos of Pope Alberto Scrivener — the former Pope — thanking the Cardinal for his fundraising. After Jarboe went through the regular introductory questions, he got to the heart of the matter:

"Cardinal, what is your role in the hierarchy of the church?" Jarboe asked.

"Well, I oversee, along with some other Cardinals, bishops around the world on behalf of the Vatican, and report to the Pope on their performance," the Cardinal said proudly.

"So the former Archbishop of San Francisco, Archbishop John Pilarczyk, who I'll call the Archbishop, whose death the jury will learn about later in this proceeding, he reported to you?"

"Yes," Cardinal Degollado nodded.

"And the Archbishop was responsible for overseeing the priests in the San Francisco archdiocese, right?"

"Yes," the Cardinal said.

"So who were these 19 dead men, Cardinal?" Jarboe asked like he didn't know the answer.

The Cardinal was dressed conservatively, the way any other priest would be dressed, with large forehead almost hanging over the front of the witness stand. His beady eyes could barely be seen, and his receding hair, which was almost parted except that there wasn't enough hair to be parted, were specks of dust on his pale head.

With his arms crossed, in an authoritative and not a comfortable posture, he said:

"They were great men, all of them," he nodded.

"Let's take Fathers Ricardo Aube, Roger MacRae, Gordon Fortier, of St. Mary's Church. Did you know these men?"

"Yes, I've personally known each of them for years. The Archbishop introduced me to them on several occasions, and I oversaw, along with the Archbishop, all of their comings and goings in the church, and had the enjoyment of having them as my fellow servants of Jesus Christ," he closed his eyes and nodded. His small oval silver glasses made him look like God's librarian.

"Did they have any problems in the Archdiocese, any reports of misconduct by any of the parishioners?"

"No," the Cardinal shook his head. "I never received any reports from the Archbishop about these three men."

"So, for there whole time as servants of your Archdiocese, they have had spotless records?" Jarboe looked down onto his notes to make sure he was getting all of his questions down.

"Yes, they have been some of the best priests this Archdiocese has ever had, and the people just loved them," he looked down into his lap, "which is why I was so sad and disheartened to hear about the horrible things that were done to them."

"I understand," Jarboe said as he looked back at the audience, "it is not often that you would find men like this willing to serve such a lofty cause," he then looked back at the Cardinal and just paused for a moment to gather his thoughts.

"Everything you have said about these men, the same can be said about Zachery Connor, and Jerry Paralta of the St. Theresa Avila Church?"

"Yes," the Cardinal nodded his head again in confidence, with his arms confidently crossed. "They, too, were immaculate servants of the Lord," he looked down ever so briefly to his feet, and then up. "They, too, will be impossible to replace."

"And, just to confirm, you were the Cardinal associated with Vatican who oversaw archbishops, including those in San Francisco, at the time that the defendants joined?" Jarboe asked.

"Yes," the Cardinal nodded.

"And were you aware of any alleged criminal conduct by the defendants before they joined the Diocese?" Jarboe asked with pleasure.

"Objection, your honor," Hyman said as he scratched his ear with his pencil, "Assumes facts not in evidence."

"Mr. Jarboe," Judge Parker looked over to Jarboe, "you have witnesses who will be testifying about this criminal conduct, correct?"

"Yes, your honor," Jarboe said with a snarky grin.

"Overruled, counsel."

Hyman shrugged his shoulders like he could care less, and scratched his other ear with the pencil.

"Well," the Cardinal unfolded his arms and changed his posture in his seat, "I wouldn't have allowed them in if I had known anything like that, so the answer is definitely no."

"I understand, Cardinal. Now, going back to these five priests of the St. Mary's and Avila Churches, did they have any other duties to the Archdiocese other than tending to their respective flocks, doing mass on Sundays, doing communion, baptisms, and such?"

The Cardinal sat back in his chair. The question seemed to comfort him. He folded his arms again. The wrinkles on his massive forehead, like a blank sky over the Pacific getting muddled by clouds, creased as he said:

"Yes, they were part of the Gold Rush Commission."

"And can you tell the jury, Cardinal, what this commission was responsible for doing?"

"Yes, of course, we authorized the Archbishop to form a commission to investigate and regulate the influx of dirty money into the church coffers from gamblers, whoremongers, and others who have come into this clean state of ours and have been ruining it, just ruining it," he shook his head.

"So you are saying that the church leaders were concerned about money being donated to the church that came from morally questionable sources, like the gambling parlors that have popped up all around San Francisco?"

"Yes," the Cardinal nodded. It was obvious that Jarboe and the Cardinal had prepared before trial, two cogs working in the wheel. "People come here from all around the country, make it big when they find gold, and then go gamble it, buy booze, women, or, our concern, to contribute that money to the church."

He paused.

"We don't want this money in our pure sanctuary, which is reserved for those who want to worship God with our assistance, the clean clergy," he said.

"When did you authorize the commission?" Jarboe asked.

"We issued the formal authorization, called Stop 666!, on January 24, of this year the Cardinal said, "and the Archbishop started choosing the commission members shortly after that."

"The archbishop directly oversaw the commission?"

"Yes."

"And who were the members of this commission?" Jarboe asked with his hands intertwined, like he didn't know.

"There were eighteen members of the commission," the Cardinal answered, "not including the Archbishop. But all of them have either been murdered or have disappeared."

"And the defendants are alleged to have killed the 18 commission members. Isn't that right?"

"Yes," the Cardinal answered.

"And did this commission report to you, Cardinal?" Jarboe asked.

"Not directly. They first made their reports to the Archbishop, who then sent the reports to me."

"From those reports, can you tell the jury which parish was the most worrisome in terms of how much of this crooked money was coming into its coffers?"

"Yes, it was the Mission Dolores," he said.

"And the defendants sitting over here," Jarboe looked over to the defendant's table, "they were all responsible for running the Mission Dolores?" Jarboe now stared at the Cardinal waiting for his answer.

"Yes, they were," he Cardinal nodded.

Happy that he got the testimony he wanted, and that he obviously got a rise out of the jury, Jarboe confidently said:

"That's all for this witness, your honor," he then walked calmly back to his table as he looked over at Hyman, who was whispering in Blue's ear.

"Any cross?" Judge Parker said.

Hyman put up his hand, almost as if to tell the judge to not interrupt him as he spoke to Blue, and then he put it down without seeing the frown on Parker's pitch white face.

"Yes, your honor, I have a cross," Hyman pushed his chair out, in an inelegant way so that it made a big screech which echoed throughout the whole courtroom. All of the jurors grimaced when he did it.

Hyman didn't say a word as he waddled over to the Cardinal, who was still sitting with his arms crossed, the castle that Hyman was going to try and topple. He stood in front of the Cardinal for a moment, looked over towards the audience in the courtroom, and then stared at the Cardinal for a moment.

I had seen dogs do this — not humans. I guess there is a first time for everything.

Didn't see who blinked first that day.

"Are you aware of the leak of documents from the Vatican that occurred on December 25, 1875, Cardinal?" Hyman asked.

Didn't need to see who blinked. Right after Hyman finished asking his question, the Cardinal uncrossed his arms. He looked at Hyman, surprised. He reacted — so that was as good as a blink.

"What do you mean?" The cardinal asked.

"On January 8, 1876, there was an article in the *San Francisco Chronicle*, entitled *Underbelly of the Church*, about documents that were leaked to various newspapers from, it seems, someone inside the Vatican. That leak, Cardinal," Hyman said confidently as his pants started to move down his left leg.

"Yes, I'm aware of that article," the Cardinal said as he leaned forward in a sort of aggressive tone.

"Isn't it true, Cardinal," Hyman looked into the nothingness towards the ceiling, like he was some Roman actor, annoyed he was doing this instead of playing poker, "that the leaks revealed that the Vatican had a worldwide policy of protecting priests," he stared into the Cardinal's eyes now, "who have been indicted or convicted of crimes against Mother Nature by transferring them to dioceses or jurisdictions where they wouldn't be prosecuted?"

The Cardinal just sat there saying nothing.

"And isn't it true that the leaked Vatican documents show that the Vatican actively oversaw the transfer of some priests from other dioceses who had histories of crimes against nature to this one, something that has been commonly referred to as 'priest shifting' as an almost term of art within the Church?"

"It's irrelevant what the 'leaked' documents show," the Cardinal then said with his fingers making quotations marks around the word "leaked" and looked at Hyman with a whiney face. "Those documents were just made up, fabricated, to make the church look bad."

"So these documents," Hyman passed around duplications to the judge, Jarboe, and the Cardinal, "these documents are frauds, Cardinal, even though they have the Vatican's seal on them?"

The Cardinal just sat there for a moment looking at the documents.

"I can say I've never seen these documents before, I am sure that you won't find anybody else in the Vatican who has seen them before," he put the documents back down on the little wooden witness stand fence.

"Very well, Cardinal, that's very nice, but did you know, Cardinal, that Fathers Ricardo Aube, Roger MacRae, and Gordon Fortier were convicted in Boston, Milwaukee, and Philadelphia respectively, for touching children in ungodly ways?" Hyman asked.

The Cardinal again just sat there.

"Your honor," Hyman looked up to Parker, "speaking to the ants, trees, and spiders behind my house is a lot better than this, cause at least they react," he said with his smart ass grin. "I'd ask that you direct the witness to answer the questions."

Judge Parker stared at Hyman for a moment, cause, while he was right, Parker the serious Yale man didn't like Hyman's New York humor.

"Please answer the question, Cardinal, so that we can move forward with this day," Judge Parker looked down to the Cardinal, who finally said:

"I've never known such trash, these men were good men, never knew about any convictions because there weren't any, maybe this trash is just a fabrication of some heathen, maybe the defendants over there?" The Cardinal said.

"Would it surprise you, Cardinal, if I told you that I will be having the district attorneys from those cities in the stand later on during the trial, and that they will testify as to the existence of convictions and/or the trials that led to them?"

"Yes it would, since I have never seen such horrendous false allegations before in my life time," he shook is head in disgust and looked to the jury for approval with his sad dog eyes.

"Don't worry, Cardinal, I have some more for you," Hyman said.

"Objection, your honor," Jarboe said, "he's harassing the witness."

"Ask your question counsel," Judge Parker said to Hyman.

"Were you aware, Cardinal, that the remaining two priests from the first set of murders, namely Zachery Connor and Jerry Paralta, were indicted for crimes against Mother Nature in New Orleans and Chicago?"

The Cardinal just shook his head.

"No, I was not, and I'd be surprised . . ."

"Your honor, please direct the witness to just answer my question, and not provide any of his color," Hyman looked up to the judge and said with a sharp tone.

Judge Parker looked down to the Cardinal with a frustrated tone to his brow.

"Cardinal, please just answer the question that is asked of you, nothing more, alright," Judge Parker said forcefully.

The Cardinal nodded.

"So you were not aware that these two priests were indicted in New Orleans and Chicago?"

"Yes, I was unaware," he cocked his head over to Hyman, a sort of fuck you look.

"Were you aware that the leaked documents indicate that, under the old Pope, the Vatican transferred priests to the San Francisco Archdiocese so that they could avoid prosecution . . ."

"Objection, your honor!" Jarboe got up quickly. "Those documents haven't even been authenticated yet, and, even if they were, they speak for themselves. We don't need counsel's interpretation of them," Jarboe pleaded.

"Overruled, counsel," Judge Parker said. "Mr. Hyman can use hearsay on cross, and the authenticity of the documents is something for the jury to consider when weighting the evidence."

Jarboe shook is head as he sat down and whispered to his fancy looking paralegal.

"Did you understand the question, Cardinal?"

"Yes," the Cardinal nodded.

"Then please answer it," Judge Parker said.

"I was not aware of any transferring to avoid any investigation or convictions," he cocked his head again in a defiant way to Hyman.

Hyman just stood there and smiled for a few seconds.

"Very well, Cardinal," Hyman then said. "Just a few more questions," Hyman looked back at the jury with some concern, "cause I know the members of the jury would like to be out of this sooner rather than later."

Hyman stared back at the Cardinal.

"Now, Cardinal, you were the one responsible for forming the commission that was, it has been said by the church, responsible for investigating the influx of dirty money that's been coming in from gambling money, right?"

"Yes, that is right," the Cardinal nodded.

"And this commission was formed, let me see," Hyman moved one of his notes that looked like it was just racing with the leaves on the dirt in front of the courtroom. "On February 18, 1876, right?"

"That sounds right," the slightly sweaty looking man said and nodded.

"And this commission was formed after the Vatican leaks, correct?"

"Well, let me see," the Cardinal looked into the distance and thought for a moment, "yes, that's right, after the alleged leaks," he emphasized "alleged" with his index finger on the witness stand front of him.

"And after the article, entitled the *Underbelly of the Church*, which appeared in the January 8, 1876 edition of the San Francisco Chronicle, right?"

"If that was the date of the article, then, yes, yes, Mr. Hyman, that is right," the Cardinal nodded.

"So," Hyman put his note down, "the purpose of the commission wasn't to investigate the leaks?"

"Objection," Jarboe shot up, "asked and answered."

"Overruled," Parker said from the bench, "please answer the question, Cardinal Degollado."

"Absolutely not," the Cardinal shook his head, "it was, as I have said, to investigate sinner money that was coming into the church, particularly the Mission Dolores."

"So the timing of the commission with the leaks is just a coincidence?"

"Indeed it was," the cardinal nodded.

"Why wasn't the commission formed earlier, before the leaks happened?"

Th e cardinal just sat there for a moment thinking of how to respond.

"It takes time, Mr. Hyman, to move a big ship, and the church is a big ship, larger than you can appreciate. We were meaning to form this commission for some time, but it took time to get the right bureaucratic approvals from the Vatican."

"I see, I see," Hyman smiled as he looked through his notes, "time, the other four letter word." I not too damn sure that this was lawful, or whatever they call it, for Hyman to do, you know, signal to the jury his feeling about the answer without saying nothing, cause that was exactly what he was doing. Wondered to myself why Jarboe didn't object.

"Cardinal Degollado," Hyman looked up from his wrinkled notes, "you are aware of the second and third rounds of priest murders that occurred on April 23 and May 20–21, of this year, correct?"

"Unfortunately, Mr. Hyman, I am all too familiar with these dates, and what happened on them."

"Right," Hyman nodded not caring about the cardinal's seeming sad eyes. "So do you know, sitting here, right now, that there was an anonymous note given to the police on May 24, 1876, which said," Hyman pulled out another wrinkled note and read from it, "***Dolores*** is her name, and she kills with no shame, cause she thinks she is on a ***Mission***, but she is just a killer, and you had better get her."

The cardinal thought for a moment to himself.

"I do not know about such a note, Mr. Hyman."

"Please, cardinal, take a look at it," Hyman handed the note to Degollado, who took his own survey of the note, "and let me know if you had seen this before."

"Never seen this before," the cardinal looked up.

"Right," Hyman nodded with a small smile on his face, "Cardinal, I'd like to show you something else," at which point Hyman pulled out still another crumpled piece of paper and handed it to the witness, "have you seen this before?"

The cardinal sat and looked over the piece of paper.

"Yes," the cardinal finally said.

"What is that piece of paper?" Hyman asked about the note, which he duplicated from the original on one of those new duplicating machines.

"It is, well," the cardinal turned the paper over to look at the other side, "it looks like a copy of the letter that I wrote to father Canon de Vivaldi," the cardinal said with surprise.

"So you recognize the handwriting as yours, correct?"

"Yes, that is my writing," the cardinal said.

"Thank you," Hyman said with some sort of devious happiness in his voice. "Cardinal, do you not see the similarity in the writing between the letter that you wrote to Father Vivaldi and the anonymous note?"

The Cardinal compared the two notes.

"I do not, Mr. Hyman, I am sorry but I do not," the cardinal put the papers back up on the witness stand like he didn't want them in his hands too long.

"Your honor, I'd like to hand these papers to the jury for their review," Hyman said with the two scraps in his hands.

"Please proceed, Mr. Hyman," at which point he went over to the jury and handed them the papers.

"Would you be surprised, Cardinal, that an expert handwriting witness will testify later in the trial that the style of writing found in these two pieces of paper is identical?"

The Cardinal stared calmly at Hyman. It was a calm stare, but I reckon it looked like one of those stares you get when you are stuck, and there isn't anything you can do about it.

"Of course I'd be surprised," Mr. Hyman, the cardinal said, "because I didn't write that note."

"No more questions for this witness, your honor," Hyman looked up to Judge Parker. I noticed Hyman didn't thank the Cardinal for his testimony, but just went to sit back down at defendants' table.

"Very well, counsel," Judge Parker said, "Cardinal," the intimidating judge looked down onto the witness, "thank you for your testimony today, you are free to go."

The Cardinal just sat there for a moment looking over at Hyman as he sat and whispered with Blue, who I could see was just aiming his icy blue Viking looking eye at the Cardinal.

"Cardinal, you are excused," the Judge said again, this time with a louder voice.

The Cardinal slowly got up and walked out of the court room, all the while Blue stared at him walking out, with Hyman whispering who knows what — only they do — into Blue's ear.

"Counsel," Parker looked to Jarboe. "Your next witness," Parked nodded.

I didn't need to guess who the last witness of the day was. I knew very well who it was. Heck, I interviewed him months ago for Jarboe, and knew all he had to say about Defendant Amber Francis, also known as Sister Emerald Beem, and her noose making skills. This prosecution witness's name was Abel Russell, a former lover of Amber's.

As I sat there watching Abel walk up to the witness stand, I remembered back to when I met him, and what he did — and didn't — tell me about Amber's 19 murders.

CHAPTER SIX

NOT A BOY, NAME ISN'T TOM

"Nobody could tie a tighter or more deadly noose faster than her, Father Jasper," Abel the gypsy looking Russell said to me one overcast late September afternoon that year, not long after the cardinals and bishops from the Archdiocese went missing.

Was sitting with Abel on some pieces of wood, around a warm fire, next to his horse and carriage on the outskirts of a new city called Chico, which is about 180 miles north of San Francisco. Abel Russell and his arm quilt full of tattoos — dolphins, women, crosses, a Jesus here, a wolf there, an owl here, a spider over there — was in the middle of setting up for the circus. There was nothing much around that part of town but a stage and some chairs where Abel, and the rest his circus act, was going to put on their show. We were sipping on some coffees, and sitting under the cloudy September skies that cover inner California.

"So you seen her do her thing with the rope, I mean, you know," I looked around to make sure nobody else was listening to what I saying, "making the noose and all that?" I spit some of the chewing tobacco that Abel had given to me into the fire.

Abel just stared into the fire like he was thinking about the past.

"I done seen her do it all," Abel said with some of his chewing tobacco dripping out of his mouth and over the dry crevices of his lips. "Seen her do many things no man could do, and, you know," he looked around as the clouds listened to our every word. He seemed like he was worried about others listening in, too. "Things she could do is what made me love her so much, hear me Father?" He nodded over to my direction, his skinny weathered neck making a creak sound, or at least wanting to, when his long thin head looked into my direction.

Man had brown blond Jesus like hair down to his shoulders, and a long brown blond beard on his face that went to the middle of his chest. But the rest of his body was baby bare. When the wind came through town, wasn't much on his skin to keep it just running off and going into my face, with the smoke, ambers, and smell of the burnt wood digging their hands into my skin. Burnt brown eyes of his just looked into mine, reaching out to see if I was listening to what his lips were saying, his eyes saying more than I could hear with my ears.

When I went to speak to potential witnesses like Abel about the defendants, I made it seem like I was on church business and was just going through a routine back ground check on all of our new priests and nuns.

Abel told me he didn't know Amber been a nun since February 21, 1860. I just made it up that she just joined when I first met him. Don't think Abel had seen Amber since she left the circus around January of 1859, age 17, from what she told me.

"So what type of things can she do that not many other man can do?" I said to Abel after I had my swig of cowboy coffee with those pieces of coffee beans in the bottom of the mug that get in your teeth. Nasty shit, but it was strong.

"Well, father seeing as you is doing God's work and all, right, I reckon I should be telling you what I know, don't you say?" He tapped me on the shoulder as the fire smoke invaded my priest costume. He thought we were buddies. And I suppose we were in some ways — on the surface and all.

You see, a man like couldn't just run up and get information from any man, even if I look like I am a servant of the Lord. Men in those parts of California are extremely private. They don't let anybody know the things they going to do, or have done, cause that is the California frontier way. People from all over God's good earth have been coming to that state to forage for gold, renew their lives, and, to do that, they don't want anybody knowing their dark pasts.

"You know who this Abel Russell working for?" Police Commissioner Boyle asked me that May, not long after we started the investigation into the defendants of Mission Dolores.

"Yea," I said as I sat in the Commissioner's office filled with cigar smoke, not far from Fisherman's Wharf, with the cool humid smell of the Pacific coming in through the window and blowing the smoky air to and fro.

I didn't say anything cause I knew the Commissioner didn't like anybody saying anything to him until he asked.

"Well son," he said through his big bushy mustache that hung like a cow's horns over his upper lip and drooped down on the sides. "Who this man working with?" He dropped some ash into the metal tray that he got from some Texas Ranger.

"Let me see," I said as I looked through my notes, notes I took after I spoke to Amber about Abel, which I'll get to. "He works with the Mr. James 'Grizzly' Adams circus."

"Shit," the Commissioner said as he chomped on his cigar. "You mean good old Grizzly Adams?"

"Yes sir," I said as I sat in the wooden chair in front of his desk.

"Alright, son, alright," the commissioner said as he chewed his cigar, thinking for a few seconds, and then he asked, as he looked outside the window:

"Damn, son, this Abel Russell is a bear man?"

He didn't give me time to answer.

"Them some roughnecks, them bear playing men," he said as he stared at a boat unloading it's day of fish.

I shrugged. I supposed so. The Commissioner, himself, was a rough man. He looked like a bear, standing some six-foot or so, with shoulders and wrists full of hair, and muscle, that any strong man of the circus would be jealous of.

"But we got our own roughneck life, too, don't we Jasper," the Commissioner leaned over his beat up, scarred, and sort of deformed table to stare at me with his eyes, which were over-worked, stressed, but tough as railroad track nails.

"Yes sir," I shook my head in agreement. The table was a lot like the Commissioner, cause it had been through a lot like him, seen its share of knives picking into its skin, scraping away whatever things that was protecting it from men's smoke, men's throw up, sun shining down, or whiskey spill stains.

"So where is this Abel Russell man now, you know?" The Commissioner leaned back in his comfortable chair and asked.

"Let me check, sir, let me see here," I was looking through my notes, hurrying cause a busy man like the Commissioner doesn't like waiting. "He should be in Chico, I think in Chico, next week," I looked up and sought approval from him through the cigar smoke. The sun was setting over the San Francisco bay, and it came through the windows, went through the smoke, shined off the file cabinet next to his desk, and went into my eyes.

"How you know that this Abel Russell going to be in Chico, son? How the fuck you know that type of shit on this man, you sure?" The Commissioner was worried cause he knew the San Francisco mayor was putting the heat on the Commissioner to solve the murders. They made the police look bad.

"Well, sir," I closed my notes, "I got a schedule for the Grizzly Adams circus tour here," I looked down to my little notebook with the schedule in it. "It has all the dates they going to be going, Chico, Bakersfield, Sacramento, and . . ."

"I got it, son, I got it," he put his palm up for me to stop. "And where did you get that? That pamphlet there?" He looked over the desk.

"From the tourism office. They got all of these things there like this because people coming in from all over to see California," I smiled a proud student to his teacher smile.

The Commissioner just stood there thinking. He looked the wild bear look, but he calculated like the night owl.

"Chico? Shit. Chico, that shitty little town, they going to Chico?" He played with his stringy balding hair that he tried to part on the right, but it never parted. One string was always swaying one way, or the other, a wayward piece of grass, fuck off old man, let us be free, the string said.

"Yes sir," I nodded as I kept my finger in the place in my notebook, "Chico."

"You can get up there next week, I mean you don't have anything at the Mission that you need to tend to?" The Commissioner asked.

I looked through my Mission Dolores schedule.

"No sir, schedule is open."

The Commissioner just sat there and then his burly right arm took the small pencil that was on his desk, and he scribbled some notes. I couldn't believe a man like him could even write. He looked too big for the desk, too big for the small corner office of the building that he was in, and his hands was too big for the pencil that his fingers wrapped around when he took it.

"Alright," he said as he threw his pencil down. "You should go up there, meet with him, tell him that you doing some research on our little gal Amber cause she wants to join the Church, and that it is procedure for you all to do background checks, see what you can find, before you admit someone in the church understand?" His cigar smoke camouflaged the gas that he kept dropping throughout the meeting.

Maybe him and Hyman had the same dirty quiet deadly playbook?

As he spoke, I took notes in my little black notebook, a notebook that I took with me everywhere, and wrote everything in. My best friend when I felt like I didn't have any. Putting my pencil down, I said:

"Yes, sir, I understand," I nodded. "I'll get some questions in order before I go up there, be prepared like this is something that I am doing all of the time for new recruits into the church."

"Good son, good, that's good son," he just left the lonely cigar sit there and give off its smoke. "You want to play this real smooth, cause you don't want this man thinking nothing other than what you wanting him to think, that you is a man of God and that you is doing God's work, not police work, but I guess they are the same thing, isn't that right son?"

"Yes sir, I understand," I said just as how I used to just agree with the priests when I was younger going to Episcopal school.

"Alright, Sergeant, you have your orders. You come back here and report to me when you done, you hear me?" His eyes looked at me through his freckled eye sockets.

"Yes sir," I started to get up.

"And son," he said as I opened the door to leave.

I turned around to look back at him as he picked up his cigar to chomp on it, smoke it, or both.

"Don't go fucking this up, we clear?" He crossed his arms.

"You can count on me, sir," I said back.

"Good," the Commissioner said as he turned to look out into the bay. "You can leave the door open, gets musty in here with the cigar smoke and the humidity, or maybe it's just the beans my wife put in the dinner last night," he looked over at me with a smile of relaxed confidence.

"See you when I get back, sir," I saluted him and exited his office.

The train ride from San Francisco to the California and Oregon Railroad depot in Chico, which I understood from speaking to a local Chico native, was laid just in 1870, took a few hours. The train passed through the great red woods of Northern California, inland and along the long, desolate, and untamed coast.

When I got into Chico, I got off the train with my bag and went to check into my hotel in the middle of town, which was like any other little gold rush town — one street in the middle of town with a saloon, bank, horseshoe maker, and general store.

"Good morning, father," the hotel owner, a short red headed man welcomed me, wearing those small banker glasses that had become stylish in these parts.

"Good morning, to you," I said as put my bag down.

"How can I help you?" The short man with no hair in the middle of his head said to me, a little nervous I must say, but I didn't know why.

"Yes, well, I need a room," I said as I took out my book and looked inside, "and I also need to know where the circus is setting up, the, let's see, the . . ."

"The Grizzly Adams circus you mean, right father?" He asked.

"Yes, that's it," I said as I closed my notebook.

"Easy. When you leave the hotel, you just make a left hand turn, go to the edge of town, and then head towards Bidwell Park. When you arrive, you'll see where the circus is setting up," the red headed balding man said.

"Thank you, my son," I said as I patted his hand, which was on the desk.

"Of course, father, of course," he nodded. "So let's get you settled with your room, and then you can get on your way, alright?"

"Yes, thank you."

After I got my room key and placed all of my things in the Victorian room, which was on the second floor of the hotel, overlooking the main street below, with the main saloon across the street, called "Sal's Saloon," I headed to the forest Bidwell Park, where I expected to find Abel.

Suddenly, I came upon a scene of organized confusion. There was a large tent in the middle of the opening. Some black men were pulling on the ropes of a tent, which had to be pulled up and made whole, along with white men and even some Chinamen. There were little fires all around the opening, with tents where people slept, babies crying, kids chasing each other, women tending to the fires — it was the late evening by the time I got to the opening — dogs running around chasing one another, chasing the kids, and smoke running through the open skies.

There were men sitting about taking things from their carriages and, if it weren't for Amber telling me about what Abel looked like with some detail, I wouldn't have been able to pick him out of the scene of tattooed dark eyed heathens.

"Can I help you father," a pig looking man asked me as I came in from out of the clear air and into the smoke of the circus circle. There was a dinosaur tooth hanging from his left ear, hair down to his nipples, cause he had no shirt to cover up his graying chest hair, and nothing like a cigar to make him smell less like the sewer than he already did.

I slightly turned my head to stay away from his stench.

"Yes, um, please," I said as I pulled out my little black booklet, acting like I was looking for Abel Russell's name, when in fact I was just turning away from piggy man's smell, hoping some of the smoke would help. "I'm looking for Abel, Abel Russell," I said real slow.

"Shit," he looked around as his black Scottish kilt, which went down below his knees and looked like it was made out 5 or so black sheep, twisted in the wind coming down from the mountains around. "You looking for Rat Boy?" He looked at me with his filthy face and spat a big piece of tobacco onto the ground, some dripping down onto the upper part of his graying ape chest.

"Well, uh," I put my black book back into my satchel, "is that Mr. Russell's name—Rat Boy?" I looked into the pig man's beady black eyes, surrounded by soot and wrinkles from all those times outdoors.

"You bet it, Father," he playfully slapped my shoulder with his dirty right hand. He started laughing happily, a Santa Claus laugh, but a Santa Claus who had too many whiskeys, and maybe didn't make it out on Christmas cause he was having too much fun with Mrs. Claus. "Call him Rat Boy cause he a thin, skinny, little son of a bitch, like one of them little rats that coming around and digging through your trash, you see, Father?" He pointed to some of the trash piles around the circus circle. "But you trying to fuck with any of them little vermin, and you get you ass whooped, see Father?"

He smiled and air kicked one of his muddy, grass covered, black cowboy boots into the air. His smile wasn't so much a smile. It was a crack. And through that crack he showed me, or maybe I should say previewed, the dirt on his teeth.

"I understand, my son, I understand," I couldn't help but crack my own smile.

"Well, father, enough of my bullshit, cause I got to get to working, so you can find Rat Boy right over there, he taking all of that shit out of his wagon, see him?"

"Much obliged, mister," I held my hand out.

"Love to shake your hand, father, but I just cleaning up some horse shit," he smelled his hands.

"Much obliged, ," I said as I tipped my large circular black hat, the one that the rest of the priests in the Archdiocese wear, and walked slowly over to Abel.

He saw me and said, as he lifted a black wooden box:

"Beautiful night here, don't you reckon father?" Abel looked up towards the open blue sky, just above the smoke from the circus.

"Yes, my son, beautiful," I looked up towards the sky, too, along with him. We both just stared upwards for a moment.

"Name is Abel, Abel Russell, father," he held his hand out for mine under the twilight of the Chico sky.

"Father Jasper is what they call me," I shook his strong, thin, muddy hand.

We was standing not far from his fire, which was brewing some coffee, cause I could smell it coming into my nose. He kicked some tin can out of the way with his ashy brown cowboy boot, some of the old coffee that was in the can came and wrapped itself all over his black Levis' jeans, which had holes, burn marks, and a long silver knife on its waist belt.

"Care for some of this here coffee, father? It not like that coffee you having in those big cities like San Francisco down there, but around these here parts, it does us just right."

"That would be nice, thank you," I stood there with my old satchel on my shoulder.

"Put that there bag down, father, make your holy ass at home," he threw his worn horse saddle off the large tree branch that was serving as his bench. His old world black denim shirt had its sleeves rolled up, which is when I saw all of those tattoos of his.

"Much obliged, my son," I put my satchel down and sat down on the tree bark. Looked around for a moment as he tended to the coffee, his horse in the shrubbery just to the right of me, was tied up to one of the trees, and his covered carriage was in front of me. Saw them men putting up the big tent in the background, as their kids played with each other.

"Here you go, father," he said as he gave me the coffee.

"Thank you," I said.

"You from around here, you part of the parish?" He asked and sipped.

"No, I am based out of Mission Dolores, a parish in San Francisco."

"You don't say?" He looked over at me. "What brings you up to these here parts?"

"Well," I looked around, "I came here to meet you, my son," I said.

He spit some of his tobacco out of his mouth into the fire. It sizzled.

"Shit, me? What you holy man want to do with a Rat Boy?" He looked over at me, Lucifer looking over at Jesus wondering why Jesus loves him — or the world.

"Came to ask you some questions," I said calmly.

"Shit, questions . . . you mean like how to put on the best damn circus on this side of the Mississippi?" He smiled.

"No, not that, but I am sure I'd like to know your view on that," I chuckled.

He pulled out a little tin canister of tobacco and put some more tobacco snuff into his mouth.

"Oh, shit, father, you want some of this," he held out the canister after he shoved a wad into his mouth.

"Why, awful thoughtful of you," I took a small pinch and tucked it under my lip.

We sat there for a moment watching the fire.

"So what you wanting to know from a man like me who not knowing shit?" He looked over at me.

I spit tobacco into the fire.

"Want to know what you know about a woman named Amber Francis," I looked him dead on.

"Amber, Amber," his eyes just stared into the fire. They were transfixed and then he spit a big wad into the fire, sizzle it went.

"You know her, son?" I asked.

"Know her? Shit, father, I loved her, father, just loved her with all my heart," he just kept staring into the fire. "And when you love someone, you got to know them, cause if you don't know them, you just loving what you think you knowing about them, see father?" He looked back over at me.

"Right, my son."

"So what a man like you wanting to know about a woman like her?"

"She applied to be a nun with the church, and we are doing our looking into her background and such," I looked into the fire with him, "before we admit her."

"Amber? Amber Francis a nun?" He said with excitement as we both sat there. "Who would have guessed that far out shit?"

"The Lord works in mysterious ways, my son."

"Pretty fucking mysterious to me, couldn't be more mysterious than that shit," he said. "Oh father, you have to forgive me for my mouth, it's untamed like this ground here," he looked down to the mud below.

"Please, no need. Speak openly with me."

"How'd you find me, how'd you know I was here?"

"Spoke to Amber before, and she told me about you, so I looked you up and found the schedule for the circus."

"So you knowing she was working with us?" He looked over at me with surprise, spit, and the fire sizzled.

"She told me, told me what she used to do, it's part of the application process, if you want to call it that."

"I get it, father, I get it," he said in a tired way. I could tell he didn't like talking about her, something that I gathered from speaking to Amber about their relationship.

"What do you think about her, my son? Tell me what your heart says about her?"

"One of the best women I ever done met in my shitty short life," he said. "She a rare breed of woman, Father, cause she a strong woman, not like them city dolls that you find, break, and

152

get another cause they can't be in the brush, country, darkness too long, or else . . ."

"Or else what?"

"They getting scared," he looked over at me, "or start bitching and moaning."

"I see," looked in my satchel for my notebook. "You mind if I take some notes while we talk?"

"Do your thing, Father," he nodded over to me, his beard drifting slightly in the wind that came down from Oregon. "Reckon you like some more coffee?"

"Please," I held out my cup for him to fill it up and then took a long swig. "So why isn't Amber a fragile city doll?"

Abel spit some more tobacco into the fire.

"Cause she don't fuck around, see Father?" He pulled his silver knife out of its cover, just enough for me to see it, and then put it back, as he looked over at me. She rode the horse, hung with us dudes, and did what we like doing, a real deal Tomboy.

But Amber Maggie Francis was not a boy, and her name wasn't Tom.

"What do you mean?" I asked. "What did she do for the circus, my son?

"See them men over there," Abel pointed to where the men were putting up the tent.

"Yes," I nodded.

"She in charge of all that roping, all of the roping for the circus. Putting up the tents with rope, catching our loose cattle with the rope, doing whatever we needing her to do with the rope."

I took notes in my booklet.

"What else did this Tomboy do for the circus?"

He looked at me.

"Now, Father, I don't want to say nothing that going to get Amber in trouble, cause I don't want no trouble for her."

"Son, you won't get her in trouble. We are just seeing who Amber is, you see, cause we know nobody is perfect, only God,

Jesus, are perfect. We are flawed, flawed beings, and so we want to know everything about her, her flaws, are her beauties."

This was all bullshit. But I needed what I needed.

"So, son, what else did she do for the circus?"

I already knew part of the answer to my question. Amber confided in me one day earlier that year about what she did for the circus. We were sitting under the same tree where I spoke to Shane that one water fight Sunday. Except, the day I spoke to Amber, it was Blue and Shane who were water fighting with the kids.

"What did you do before this?" I remember looking over as she sat next to me on the bench.

She paused. Her blond stallion hair came out from under her veil.

"I was a show girl," she said.

I looked at her with my eyebrows raised — surprised at what she was saying.

"Silly gooses," she looked back at the kids playing with Blue and Shane.

"Show girl doing what?"

"I worked in the circus."

"Wow!" I slapped my knee. "What circus?"

"Grizzly Adams," she said calmly.

"That's amazing," I looked over at her long slender body. "What did you do — tame the bears?" I joked.

She wasn't joking.

"Some of the time," she looked back over at me, "when they needed me to. But I also oversaw the boys and their setting up for the show, you know, the tents, all of the parts that go with that, cause my family was part of the business for a long time. Daddy knew Mr. Adams for a long time."

Had a feeling as I sat there next to her that she did more than that, and that's why I later asked Abel Russell: "what else did she do for the circus?"

He didn't seem to keen on answering the question. So I asked him again.

"Son, what else did she do for the circus?"

That's when looked over at me and said: "Well, father seeing as you is doing God's work and all, right, I reckon I should be telling you what I know, don't you say?"

And I remember saying, "yes son, yes, you should, it will only help her, cause, you know, Mary Magdalene, you know, she was a sinner, but she was one of Jesus's disciples. So I don't think she is some angel, some Mary, cause no woman is Mary, son."

"So, then, this between us now, right, between us, father?"

"Yes, son, yes, it's between us, nobody needs to know."

"Well," he looked around, "she some circus muscle."

He spit tobacco into the fire as though to put a period on the statement.

"What do you mean?"

And that's when he said, with his graveyard eyes, "Nobody could tie a more deadly noose faster than her, Father Jasper."

"Deadly?" I looked over at him.

"They all deserved it, father, deserved it, cause they was thieves, thieves I tell you, trying to take things from us, you know, coming in at night, coming into our parts, our places, taking from us," he said.

"What happened to these people, what did she do to them?"

He bent over to get some more coffee.

"Hung them all?" He said in a matter of fact way as he sipped his coffee.

I looked over at him through his fire smoke, through the smoke from the other fires that were around the circus circle, and my eyes became sore.

"And how do you know, my son?" I asked as I started writing in my book.

"Cause we was real close, father, maybe we was close in ways that God didn't want us to be, but we was close anyway," he answered.

Amber had told me some about her relationship, her love for him, him for her, and the sad end of tracks, during my talk with her while Blue and Shane played with the kids.

"You have some surprises, I see, up your sleeves, sister," I said after she told me about her involvement in the circus.

"More surprises than you know, Father Jasper, more than you know," she said with a small smile as she looked upon the playing children.

"Any love interests, any loves before you joined the church?" I smiled.

"That's partially why I joined," she said as she crossed her legs, the silhouette of her beautiful toned muscles showing through the dark long nun dress she was wearing. "I was so sad after him, so sad, that I needed something to keep my mind off the heartache, the feeling of helplessness I was feeling after we split."

"After you split from who?" I remember asking her as we sat on that warm summer Sunday, unseasonably warm for San Francisco's standards, running about 80 or so degrees, sweat dripping down her witch white skinned neck.

"From Abel," she looked over at me with sad eyes.

"What happened?"

"Love, happiness, contentment, joy, living in the moment, hugs, waking up smiling, cuddling, hair fondling, thinking about family . . . and then . . ."

She paused.

"And then what, Sister Amber?" I slightly touched her arm to get her attention.

"His older brother died, horrible accident, just horrible," she put her hand over her eyes. "Abel was such a sweet, and yet daring, soul. He was never the same after," she said as her hands covered her eyes.

"What happened, I mean what happened after to Abel after his brother died?"

"Abel broke into pieces. He went from this larger than life person, able to ride one horse then jump to the other, having all the boys from the circus cheer him, he drinking it up with them after, bringing people together to . . ."

She kept her eyes covered in her hands.

"He went from bringing people together to . . ."

"To what, sister, to what?" I asked.

"To being broken, just a broken man," she said looking into my eyes.

"A death like that can have a paralyzing affect on anyone, especially a sibling," I remember saying looking out at the kids playing.

Amber also sat staring out at the kids, and said:

"He went from being the center of the wheel, the part that kept it all together, to being a loner, staying away from the others, telling them to stay way, sleeping late, not working like he used to . . . they kept him on because of all the years that he put in, and . . . he had nowhere else to go."

"And that's when you left?" I asked.

"After a year and a half like that, I left, couldn't handle it, I felt like slitting my wrists, jumping off a cliff, pulling my hair out, anything to not see him just throw away his life, his talent, his beauty, like that," said to me softly, sincerely, lovingly.

"And that's when you joined this?" I looked around the Mission's courtyard.

"God was waiting for me, with open arms," she looked over at me with a small loving smirk on her face, "and I went right into them," she hugged herself, closing her eyes. "I have felt so safe being here since then, so good helping these little ones," she opened her eyes and pointed towards all of the children, "and now I have them, Father Shane, Father Blue, and you," she smiled in my direction.

I just looked at her with a blank nervous face. I was ashamed of myself. She was sincere, and I felt like I wasn't. I was using her heart for information. But this was the job I signed up for, so I knew I had to keep my head down. It's just that it was damn hard to keep down when I felt like I was maybe on the wrong side, seeing as this woman wasn't what I thought she was about when I first got here — cold, calculating, wicked.

"What made you join? I mean, how did you know this would be the way?"

"Came here one day, some day in January or February of 1860 or so, cause it was darn cold, to say a prayer for Abel. I smelled this incense that Father Wolf was burning, smelled so safe, so good. And it was the same incense, the same one that I smelled one day when I went to the cliffs, to look over, into the abyss, into the Pacific, and met this Ohline Injun man, on a donkey, who had the same incense with him, was burning it on his donkey."

"A traveling outhouse freshener for his donkey shit?" I smiled.

"No doubt," she smiled as she playfully pushed me on my shoulder, "but that Injun man was also a breath of fresh air to my soul," she smiled, "when I ran into him that man, by the ocean, in I think it was in Big Sur, if I remember right."

Abel had a different memory of when, and why, Amber left, the circus.

"After men was murdered, nineteen if I reckon right, word was it that they was some thieves, was when Amber done disappeared," Abel said to me next to that fire a few months later in Chico when I asked him why, and when, Amber left.

"Why do you think she left?"

"Cause she was in on it, in on directing that stuff, them murders," he said.

Spit, sizzle, the fire went.

"Don't get me wrong, now, they men had it coming, taking things that wasn't theirs, see father?" He pled with me. "Word has it that they men was bounty hunters from the south taking them escaped men from us, people who was part of our crew, people we needed for our circus, who became part our extended wacky family."

"Yes, son, yes," I nodded as I took my notes.

"Wasn't you with Amber though, didn't you know what she was up to?"

He shook his head no and answered:

"She was a mighty secretive gal. Would leave when I was sleeping, and then come back in the morning, real late, would wake me up and kiss me on my cheek," he smiled at me. I could tell he hadn't spoken about all this in a while.

Got what I needed from Abel, thanked him for his help, and told him that Amber was a good woman for protecting her flock from the southern intruders, or some quality horseshit that I made up like that to make him feel good with himself. Went, next, to meet the mayor of Chico, Hiram Treat Batchelder, to see what he knew about the Adams Circus. I knew that they traveled through Chico often going up and down the West Coast from Oregon. Went to Mayor Hiram with the same cooked up story that I gave Abel, about me being the priest, looking into Amber, and all of that.

"Father, father, please come in," the upper lip of the tightly manicured mustache of the mayor moved with mechanic precision as he welcomed me into his large mahogany office.

"Thank you, Mr. Batchelder," I said with appreciation as I walked in.

"How can I help you?" He said from behind his massive ornately designed desk, which had heads of bison, horses, stars, ocean, and fields of wheat etched into its side.

"Well, Mr. Batchelder," I said as I started putting my satchel on the wooden chair next to me.

"Please call me Hiram, father, just Hiram," the stout short mayor said as his beef shoulder thick hands rolled up his sleeves.

159

Remember it was a warm day in Chico, running about 85 degrees, which was unreal for the month of September.

"Thank you, Hiram," I crossed my legs comfortably. "I am here doing some back ground research on a woman who recently sought an application to be a nun in our Archdiocese," I opened my book like I didn't know her real name, "let's see here, her name is . . . Amber . . . Amber Maggie Francis is her full name."

"Can't say I know her, father," he spun a little in his chair.

"Didn't think you would, but," I closed my booklet, "it appears she used to be with the Adams' Circus, and that her family was, from I am told, heavily involved with them."

The mayor stopped spinning in his chair.

"You sure she worked for them?" He said as he leaned over his long brown desk.

"Positive," I nodded.

"Shit," he said as he looked down underneath his desk at his fancy looking cowboy boots, shined to make them look less country and more city, "that's too bad."

"Why do you say that?" I leaned over to ask.

He put his gaze upon me.

"Cause that circus group, that Grizzly Adams Circus, they was a group of troublemakers."

"How so?" I took out my pad to start taking notes.

"Word has it, from the sheriff's office, that there was nineteen men who was found murdered around the time that a number of circus hands, including a 17 year old or so expert knife thrower and roper, left the circus."

"About what year was this?" I asked.

"I reckon it was sometime in the start of 1859."

"January?"

"That sounds right," he said.

This checked out with what Amber told me, which was that she left the circus when she about 17, if my notes are right.

"So where did these murders take place?" I asked with my notebook out.

"On the circus grounds somewhere in Bakersfield, which is before my time in office here," the Chico mayor said.

Bakersfield is a town south of, and inland from, San Francisco.

"Who were the dead men?"

"The sheriff didn't know for sure, guess he spoke to the sheriff in Bakersfield," Hiram leaned back in his chair and put his arms over his head. "They wasn't able to identify who the men were, but, let me see . . ."

We just sat there for a moment as Hiram thought with his eyes closed.

"Sheriff told me," Hiram continued when he opened his eyes back up, "that there was a lot of bounty hunters from the south, states like Louisiana, Virginia, Mississippi, coming up around these here parts looking for escaped slaves."

"Bounty hunters?" I said with a mystery to my tone. "They was looking for criminals, folks who escaped bail, from those states, they was hiding with . . . the circus?"

"Father, don't know for sure, but, from what the sergeant told me, they wasn't looking for criminals in the way you was using the word just now."

"What you mean, the way I was using the word just now, how you mean?" I turned in my seat, feeling like I was maybe discovering something that I hadn't expected to discover.

"You see, father," Hiram the mustached man leaned over his inland California wide desk, "the circus was rumored to have run an Underground Railroad which transported escaped slaves from the south and got them a place to work here in California."

As Hiram spoke, I remembered back to when I came to the circus grounds to meet Abel, remember seeing those covered carriages, like there was something on the inside that they didn't want others to see.

"Yup," mayor Hirman took some lint off of his pleated Levi's black jeans, the bottom half of a cowboy tuxedo. "Word has it, too, that they smuggling them peoples in covered carriages to California."

"So how does that help you tell who those 19 dead men were?" I asked.

"According to the sheriff, father, once they figure out what states these bounty hunters is from, they can then inquire with local authorities in those states because all bounty hunters need to be licensed, bonded, and they generally report their out of state whereabouts to the local police."

He leaned back comfy like in his chair.

"I see, I see," I was writing my notes down. "Appreciate all of this, Hiram, really do. Just one more question before I leave.

"Sure, father, sure," he nodded with hospitality.

"How did the men die, those 19 men?"

"From what the good old sheriff tells me, they thinks the men was hung, hung on some trees close to the circus grounds in Bakersfield."

Hiram swiveled in his chair.

"Sheriff suspects that the hunters kept coming in waves of two after the first set didn't come back, that these circus freaks collected them in their covered wagons, and killed them en masse," he stopped for a moment. "Is that French?"

"Is what French?"

"En masse?"

"Sure sound French," I shrugged not caring, but wanting to flatter the fat sweaty mayor.

He smiled proudly.

"So, what I was saying, yea, that they was killed en masse in Bakersfield."

This didn't help me as much as it did before. Before, I knew that, if they were hung it could be linked back to Amber from

Abel. The thing is, Abel didn't know anything about this slave stuff, or maybe he knew but he didn't tell me. I remember thinking about what Hiram told me, and I thought to myself that maybe it wasn't Amber that done all of this, but maybe it was those massive, muscular, and menacing looking men putting up the tent who killed those 19 bounty hunters? But, then, again, maybe Amber directed them all?

The Hiram man twisted things even further.

"Other folks telling me that the bounty hunter men wasn't only hung . . . but that they was . . ."

"They was what?"

"Don't really want to say, father, seeing as it's very un-Christian what I going to tell you."

"Please, Hiram, please do tell, we like to know what type of people we are thinking about admitting into our house of the Lord."

"Some other folks, not the sheriff's office, but some older folks who came up here from Bakersfield, who moved to Chico from there, said grizzly bears ate parts of those men before they was hung, which is why their bodies, was so mauled up, chewed up, when they was found on the trees, like bear beef jerky."

Hiram paused again.

"They also say that the reason why these men's hands was missing, being cut off and laying on the ground underneath some of their mauled bodies, was because someone cut off those hands to send a message to the southerners: keep your bounty hunter hands out of California."

I grimaced at what he just finished saying as I wrote in my notepad.

Wonder how that bear beef jerky tasted to the grizzly bears? Sweet, sour, or both?

Then I asked the mayor:

"Any connection you know of, Hiram, between Ms. Francis and these killings?"

"Only connection, father," he leaned back over, "is guilt by association, cause she hanging with the crew that sheriff is thinking did these things, you see?"

"Right, right, I do see. Before I go, do you know who did the rope lasso shows for the circus?"

Hiram shrugged his shoulders.

"More or less, cause most of them been with the circus for a long time now, and I seen the circus before many times when I was living in Bakersfield, before I moved up here to Chico."

"Well, who did their rope shows?"

Hiram looked up to the ceiling to think.

"Come to think of it, know that this Amber Francis was quite the artist with the rope, but, there was another one who was in charge of the rope show, could lasso a bear I tell you. What's his name now? Oh, that's it, yes, his name is . . . Russell . . . Abel Russell. Could lasso, noose, you name it, he did the show with her, much faster and more skilled than her, seeing her stare at him sometimes cause he was so fast, so tight, like he was possessed."

I remember leaving Hiram's office more confused, in some ways, than I had been when I had gone in there. It was like a thick cloud of battle, bullets going this way, going that way, and wasn't sure what was up or down.

But, as I sat there in the courtroom listening to the closing words of Abel Russell's testimony, the jury wouldn't hear from Jarboe all of the things I heard from the mayor about the Underground Railroad, the mauled bodies, or the fact that Abel was just as good as, or much better than, Amber at making nooses.

That's cause Jarboe wasn't going to let inconvenient truths get in his way.

After Abel got down from the witness stand, Judge Parker said: "That's it for these second day of the trial, ladies and gentlemen of the jury. Please be back here tomorrow at 9:00 a.m. sharp.

And, as before . . ." As the judge made his final instruction for the day, I tried to make peace between the two visions I had in my head of Amber: angel of Salem, or angel of death?

The third day of the trial only made my pigeonholing chores harder when I heard testimony about Father Shane's long sharp hand saw, the one that Poncho Sanchez found underneath Shane's bed.

CHAPTER SEVEN

CHRISTMAS ORNAMENTS

"I remembering the bodies, they is, how you say, they is, floating in the San Francisco bay," the salty Italian fisherman, Gerald Medici, testified at the start of the next day.

His wrinkled hands and dirty fingernails covered his eyes.

He took his hands off of his eyes to look at Jarboe, who was standing next to him, thumbs in his vest, pocket watch dangling, watching the trial with the rest of the courtroom. Jarboe was proud that the witness was telling it all, proud in his preparation, proud that he was on the right side.

"Mr. Medici," Jarboe said in with a calming voice to the witness, "I understand the difficulty, the difficulty in remembering what you are remembering, and seeing what you are seeing in your mind's eye," Jarboe pointed to his own forehead. "Both myself, and . . .," he looked over to the jury, "the jury appreciate that you are here today."

I remembered thinking that Jarboe's Christmas cards must have been so sweet.

"What were you doing on the morning of April 23, 1876 when you came upon those bodies?"

"I am the fisherman, I was doing the fishing, this is what I do, like you doing the lawyering, I do the fishing, understand?"

"Yes, thank you, sir, now . . . about where were you when you saw these bodies?"

"I was, out there," Medici pointed out towards the Pacific, "I was in the bay, the San Francisco bay, cause this is where I do my best fishing."

"Okay," Jarboe nodded his head and tightened up his hands in his vest, "about where in the bay were you, I mean far out from the coast?"

"Yes, I was, let me see," the fisherman played with his grey black raspy looking beard, "I was about in the middle, in the middle between San Francisco and Oakland, so, how you say, pretty . . . fucking . . . far . . . out?"

Some jury members giggled.

"Alright, Mr. Medici, alright. Now, going back to that day, the morning of April 23, 1876, what time did you get out into the bay?"

"Oh, let me see, I say about 7 in morning, something like this."

"And when is it that you saw these bodies?"

"Is was later, later in the day, I thinks."

"About 10:00?"

"Yes, something like this, about this time."

"What did you first see, specifically, at that later time in the morning, in the ocean?"

"Eh, I was with my son, Pepe, and was going on the boat, is the currents which is strong, going back and forth from San Francisco to Oakland, when we see these bodies floating in the ocean."

167

"How many bodies did you see?"

"They was five, they was five in all."

"Close together, I mean were they floating next to one another?"

"No, we seeing them in different parts of the ocean, one here, one there, then another, you see, you understand?" The Moses bearded Italian leaned over the witness stand.

"Yes, sir, I understand," Jarboe nodded comfortingly. "So, Mr. Medici, please tell the jury, were the bodies dressed, I mean, were there any clothes on them?"

"Eh, Mr. Jarboe, this is the difficult question to answer, you see, it is difficult."

"Why? What is it difficult?"

"Cause, you see . . ." The pirate looking Italian put his head in his hands in despair. While he was in the cave of his hands, he started mumbled something, "they . . . is . . . not . . . the . . . they . . . is . . . not . . . all . . . oh . . . together."

"Sorry, sir," Jarboe said, "could you please speak up?" Jarboe moved over to put his hand on the fisherman's shoulder. "I know, I know what you saw is hard to relate, but it will help us find out the truth."

The bearded Italian looked up from his hands.

"Yes, okay, what I trying to say is that they was not complete, their bodies, they was missing the things, you see, the parts of the bodies."

"What parts? What parts were they missing?" Jarboe leaned back to give the witness some room.

"The hands, the feet, the . . . oh my Lord, Lord Jesus Christ," the man did a cross over his chest, "their heads, their heads was, how you say, they was not there, on their bodies, you understand me?"

"Yes, Mr. Medici, I do, thank you." Jarboe looked over his notes that were resting on the little fence between him and the witness, and then continued.

"So their torsos, more or less their torsos, were floating in the ocean, right?"

The man shrugged.

"I not know what you mean by the torsos, but I know what I see, I see nothing other than those bodies, doing the floating."

"Right, right, sir, now, let me see," Jarboe looked into his notes, "did their bodies have any clothing on them, anything at all?"

"Um, let me see," the sailor looked up to the ceiling, thinking back, "if I thinking back to this right, thinking back to what happened right, yes, they was wearing the black things, the black dress of the priest, you understand?"

"Yes, all too well, Mr. Medici," Jarboe nodded in despair.

As I sat there listening, I knew that the Italian was telling the God's honest truth. When the police precincts in the two parishes where the five dead priests were from — Fathers Ricky Vasquez, Timothy Cruces, Felix Trupia from Star of the Sea, and Lou Tugade and Doug Teta from Saints Peter and Paul Church — investigated, they discovered that their holy vestments — clothing — were gone from their bedroom closets. Whoever the killers were, I remember thinking to myself as I sat there, must have dressed the men up before cutting them up.

"So, Mr. Medici, these bodies or, more accurately, torsos, were fully clothed in the garb of the priesthood, with all of the fixings?"

"Yes," he nodded his head. "This is the way it was."

"And you didn't know, upon discovering those floating bodies, what happened to their body parts, the body parts that were missing, did you?

"Eh, no, I see them things, the bodies, but knowing nothing else."

"What, if anything, did you do with the bodies after you saw them floating?"

"Eh," he shrugged, "we picking them up, me and Pepe, picking them up out of ocean, putting in the boat. Is not the

Christian thing to leave them in water like this, see, and then we brings back to the police when we coming to shore."

"Thank you, sir, that's all for now," Jarboe nodded.

At this point, Jarboe tendered the witness to Hyman, who, during Jarboe's direct, just sat there whispering in Blue's ear like two nerdy little schoolgirls who get away with playing hooky along the coast during a warm spring day.

"Counsel," Judge Parker looked sternly in Hyman's direction, "I don't mean to interrupt your conversation there," he said with a sarcastic tone, "we don't mean to waste your time, as it looks like you are enjoying it, but are you intending on doing a cross?"

"Oh, yes, yes, your honor," Hyman threw down his pencil on the defense counsel's table and inched for what seemed like days, over to the witness.

As he did, I thought to myself: three people, killing and dismembering five men, in different parts of the city, in one morning? It seemed unrealistic. There had to be more involved. But then, after I thought about it for a moment, I nodded my head as I walked through the sinister steps.

Take the first three priests from the Star of the Sea Church. As with the first set of priest murders, Amber, Blue, and Shane would enter the priest's separate bedrooms during the middle of the morning. This time, however, Blue would slit the first priest's throat while he slept, which explains the blood on the beds that we found. Then, either the priest would be dressed, or they would cut the next two priests' throats, and then dress them all afterwards.

In either case, Shane would then dismember them holy bodies with knives for the fingers, and a hand saw for the meatier parts. I could picture Shane sawing off the arms, and then the legs, of each body with such force, such focus, that both bodies would be cut up within 10–15 minutes. After that, Blue and Amber would take over with the fixings, preparing the fingers and so on for hanging.

After the bodies were cut up, the three would put the torsos in their carriage for transportation to the next church, where they would do the same thing to the next two priests, only to end up at the frigid waters of the San Francisco bay where the torsos were laid in the water. All in all, with transportation and killing time, I see the operation taking 3 to 4 hours, tops.

"Mr. Medici," Hyman all of a sudden said, "my name is Benny Hyman, and I represent the defendants sitting behind me," he said wearing the same outfit he wore yesterday, and the day before.

"Okay, I am here to answer these questions, okay," the salty sailor nodded.

"So," Hyman walked close to the witness stand, "I understand you are a fisherman, right?"

"Yes," he said.

"And that the first time you saw these men, these dead men, was in the bay?"

"Yes, this the first time, the first time I seeing them," Medici nodded in acknowledgement.

"So you don't know how they got there, in the ocean, do you?"

"No, I have the no idea," the witness said.

"Were you on your regular route, your regular fishing route, when you came upon the corpses?"

"Yes, I taking the same route, with some places that is changing sometimes, when I going with my son into the ocean."

"Thank you," Hyman thought of his next question. "As far as you know, were you the only fisherman who took that particular route during that time of the day?"

"Yes, I thinks so, cause I see nobody else."

"Where is your business based, I mean, where is the location of your dock?"

"Eh, eh," he almost pleaded with Hyman.

"Objection, your honor, relevance," Jarboe said forcefully.

"Overruled," Parker quickly batted down Jarboe's fly of an objection.

"Well, it is not far, is between the Marina, this place called the Marina, and the North Beach, the place where many of my peoples is living."

"Your peoples being the Chinese?" Hyman asked with a slight smirk.

The audience laughed. Even the man next to me laughed. When I caught him, though, he stopped.

"Objection! Objection! Harassing the witness, your honor!" Jarboe got up.

"Relax, relax, Mr. Jarboe," Judge Parker said, "it's just a little humor, it isn't going to hurt nobody, especially you," the Judge said. "That being said," Parker looked over to Hyman, "one more wisecrack like that about a witness, and I'll hold you in contempt, do you understand?"

"Yes, your honor, I hear you loud and clear," Hyman responded.

Jarboe sat back down.

"Proceed, Mr. Hyman," Parker said.

"No offense, sir, just a little humor," Hyman said in a con-ciliatory tone to Medici.

"Is okay, I like the humor, is good, is good for the heart," he pointed his chest and smiled.

"North Beach, this is where many Italians live, right?

"Right," the seaman said.

"And do you live in North Beach?"

"Yes, I am living there with my wife and the two sons."

"So, going back to your dock, is it walking distance, walking distance to the Star of the Sea Church?"

"Relevance, objection, relevance!" Jarboe got up.

"Mr. Hyman?" Parker asked.

"Your honor, Mr. Jarboe will eventually show," Hyman said as he looked at his notes, "That these first three priests were from Star of the Sea Church, and that the second set, they were from . . ." Hyman looked down . . . "the Saints Peter and Paul Church, which he'll show later on is in North Beach."

Parker looked at Jarboe, who pleaded:

"This is all true, your honor, but where is he going with this?"

"Let's see," Parker said, "let's see," he looked over to Hyman, the two insiders — Parker and Jarboe, who are rumored to play chess together — reviewing Hyman, the outsider, who is rumored to play chess with folks related to former Barbary coast pirates, among others, in some of the more colorful parts of town.

"Thank you, your honor," Hyman graciously said. "Now, Mr. Medici, is your dock walking distance to the Star of the Sea Church?"

"No, no, it's a good ride on horse," he said.

"And what about Saints Peter and Paul Church," Hyman persisted. "Is your dock walking distance to that church?"

The fisherman played with his beard for a few seconds.

"Listen, Mr. Hyman, this all depends, eh, what you carrying, so if you not carrying, the nothing, you can be walking to both very easily."

"I see," Hyman nodded as he reviewed his notes, waiting to deliver the next question. "So, now, if you are carrying a heavy load to or from your dock, where you put your boat, to either church, would it then be walking distance?"

The Italian sailor sat there, thinking of where Hyman was going with this.

"Eh, no, this as too long, too long the walk, you need the horse, the horse is the need for this."

Hyman made a note in his notebook.

"Do you own a horse?"

"Objection, relevance," Jarboe shot up. "Where is he going on this wild goose chase?"

"Overruled," Parker said quickly.

"Please answer the question," Hyman continued.

"Uh, no, I not owning any horse, only the bicycle, no horse."

"Do you know any of these defendants sitting there," Hyman asked as he pointed to the defense counsel's table.

"No," the fisherman shook his head as he looked at Blue, Amber, and Shane.

"Did you know any of the five dead priests that you saw in the bay?"

"Eh, not when I seeing in them in the ocean, cause I don't see nothing other than some bodies, you understanding?"

"Yes, yes, so what about afterwards, when the bodies were identified as Fathers Ricky Vasquez, Timothy Cruces, Felix Trupia, Lou Tugade, and Doug Teta. Did you know any of these men?"

Medici just sat there with his head held up to the ceiling and his eyes closed.

"Mr. Medici?" Hyman asked.

"I just remembering back," Medici said with his eyes closed. "Yes, I knowing these men, I know them cause I selling fish to them, to their parishes, you see?"

"Right, thank you. Were you aware that Fathers Tugade and Teta were priests at the Catholic high school in the St. Peters church in North Beach?"

"Eh, no, I not having the idea."

"Mr. Medici, isn't it true that your two sons attended high school at St. Peter's?"

"Yes, yes, yes, this true."

"Weren't Fathers Tugade and Teta teaching at the school while your sons attended?"

The fisherman sat thinking.

"I not knowing if these men was there, cause my sons never had them as teachers."

Hyman sifted through his many notes resting on the witness bannister.

"Sir, I have here your son's attendance records at the school, and the records show that both of your sons had these dead priests for American history and math."

The shitty looking but Machiavelli acting defense attorney handed the fisherman duplicates of the records, after handing some to Jarboe.

"Objection!" Jarboe shot up after he quickly reviewed the records. "These documents are hearsay!"

"Overruled, counselor, this is cross," Parker dismissed Jarboe. "Please proceed, Mr. Hyman."

"Do you still maintain that your sons never had these two priests as teachers?"

"Eh, maybe, eh," he shrugged his shoulders, the same shoulders he would use to haggle with buyers at the market were now haggling with Hyman. "Maybe they did, but, uh, I not remember this."

Hyman smiled with amusement.

"Are you aware of the priests' histories of molestation?"

"Me, oh, no, I not knowing nothing," Medici shook his head with his eyes closed. See no evil, hear no evil, then there is no evil, is what the man's gestures said. But Hyman knew better, and the fisherman's denial wasn't going to show otherwise.

"Very well, that's all for this witness, your honor," Hyman looked over at Parker, "thank you for your testimony, sir," Hyman then looked back at Medici.

The next witness, a stout English-Scot started walking to the front of the courtroom in his overalls, ripped here and there, but freshly shaven, a gentleman in the closet, perhaps, I thought when my eyes saw him.

That gentleman in the closet came out during testimony.

"Their parts, their toes, their . . ." The man, whose name was Otto Hale, trembled as he looked outside, his thinning gray hair sneaking down to the sides of his head, shaking, too, at what he was forcing himself to remember.

His large brown fedora was hung on the back courtroom wall.

"What is it, sir, what is it Mr. Hale?" Jarboe prodded. "Please help us understand what happened?"

Hale's hands, which weren't thick like the Italian's, but thin and powerful, covered his eyes. Hale's distribution business was responsible for shipping most of the city's booze in and out of the ports, and then to the rest of the city. Hale's face had the same weathered look as the Italian's, but there was some hidden refinement to them, a manicure that happened here, or there, sometime during the past, once, twice, maybe every week.

After Hale gained his composure:

"Toes, heads, ears, hands, fingers . . . they were . . . hanging in those trees, those trees," he pointed towards where San Francisco was located. There was more to the man than met my eye. His brooding eyes briefly glanced over my way, and I had the feeling something big was going to happen, a big explosion, something that I didn't expect.

"What trees?" Jarboe asked.

"The trees," the strong beanpole of Hale adjusted himself, "the trees surrounding Star of the Sea Church."

The people in the audience made noises of disgust, and so did the jury members. It was all so gruesome, so dark, I closed my eyes to escape into the rhyme that my mother, whose family was originally from East London, used to sing to me with her Cockney accent when I was younger growing up in Rocky Mount as she played with my toes:

"This little piggy went to the market," she wiggled my big toe.

"This little piggy stayed home," she wiggled the next one.

"This little piggy had roast beef," onto the next.

"This little piggy had none," she wiggled the next to last.

"And this little piggy," her tall elegant silhouette leaned over me, with her blond brownish hair dangling into my eyes, and smiled with one of the warmest smiles I have ever seen, as she said "cried wee wee wee all the way home."

My eyes opened back up in the courtroom, and I was rudely brought back to reality, when Jarboe asked:

"On what date did you see these body parts, toes and such, on those trees in front of the Star of the Sea?"

"Oh, let me see," the stealthy elegant booze distributor rubbed his chin, "I suppose it was April 23, 1876, it was the morning."

"About what time?"

"I think it was something like 8:00 or so in the morning."

"What time did you start your work day that day?"

"About 6:00 a.m."

"So how do you know, I mean," Jarboe looked over at Hyman, "how do you know it was about 8:00 a.m. when you saw those bodies?" Jarboe looked back at the beer man.

"Cause that is my route," he pointed towards the city, "Don't nobody else take that one except me," he pointed to the tuff of white chest hair popping out from underneath the neck of his white t-shirt, "and I was on my second trip to the wharf, which usually happens around 8:00 a.m. on days when I make a second trip."

"So, Mr. Hale, tell us what you did that morning when you came upon the Star of the Sea church, what did you see first?"

"The trees," he nodded.

"Yes, but what did you notice in particular about the trees, I mean did anything seem out of the ordinary about them?"

Hale, who was German, sat there for a moment and thought to himself.

"There were what looked like things hanging from their branches, like you see when ornaments hang from the tree on Christmas," he held his hand up like he was hanging an ornament, "just dangling there and swinging in the wind that was coming in off the Pacific."

"What did you do next?"

"I stopped my buggy, cause I couldn't make out quite what I was seeing, so I parked my buggy and lassoed up the horses."

He stopped to gain his composure.

"I walked slowly up the trees, to the trees in front of the church," he said as he closed his eyes in pain, "and that's when I saw them."

"What's them, sir? What do you mean by them?"

"Toes, they was each . . . they was each . . . they was each wrapped up so neatly with little pieces of rope that you think someone was making this a special thing, you know, like a present, cause they was each wrapped and knotted with rope, and hung up," he put his hand over his face.

"And what about the rest of the body parts you found, if any, were they also wrapped in the same way?"

Mr. Hale didn't respond. He just sat there.

"Mr. Hale, would you like some water?"

"No, no, no thanks," he said as he waived Jarboe away.

"They all had this rope around them, like the heads," he said he took his meaty hand off his eyes, "the heads had a rope running all around them, and then they was hung up on the trees, just like . . . just like . . ."

"Yes, sir, please tell the jury," Jarboe encouraged the witness.

"Just like they was sitting there, Christmas presents for someone to see."

"Approximately how many heads did you remember seeing?"

"There was, let me see," he looked down to think, "there was about three."

"And what about fingers, if any?"

"Ah, sir, I can't say for sure, but there must have been thirty or so fingers, a bunch."

"Same with toes, if there were any?"

These were all leading questions, but Hyman didn't care. He sat there leaning back in his chair whispering with Shane, smiling here and there, as they used their hands to make gestures as if they were playing a secret game of rock, paper, and scissors.

"Yes," he nodded slowly, "about the same number of toes."

"Were these parts, were they neatly cut, as far as you could tell?"

Suddenly, Hyman lazily objected:

"Objection, calls for speculation, vague and ambiguous as to 'neatly cut.'"

"Overruled, counsel," Parker quickly ruled, "please continue, Mr. Jarboe."

"What do you mean by neatly cut?" Hale asked Jarboe, who responded:

"Did they look like they had been torn from the bodies from which they came, like how you tear a piece of chicken?"

Hale shook his head.

"Mr. Hale, please answer yes or no."

"No, no, they looked like they had been cut, real clean, cause I remember seeing how neat the edges on the wrists of the hands, and the tops of the ankles, were, there wasn't any skin sticking out, nothing, not like they was pulled from their joints or something," Hale shook his head. "Nope, was more like," he looked out into the audience, "like how you see, let me see, how you see a butcher cut meat, you know, like that," Hale made a slicing motion, like a saw, with his right hand.

"So it would be fair to say that you believed that the parts were cut, not pulled apart?"

"Yes," Hale nodded in agreement. "Cut by a knife or some sort of blade . . . maybe like a saw," he said.

"What type of saw would you say, Mr. Hale?" Jarboe asked.

"Objection, calls for speculation," Hyman said as he sat. "This witness," Hyman nodded to the distributor, "he's no expert in meat cutting."

"Overruled," Parker quickly snipped. "And, next time you want to make an objection, you stand, counselor, you hear me?" Parker leaned over.

"Yes, yes, of course, your honor," Hyman slowly stood as he spoke.

An opium addict moved faster.

"Please answer my question, if you can, Mr. Hale, as to what type of saw would you say cut off those hands?"

"Well, let me see . . . let me see," Hale's black and blue eyes looked outside the court room window for a moment, "I know, when I go to the butchers in town, they use this . . . wait . . . yea, they use this big hand saw when they are cutting meat, you know, bone, skin, and all that, from the cows. That's what I see Moe, my butcher, use when he makes the steaks for me. So . . . sitting here . . . I'd think it was something like that, you know, a saw, some type of handsaw," Hale looked at Jarboe in a trembling terror at the thought of what he just said.

Calmly, Jarboe just stood next to the witness fence.

"Before we move on from what you saw in the tress, Mr. Hale," Jarboe said, "let me ask you something about the heads, if you remember."

Hale nodded his agreement.

"They were cut off, right?"

"Yes," he nodded. "They were just hanging there."

"Did you see any marks on the necks, I mean, around the throat area, like the throats were cut?"

Hyman got up, slowly. "Objection, same grounds, your honor, and also improper form, cause counsel is leading the witness."

Fed up with Hyman, Parker barked: "overruled, counsel. Mr. Hale can give us his lay opinion about what he saw. Please answer the question, Mr. Hale."

"Was real early in the morning, you know," Hale flicked some dust off his knee, "but I remember seeing a mark, like a knife mark, around the throats of the heads, right above where they were . . . where they were," Hale paused uncomfortably, "severed."

"Thank you, Mr. Hale," Jarboe smiled satisfied.

It makes sense that Hale testified the way he was testifying — it was the truth. We — that is, the police — knew from speaking to the priests and nuns of Star of the Sea that the beds of the three missing priests — namely, Fathers Ricky Vasquez, Timothy Cruces, Felix Trupia — were full of blood, as I had mentioned to you earlier when I was imagining how this second set of murders went down. We took this to mean that the men had their throats cut in bed. Someone must have held their hand over their mouths as their throats were cut, or heads cut off, so as to not awaken anybody from their 7–8 hours of healthy sleep.

"Now, did you look under the trees at all, Mr. Hale, after you saw what was up there hanging?"

"Well, um, well," Hale just played with his overalls for a moment, tinkering with the straps, "I remember seeing, seeing, what looked like some type of crushed tobacco on the ground."

"Crushed?"

"Yes," Hale nodded, "like when you step on a cigarette or cigar."

"Can you tell us, did the tobacco look like it was from a cigarette?"

"No, it looked more like that dark tobacco that you see in cigars, cause the wrapping, the cigar wrapping was dark, not like I seen on regular cigarettes."

"Very well, Mr. Hale, "Jarboe said, "what did you do after you saw this tobacco on the ground?"

"Embarrassed, embarrassed to say it, but I walked away from the tree and, well, I threw up, threw up all of the eggs, bacon, and beans that my wife just made me that morning."

"And after that?" Jarboe asked.

"That's when I went to, went to the police precinct to tell them what I just seen."

Jarboe paused to look over his notes on the witness stand bannister.

"Thank you for your testimony, Mr. Hale," Jarboe said with appreciation, "that's all for this witness, your honor," Jarboe said to Parker.

"Your cross, Mr. Hyman," Parker said in Hyman's direction.

"Never leave home without it," Hyman said under his breath as he started to take his notes to get up.

"Excuse me, counselor, what did you just say?" Parker looked down disapprovingly at Hyman.

"Nothing, your honor, just saying how I never leave home without my trial notebook," he held it up to the judge.

Blue, Amber, and Shane were all smirking, their mouths taut to hide their laughter at what Hyman said under his breath but nobody heard — except maybe for them and me.

"Get on with it," Parker growled at Hyman.

"Yes, yes, of course," Hyman said. After his customary introductions, Hyman got right to it.

"Mr. Hale, did you see how these body parts arrived on those trees?"

"No sir, no idea."

"So you only saw them after they had been placed up on the trees like Christmas ornaments?"

"Yes, yes, that's right," he nodded.

"Do you know when those parts were put up there?"

"No sir, no idea," Hale shook his head.

"Could have been anytime before you saw them?"

"Right, don't know," Hale responded.

"Thank you," Hyman looked down onto his notes as he crossed his legs comfortably while standing. "What about the bodies that corresponded with those parts, know what happened to them, when you came upon those parts that morning?"

"No sir, no idea," his head shook.

"Okay, now, please tell the jury how you do your routes in the morning, where do you go to pick up your beer and booze?"

"Let me see, well," Hale paused to think. "We first pick up everything from the ships, the ships that dock off the port of San Francisco."

"And that's along the bay, along the bay of San Francisco?"

"Yes."

"Those ports, they are located over by Fisherman's Wharf, right?"

"Yes," Hale nodded.

"And how far is Fisherman's Wharf from Star of the Sea Church?"

"Quite far."

"Not walking distance?"

"Well, not really, but I guess it could be done."

"With a heavy freight on your back?"

"Not likely," Hale shook his head.

"And what about Saints Peter and Paul Church in North Beach, is Fisherman's Wharf closer or father to that church?"

"It's closer, much closer."

"Is Star of the Sea Church on your route?"

"Yes, yes it is," the six foot man nodded.

"What about the church in North Beach?"

"Your honor, objection, relevance," Jarboe shot up. "Where is he going with this, I mean we don't have all day for him to fish here."

"Counselors, please come up to the bench to speak with me," Parker said.

Jarboe got up and walked over to Parker, with Hyman slowly inching over to do the same. After a short-lived conference where there was whispering, some yelling, with Jarboe shoving his hand on the table, and the three broke their huddle.

"You may answer the question," Parker instructed Hale.

"What was the question again?" Hale asked.

"Is the Saint Peter and Paul Church in North Beach along your distribution route?"

"No, that church isn't on my route."

"But that church is on the route for, let me see, your son Knox Hale, correct?"

The witness just stared a "how did you know that" look at Hyman.

"Yes, correct," he adjusted himself in the seat, not in a getting comfortable way, but in a something is hot underneath the seat type of way and you want to get away from it — your ass, that is.

"So you and the boys, including Knox, separately go to Fisherman's Wharf, you pick up your product, and then what do you do?"

"We go and deliver the product throughout our city routes."

"Okay," Hyman nodded, "do you only make a one way trip? I mean, do you go and pick up what you need from the port, make your deliveries, and then go home?"

"No," the witness shook his head. "We sometimes need to make a few trips during the day."

"How many?"

"Can be up to two, sometimes three."

"And how big are the carriages in which you put the booze that your horses carry?"

"What do mean?"

"Well, let me see, how many people could you fit in the back of one of those carriages?"

"Your honor, objection, any relevance here is outweighed by prejudice!" Jarboe jumped up.

"Sustained," Parker said. "Counsel, rephrase your question."

"Sure, your honor," Hyman paused to think, "take a full grown horse, without legs, could you fit one of those in the back of your carriages?"

"Let me think, well, um, yes, I think that would be doable," he said as he calmly removed some lint from his pants.

"How about two?"

"No, probably one and a half in there," Hale nodded.

"So, approximately, about how big is the back of your carriage?"

"Don't know for sure, but it can fit up to six adults easy."

Jarboe threw his pen on the prosecutor's table.

"And what about cover, are your carriages covered?"

"It depends. If it's raining, we cover them, but when we want to fit more in them, we don't cover them."

"The day that you saw those body parts on the trees, that is April 23 of this year, was it raining?"

"Let me think . . . let's see . . .come to think of it, it wasn't raining that day, but it rained the day before."

"Did you have a cover over your carriage that day, that is on the morning of April 23, 1876?"

Hale paused and looked like he was trying to remember, squinting his eyes.

"Yes, sir, I think it was covered, cause there was still some mist in the air."

"Thank you, Mr. Hale, only a few more questions."

"Did you make any trips back to the Fisherman's Wharf that day after you made your delivery to the neighborhood around Star of the Sea?"

"Yes, was a busy day, people drink more when it rains, so we had more deliveries to make that day," he nodded.

"When you saw those parts in the trees, were you heading from Fisherman's Wharf?"

"No sir," he said.

"Were you heading back to Fisherman's Wharf?"

"Yes, sir."

"To pick up more shipment?"

"Yes, it was a very busy day."

"Was that before you made your report to the police?"

"No, no, I headed back to Fisherman's Wharf after I made my report."

"And about what time did you make your report?"

"Well, um, let me see, it must have been around 8:30 or so in the morning," he said thinking back.

Hyman looked over at Jarboe, who gave a "go fuck yourself" look at Hyman.

"Only a few more, Mr. Hale," Hyman started back, "don't want to make this a trip to the dentist here," Hyman smirked.

"We all need to get our teeth cleaned once in a while," Hale said.

"Right, right, so, now, do you know any of the defendants sitting over there?" Hyman asked.

"No sir."

"And did you know the dead priests, namely Fathers Ricky Vasquez, Timothy Cruces, Felix Trupia, Lou Tugade, and Doug Teta that were killed on April 23?"

"Only knew two of them, Fathers Lou Tugade and Doug Teta, cause my son, Knox, went to the Catholic high school in their parish."

"You mean Saint Peter and Paul parish in North Beach?"

"Yes, that one."

"The church that's not on your route, correct?"

"Correct."

"But is on your son Knox's route, correct?"

"Yes."

"Did you like those dead priests?" Hyman asked.

"Didn't know them well enough to like them or not, just know they were responsible for running the parish where my son went to school."

"Did you know that Fathers Tugade and Teta have convictions in other states for crimes against Mother Nature with children?"

Hale just stared at Hyman for a long time.

"Mr. Hale, please answer the question," Judge Parker said.

"No, I didn't know," Hale finally answered.

"Mr. Hale . . . do you read the *San Francisco Chronicle*?"

"Yes, its one of my favorite things to read when things are slow."

"Okay," Hyman gave Hale a I have you in my sights smirk, "did you not see the article, entitled *Underbelly of the Catholic Church*, which was on the front page of the January 8th edition earlier this year?"

Hale paused again. He didn't stare at Hyman. He just stared at Jarboe.

"Mr. Hale, the prosecutor may be a good dresser, but his fancy window dressing won't help you answer the question."

"I don't recall, I just don't recall," Hale said slowly.

Hyman just stared at the witness.

"I have no more questions for this witness, your honor," Hyman concluded.

Jarboe called the next witness to the stand, a young buck named Chip Lantz, a medium height and powerfully built barista of the coffee house just next to the Saint Peter and Paul's church in North Beach, called *Cefalu at the Park I*. Lantz was a famous local character cause he played professional baseball for the Chicago White Stockings, and he worked with local kids from the Beach — as they called it — teaching them baseball, and mentoring them.

"And when did you notice something peculiar about the trees in front of the church?" Jarboe asked Lantz after the customary introductory remarks.

"After I got in, started setting up shop, around 7 in the morning or so, I always look across the street to check out the pretty trees in front of the church," Lantz's baseball bat gripping fingers indicated as he spoke. I could see why the kids liked him. He looked like a mix between a rough dockworker, a musician, and a mountain shepherd.

"Where is your coffee shop," Jarboe looked down onto, "*Cefalu at the Park I*?"

"On Stockton Street, just between Union and Filbert Streets," Chip used his hands to show Jarboe.

"Okay, so you get in normally, get into the coffee shop, set up, look out the window, so what, if anything, was different on the morning of April 23, 1876 about the trees that you saw outside?"

"I can't, I can't, I just can't really explain what I saw," Chip put his head into his hands, shaking his head, like he couldn't go on.

"Take your time, take your time," Jarboe said in a confiding type of way to the witness.

Lantz took his head out of his hands, and there were tears brewing.

"Saw things, saw things, saw some things hanging from the trees, blowing in the Pacific wind. Was drinking my morning espresso, and I remember just stopping, stopping my sipping, and just stared."

"Did you know what you were staring at, as you stood there at, through the window?"

"Didn't quite know," Lantz said with a shell-shocked face, "didn't quite know until . . . I saw . . . until I saw," he just sat there with his mouth open.

"Until you saw what, Mr. Lantz, until you saw what?"

"The . . . the . . . the . . . uh . . . the heads, the two heads that were hanging on the trees, on the trees in front of the church." Lantz sat with a blank look on his eyes and looked onward.

"What church?" Mr. Lantz.

"Saints Peter and Paul Church, the one that is on Filbert Street, at the end of Washington Square Park in North Beach."

"And, just for clarification, that's between the park and Fisherman Wharf, right?"

"Yes, yes," Lantz said quietly.

Jarboe drew out testimony from Lantz about the ears, fingers, hand parts, feet cut around the ankles, and toes hanging from the trees via tightly knotted pieces of thin rope, and that Lantz had no idea how the parts got up there.

Hyman then slowly walked up and did his cross.

"Mr. Lantz, you have another Cefalu Café, do you not, by Star of the Sea Church, right?"

"Yes."

"And that coffee shop of yours is located," Hyman looked down on his notes, "on the corner of Geary Boulevard and 8th, right?"

"Yes," Lantz nodded.

"That is right across the street from Star of the Sea Church, right?"

"Yes."

"And that café is called *Cefalu at the Park II*?"

"Yes."

"Do you have an individual by the name of Katya Stravinska who works there?" Hyman asked, not because he didn't know the answer, but because he did.

"Yes," Lantz nodded.

"And, as part of her employment, she is responsible for getting into *Cefalu at the Park II* at what time every day?"

"Around 6:30."

"Do you use thin strong hemp rope to close the tops of the coffee bags at your stores, the ones that you store coffee beans in?"

"Yes."

"Is this," Hyman pulled out a piece of rope, "does this look like the thin rope that you use?"

Lantz paused to inspect the thin rope.

"Yes," Lantz said.

"Exactly like the rope you use?"

Lantz inspected the rope closer.

"Yes," he nodded.

Hyman took back the rope, walked over to Jarboe, and handed it to him.

As Jarboe inspected the rope, Hyman said to Parker:

"Your honor, I'll represent to the court that this is an actual piece of rope from one of Mr. Lantz's coffee shops and obtained by my private investigator, Mr. Wu, who will later testify."

"Counsel," Parker said in Jarboe's direction, "do you have any objection?"

"No," Jarboe said as he handed back the rope to Hyman.

"Mr. Lantz, were you aware that the same rope, the same hemp type of rope, that we just looked at was used to tie those body parts up on those trees in front of the Star of the Sea Church?"

"Objection, your honor, assumes facts not in evidence!" Jarboe shot up.

"Overruled, counsel," Parker quickly said. "Please answer the question, Mr. Lantz."

"I was not aware that the same rope was used on these men," Lantz shook his head.

"Do you tie your own knots, using that hemp string, Mr. Lantz for your coffee shops when the bags come in?"

"Mostly, with Katya's help."

"Is that why you have them callouses on your hands?" Hyman looked to the witness's hands.

"Partially, and because I play a lot of baseball with the kids," Lantz smiled.

"Thank you, Mr. Lantz, I have no more questions."

Jarboe's last witness of the day, Poncho M. Sanchez, the Mission Dolores janitor, then came to the stand and shocked the jury.

"And where did you see this bloody hand saw, Mr. Sanchez?"

"I saw it, I saw it," the wrinkled mustached Mexican man's face cringed, maybe in pain about remembering what he saw, "underneath the bed, in a white cloth, with . . . with . . . with blood."

"Underneath whose bed?" Jarboe leaned over to emphasize the question.

"His," Sanchez pointed to Defendant Shane Egan.

"Your honor, let the record reflect that the witness pointed in the direction of Defendant Egan."

"The record is duly recorded, counsel," Parker nodded.

"And what did the saw look like?" Jarboe asked.

"It was like from your elbow to your fingers," the janitor used his index fingers to show the width of the saw.

"Your honor, let the record reflect that the witness it indicating a distance of roughly 15 inches in length."

"The record is reflected," Parker nodded.

"Did it have a handle on it?" Jarboe asked the witness.

"Yes," the janitor said, "made it all look super easy to use."

"About how tall was this saw?"

"About this tall," the janitor used his hands.

"Let the record reflect that the witness is indicating a distance roughly between his wrist and the tip of his fingers," Jarboe said.

"Duly noted," the judge said.

"Have you seen such a saw before, Mr. Sanchez?"

The janitor paused to think.

"I think, I think I seen it at the butcher, this butcher man in my hood using it to cut shit up," the witness made a cutting gesture with his hand, "like some meat artist."

The jurors looked at one another with fear in their faces.

"No more questions for this witness, your honor," Jarboe concluded.

While Jarboe appeared to have established an airtight record against Shane Egan, air sneaked back in when Hyman got his crack at bat.

"Mr. Sanchez," Hyman asked with a cynical I don't buy anything I can't touch, taste, and see tone, "didn't your nephew, Julio, attend Star of the Sea Church for elementary school?"

"Yea, so what mister lawyer man, got to send them to school somewhere, and the public schools around here suck my old nasty mold beans."

Sanchez grabbed his private parts as he smiled, not caring that the jury was horrified. That's cause he shrugged.

"Did you know that Father Trupia taught your son?"

"No, man, didn't know anything like that!" Sanchez's eyebrows went up to his forehead as he looked at Hyman like he was sick, like he had some snot dripping down his nose, or was otherwise high on peyote. But, really, Sanchez was just shocked.

"Mr. Sanchez, weren't you previously convicted for aiding and abetting tax evasion?"

"Never, man, what you talking about you gringo!" Sanchez waived his hand towards Hyman. "Wait, but you a Jew," he scratched his head, "so you maybe you not a gringo, but that's all still bullshit what you just said," he said pointing his finger at Hyman.

"I have a record here," Hyman looked down in his hand, "which shows you were convicted in Texas on May 24, 1869, of aiding and abetting the tax evasion of a criminal organization out of Mexico called San La Muerte, Inc., by hiding money and preparing fraudulent tax returns."

"What, what, that's a bunch of . . ."

"Mr. Sanchez, please watch your language in my courtroom," Parker looked down at the witness. Sanchez looked up at Parker, obviously pissed off.

"Here is a duplicate copy of your conviction," at which point Hyman handed the copy to the witness, then to Jarboe.

Sanchez just stared at the conviction, a bad report card he didn't want to tell his parents about, but which they found out about anyway.

"Were you aware that this organization, San La Muerte, Inc., was known by the Rangers in Texas to have killed its enemies in the very same ways that the priests were killed, that is, by dismembering their bodies, hanging them in trees, and putting torsos in the bodies of water, like lakes or rivers, around the site of the killing?"

"Man, mister lawyer man, I was framed for this, like totally framed, you know, like when you coming out of some house that not your woman's, and your woman sees you, thinks you is cheating, but you is, uh, just getting like a massage?"

"Mr. Sanchez," Hyman asked the pot bellied Mexican with slickly parted hair and finely manicured mustached, "did you receive any compensation for your testimony today?"

"Eh, what you getting at? No, never," Sanchez crossed his arms.

"You never met with Cardinal Degollado to receive money from the Archdiocese?"

"Never, never," the janitor said emphatically.

"Would it surprise you, then, that Mr. Katsumi Yamamoto, the Mission's gardener, will testify later on in trial that he saw you meeting with the Cardinal and receiving cash from him, not long after the Stop 666! Commission was formed, and then continuing to receive cash from him until the start of the trial?"

"Shit, that dude is like totally lying, lying!" He uncrossed his hands and put them on the witness table in front of him, slamming them several times.

"Would it also surprise you that Mr. Yamamoto will also testify to hearing you brag about: how much cash you had made with the Mexican organization I had mentioned earlier, how you had hid a all throughout California and laundered it through your baby clothes side businesses, and the creative ways in which they killed people who stole from them?"

"What? What?" The janitor slammed his hands on the bannister. "That guys is full of, well," he looked up to Parker, "you know what he full of, that Jap mother . . ."

"Order, order," Parker slammed his gavel on the table, interrupting Sanchez's tirade. "I told you I will not have such language in my court!" Parker stared at the now sweaty faced Sanchez.

Hyman just stared at the defeated looking Sanchez.

"No more questions, your honor," Hyman smiled he slowly pulled his knife out of Sanchez's stomach and went back to sit down.

Testimony from the day's final witness, Sun Tzu, the Chinese cook for Shane's family's in Pacific Heights, wouldn't be so easily dealt with by Hyman.

I should know. After I got back from Chico, CA, I interviewed Tzu, who had plenty to tell me about Shane's quiet murderous past before he became a priest.

CHAPTER EIGHT

SLEEPER GRIT PINK

"**H**ow did they scare the competition, the Egan family?" I asked Tzu.

Tzu shook his head in fear as we stood in a wet downtown San Francisco alley.

"I don't know how I say, don't know how I say, father."

He looked down into the alley's muddy waters on that cold day, only a few days after the priest disappearances that took place on September 3–4 of that year.

"Is hard to say in the English, father," Tzu shivered against the red brick wall and pulled his hands out to blow hot air from his mouth onto them.

"Try, try your best," I said. "Cigarette?" I held out a pack for him to take one.

The sun from the Pacific Ocean edged itself around the corner of the alley.

"Yes, yes, thanks very much," Tzu said as he took one.

"Is not against the wishes of Jesus, your Jesus, to smoke this?" He asked wondering how I could smoke.

"Nah," I said. "I'll just say confession, Jesus will hug me, and I'll be forgiven."

Tzu looked at me with surprise.

"Ah, okay, Jesus is pretty, how you say, the fuck cool guy?" He broke a happy smile on his face, like he got his savory barbeque after a long day.

After lighting Tzu's cigarette, and after a few puffs, he relaxed.

You might ask how I got to Sun Tzu? I got to him through Shane.

"When you were growing up," I asked Shane one day earlier that year over the table as we ate some sweet and sour soup with dumplings that Amber had made, "did you eat anything as good as this?"

"Better than this," remember him smiling over my way as he sipped the broth.

"Oh, how so?"

"We had this cook, Sun, name was Sun Tzu, and he made the best sweet and sour soup with dumplings I have ever tasted."

Sometimes, answers to your questions fall right in your lap.

Did some digging around after speaking to Shane, and found Tzu working construction downtown with a large crew of other Chinamen. Wore my bullshit priest outfit, same as I did with Abel Russell in Chico, and went to ask Tzu questions, like I was doing the same type of background check into Shane that I did on Amber.

"Are you Sun, Sun Tzu?" I went up to him as he stood during his lunch break smoking a cigarette in the alley across from the construction site.

"Yah, yah, father, why you ask me?" He looked at me nervous.

"Please call me father Jasper," I held out my hand for him to shake.

Tzu shook my hand nervously as his grey hair, which was parted down the middle, shook on each side of his head. Couldn't believe this potato of a man did Kung Fu, as Shane told me, but maybe he was one of the sleeper types? He hits you with his palm, you think nothing happened, and then you start bleeding internally a day later while you are trying to make love to yourself.

"Okay, okay, father Jasper," he took his hand down and looked nervously around. "What you wanting from me? What you wanting?"

"Just to ask you some questions," I put my satchel down on the ground next to my leg, "about Shane Egan."

Tzu looked at me with surprise.

"What you want to know about him, why you asking Tzu?"

"Shane said I could ask you questions about his family, said you knew things about them, about his background, could show the type of man he is," I put my hand on Tzu's shoulder, "how he has turned towards the light of the Lord, away from sin."

I was getting good with my lies. Quite proud, I must say, about how I could make this crap up on the spot. Suppose I got if from poppa, who was known around Rocky Mount as the wordsmith. Could cook up stories to tell anybody who wasn't from Franklin County, Virginia, so that they either wanted to move to the county, or never set foot in it.

"Me want no trouble, no trouble," Tzu protested, "me need to go back to work," he started to move towards the street.

"Please," I put my hand on the chest of the five foot five Chinaman, softly, in a non-threatening way, "I'll make it worth your while," at which point I took out a five dollar bill and showed it to him.

"You pay me?"

"Yes, I pay you."

"Okay," he backed up to where he was standing against the wall, "I stay," he crossed his arms.

"You want the money?" I asked.

"After," he waived his hand effortlessly, like a sorcerer waving a wand. "Now, what you want to know from me?"

"Okay," I took my notepad out from my satchel, "could you tell me when you first started working for the Egan's family?"

"Oh, let me see," he put his brick shit house sturdy hand, the one that could flip you with a Kung Fu twist, on his chin. "Sometime like in 1866," he said.

"When did you leave?"

"Not long time ago from today."

He shrugged his shoulders.

"So about 10 years, 10 years you were with them?" I asked.

He nodded.

"And you were their cook?"

He nodded.

"Did you cook for the whole family?"

He nodded.

"Did Shane have any sisters, brothers?"

"He having the sister, her name, what is her name?" He paused. "Cara, yes, this her name," he said.

"So you knew Cara, and Shane's parents, Mr. and Mrs. Egan, for all that time?"

"Yes, seeing them every day, Tzu seeing them every day."

"At their Pacific Heights mansion, that's where you were based?"

"Yes," he said.

I looked down on my notes. I needed to take good ones as I knew I was getting this information for Jarboe, so that Jarboe could decide whether to subpoena Tzu the cook to testify at trial. I had my notes separated into headings, "money — source," "fear — methods," "Shane — role." It was well known in the community that the Egan clan, originally from South Boston, and, before that, from County Cork, Ireland, had expanded their construction and booze empire to Northern California in or about January of 1866 so as to take advantage of all the new money that flushed into San Francisco from the Gold Rush, which ended about 1855. While they ran a tight ship, paying their employees well, and not ever having to call us — the police — to clean up their messes, it was rumored that they were vicious when they were double crossed in business dealings.

Shane's father, George Bernard Egan, wasn't only known to be smart — but he also had a reputation for being a mean son of a bitch. Other officers and detectives told me he was well read, knowing the methods used by world history legends to intimidate enemies.

"He a filthy mother fucker," Dougal, a dirt under the fingernails dark complexioned Irish-Scottish detective, told me over lunch one day.

"How so?" I asked as we sat on the steps outside of the precinct on an overcast Friday afternoon in San Francisco.

"Well," Dougal put his sandwich down on the steps, licked his soiled fingers clean, and looked around to make sure nobody was listening, "have to be careful, lad, cause don't want me words to hit the wrong ears."

He leaned over to whisper in my ear.

"So, word has it lad, that the Egan clan gives a lot of money to the mayor's office," Dougal looked back to the building. "So," he said looking with an intense focus on the street, "the word is that the old man."

"You mean the old man Egan?"

"No, the old fucking man who delivers presents on Christmas, who the fuck else do you think?" He slapped me on the shoulder playfully, but sort of not playfully.

"Right, ok," I said.

"Now, you got me off my focus, where was I? Ah . . . yes . . . so I was told by some lads who work back in Boston, who work the organized crime beat there, that the old man Egan was double crossed on a big deal . . . the buyers committed to a big purchase of whiskey and other things, and the old man didn't have nothing on paper, just a handshake."

Officers were walking up and down the steps all around me and Dougal in their uniforms, some just plain closed, "what's up fellas," "good day lads," "having a good date, boys?" they would say as they came by and saw us sitting together.

"So the old man has his Mick hoodlums deliver the booze, word has it from my Boston connect, to the Chinamen down in Five Points, Five Points Manhattan, but, get this," Dougal slaps my shoulder, "the delivery boys don't come back with the money they was supposed to getting from the chinks."

"Why?" I took a big bite of my San Francisco sourdough ham sandwich.

"The chinks surrounded the Egan boys with bats, knives, you name it, and told them to get out of the Points before they could never make it back over the river."

"So the Chinamen, they made a profit on the deal, eh?" I licked my fingers.

"For that moment lad, for that moment. When old man Egan got wind of what happened, he waited, I was told, a year or two, so that there wasn't anything that he could telegraph and," the burly Scot shook his head, "then he did some sinister shit to them chinks."

"What, scalp them?" I asked Dougal.

"Worse," he said in my direction with his beady eyes, "he had all of the members of this chink crew, forgot their name, maybe it was the Dragons, but, whoever it was," Dougal shrugged his shoulders and looked back on towards the street, "their corpses . . . were cut up . . . and their torsos was found floating in the East and Hudson rivers, about 50 or so, 50 or so of the whole crew was found."

I looked over to Dougal.

"And what about the rest of their bodies, hands, heads, feet?" I just held my sandwich in my hand. Didn't feel like taking another bite.

"They was found hanging all around Five Points, a chink head there, feet over here, toes on trees over there."

Just closed my eyes at the horror of the image in my head.

It was then that I knew that old man Egan wasn't only wicked, but he was wicked in a refined, horrible way, something from the medieval times that I thought were long gone, blending modern cutting methods with old world brutality. I wanted to know whether Tzu knew of such brutal acts by the Egan clan, the ones that Dougal told me.

"So you see them every day," I said to Tzu in the alley that cold fall day in September after speaking to Dougal, "the Egan clan, but did you know anything about the senior Egan, how he made his money, what he did to protect it?"

"Oh, I know many things about the Egan money, what they doing to keep others from taking."

Tzu looked at me like we were going into dangerous territory.

"So, Tzu, how did they get their money, what was their business?"

"The many things, the many things, father Jasper," Tzu put his cigarette out on the ground.

"Like what?"

"Well," Tzu shrugged, "I knowing that they doing much of the business in the whiskey, vodka, gin, but, under the table, they sell the hard things, like the China opium, import and export to New York, you see?"

I didn't look at Tzu because I was taking notes in my notebook as fast as I could.

"Yes, I see," I said as I kept my head down, writing. "Did you ever personally see them ship any of this white opium stuff, or talking about it, in the home?" I looked up.

"I hearing the old Egan, the old man, he talking about the shipments, doing the shipments to China, for the when-shee . . ."

"What the fuck is when-shee?" I asked with the notebook and pen ready in my hand.

Tzu looked at me with shock, his cigarette dangling from his mouth, when I cussed.

"Sorry, I just hate sin," I took a long puff off my cigarette, "and this is all sin, so I get frustrated being around it."

He just stood there inspecting me along with his dangling cigarette, and then:

"Is okay, father, is cussing for the good cause, yes?" He slapped my shoulder to comfort me.

"Yes," I nodded.

"Oh, when-shee is the name, the Chinese name for opium," he nodded.

"So you heard old man Egan use this term?"

"I hear, I hear, yes," he said.

"Interesting," I said as I licked my pencil and kept writing. After I finished writing my thoughts, I looked back at the wrinkled strong-bodied Chinaman, who was waiting for me, now with his arms crossed.

"So what about security? How did the Egan family make sure others didn't come in on their business, steal things, and all that?"

"Oh, piss myself, oh, shit yourself, when old man Egan, when old man Egan," Tzu took a drag off his cigarette that he had between his fingers, "when he putting his war paint on, there nothing that stopping him except for Satan himself," Tzu spit on the ground.

"Did you personally see any of the things that the old man Egan did, I mean in and around the house?"

"I never see, never see, cause the old man never doing nothing, nothing himself," he shook his head. "He have his men, his men doing this things for him, outside the house, far way, so nobody seeing, knowing, what he quietly doing."

"Did you hear of him talking about doing things while he was in the house?"

Tzu just looked up to the dark clouds above and thought.

"I remember, I remember," he looked back towards me, "that old man talking about what he want done, what he wanted done to these Chinamen in New York."

And then I asked: "what directions did you hear him give?"

"I hearing him giving evil directions cause they taking the products and not paying, you see?"

He held his dirty wrinkled hand with the cigarette in it up to my face.

"Oh, I not like this, not like this, I have do go, have to go," Tzu said with worry.

"We are almost done," I patted his arm, "just a few more questions, we'll make it worth your while, very important information I am getting on Father Shane, shows how far he has come from living a Lucifer life."

I pulled out another five dollar bill, offered it up slyly down below my waist to him, and Tzu took it while looking around, making sure nobody was seeing.

"So what were George Egan's directions?" I asked him.

"Oh, this the bad things, the very bad things," Tzu shook his head in distress, "he wanting done to people."

"Doing what?"

"He telling, telling how he want the bodies cut, where, just where he wanted them cut, and where he want . . . where he want . . . where he want," Tzu took a long drag like he was hyperventilating.

"Where he want what?" I put my hand on Tzu to calm him down.

"The parts," Sun looked into my eyes with fear. "Where he wanting the parts of the bodies put, hung, around Five Points, and where he wanting the big part, the, how you say . . . um . . . the chest, belly, this part, what is called?"

"The torso?" I asked.

"Yes, this the big body part, he saying to them where he want this big body part, he wanting it in the river water, to floating so the peoples can seeing."

The methods of the old man Egan were chillingly similar to way in which Fathers Ricky Vasquez, Timothy Cruces, Felix Trupia, Lou Tugade, and Doug Teta were killed.

But the most troubling news was yet to come. I asked Tzu:

"Who was old man Egan giving the directions to, who was listening to him?"

"Oh, I don't wanting the trouble, don't wanting the trouble," Tzu shook his head.

"There is no trouble here, just wanting to know more about Father Shane. As I said, he is a good man, has turned his eyes and heart towards the Lord," I looked above, "and we want to see how far he has come, from where he came from, see?"

"I understand, I understand, he is the boat who go in the right direction, from the wrong, yes?"

"Exactly," I said.

"The old man, the old man Egan, he sitting at head of table, in the big room where they eating the dinner, and the rest of them men, they was sitting around the table, but the main man, the main person that doing the dark things like this for the old man was . . . was . . . a wolf eyed Siberian in the winter, he the meanest man I seen, and, sitting right next to this Siberian was master Shane, who was taking notes, writing in his book."

"Wolf eyed Siberian — head of security/enforcement" — I wrote in my notebook. And then I stopped writing to think:

But Shane? A mass murderer, a butcher, a man with so much caring, softness to his looks, his spirit, a gritty man like that, underneath the covers, the grit sleeping until it is awoken from its slumber? Only then he becomes this monster?

It was hard for me to believe as I stood there listening to Tzu.

I wanted to dig further, wanted to dig more, as I gathered evidence to submit to Jarboe so that he could impanel a grand jury and indict Blue, Shane, and Amber. Since there wasn't an indictment yet, nobody knew that Shane was a target of our investigation. After I finished interviewing Tzu, I asked around among some of the Russian police officers, and folks who informed for us that lived in San Francisco's Russian Hill neighborhood, about this wolf eyed Siberian who evidently worked as head of security for the Egan family.

His name was Sergei Orel Stravinska, and that he split his time between Moscow and San Francisco. From what some of the Russian officers have told me, he is related to an old line of bandits from Siberia, the backwoods of Russia, who are famous — or infamous — for stealing from the Czar government. This explains why, according to police records, we have had Sergei under close surveillance since he came into the country.

But, oddly, all we have seen him doing is swimming in the San Francisco Bay, practicing piano in his Russian Hill home, playing free piano concerts in the local park, having coffee (or vodka) with friends in North Beach, going to hear live music with his Russian girlfriend, playing chess at the chess club, strolling in the park and collecting flowers, doing yoga, or sun bathing, not in that order.

A week or two after speaking to Tzu on that cold September day in 1876, I went to meet Sergei.

"Mr. Stravinska?" I remember asking the wet Russian after he got out from swimming in the frigid waters of the San Francisco bay, and was drying his tattooed chest off with his black embroidered towel, "SOS" written on it in fancy pink handwriting.

He turned slowly around to look at me without saying a word.

"They call me Father Jasper," I held out my hand.

He just stood there, slightly wet, looking me up and down. Then he growled to me in his thick Russian accent: "what . . . the fuck . . . do you want . . . father?" As he continued to dry his legs, he then said with a crocodile smile as he offered me his hand, "I just kidding, how can I help you?"

"Sir," I said after shaking his freezing cold hand, "Father Shane Egan is up for promotion in the Mission Dolores, and we are doing some background research on him, his upbringing, to see just how far he has come in his spiritual journey from where he as before, and I need your help," I pleaded with the cranky Russian. "I'd go to the police, but . . ."

Sergei interrupted me.

"No, the police are whores to the highest bidder. Pay them and they dance to your music, even if it is shitty music," he said to me like he knew how my music would sound.

"What?" I said.

He ignored me.

"Dah, I help you, Shane the strange boy, but he is good boy," Sergei said as he finished drying his polar bear white skin that was rattled with tattoos, with two stars tattooed on his upper chest. We went to sit on the bench close to a part of the bay where swimmers from all around San Francisco came to swim. The water was frigid and I didn't understand how a human could swim with the sharks in them.

"What is, what you want to know about boy, father," Sergei swept the sand off his ankles and mumbled what sounded like cuss words to himself in Russian.

"Well, I, let me see," I continued with a gulp in my throat, "I spoke to Sun Tzu, the cook, and he . . ."

"That man is the big piece of poodle shit!"

"Why? Please tell me."

"Father, this man, this Tzu, he is in family of the Triad," Sergei looked towards the bay, "and Sun Tzu is only one of his names, cause he also using Dr. Shun Ling, Dr. Wang Long, Dr. Big Bong, among the other shitty names he using."

I knew who the Triad were from my investigation work with the police, an organization originally formed in China to restore the great Ming dynasty to power, they had become a massive organized crime organization in and out of San Francisco, among other cities around the world.

But I couldn't let Sergei know I knew such things, so I acted dumb.

"Triad? What's that?"

The husky five-foot seven or so Russian looked over at me, his blond hair and cleanly shaven white face contrasting with his marked up body full not only of tattoos, but knife marks and what looked like bullet holes, and explained Triad history.

After he did, I got straight to it.

"Tzu told me, he told me," I looked at my notes to review them, "that Shane took down written orders from old man Egan to do, how can I say this, to do . . ."

Sergei put his heavy hand on mine and interrupted me.

"Father, pozhaluysta . . . please . . . I know the lie Tzu told you, I know cause the Triad, they is the ones, they is the ones that ubit' . . . kill . . . like this, not the old man Egan." Sergei pointed into my eyes for emphasis and looked fiercely at me, "not his family." He put his hand back down and then regained his cold watered look towards the ocean. "His family is the good sem'ya, the good family, and Shane is the good mal'chik . . . the good boy," Sergei nodded as he spoke to me but stared at the sea.

I wrote in my notebook, "why would Tzu lie? A frame up, but why?" I looked over to Sergei and asked:

"Why would Tzu lie about Shane like that?"

"Cause Tzu's family, they fighting for the den'gi . . . the money . . . for the Triad, who want Egan's business, ponyat' . . . understand, father, not very complicated chemistry here?"

His bare-knuckled manners didn't surprise me. According to my Russian comrade on the force, Sergei's Virgin Mary tattoo on his back meant he was a criminal from the early days of his life.

"Sergei — open up more questions, less than answers," I wrote in my notebook. While Tzu, or whatever his real name

207

was, may have been lying about Shane, his father George wasn't an elementary school teacher. I then asked Sergei:

"And the Egan money, it's from their bars?"

"Father, this is the big time fucking boring. We go to my apartment, in Russian Hill, and we have the drink and talk more," Sergei wiped himself completely off. "And I must practice for my concert zavtra . . . tomorrow . . . for the deti . . . the children in the park."

"Okay, Sergei, but I don't want to impose."

"Eh, no, I love the guests in my place."

Sergei put on his black Levi's jeans, t-shirt, workman boots, and we walked, without saying one word, kind of uncomfortable moments of silence, like an awkward date, slowly up to Russian Hill.

We arrived in his 20 feet or so high ceiling apartment overlooking the San Francisco Bay, with decorations from all over the world — a bear rug, Persian carpet, fine French crystal chandelier, Mongolian armoire, and some Japanese Samurai swords on the walls. A large black Steinway piano was in the middle of the apartment as little Japanese looking lights hung from the ceiling above on small strings. After I passed through the front door, I saw a tall blond Russian woman in the kitchen preparing drinks.

She was apparently expecting us.

"This my girlfriend Maya, Father," Sergei said as he put his keys on the table next to the door and kissed her on both cheeks as she came out of the kitchen.

The stunning Maya, who was wearing a red silk kimono, came to introduce herself:

"A pleasure, Father," she held out her long white toned arm for me to shake her hand.

Whoa, I thought as I looked up at her ever so slightly, she could possibly crush me in a wresting match — or at least she had me on the reach in a boxing match, keeping me at bay, as

208

she'd just jab me, jab me, and then come in with a knock out punch.

But what's better than being knocked out by a knock out?

"Come, Father, we sit and have some vodka while I play some," Sergei said, "but please, no shoes in the house," he said as he looked down at my cowboy boots. I took them off and left them next to his large black doors.

Sergei sat at the piano and started sipping his vodka. I just stared at my glass of vodka.

"Father, please, I won't tell your boss if you drink some," Sergei smiled as he put his index finger up to his lips.

What the hell, I said to myself, as I moved my hand to pick up the vodka. Maya came to sit on the black buffalo looking leather couch. Sergei had his bare feet on the pedals of the piano as he started to sing this song that was mighty popular at the time, "Good-Bye Liza Jane."

"Swing ma, swing pa, goodbye, goodbye swing that gal from Arkansas, good bye Liza Jane," Sergei sang as Maya drank her vodka tapping her pretty bare foot on the wooden floor.

As I sat there listening to this tattooed winter wolf singing, I thought: what the fuck? Could Shane be an enforcer, the type of person that would cut people up like those priests were cut up? Or was it all Sergei?

Sergei sang more, I drank more, and, after another song, I think it was "Poor Little Gypsy," Maya had filled up our glasses about three times. As she poured the fourth glass, Sergei suddenly stopped playing and looked over at me, with serious eyes, like he wasn't fucking around, the eyes the wolves have when they are about to pounce on their prey, and said, "so, you want to know where the Egan family money is from, dah?"

Didn't answer him right away. He was answering a question I had asked hours ago, as a chess player would, I thought.

"Uh, yes, please, Sergei," I took a big swig off my vodka, not really caring anymore about why I initially went to see him, cause, well, I was actually having a blast. I adjusted myself in the couch and asked again:

"So, is the Egan money is from booze?"

He looked at me with a small smile on his face.

"Dah, legal bars," Sergei said a he slowly sipped — didn't shoot — his vodka. "Nochnyye kluby . . . the night, um, what you say, clubs," Sergei stared towards the bay through his large glass windows, then looked back at me. Maya had the same smile on her face.

I've been in the force long enough to know when someone is answering my questions, but not really answering them all of the way. I left Sergei and Maya that evening without a clear idea about whether Tzu's testimony at trial would be truthful — or full of cut corners, under the table facts that don't get put on top, and winks that never show up in court.

Speaking with Shane one morning in October of that year, after I had interviewed Sun Tzu and Sergei Stravinska in September, didn't clear things up, either.

"I could have taken the easy way out," Shane said shyly to me over the same country mess hall table that I had spoken to Blue about his outlaw past.

"What do you mean you could have taken the easy way out?" I asked as I wiped the steak and eggs off my mouth.

"Well," he looked around to make sure nobody was listening and leaned over our breakfasts, "I don't know if anybody knows this," he put his soft skinned hand on mine from across the table, "but my family lives in Pacific Heights."

"A poor family from Pacific Heights," I smiled sarcastically.

"We are black Irish, but we aren't poor," he smirked back and fixed the straight part of hair on the right side of his head. It was a secretive smirk. It was the same smirk that Sergei and Maya gave me that night in Russian Hill, like they all knew something I didn't.

As representatives of God, Jesus, the Holy Spirit, and Santa Claus we weren't supposed to smoke. And, of course, nobody was supposed to smoke inside the church. But I knew that Blue broke the rules with his smoking, that Sanchez the janitor smoked his cigarettes, and I don't know anything much better than smoking a nice smooth cigarette after a meal.

So, after finishing my breakfast, I pulled out my bag of tobacco, rolling papers, and put them on the table.

"You like smoking?" Shane said with a sweet smile as he pointed to the bag of tobacco. I looked back at him like he was going to tell on me, or say something.

"Make me one too, while you at it?" He winked his calm right green eye secretively at me. He had deep scars above his eyebrows, like he had done some fist fighting in his life. They drooped over his eye sockets, kept them shaded from the sun, perhaps. His wire rimmed round librarian eyeglasses camouflaged the anarchy in the scars.

I smiled back as I rolled his cigarette.

"So how did your family get to live in Pacific Heights? I mean, that's quite the neighborhood."

"Yes, yes, it is," the fingers of his right hand slowly played an imaginary piano as he waited for the cigarette, "my family did a lot of work to get where they are. Came from County Cork, Ireland, originally, settled back east in South Boston, and then came out here to make a better life for themselves," a slight tinge of an Irish accent was scattered among his words.

"What is their main business?" I asked as I completed the cigarette roll.

"Construction and some bars back east," Shane said quietly and calmly, "then they got into the business out here, what with all of these folks coming to find gold and making homes all around the city." I finished rolling the cigarette and handed it over to him.

211

"Obliged, Jasper," he took the cigarette and lit it with a silver lighter he had in his jacket.

For a moment, I sat there watching Shane calmly and serenely smoke.

If you remember, from the way I have told it so far, Blue and Amber were mostly the ones doing the playing with the kids, while Shane just stood under the shade of the tree and watched. I could tell he didn't like being center stage, cause he was one those fellas who liked being in the background of things.

You see, I never much like being in the limelight either, cause that is the place where people will pick you apart. Even when you are doing something right, or great, people going to call you out and say you doing wrong — cause they jealous, don't like seeing anybody happy when they aren't, or doing things they can't do.

Shane now took that smoke into his lungs.

As he did, I sensed this man with the fair Irish skin, prim style, and nice smile had something dark that I could not see brewing underneath, just like the darkness under those trees during my camping trip to Big Sur, California.

My face would be nice and warm underneath the sun, and I could hear the crashing waves going up against the rocks while my soul felt calm and at peace. But, when I looked around behind me, I could see the trees, the big red wood trees, rising up a mile into the sky. Couldn't see underneath them trees, underneath the branches, where there was a dark shade. In that shade lived the spiders, bears, and wolves of the forest. And they would eat you alive if you weren't carful, thinking the forest is just all sun and fun. But I didn't want Shane to think I was feeling things in him that he didn't want people to feel, just like how the spiders, bears, and wolves wanted to stay in the shade, with nobody bothering them, especially us humans.

So I said to Shane, as I started to roll my own cigarette, real calmly:

"What type of construction your family doing?"

"Commercial office buildings where there is a lot of storage space," he shrugged his shoulders like he didn't care, "like all of the office buildings the Chinese workers have been making downtown," he pointed towards the San Francisco business district. "All of the big gold and oil businesses are clients of my family, making all of their big buildings in New York, New Orleans, and San Francisco with architects, construction outfits, you name it that my family provides."

When Shane said "storage space," I immediately thought of the things that Tzu said to me, a place where George Egan's opium could be stored, but that was my suspicious mind working.

"It sounds like your family is very powerful," I said to Shane as I lit up my cigarette.

"They are powerful, Jasper," he agreed, not seeming to want to talk about it.

"Why didn't you go into the family business, I mean, take it over?"

"Was in it for a while, before I went to divinity school," he nodded as he dropped some ash of his cigarette.

"Divinity school?"

"After I got out of college," he held his right elbow with his left hand, and had the cigarette dangling from his right bent wrist, a position I'd seen many women make, but not men, "I helped my old man with the business for a few years."

"Where you go to college?"

"Yale," he nodded.

"What you study there? You a smart lad, eh?"

"World history, with an emphasis on empires, what makes them tic, what leads to their downfalls, and how to keep them going," he said in a very not impressed with himself, unlike the way others from Yale I had met.

Maybe this is what led to the rumors about his father using ancient terror tactics.

"So you worked in the business, helping your old man, and what did you do for him?"

Shane took a long drag now.

"Everything," the smoke hit me in my face, "everything and anything he needed, I did," Shane said.

"Travel a lot?"

"Yes, back to New York, also to Chicago, cause we had offices, outposts, in both cities," he said.

"So you was, you was like your pop's right hand man, or something like that?"

"Not really, cause Uncle Sergei was my old man's right and left hand man," Shane blew some more smoke out as he looked outside the stained glass mess hall window to the church backyard.

He paused as he stared.

"But there were times," he looked over at me, "when I was the one who had better ideas of how to solve problems than both of them put together," he smirked the Sergei and Maya type of smirk.

When I heard this, I immediately thought about what Tzu told me. I wondered to myself whether it was Shane, and not his father, who was the one who was the one giving directions about how to deal with the Chinese, using his education and training to drive company strategy.

"So why didn't you want to stay, take over your father's business? Sounds like you was good at it."

"Cause," he leaned back a little more with his legs crossed and pushed up against the bottom of the table, "I've never been the marrying type, and that's what poppa wanted from me, to have a family, take over the business."

"So what did you do, what did you do to get out of . . ."

"The suffocation?" He interrupted and looked at me with sad eyes.

"Right, the suffocation," I said.

"Went back to divinity school," he moved the almost finished cigarette to his mouth.

"Where?"

"Harvard Divinity School, for my doctorate in theology," Shane nodded to me.

"And then you joined the priesthood after?"

"Yes, cause I knew that, by being this," he pointed to his priestly neck, "my old man wouldn't have the fantasy that I was going to start a family and take over the business."

Shit, I thought, Father Vivaldi was the type who probably would have done both.

Didn't understand what was so different about Shane when we sat and had that talk sometime in early October of 1876, and why he was so against his father's wishes, but I soon understood a day or so later.

It was a sunny Sunday October morning, as most October days are in San Francisco. I had run out of my shoe polish. Blue, Shane, Amber and I were sitting at the table eating some morning grits and drinking coffee. The sun was coming in through the windows real nice, making the whole room look pretty, shiny, and bright.

"Oh Lord," Amber said as she took a big spoon full of her grits, "it is going to be a glorious day for me to do his work," she swallowed the grits real slow and calm. "We going to have one of the biggest turn outs today for mass," she smiled a sweet chocolate smile. "Hope y'all ready," she played with the silver cross that was over her heart, resting softly over her frontier like blouse that had some dirt and other grit on it that she used to like to wear in the mornings when she ate.

I remember Blue smiling as he patted Amber's hand.

"Shit," Blue said in an Army of Jesus type of way to Amber as he wiped his face clean of grits, "not never been more ready to do the Lord's work," he smiled and showed his rotten teeth.

"I got my shoe polish ready, I got them fresh razors, my comb is ready to make this here wild tree of hair," Blue tussled his hair like you would do to your little brother in a playful way, "nice, neat, welcoming, just like the spirit of Jesus." He made a smile that covered up the fact he had been ah outlaw before coming to San Francisco.

Something I knew — but nobody else did, or so I thought at the time.

"Oh Lord!" I suddenly said out loud cause I just remembered at that time, in that day, that I ran out of shoe polish.

"What's wrong there, Father Jasper?" Blue, who I knew as Father Wolf at the time, looked over at me.

"I just remembered that I ran out of shoe polish, and that I'm going to need to head down to the general store to get some more."

I started to get off the bench.

"Please don't go, Jasper, you can take some of mine, I have plenty," Shane cracked a small smile and said softly as his head rested against the brick wall. He was wearing his sleeping gown, and nothing more, cause, like the rest of us, Shane just got up.

"You sure?" I asked as I stopped.

"I am sure," he nodded his head. "There some extra polish in the shoe box under me cot in the room," he said with some Irish accent peeking out and nodded over to where his bedroom was. "Take as much as you need," he finished.

"Much obliged," I said as I headed over to where he told me to go in his bedroom. I walked past the photos of previous priests from the Mission and then came to Shane's large wooden bedroom door that seemed to come from the time of Martin Luther.

I opened the large door to the small room that was Shane's, and it was all like a garden that you see in front of those folks who have pretty little white picketed fenced houses. His bed was made and there wasn't much going on around his little room.

The closet that kept his suits was open, and I saw inside that he had his church clothing nicely and neatly hung.

Over his pillows was a large cross with Jesus Christ on it, plus a Bible on the nightstand. I slowly walked over the Spanish tiles in his bedroom with my bare feet to his bed. I kneeled down to feel under his bed, but I couldn't feel where the polish was. So I leaned down and looked underneath.

There were two boxes. One was an old beaten up shoebox that looked like it had some fancy shoes inside it — on the front it said, "Frye — Marlborough, Massachusetts." The other box was fancy and looked like one of those boxes you would see people put jewelry inside of. It had the name "Tiffany & Co — New York, New York" on it.

I took the old shoebox with "Frye" written on it and placed it on Shane's bed. The sun shined softly on the Puritan looking blanket that was spread over his bed. I opened the top of the shoebox. Inside was what Shane said would be on the inside — a brush, some extra bottles of shoe polish, a dirty rag. I took one of the bottles of shoe polish, closed the shoebox, and then went back down into the darkness that was underneath the bed to place the box where I had found it.

And that's when I had the choice.

Should I look inside the fancy looking box with Tiffany & Co. on top of it, or just leave it where it was because it wasn't my business? And then I remember reminding myself why I was there. I wasn't there to be Shane's friend. I was there to do my job, and that job was to investigate the murders that made us police in San Francisco just look downright silly, like we didn't know shit about police work, like a bunch of idiots, like, well, you get the picture.

So I went with the police self of me.

The fancy box was further underneath the bed and so it was in a darker place. Light was shining all around the bed, and seemed to creep inside from the bed's edges of the bed. But as my long skinny arm got deeper and deeper underneath the bed, the darker it became, just like that dark forest close to Big Sur, California, I told you about before. My right hand grasped the fancy box, while the rest of my body was in the shining sun. There was no dust to get onto my right elbow cause the floor underneath his bed was, to be expected, clean as a plate after a cowboy eats everything off it when he comes back from rustling.

I slowly placed the Tiffany box on top of the sun-drenched bed and took the top off. Photos and photos flowed out of the box. They were waiting to get out, and this was their chance. A few scattered to the right, and a few fell to the left, of the box. The top photo was of a taller pale blue-eyed skinny young man, around 28, with his shirt off, but couldn't see his face too well cause he was turned to the side. Seemed like he was smiling, couldn't see hair on his chest cause there was none. No real big muscles like I could see on Sergei the Russian pianist, cause the boy didn't have any big muscles, more like those muscles you might see on some gymnast, I reckon. This young skinny pale boy in the photo was in front of the ocean, with some jeans on, nothing else, it seemed, even underneath cause his jeans were hanging low below his waist — and I didn't see any underwear.

Was this Shane's brother? If so, why did Shane have a photo of his brother looking like this? Why didn't he have any clothes on — other than his jeans?

I kept looking.

After I put that photo to the side, I saw that Shane had ripped out a picture of a man that was in an article from a Boston newspaper. The Gaelic looking man was wearing a full suit, had riding gloves that he had put to the side, a nice overcoat, and with a proper top hat. There was some horses in the background, like the man owned them or something.

Maybe that was picture of George Egan, Shane's father?

After I moved that photo to the side, I then saw a photo of Shane and the same pale skinny blue eyed young man with the sagging jeans below his waist. This one was pretty damn risqué, I remember thinking to myself. The skinny gymnast muscle mystery young man had his shirt off, and he was sitting on Shane's lap on a bench by Ocean Beach, here in San Francisco.

I know that beach well cause I go there all of the time with my dog.

So, anyway, didn't think anything of the first photo until I saw the next one. In this one, Shane and the skinny blue-eyed young man was at the same beach, and they weren't wearing any shirts in this photo. I remember my mouth opening when I saw that they were kissing each other in their mouths, and that they were hugging one another.

Right then I realized something that I never would have known had I just looked at Shane: he was a Mary! He liked men, not women, for his pecker time. Nobody would every have thought that by looking at him. Yes, Shane had this sweet face that looked like it would have been the face of your high school or grammar school teacher. Yes, Shane had this massive body, with forearms that looked like they had done much construction and lifting of other heavy things in their life. No, you didn't put the face with the arms and think that the man was a Mary.

Standing there over the bed, I just stared at the photo of Shane and this other man. I took my gaze off that photo and looked at all of the others that was behind them, and which was spilling all over the top of the bed from the middle of the box. I looked at all of them photos kind of like how you look at the stars when you in the middle of the country at night and just see stars, stars, stars, and stars looking down on your from everywhere. All of the pictures was of men, or of Shane with men, and none of the pictures was of women — or Shane with women.

And then I realized something else.

This 28-year year old or so skinny man, this mysterious man that Shane was kissing, he was someone I thought for sure I had seen before. Couldn't put my finger on it. Knew I had seen a man of his height, strength, in the neighborhood. Was it at the market or the locksmith?

All of a sudden, I heard footsteps on the wooden floor behind me, the slightly closed, but slightly open door, to Shane's bedroom.

"Hey there, Jasper," I heard Shane's voice from the hallway, "you find that shoe polish I was telling you about?"

Quickly, I started getting those photos together and putting them inside the box. I was nervous cause I thought if he knew that I dug up those photos, he wouldn't trust me.

By the time I heard the door creak open, I had just put the fancy Tiffany box with the pictures in it underneath the bed, although I guess not as far as I had found it cause I didn't have the time.

"You have some great polish here," I said as I heard Shane come behind me.

He came along my side, looked over at me, and said:

"Yep, been keeping a collection of fancy shoes for a long time now, and I take great care of them," he said as he shot me a smile that one bandit gives to another riding together under the midnight moon.

Right there, right then, Shane knew I knew who he really was.

As I slowly put my right hand on Shane's shoulder, I said:

"Thanks for lending me your shoe polish," I made a small smile as I held up the show polish, "I can see you know what you are doing."

Shane looked over at me and nodded without saying a word.

I knew then that Shane trusted me. He trusted me because he could tell, when he looked into my eyes that day when he knew that I looked inside the Tiffany box, that I would not tell his secrets, or judge him for his sexual taste. I did this cause I wanted him to tell me about other things, about his family, about him, Blue, and Amber. I didn't say anything not because I really cared if Shane liked me, but because I was doing my job.

That day, after seeing what I seen underneath Shane's bed, I knew that he couldn't have been this vicious man that Tzu told me about, cause Shane was a Mary. And these types don't go around cutting people up, hanging them in trees, and ordering their bodies thrown in the ocean.

"Shane is a Mary. He didn't do the cutting. A Mary doesn't do that. Need to find who did it then," I wrote in my journal on that October day of 1876.

My conclusion changed a few days later.

We were all cooking in the kitchen, having chicken, some vegetables, and some pig. Shane was at the cutting board, a big one that we had in the kitchen.

"You need some help?" I asked him.

"Got it all, thank you," he pulled out the full chicken, which he had gotten from one of the parishioner's farms. Shane took out a large hatchet, and cut the chicken up into little pieces faster than I had seen a butcher do, starting with the chicken's head.

We were sitting at the table and I couldn't help but peek at Shane's face when he was cutting. It was like one of those stoic stone sculpture things you see with no emotion. His eyes were looking down, focused, like he was killing the chicken, again, even though it was dead already. He threw the pieces to the side, and then continued to cut it like a machine.

He caught me looking at him, and he just stared at me, the same way Sergei the Russian did when he said "what the fuck do you want?" Shane didn't smile, and his jaw was clinched. I felt a shiver come through my body.

It was then that I changed my mind back to what I had originally thought. While Shane may have been a Mary, something I didn't know before, he had sleeper grit. Yes, sir, I was right about him. He was that shade where the spiders, bears, and wolves lived. You couldn't see, or hear, them. But they were close

221

enough so that you knew, in your head, what would happen if you crossed them.

So I knew that about Shane — but the jury didn't.

All the jury heard was Sun Tzu's testimony.

When Hyman did his cross-examination of Tzu about the Triad crap, it was just as before with the janitor's testimony. Jarboe scored a point, but then Hyman took it away by exposing Tzu's Triad connections, and the fact that they often killed their victims in the *same way* as Shane was alleged to have killed the priests.

But it didn't matter.

I knew that the government's next witness was going to help link Blue to the third set of murders, cause Blue cut his victims' stomachs open, bled them out, and fed them to prolong the torture, when he was back in Illinois. There wasn't anything that Hyman would be able to do about it once Blue's heathen past — a past he told me about that one day in June earlier that year — came out into court.

Or so I thought.

CHAPTER NINE

WILD
WEST
NINJA

"**M**en with black bandanas on their faces grabbed Father Chris Murphy off the street," said the government's first witness, a white haired Puritan grandmother, the next morning. "And then they shoved that poor priest into this waiting black carriage which sped off before I could scream," she said shivering wrinkled hands.

The local sandwich boy, Jarboe's second witness, testified as he grasped his cross, which was hanging around his neck, clasping it for safety, "One moment I saw Father Gary Keisle walking on Market Street, and then, and then . . . and then," the boy stuttered and paused to gain his composure. "And then the next thing I know, that holy-father was being pulled into this black carriage. I couldn't even see through the windows because they were they were, um, tinted black. Then he was gone, just like that!" The sandwich boy snapped his fingers as his worried eyes peered into the jury.

A Russian lady with sagging arms swaying, and tits hanging to her belly, was the third witness to testify for the government that morning. In a thick Russian accent that reminded me of Sergei's, she said: "These two lyudi . . . dah, men . . . was wear the . . . chernyy . . . dah, dah, black bandanas over mouths, black hats, this dark . . . how you say . . . sunglasses for the sunlight." She covered her mouth as she recalled the scene, and then spoke. "These bandity . . . bandits . . . steal the svyashchennik . . . stole Father Jose Maciel off the street on that Sunday morning when I getting my vegetables."

"Did you see how tall the bandits were?" Jarboe asked.

"Nyet, no," she shook her head. "I know one was is . . . boleye vysokiy . . . oh, how you say, yes, taller than the other, the other was smaller, you see."

"Did you see their eyes?" Jarboe asked.

"Net, no, is too fast for me to see nothing, and they wear the black sunglasses on eyes."

Then there was the rough looking construction worker, government's fourth witness, who testified about Father Jerry Hargadon's abduction:

"I heard this motherfucker yelling, shit, was a God damn Sunday morning, and I thought, what the fuck," the worn and wrinkled hands of the worker grasped each other for security as he testified. "I said to myself 'what the fuck is going on over there,' and, then, I turned the fuck around, and, eh, shit, shit, counselor," the tough jawed looking man looked away for a moment, "I saw Father Hargadon's motherfucker's legs being pulled into this black carriage, like he was being eaten by a . . . by a . . . fucking . . . um, that's it, a black widow spider."

224

Finally, a thick cowboy from Bakersfield testified about Father Steve Hahn's kidnapping, the fifth priest who got ripped from the streets of San Francisco:

"Oh man, was walking with the little lady, was a pretty Sunday morning, she in the audience you know," the mustached man looked out into the sea of people to find his lady, looking back to Jarboe, "then, smack!"

The cowboy smacked his hands together.

"I done see Father Hahn, he was on the street, then he wasn't on the street no more mister, cause that black carriage, shit the damn thing look like night itself, you know, real dark and shit, like there not no stars out, you see mister, and that carriage done race away."

Cardinal Degollado then testified about the missing person reports he filed for those five priests taken from the San Francisco streets during the weekend of May 20–21, 1876.

"Father, when did you first become aware that these five men, that is Fathers Chris Murphy, Gary Keisle, Jose Maciel, Jerry Hargadon, and Steve Hahn, were missing?"

"Well, let me see," the balding seventy year old something priest thought with his hand on his chin, "I think it was May 22, it was probably May 22, but it may have been May 23."

"And why do you say that date?" Jarboe asked.

"Because that is the first day that I received a report from one of the nuns in their parishes that these priests didn't come back that weekend . . ."

"Which weekend," Jarboe sharply interjected.

"Oh, yes, that would be Saturday-Sunday, May 20–21."

The thing is, the black widow carriage, and the people inside, must have done the abductions fast. To me, this meant that someone was driving, and that there was two men who were strong enough to take a man off the street, against his will, and throw him, like a rag doll, you know, one of those little things that kids play with, into the carriage.

225

Ms. Fanny Porter, Jarboe's next witness, testified:

"It was when I heard the screaming," Porter put her left leg over her right, like she actually was making herself feel comfortable, "it was when I heard the screaming that I went downstairs."

"And where is downstairs, Ms. Porter?" Jarboe asked.

"In the basement of my building," she calmly said as she moved her black-laced cape further over her left shoulder so that she could fix the bun on the top of her well manicured hair.

"And on what date was this?"

"Well, um, let me see, it was the morning of Friday, May 26, I think."

"Thank you, Ms. Porter. Now, could you please tell the jury where this building is located?"

"Yes, its in downtown San Francisco, on the corner of Buchanan and Post Streets."

"And do you own the building, Ms. Porter?"

"No, I don't."

"Who is the building owned by?"

"A New York corporation, I don't know who runs that, but I do know it's owned by a New York corporation."

"What is the name of that corporation?" Jarboe asked with curiosity.

"Quiet Hospitality, Inc." she said.

"Thanks, Ms. Porter," Jarboe said as he reviewed his notes for his next question. "Now," he put his fancy pen in his mouth like he was in thought, "before we get to where you were when you heard those screams, what is it that you do in this building?"

She smiled enjoyably, like she was proud to tell the jury about what she did.

"The building is home to one of the finest, most exclusive, classiest hotels in San Francisco," she said as she fixed her hair again, which was funny because it looked perfect to me, "and I am the manager of the hotel."

"What is the name of this hotel, Ms. Porter?"

226

"Dimples," she said proudly. "It's called Dimples," she said again with a small pleasurable smile.

"I see," Jarboe said as he made a note in his book. "And what type of clients do you have in this hotel?"

"Oh, well, let me see," she played with the other part of her cape, moving it not so much because it was annoying her, but almost to attract more attention. "We have mostly businessmen, traveling businessmen from all over, you name it . . . Tokyo . . . let me see . . . New York . . . um, Austin," she was moving her hands out to indicate all of the places her clients came from. "Oh, and, yes, sometimes we have local clients, natives of San Francisco," she calmly said.

"Any families ever stay there?" Jarboe asked.

"That's a good question," she leaned her head closer to Jarboe, "cause we do have families sometimes staying up in the upper floors, you know, men who come to town with their families, they stay in the upper floors."

"But not on the lower floors?"

"No, the ones with the money usually stay above, cause that's where the views are, views of the bay, and all of the city."

"Thirteen, thirteen floors," she quickly said.

"Okay, okay, so, now, going back to these screams, on which day did you hear them?"

"Let me see, let me see here," she counted her fingers. "It must have been May 26 if I remember right."

"And that was a Friday?"

She sat for a moment.

"Yes, it was, was a Friday."

"And how do you know that, Ms. Porter?"

She looked out into the audience and basked in the limelight.

"Cause I remember that's when the cleaning lady asked me if she could clean the five rooms in the basement, which hadn't been cleaned for about a week."

227

"How often are the floors normally cleaned?" Jarboe asked like he didn't know. He prepared with Porter before the trial, just as he did with all of the other witnesses.

"Every day, every day the rooms on each floor are cleaned from the night before, unless someone puts a 'do not disturb' sign on the door."

"Cleaning, meaning the sheets are changed, the dust is picked up, the . . ."

"You name it, mister, you can eat eggs and bacon off the floor in those rooms after my girls get done with them," Porter looked intensely at Jarboe with her dark brown eyes.

Or you can eat black bear meat off them, I thought.

"That's a mighty clean floor," Jarboe smiled.

The audience laughed slightly.

"So, going back to that day, the cleaning woman comes to you, asks you if she can clean these five rooms in the basement, right?"

"Yes."

"And why did she ask you?"

"What do you mean?" Porter looked at Jarboe with questioning eyes.

"Did those rooms have 'do not disturb' signs on their knobs?"

"Yes," Porter nodded.

"So why did the cleaning woman ask you to clean them?"

Porter paused for a moment. It was the first time in the trial that I had seen here look even slightly uncomfortable. It's like she had seen a ghost, the way her eyes looked, the way she swallowed her spit.

"Ms. Porter?" Jarboe asked. "Why did the cleaning woman ask you if she could clean those rooms?

"Because," she sighed to breath, "because of the awful smell coming from them."

"Can you tell the jury when was the last time that those rooms were cleaned before that Friday?"

"I think . . . I think," I could tell the subject now got to her because she wasn't as natural as before, "it had been a few days, I think it was the Saturday morning before that the rooms were cleaned."

"So that would be Saturday morning, May 20, 1876, correct?"

"Yes, yes, that is right, mister."

Jarboe moved his body weight onto his left long leg, away from his right. A stork who tires of the same leg, the same perspective, perhaps, and moves to another.

"So the cleaning lady asks you to clean the rooms, the five rooms, in the basement, and where were you when she asked you?"

"I was up on the 13th floor, going through the previous night's receipts."

"The previous night being Thursday, May 25, 1876, which is the day before?"

"Yes."

I looked over to the defendant's table. Hyman was leaning back in his chair, and was speaking with Amber. She seemed to be making a point, an important one, to Hyman, who was intently listening, taking a note here, taking a note there, as Amber spoke. Blue and Shane just listened, with Blue looking sort of bored, doodling on something on the pad in front of him, Shane looking around, checking out the audience, the jury, like he was exploring their fashion sense.

"So," Jarboe continued, "you are going through the receipts, and then the cleaning lady, her name is?"

"Dora."

"Ok, so Dora comes to you, and what does she say?"

"Objection, calls for hearsay, your honor," Hyman, a slow pitching pitcher, interrupts his conversation with Amber and stands up.

"Overruled, counselor," Parker quickly retorted. Dora was going to testify later in the trial, something that both Parker and

Hyman knew, but I guess it was a little game to see who is being alert. "Please answer the question," Parker said.

"She said something like, the five rooms, 1–5, on the basement level are starting to smell, and she wanted to know if she could clean them, or at least see why they are smelling. Other guests were complaining, she told me."

"And what did you say?" Jarboe asked.

"Yes, I said yes, check them out," she said calmly.

"And then what happened next?"

"Dora went downstairs, went downstairs, and then . . . she . . . um," I could tell Porter was about to jump off a cliff into cold water that she didn't know how cold it will be, "that's when I started to hear Dora's screaming."

"And then what did you do?"

"Went downstairs, to the basement floor."

"What did you see?"

Porter just stared into space. She stared like Mr. Williams, the mail carrier, into the air between the witness stand and the eyes of the audience members, the jury members, the judge, the attorneys, all of them. I felt like Ms. Porter was transmitting, through her look, the things that she was thinking, but had yet to say. I looked around to the people in the audience, and they just sat there, with their eyes aimed at Porter.

"Ms. Porter, what did you see?"

"I came down the stairs, and , just screaming at the top of her lungs, crying, with her hands to her eyes, crying like I haven't seen anybody crying."

"What did you do next?"

"I took Dora into my arms, hugged her, and she just kept crying and screaming, and I just kept telling her, as I pet her head, 'it's going to be alright, I'm here, I'm here,' I said over and over again."

"And then?"

"I looked," Ms. Porter looked down for a moment, an almost moment of silence, "I looked over and saw the door to room one slightly open."

"The rest of the doors on the floor, were they closed?"

"They were all closed, all closed," she nodded with certainty.

"So what did you do, what did you do after you saw that door to room number 1 open?"

"I told Dora, stay here, stay here, and I'll be right back," Porter said not in the direction of Jarboe, but to the jury, and then to the audience in the courtroom. She swallowed her spit. "And then I slowly walked over to the slightly open door, the lights in the hallway were on, but there was no light, not a light on in room number one."

"Does room one have any windows?"

"No," she shook her head, "no windows."

"And what about the rest of the rooms on the basement floor?"

"None of them have windows, either."

"And so, you walk towards the slightly open door for room one, and what did you do next?" Jarboe asked, almost nudging her forward, urging her to continue.

"Walked up to the door, slowly pushed it open, and the light from the hallway . . . the light from the hallway," she stuttered with stress, "came in and lit up the dark room," she paused as she breathed heavily.

"And that's when I saw it."

"Saw what, Ms. Porter?"

"That's when I saw it," Porter said again.

"Ms. Porter, saw what?"

"The eyes, the eyes, the eyes of the priest, they were, they were, they were . . . still . . . open."

"What priest, what priest Ms. Porter?"

"The priest that was . . . he was . . . lying on the bed."

231

"How did you know he was a priest?

"Because he was wearing his priest outfit, his, um, his dark suit, his, um, things, you know," she put her forehead in her right palm.

"So you saw the eyes of the priest, and what else, what was he doing?"

"Oh God, God, mister, he wasn't doing anything, he was just lying there, with his mouth open, like it was stuffed with something, lying there in sheets that were . . . that were . . . drenched with blood."

The members of the jury made noises of disgust. The people around me just made noises of aching and pain, like they had just seen the scene themselves.

"So the priest was dead?"

"Yes," she nodded.

"What did you do next, Ms. Porter?"

"I opened the door all the way, and had to hold my hand over my nose, my mouth, because of the stench, the absolute smell of a rotting dead body."

"And what did you see when you did that?"

"I saw leather straps, straps that were on the man's ankles, his wrists, he was strapped down to the bed, with his stomach, how my Lord," she started tearing with emotion, "his stomach was exposed, his shirt lifted up, and there was a gash, a neatly cut gash, that was cut across his stomach, just cut across, like someone had sat there and neatly made the cut."

"Why do you say that?" Jarboe asked.

"Objection, calls for speculation," Hyman jumped up and said.

"Overruled," Parker said. "Please answer the question, Ms. Porter."

Jarboe handed Porter a tissue to dry her tears.

"Thank you," she said as she wiped her tears to the side.

232

"I say that because, because," she finished wiping, "the gash wasn't really that big, it wasn't like that thing you see when men have their throats cut, you know, it was like someone made it big enough for that blood to spill out, but not so big that the blood would . . ."

"Your honor, this is ridiculous," Hyman jumped up. "With all due respect, Ms. Porter isn't an expert, and she is going way beyond . . ."

"Counselor, state your objection and shut up, or I'll hold you in contempt, do you hear me, read my lips?" Parker barked back.

"Yes, your honor," Hyman nodded, "but this testimony is pure speculation, just pure speculation, how the hell . . ."

"Counselor, watch the language, I'm warning you," Parker pointed his finger.

"Sorry, your honor, how on, um," Hyman looked up the ceiling, "how on earth can she know if it was cut for that purpose, and not another one?"

"Counsel, its lay testimony, she is expressing her opinion about what she saw, nothing too fancy here," the judge said.

"Sure sounds fancy to me, your honor," Hyman pleaded, "mighty fancy for a hotel manager."

"You can raise that fancy point in your appeal papers counsel, now sit down."

Hyman sat back down, as Parker looked over to the witness. "Please continue, Ms. Porter." She looked at Jarboe, who nodded for her to continue.

"It was my opinion, when I saw that gash, that someone made it, made it purposefully so that it wasn't so big that the man would die quickly, cause there was just blood all over the bed, all over I mean, like the bed was some sponge."

"Did you see anything else, anything else in the room that wasn't part of the room, that whomever was there left behind?"

She thought to herself.

"Come to think of it, yes, there was, let me see," she closed her eyes, then opened them. "There was a nightstand next to the bed and, on top of that, was an ashtray. In it was what looked like a bunch of burnt . . . they weren't cashed cigarettes, they looked more like . . . more like . . . more like cigars," she stuttered again from the stress.

"Alright, Ms. Porter, you are doing great, now, did you see anything else in the room, on the nightstands?"

She sat thinking.

"Yes, yes, there was . . . let me see . . . there were what looked like pieces of food, and some glasses of water, on the nightstand."

"Was the food eaten?"

"Yes, there was I think some fruit, and some of other things, like some pieces of chocolate and a canteen of water, or something like that, on the nightstand."

"Did you see any of the food on the bed, any pieces of food on the bed?"

"If I remember, if I remember right, there was some orange peels and pieces of chocolate around the man's face, right next to his face, like he had eaten some oranges, and then there was some nuts, nut shells, that was left around the same place, next to the man's head."

I remember seeing the circus come through Franklin County as a boy, and seeing the messy monkey cages full of food like this. Maybe these mysterious killers were a band of genius apes loose from Amber's circus? Or some wicked smart grizzly bears who smoked cigars? You'd be surprised how smart Mother Nature can be.

Jarboe nodded his head as he listened to the Porter's testimony, and made notes in his trial notebook.

"Ms. Porter, do you know how long the do not disturb sign was on the door of room one?"

"Well, let me see, um, I think it must have been from the Saturday before, cause I remember the maid last cleaned the room the previous Saturday morning."

"So you mean, when you say the Saturday before, you mean May 20, 1876, right?"

"Yes, I suppose that's right," she nodded.

"And the day you went downstairs to room one on the basement floor, that was May 26, which is a Friday morning, seven days after the room had it's do not disturb sign on it, right?"

She sat there and did the calculation in her head, and on her fingers.

"Yes, right," she agreed.

"So it's safe to say, then, that this man, in room one, was in there for seven days?"

Hyman got up.

"Objection, your honor, calls for speculation," he stood annoyed and waiting for the judge.

"Overruled," Parker quickly batted Hyman's objection away. I could see Hyman's right hand softly wave the judge away as if to say, "your are full of shit." "Please answer the question, Ms. Porter," Parker then said.

"Yes, I'd say its safe to say that body was in there for seven days."

"Ok, thank you," Jarboe nodded. "So did you believe at the time, upon coming on the scene, that the food that was in the room, that it was being eaten by whomever the killer is, by the dead priest, or by both?"

"Certainly looked that way," she nodded, "by both I mean."

"And did you believe, when you came upon the scene in room one, that this man, this dead priest on the bed, was tortured?"

She stared for a moment without answering.

"Ms. Porter, do you want some water?"

"No, thank you, thank you," she finally responded.

"Could you please answer my question then?"

"Yes, when I came into that God awful room, I was so disturbed because of that reason, it was like whomever did this, was sitting there, feeding the priest on the bed, prolonging his life, while, at the same time, torturing him."

A Harvard medical school graduate who did forensic work for the San Francisco police department later confirmed this. The gashes on the priests' stomachs were carefully tailored, the expert testified, so that the priest would bleed, but not so much bleeding that the priests would die swiftly.

"Just a few more questions, Ms. Porter," Jarboe said as he did some check marks on his trial notebook. "Now, did you know this dead priest, the one lying there on the bed in room one?"

"No, never seen him before in my life."

"Ok, thank you. Now I'd like to turn your attention to the next room, room two. You said earlier that the door was closed. Was this another room where this stench that the other tenants were complaining from came from?"

"Yes."

"To be clear for the record, the stench was coming from rooms 1 — 5 on the ground floor, right?"

"Yes."

"And each of those rooms had do not disturb notices on their doors, right?"

"Yes."

"Did each of them have those notices put on their handles the same day?"

Porter pondered the question.

"I don't think so, I think room one was . . . it was . . . the first one to have it put on . . . put on . . ."

"That do not disturb sign was put on door one on Saturday, May 20, right?"

"Yes."

"Do you know what day room two had its do not disturb notice put on it?"

"Yes, I think it was also Saturday."

Jarboe then went through the same questions with Ms. Porter about rooms two, three, four, and five as he did with room one. For all, the answers were the same, except for the dates, of course, cause rooms #3–#5 had "do not disturb" signs put on them on Sunday, May 21. Sitting there listening to the testimony, it was hard for me to believe that three people could have done such things all by themselves over a two day period.

But then, when I thought about it more, I suppose these aren't three regular people. Amber would have been the driver. She would roll up to the first priest, and then Blue and Shane, both disguised with their sunglasses, bandanas over their mouths, and black hats, would come out and grab the unsuspecting victim off the street, not too difficult of a feat for two men of Blue and Shane's size and strength. Once they had the victim in the carriage, they would knock him out, wrap his hands together, cover his eyes, and stuff his mouth.

Upon arriving at the hotel, of course, they had to use a back door like some Wild West ninjas, some way where they wouldn't be detected, to get to the basement rooms. This is the one thing I hadn't figured out yet, but soon Hyman would bring it out. Then, once they had the priest in the room, they would prep him by strapping him down, putting the do not disturb on the door, and then go out for their next priestly fish, or maybe they did this to the priests in succession — putting one and two into the carriage and then unloading them. The same would be done to priests three, four, and five.

But it wasn't until that Hyman crossed Porter that I discovered she wasn't telling everything she knew to the jury.

"Ms. Porter, where do you live?" Hyman asked after he introduced himself.

"Objection, relevance," Jarboe shot up.

"Overruled," Parker shot back. "Please answer the question."

"I live at 777 Mission Street."

"That address is located in the St. Patrick's Parish, right, which is on 756 Mission Street?"

"Yes," she nodded.

Hyman didn't bring his whole notebook up to the stand. Just some loose leaf papers that he had his strategy notes on. He looked more disorganized than Jarboe's neat window dressing, but Hyman was just as, if not more than, prepared. He seemed to ask questions like he didn't know the answer — but I think he knew all the answers, waiting, like that black carriage, to jump on the witness when he or she was caught in an inconsistency.

"Do you have any children, Ms. Porter?"

"Yes," she nodded.

"How many children do you have?" Hyman asked.

"One."

"A daughter?"

"No, a boy."

"His name is Oscar, right?" Hyman stated more than asked.

"Yes," she looked at him surprised.

"And Oscar is 8 years old, right?"

Again, with surprise in her eyes, she nodded yes.

"Oscar goes to the Catholic school, the local St. Patrick's parish Catholic school, doesn't he?"

"Yes," she nodded.

"Were you aware that one of the priests found dead in your hotel was none other than Father Gary Keisle, who is a teacher at your son's school?"

She didn't know how to answer this one. On direct, she told Jarboe she didn't know any of the dead men. But she answered anyway.

"No, I was not," she shook her head.

"Is it not true, Ms. Porter, that Father Keisle was one of your son's teachers?"

"Not that I was aware of," she denied with a straight face.

"Would you be surprised, then, that one Father Timothy Allen, who is a teacher at your son's school, will testify on behalf of the Defendants that Father Keisle was, in fact, one of your son's teachers?"

"I would be because I never heard his name before," she looked away from Jarboe's fierce eyes.

"Are you aware that Father Keisle was convicted in Charleston, South Carolina, for indecent relations with minors?"

"I am not," she shook her head.

Hyman looked over his loose pieces of paper to make sure he covered all of his points, shifting from one to the other like cards at a poker table.

"Ms. Porter, isn't it true that you have a conviction on your criminal record . . ."

Jarboe shot up before Hyman could finish his sentence.

"Objection, your honor, objection, irrelevant, this is just irrelevant," Jarboe slammed his papers down on the table.

"I'll defer ruling on your objection, counsel, until I hear where Mr. Hyman is going with this," Parker quickly shot back. A Yale law school educated legal mind who had his share of trials in the halls of San Francisco, Parker was no stranger to the ins and outs of courtroom jousting. "Please continue, Mr. Hyman," Parker said.

Hyman looked away from Parker and back to the witness.

"Don't you have a conviction on your record, Ms. Porter, for being a prostitute when you were, let's see, 21 years old?"

Porter didn't know what to say. If she denied it, Hyman would introduce the conviction.

"Yes," Porter said with hesitation.

"And isn't it true that before this trial began, Ms. Porter, you were being investigated by the police for, let me see," Hyman looked at this note, "running an establishment, that is the Dimples establishment, of ill repute?"

"I was not, never heard such a thing!" She slammed her hand on the witness bannister.

"Officers from the local precinct didn't come to investigate your establishment on, let me see, on about a week before those bodies were found, asking you questions about Quiet Hospitality?"

"No, they did not."

"Would it surprise you that we'll have a New York City Police Department detective testify on behalf the defendants that Quiet Hospitality is known in New York City for running the highest end brothels there, in addition to other cities, like San Francisco, around the country and that they are known to have vicious security personnel enforcing the house rules — including by slicing men's stomachs open who don't follow those rules?"

I thought to myself: guess the hospitality they offer wasn't so quiet?

Porter then answered Hyman's question:

"We run a hotel, not a brothel. Why are you . . . ?"

"Ms. Porter, just answer the question please," Parker said sternly in her direction.

"Yes, yes, your honor," she said.

Hyman, shuffling through his questions written on the pieces of papers, got ready for his next pitch.

"Ms. Porter, do you recall who the five rooms on the ground floor were registered to for the days in question, that is, Saturday, May 20, to Friday, May 26?"

This is something Jarboe didn't ask about.

"I do not."

Hyman had his sheets of paper in front of him, and read from them:

"According to your records, this is what I have: Room one, registered to one Alan Smith, of New Orleans; room two, registered to one Brian Whitfield of Columbus, Ohio; room three, registered to James Elroy, of Boston, Massachusetts, room four, registered to Gregory Odom, of Savannah, Georgia; and room five, registered to Ronald Shannon Jackson, New York, New York," Hyman finished. "Ms. Porter, do you know of any of these men?"

"No, I do not."

"Did you know that these men were listed as the owners on the corporate papers with the New York Department of State for Quiet Hospitality?"

"No," she shook her head. "I just do my job at the hotel, don't deal directly with the management ever back in New York."

"Did you know that, when I had my private investigator look into these men, he discovered that they all died, were reported to have died in the Civil War, with death certificates and all?"

There was a stare in Porter's eyes that made me think she knew more than she was telling. I suppose it's because she didn't answer the question right away. She just delayed for a moment. And I think that is what Hyman was looking for — that flinch so that the jury would think that she was hiding something, something that she didn't want to open up to the eyes of the public, or the system. She finally admitted:

"I did not know that."

"Who, if anyone, did you deal with at Quiet Hospitality?"

"Just this very proper sounding English woman, named Iris, at their office in New York. She is the only one I had contact with at the company."

"I see, I seem," Hyman looked through his notes. "You mean Iris Colchester, of Park Avenue, New York, New York? Does that name ring a bell?"

"Yes, yes, that sounds right," she nodded.

Hyman just looked at her for a moment, that moment when the predator sweeps down on the helpless prey, and goes in for the kill.

"Were you aware, Ms. Porter, that Ms. Iris Colchester, of New York, New York, was a nurse for the Union and that she died in Virginia not long before the end of the civil war, in January of 1865?"

There are some coincidences in life, but too many makes anybody think, especially those in the jury, that they aren't just coincidences.

"I was not aware of that."

"So, is it accurate to say, Ms. Porter, that you have been working with Ms. Colchester and that you never knew she wasn't who she said she was?"

"Yes," she nodded, "that is accurate."

"And how long, how long have you been dealing with Ms. Colchester?"

"For, um, let me see," she looked up to the ceiling, pausing to think, or at least see where Hyman was going, "10 years."

There was more whispering in the audience now.

"Order, order, order in this court," Parker forcefully said.

"So, for 10 years, you are going to ask this jury to believe that you were dealing with Quiet Enjoyment and that you never knew, or had reason to know, it was one big front made up of dead people?"

"Yes, yes, because that is the truth."

"Right, I'm sure it is," Hyman said under his breath, "just like how me and the pope drank whisky and got some lap dances from dancing bears before we played chess last night."

"What did you just say, counselor?" Parker barked.

"Nothing, your honor, just mumbling to myself."

Hyman shuffled through his notes.

"Just a few more questions, Ms. Porter. Did the people who rented those five rooms, that is room #1–#5, order room service during their stay?"

"I don't recall."

"Do you know if any of the food that you saw in those rooms was from the hotel?"

"I do not."

"Does your hotel sell fruit, apples, oranges, in addition to nuts and chocolate?"

She hesitated.

"It does."

"So that food could have been from your hotel?"

"I suppose so, yes."

"If the food was from your hotel, you would have charged the accounts for those rooms, right?"

"Yes."

"Did you?"

"I don't know."

Hyman glared at Porter.

"And that smell you told the jury about earlier, that small you mentioned, this would have hit the hotel worker, whoever delivered the items, right in the face, wouldn't it have?"

"Seeing as it went through the doors, yes, it would have smelled to someone making that delivery."

"Right, thank you, just a few more questions. Now, there is a counter next to the front door of the hotel, next to the entrance, where people check in, right?"

"Yes," she said.

"Are there any other ways of getting to those basement rooms other than through the front door, where people check in?"

"Yes, through the back door, where deliveries to the kitchen are made by carriages that bring in the daily delivery of fresh fish, beef, and so on."

"Is that back door guarded by security, I mean, do you have someone there vetting who comes in, and out, of that entrance?"

"Yes, we have a security guard there, we have a security company who watches the door."

"Iron Clad security?" Hyman asked.

"Yes, that sounds right," she nodded.

"Do you know who runs Iron Clad security?"

"I don't."

"Did you contract directly with Iron Clad, or did Quiet Enjoyment?"

"Quiet Enjoyment did, I didn't have much interaction with the security company, as they have different men coming in and out all of the time."

"Did you know, Ms. Porter, that, according to the corporate filings on file with the Department of State in New York, the owner of Iron Clad security is a man by the name of Sunny Robinson, from Brooklyn?"

"I did not know that."

"Did you know that, like with the owners of Quiet Enjoyment, Sunny Robinson, of Brooklyn, New York . . .," Hyman looked back to the audience, "died years ago, in Mississippi, on May 31, 1862, a year after the Civil War started?"

She just shook her head.

"Did any of your front desk people report seeing any suspicious activity on the dates in question, that is, from May 20 to May 26?"

"No," she shook her head.

"What about the people manning the back entrance, no suspicious activity reports on those dates to you?"

"No."

"If there was suspicious activity, they would have reported it to you, right, you being the manager?"

"Yes, of course," she nodded.

"Ms. Porter, is it fair to say that, had the folks responsible for these gruesome killings wanted to keep a low profile, that it would have been better for them to have gone through the back instead of the front entrance?"

She shrugged her shoulders.

"I suppose that is a fair statement."

"Thank you, Ms. Porter, no further questions for this witness, your honor."

Damn sure wasn't clear to me whether Porter was an innocent pawn in someone's game, provided them with their torture chamber, or, shit, did the damn things herself cause of her child

Oscar maybe had been touched by this priest in his school. She definitely had the capability, as manager of the mobbed up New York managed hotel, and might have had the motive, I sat there scratching my head and thinking.

It didn't really matter though, I thought at the time.

Jarboe was about to call the mayor of Vandalia, Illinois, and a federal prosecutor based in Chicago, as his next two witnesses. I thought for sure their testimony would put a nail in Blue's conviction for abducting those priests off San Francisco's streets and torturing them in Porter's hotel.

I should know.

After I spoke to Abel Russell, Sun Tzu, and Sergei Stravinska in California, I travelled to Illinois that October, or maybe it was early November, to interview the mayor and prosecutor about the man the Illinois Injuns affectionately called "morning star" or "planet Venus."

That man was none other than Blue Hardin, also known as "Father Luther Wolf."

I wanted to buy a bible and keep it with me at all times after the Vandalia mayor told me what "morning star, planet Venus," meant.

CHAPTER TEN

LUCIFER'S PUPPET MASTER

"Them Illinois darkies, you know, them dirty heathens, they used to call Blue Hardin 'morning star'" said James P. Hastert, the seventy or something Mayor of Vandalia, Illinois, over beer in a local Vandalia saloon called Tick Tock.

"Darkies?" I asked.

"You know, sergeant, them God damn savages we had to clear on out of here so we could live the good Christian life," the chunky hair parted on the right mayor said as he sipped a new beer that came out that year called Budweiser.

"You mean the Injun," I said as I broke a peanut open.

"You god damn right I mean them fucks!" He slammed the checkered table with his wimpy fat weasel hand that hadn't done a day of manual labor in their lives.

Took an "extended sabbatical," or so I told people at the church, to further investigate Blue. That way, I could submit all of my evidence to Jarboe, who'd then get this jury together to indict the defendants. Didn't need to wear my priestly suit to do my duty in Illinois, but just regular old beat up black Levis, my old jean shirt, and shitty cowboy boots. Came on official police business, and the good city mayor was happy to oblige. Seems he had a particular bad taste in his mouth for Blue Hardin.

"They call Hardin anything else?" I had my notebook in front of me on the table.

"Well, um, let me see," Hastert's fluffy grey hair edged to the right side of his head as he moved his hand to his cheek to think.

"Oh yea," he quickly snapped his fingers, the quick way I could see him do when he was the first one to raise his hand when asked by the teacher: who wants to be class president? "They used to call him the 'planet Venus,' too," Hastert said.

"Huh," I said as some peanuts dripped onto my dark police pants and as I wrote the words "morning star" and "planet Venus" in my notebook. "Why those names?"

Hastert leaned over the table, like I should have known.

"You never studied your Bible, did you sergeant?" He said upset at me.

"Well," I shrugged my shoulders and looked over the bottles of whisky behind the bar, the dancing girls who just got off flirting with the local merchants, and some frontier looking men sitting all around me who looked like they just came back from weeks of dirt, lakes, bears, and rain, "I read the bible some."

"Not enough," the suited up Hastert leaned back on the wooden chair. "You a Christian, aren't you?"

"Yes sir, Episcopalian," I said as I sipped my Budweiser.

"Didn't they tell you about you know who?" he asked.

"Who?"

"I mean you know, you know him?" The mayor asked with increasing frustration.

"Who is him? I thought it was a who?

"Dammit, sergeant, you know who I am talking about," he said looking around like he wasn't supposed to say. He then looked back into my eyes with some anger.

I shrugged.

"Sorry, Mr. Hastert, I just don't follow you. I'm just, you know, a former beat cop who graduated to a higher rank." Sipped my beer real slow.

"Alright, alright," the mayor with the public reputation said to me. He leaned over and had his index finger up urging me to pull me closer to him.

"What?" I asked.

I leaned over towards him. He looked around, again like he was telling me something top secret, something that nobody knew, and then whispered:

"Lucifer is who I am talking about," he said and then went back away from the table, a fine hand of poker he just played.

"Who?" I asked sarcastically.

He didn't like that.

"Don't play with me, sergeant," he said with seriousness in his voice and then he sipped some of the Budweiser that I bought him.

I wasn't, and I was. I knew that "Lucifer," the word, came from the late fourth-century Latin translation of the Bible, and technically means "the morning star, the planet Venus." Oddly enough, the word also means "bearer of light," even though Lucifer, God's fallen angel, was supposed to be a bearer of darkness after his fall.

"Just trying to add some levity, Mr. Hastert," he never asked me to call him by his first name, so I kept up with the "Mr." thing. "Meant no harm."

He nodded.

"No harm taken," he adjusted the pocket watch in on his vest as he sipped.

"So, let me ask you," I leaned over getting back to brass tacks, "why did they call Blue Hardin 'morning star' and 'planet Venus'?"

Hastert started his story with how, after Blue's adopted family died, he was adopted by an Indian tribe who raised him as one of their own, something I knew from my talk with Blue that day at the Mission in San Francisco. But Hastert told me details about Blue that I didn't even know.

"You know what happened to his spirit family?" Hastert said this with a self-satisfied smirk, someone who finds pleasure in another person's struggle, or who, when seeing someone else is being entrepreneurial, ambitious, and chasing their dream, says something like "that's a shit pipe dream."

"Spirit family?" I asked.

"Yea, his damn heathen family, the ones who adopted him after his parents died," he said.

"You mean his Injun family?"

"Animal, heathen, whatever you want, you get to the same place," he said.

"Yeah, I know," I nodded.

"Did you know," he looked around again, "did you know what he did after, after his Injun family is gone, starting around 13?" His eyes were bulging at this point. I noticed Hastert didn't say why Blue's Injun family had left this world — that they were massacred in the Trail of Tears.

"No," I sipped my beer and said, "don't know what he started doing."

He leaned back in his chair. It's like he was getting ready for his pitch.

"Well, there, son, from about 13–16, this sorry excuse for a human was pick pocketing, then 16–18 he done murder for hire, 18–20 he was doing the bank robbing in my town, then went up to Chicago where he hit the big leagues," he said like he was happy he knew, the hall monitor who gets off on catching those playing hooky and making out in the bathroom like I used to do with my friends in elementary school.

"Whew," I said with the pass of my hand like I didn't know and said sarcastically, "junior varsity."

He stared at me and just sipped his beer, ignoring my comment.

"Yup, you know it. Started running with this clan, don't quite remember their names, but this clan of bank robbers from Illinois and Missouri, hit all of the major banks that had insurance in Southern Illinois, Northern Missouri, then some big ones in Chicago, nineteen in all."

"At least they had insurance," I shrugged.

Hastert stared. He didn't like what I just said.

"These outcasts, God damn outcasts," he tightened up his tie, "some of them was even niggers, and they would dress up, like bums, like God damn homeless people, no shame," he shook his head, "come into town here, and other towns, do their crimes, take off their clothing out of town, and then be on their way, God damn cowards."

"Anybody killed?" I asked.

He didn't know why I asked, but he answered anyway.

"No," his eyes looked into mine. I made a note in my book: "Banks robbed — 19 — all insured — no dead."

"Why you want to know if there was deaths?" He asked.

"Just seeing how, um," I thought out loud as I looked up to the embroidered ceiling above me, "prepared they were."

"Sergeant," he said rubbing some of the peanut shells on the table, "there is a reason why they warned you about Lucifer in school, and that's cause Lucifer is smart, still has those skills of the angel, but he uses them for Evil, just plain Evil, and that's it," he cut his hand in the air as though to stop the conversation.

During the conversation, I had told Hastert what was happening in San Francisco, the murders, the indictment, and the pending trial. He wasn't shocked one bit when I told him that we, the San Francisco Police, believed that Blue was the mastermind behind it all, while operating under the name "Father Wolf" at Mission Dolores.

"Were they ever caught, I mean for the bank robbing?" I asked.

"Well," he said as he finished his beer, "we did catch them, these hoodlums, and this one that you wanted to come out here to ask me about, this morning star piece of shit, this Blue, you bet he was locked up, locked up good," he started opening up some more peanuts and leaving the shells in the table. "Had him and him is crew tried and convicted," he shoved some peanuts into his clean mouth, with his clean shirt being afraid that some peanut shells would get on it.

"Can you get me a copy of the conviction for Blue?" I asked with eagerness.

"That's going to be hard to do, sergeant," he said with displeasure in his eyes.

"Want another beer?" I asked.

"Yup," he held up his beer.

Asked the waitress, who was the type of waitress you wouldn't want to skip a bill on because she looked like she had a shotgun behind the bar, and she went to get the beer after writing out our order with her tattooed arms on the little sheet of paper as she chewed her toothpick.

"Coming right up, sugar," she said and winked.

"So," I said as I picked my notebook back up, "what's the problem, why can't I get a copy of it, the conviction I mean?"

"I'm sort of . . . sort of . . . embarrassed," he said looking away, the boy who comes home with a bad grade on his report card and looks away when his parent confronts him — or her — about it.

"Why?" I put my pen down.

"The thing is, there was a fire in the room where his conviction, and those of the others, were being stored, so I'm afraid . . .

afraid . . . that there isn't a copy any more," he shook his head as the waitress placed the beers on the table.

"Fire, a fire?" I picked up my beer and took a long sip to think.

"Yup," Hastert said as he took a long swig off the suds, "a fire."

"Where is this file room, I mean where does the city normally keep copies of convictions?"

"In the basement of the city hall, which is where we have the clerk's office."

"Isn't that guarded, I mean, they have officers out front checking people who go in, and make sure they have nothing on them, no?"

"Yes," Hastert agreed, "but the fire was caused, it appears, because a candle fell and started the fire in the row where Blue's info was located."

"Did you conclude that the fire was accidental?"

"Between you, me, and the table, I think someone on the inside caused it, but I can't prove it, just a feeling I have."

"Funny, that's what I was thinking," I smiled.

I made a note in my book. "Blue — bank robber, convictions burned, by insider."

"So, Mr. Hastert, can you tell me about these murders for hire Blue did when he was, what," I looked into my notes, "between 16 — 18 years old or so?

Hastert looked at me with a frozen look in his eyes. You are about to lose the first person in your family to the angel of death, to cancer, to a carriage accident, and you just look into the space, not wanting to accept what is about to happen.

"Mr. Hastert," I leaned over the table, "are you alright?"

He kept staring. He kept staring the way you stare when you hear something in your house, apartment, wherever, in the middle of the night, and wonder if its someone trying to get in touch with you, a spirit you wronged.

"Yes," he said staring forward, "I am alright." But he nervously sipped the beer, his hand slightly shaking. "You don't know what this man is capable of," he said after sipping. "The sin, the sadist, the monstrosity of this man," Hastert said in fear.

"Try me," I said, the freshman in high school eager to get a beating, never having had such a beating before.

Hastert just sat there, getting ready.

"Nineteen men, nineteen of God's children this man, this animal, killed in cold blood, tortured, kept alive to torture," he shook his head in disbelief. I've seen bullshit preachers, and this man could have been one of them, fake looking teeth, promise of the perfect world if you give him — and Jesus — all of your life savings. Didn't know if I believed this Hastert, but I listened.

"Where were these men killed?"

"Some down here in Vandalia, some up in Chicago," he said.

"How, how did Blue kill them, like he bled those five priests out in the basement of that San Francisco hotel?" I asked with my notebook at the ready to write.

"Pretty much . . . pretty much," he stuttered and sipped his drink slowly to escape.

"Any different? I mean," I leaned over to emphasize, "any different?"

"Not much," he cracked open a peanut and nervously shoved it into his mouth — not because he wanted the peanut, but because his mind wanted the distraction.

"Tell me, tell me what Blue did," I sat at the ready.

He looked around again, the nervous cat thief at nighttime.

"He'd get them in their sleep, when it was all dark," he pointed to the black on his boots.

I took notes.

"Broke in to the victims' homes, real quiet, cause he knew how to pick locks and would head to their bedrooms while they slept."

Hastert sipped his beer.

"And then he'd see the victim, sleeping, snoring, at which point he'd do it."

"Do what?" I stopped writing and asked.

"Knock them out, just hit them with something across their head," Hastert made a striking move with his hand, "and they were out, like that," he snapped his fingers again.

"And then?" I asked.

He took an even longer sip of his beer, going half way down the mug.

"Then he'd stuff something into their mouths, strap them onto, strap them onto the bed, wrists to the headboard, ankles to the end of the bed."

"So they are stuck, the victim is stuck there, and?"

Mayor Hastert looked out onto the bar of women and men drinking, sharing stories, laughing. As he did, he explained.

"Seeing as this Mongolian excuse for a man's father, Pate Hardin, was a doctor, doing surgery on folks in the part of the town over there," Hastert pointed to the part of Vandalia that was across the tracks, in the backwoods, away from the more populated part of town, "this Blue knew how to cut, how to cut people open, and that's what he'd do."

Some sweat dripped down Hastert's forehead.

"Cut how? Like how I told you these priests stomachs were cut open in San Francisco?"

"Sounds like it. I mean, those 19 men were found with their shirts up, just slightly up, you know," Hastert pointed to the part of his rib cage where the shirts were lifted up to, "and then there was a small cut, a sliver of knife cut, on their stomachs which caused them," he paused to look down towards the sawdust on the ground, "to bleed out."

He covered his eyes.

"I thought a cut to the stomach would kill you immediately?" I asked.

"No," the mayor took his hands off his eyes, "if you make a cut which avoids all major vessels, then death can take days, and sometimes weeks," he said with sick eyes.

"Days, weeks? How did Blue know where to cut, I mean major vessels are all over the body?" I asked.

"That's why," Hastert played with the water beading up on the side of the mug, "this man is such a sick fuck. He knew where to cut cause he knew where the vessels were form his father's work, word has it that he was like a nurse for his father during operations, so he learned first hand," Hastert took some water off the mug and took another long sip. "Plus, he somehow knew his victims' families' schedules, maybe from their mistresses or maids, catching the men when they were sleeping alone, families away for vacation."

"So this man was a professional killer?"

"Whatever you might say about him, 'idiot' isn't one of the words that comes to mind, sergeant."

"Mr. Hastert," I took some more peanuts in my hands and cracked them open with my right hand, as my left index finger kept my place in the notebook, "weren't there any witnesses?"

"Nope. The victims were found strapped to their own beds in mansions throughout Vandalia and Chicago. Some were found in their sleep, but others, well," he nervously played with a piece of paper on the table, "they were just grabbed, like that," he snapped his fingers, "off the street."

"Who grabbed them?"

Hastert shrugged.

"Word has it that it was a bunch of niggers, but others say this a bunch of hogwash, cause some of the folks that seen the culprits say they wasn't niggers, but a bunch of white devils wearing black face, making them look like niggers done it."

"Or maybe a little bit of both, a lethal chocolate swirl?" I wondered out loud.

He nodded in agreement as he pulled out a pack of cigarettes.

"Want one?" He held the box out to me.

"No thanks," I said.

As Hastert lit up his cigarette, and took a long puff, he continued.

255

"Plus, Chicago police found some black make up crap at one of the murder scenes, one of the later murders that was done."

I was taking notes as fast as I could.

"Tell me," I looked up at the proper looking Hastert, "what else did they find at these crime scenes?"

"Yup," he nodded in my direction, adjusting himself in his seat. "The men who was abducted off the streets was found in brothels, dirty brothels, that was throughout town. One thing," he sipped his beer, a breather during a talk that was heavy and made you feel like you couldn't breath, "one thing they did find, which made me know this man, this Blue, was just sick in the head, and that was some food and cigars that was found next to the bodies in those brothels."

"Food and cigars?"

"Yea, turns out that this death monger Blue, this disgusting soul, sat there smoking his cigar and eating peanuts, apples, and some fancy chocolate bar while these men laid there, pleading for their lives to be saved, can you imagine?"

"I can't," I shook my head as I wrote in my booklet: "Blue — Illinois — torture, cigars, wholesome food, water, next to the bodies."

"And for these crimes, for these murders, Blue was convicted?"

"You bet your bottom dollar he was convicted, you bet your bottom dollar," he said with force. "It was a two week trial, and the evidence was overwhelming, got one witness who overheard Blue bragging about the murders at this here saloon, another who was in the same cell as Blue and said that Blue told him how he went about cutting the stomachs of his victims, just right," Hastert made a cutting motion with his hand.

"And those convictions, they were all burnt in the fire?"

Hastert nodded "yes."

"What about hanging? I mean, wasn't Blue set to hang for these killings?"

"Yes, yes, he was," he nodded, "but you know about these blue eyed mongrel types, they is harder to grab a hold of than a pig in a bunch of mud and shit."

Hastert paused.

"Seems Blue had some friends on the inside, or someone he knew had some friends on the inside, cause when he was being taken in a steel carriage with bars, taken in a carriage to the site where he done going to be hung, outside of town cause of security concerns and all, and this route was top secret mind you," Hastert looked and pointed in his finger in my face to show that secrecy was the norm. "Then word has it that a bunch of bandits, I mean a swarm of them, surrounded the carriage, took the riders hostage, and threatened to torture the police men and their families if Blue wasn't freed, see?"

"Yea, got it," I made a note in my book. "Blue — escaped — friends on the inside, maybe."

"Do you know where he went, Blue, after?"

"You won't believe this, won't believe it," he finished his beer.

"What, believe what?"

"Lucifer's puppet master joined the God damn U.S. Army, to fight against the Mexicans, is what we learned later on, few months later."

"How did he do that?"

"Damn military police and federal investigators from Chicago swarmed this town, I mean came down on it hard, and was saying how he had joined the army under an assumed name, think it was Eden something, but then fought with the damn wet back Mexicans, can you believe that? I mean, why they let him in the door in the first place?"

I shrugged.

"I think they needed the bodies," I said dryly.

He looked at me with an almost helpless look. All the power of his position, the prestige — many people had come into the bar and saluted or tipper their hats to mayor Hastert — couldn't get rid of the dirty sour rotten taste in his mouth from Blue.

"Mr. Hastert, can you give me the info on the Chicago federal investigator who came to town looking for Blue?"

"Sure, um, let me see, what was that guy's name?" Hastert tapped his fingers on the table.

"Something like Dick Holder, he is an attorney with the federal government, you know, investigating things like this."

"And where is he located?"

"I think, let me see, I think he is in Chicago, takes care of this whole thing for his boss in Washington D.C., I think, I think that's what it is."

"So, Mr. Hastert, just to be clear, you are willing to testify about the convictions at trial for the prosecution of Mr. Blue Hardin when it comes up in San Francisco?"

Hastert leaned over. It was the lean over you do when you are about to arm wrestle with someone else.

"You name the time, and place, and I'll be there. I want to nail this son of Satan to the wall, you hear me sergeant, to the wall!"

"Understood," I nodded.

"You men alright?" The waitress with the tattoos, who was just standing earshot from us, came over to ask. "You want another beer to whet those thirsty pallets," the flirting waitress, with grit charm, smiled and tapped my shoulder with her index finger.

"Mr. Hastert, want another?

"I've had my fill, thanks sergeant," he put his hand up.

"I'll settle up the tab," I said, "thanks."

"Thanks for the drink, sergeant."

Hastert held his hand out for me to shake.

"I'll be in touch, Mr. Mayor," I shook his hand and then he was gone.

Turns out mayor Hastert had cracks in his armor of perfection.

"Can I sit here for a moment, mister?" Asked the fine-tuned muscled waitress — whose name was Charley — that had been serving us.

"Sure, sure," I offered her the seat that Hastert was just sitting in.

She took her serving tray, placed it on the table along with her dirty towel, and yelled over to the other bartender: "bring me a tequila, Honey Bear, you know, the way I like it." Honey Bear, the burly mustached Injun looking man with a flannel shirt buttoned up all the way to his atom's apple, nodded. "You want anything else, mister?"

I looked at my empty mug of beer.

"Yes, yes, please," I nodded.

"Honey Bear," Charley turned back around towards the bar, "another Bud for the mister here," then she turned with her brown Irish eyes to look at me.

Charley was one of these frontier women who didn't take to liking all of those rules that cities placed women. A whiff of her patchouli smell hit my nose. That smell calmed me cause it reminded me of Franklin County's back woods.

"Charley, Charley Parkhurst is my name," she held out her pretty strong dirty hand.

"Sergeant Jasper is my name," I shook her hand.

"You not from round here, is you?" Charley said as she released my hand, taking me out of my worried mind.

"Nope, from rural Virginia, but I now live in San Francisco."

"You a Virginia born cop in San Francisco, so what you doing here in Vandalia, Illinois?"

"Investigating a murderer," I said.

"Murders that happened here?"

"Nope, in San Francisco."

I briefly told her about the 19 priest murders, and then Charley hit me with it:

"And you really think Blue Hardin did them 19 killings?"

The grizzly bear sized bartender came over with my beer, and her tequila.

"Thank you," Charley said.

"How, how, how did you know, we suspected Blue Hardin?"

We did a small cheers and started sipping our drinks.

"Was listening to you speak to Mayor Hastert, was standing there for some time listening to him tell you all those lies."

"Could have invited you to sit with us if you was keen, I mean, wouldn't have had to stand for so long," I smiled.

"I like standing, but I don't like standing or sitting with a liar," she looked at me intensely, "but thanks anyway," she swallowed more tequila.

"So you know Blue?" I asked calmly.

"Since we was little, little ones, grew up just outside of town together," she smiled proudly thinking back to those times, it seemed.

"Is that so?" I took my notebook out back from my satchel. I had put it away cause I thought my investigating was done.

"So what you know about him, I mean what was he like when he was little?"

"Blue was just sweet as Georgia peaches," she said as she looked at some travelers coming in through the front door, dusty from their travels with dry lips. "He was one of my best friends growing up," she then started playing with the little napkin on the table.

"Sweet as Georgia peaches?" I thought to myself as I leaned back in my seat. When she said this, I heard her say "His shit smells sweet a peaches."

"Really, sweet as peaches?" I asked her.

"Did, did, did ... I ... s ... t ... u ... t ... t ... e ... r?" She said and glanced at me with a fuck you stare.

"Yes, he was," she swigged some more tequila, "we played all of the time, you name it, chess, hide and go seek, tag, spin the bottle, Halloween dress up," she was now playing with a quarter in her hand, flipping it not nervously, but very calmly, in her right hand.

She looked at the quarter going up and down for a moment while I waited for her to continue.

"I loved being with him and I trusted him."

I wrote in my book: "Blue — trustworthy?"

"What did he do, what did he do to make you trust him?"

"What didn't he do," she said as she stopped playing with the quarter. "Remember one time, there was some kids in elementary school, some group of girls that made fun of me, cause I didn't have the shoes they had, didn't have all the nice things they had, cause my family didn't have the money to get them."

She looked at me with sad eyes.

"Those girls was all around me, three of them, saying things, not nice things, making me feel like," Charley looked down with shame at her cowboy boots.

"Like shit?" I responded.

Charley nodded "yes."

"So," she continued, "these three bitchy girls, the cool girls, the ones who were the popular ones, around me, saying mean things, and meaning it, and I was about to cry, just get down on the floor and cry, and then, I couldn't believe it."

She had a small tear. It started dripping down from the corner of her eye.

"Here," I handed her an old napkin that was on the table.

"Thanks," she wiped her tear away, a tough girl, with tough muscles, and a tough mind, but that little girl was there underneath.

"So, um," she took another swig, "Blue comes along, they didn't see him coming, cause their backs were turned to him. With sad tearing eyes, he said with a tremor to his voice: 'you leave her be.'"

Charley looked outside the bar when the front doors opened and the sun came in. She continued to talk as she looked:

"Those bully girls looked behind and saw Blue, in his black shirt buttoned up to the top, he always wore a black shirt, with his crapped out black denim pants, long hair down to his waste that hadn't been washed," Charley was playing with the paper on the table now, "and black suspenders holding up them old pants."

Charley looked back at me.

"His eyes, they was just gazing at them girls, almost without blinking, with his little hairs on his face . . ."

"How old was you all when this going down?"

She shrugged.

"We was about twelve years old, I reckon when I think about it, cause his Injun family was still alive."

"So what happened?" I asked.

"So them three girls turn around, and see Blue's midnight blue eyes staring at them, and his teeth, I'll never forget his teeth, it was like them bears who show you them teeth, you ever seen them?"

"Never."

"You don't want to see it. Those bears get on their hind legs, get taller than the tallest tree you ever seen, and then their teeth, they show you their teeth, they not needing to say nothing more, nothing more need to be said, cause them teeth, they looking at you and, when you see them, they saying to you . . ."

"We are about to rip you apart alive," I finished her thought.

"Yes, yes, exactly," she leaned over the table and put her hand softly on mine. "Part of me was so happy he was there, but part of me was scared," she pulled her hand off mine, "that he would do something he wouldn't be able to get away from for the rest of his life."

"What did the girls do?"

"They looked at him in horror, just in absolute horror. They stared at him for a second, thinking he was kidding, like they could talk themselves out of it, their daddy going to come make it better with his money."

"But nobody came?" I asked.

"Nobody came and Blue, the scary monster he can be, just stood there staring at those girls, didn't say nothing. His clinched his fists and snarled his teeth."

"Did you think he was crazy?" I asked.

"No. I thought he was one of those smart fucks," she looked at me with serious eyes so that her gaze sunk in. Charley was a waitress, but she could see where I was going with this. If he was crazy, some insane man, then he could easily be put in that box where people say he crazy, just some crazy fuck, instead of a smart fuck who sees things other people don't see.

The word "crazy" made all of 12-year-old Blue's actions seem random, whereas "smart fuck" made the same misunderstood actions way ahead of their time.

"And I thanked God he was scary smart, thanked God he was there for me, cause them girls, them girls, when he stood there, when he kept staring, they knew if they did anything more, said another hateful word, lifted another finger in my way . . ."

"Blue would have been a bear," I said.

"Yes," she nodded.

"And so they left?"

"Not yet. They looked at him like 'you can't be serious,' or 'you crazy,' or nothing. Cause they knew that any little word, little move, would be like that little rock . . ."

"That set off an avalanche?" I asked.

"Right, one you never come back from," she said with sad eyes. "And so, after they saw this side to a normally quiet boy, they knew he wasn't going to walk away without putting them on the ground."

Charley swigged some more tequila, not sure out of fear or celebration — or both.

"So those girls walked away, real slow, watching behind their backs to make sure he not going to come after them from behind," she looked at me, finished her tequila, and then said, like a man: "I got to use the head." Many ways she was like a man, but in the most important ways she wasn't.

She walked to the back of the bar, sawdust on the ground, men sitting at the bar with pistols on their sides and disappeared into the back.

"Blue," I wrote in my notebook, "Loving/Trustworthy, Quietly/Ruthless."

I thought some more. I thought some more about when I spoke to Blue that first time in June of that year about his outlaw past. What made him go from a quiet good boy to being the person who everybody thinks is a sinner?

Charley came back from the bathroom and sat down.

"Thanks for sitting with me, Charley," I said as I put my pen down.

"I sat with you, mister, cause I think you need to hear what I got to say, so I thank you for sitting with me."

I raised my glass in appreciation and took a long swig.

"So, um, what were Blue's parents, his real parents, like?"

"Sweet people," she nodded, "they was, forgot what it was," she looked up to the ceiling full of wood beams, "Quakers," she looked at me. "Some type of folk who didn't have no real religion, called non . . . non . . . conformist, something," she tapped her cowboy boot a few times on the floor. "They was some out there people, must say," she said with a smile to me like I didn't know what I was getting myself into, a black type of cave that calls you, you go in, and you can't get out once you in.

"What you mean, they was out there people?"

"What you maybe didn't know," Charley looked around to make sure nobody was listening, then back at me, leaning over the table, real quiet, "is that Blue's parents, they, they, how I gone done say this without sounding stupid, cause people use the word all the time, but, mister," she leaned more over the table real quiet, "they was some genius types."

I wrote down into my booklet: "Blue — Camouflage master."

"What did they do, these geniuses?"

"Blue's Father was a village witch doctor and surgeon, took care of the local families, kids and all, and his momma was one of the local school teachers. They was from some American Revolutionary stock."

Blue? A father who was a doctor, a mother who was a teacher, family from Revolutionary stock? This couldn't be true.

"Blue Hardin? We talking about the same Blue Hardin?"

"No, I am talking about the other Blue Hardin, the one from France, you don't know that one? He is from Paris," she leaned back into her chair.

"Well, I . . ."

"You officers, you all the same, too serious, taking things too seriously," she said as she stuck her finger into the tequila and licked it. "I am talking about the Blue you seem to know."

"What happened to them, Charley, to his parents I mean?" I asked.

"Word has it, they was killed, by that fever that done come through here, forgot the exact date, but they was killed when Blue was bout 9 or 10 years old."

"Blue — Orphaned at 10 years old" — I wrote in my book.

She looked around again to see if anybody was listening.

"Secret information you giving me?" I asked.

"No," she said looking at me. "Just don't like nobody listening to what I got to say."

"Who took care of him, I mean, after his parents died?"

"An Injun family," she took some more booze to make her lose maybe her memories, or maybe be able to get them back better. "Let me see, let me see, what their names now," her dirty black cowboy books was tapping again on the floor, "oh yea, yea, they was named Waya and Yona, Waya was the poppa and Yona was the momma, they and their little ones took Blue in when he little."

"Waya and Yona? What do they mean?" I sipped some of my beer.

"Waya means wolf, and Yona means bear," she said with intense eyes.

I wrote down the translation.

"Did Waya and Yona have other children — I mean did Blue have adopted brothers and sisters?"

Charley counted on her hands.

"Yes, he had two brothers, one sister."

I had known from speaking with Blue that day so many moons ago that an Injun family raised him, but I didn't know the details that Charley was giving me.

"What was Blue like after his Quaker parents died?"

"Sad and angry, sad cause he loved his parents, remembered him talking about having suppers with them, the talks and laughing they had, and he angry at God, I guessing, cause God took them away from him," Charley stopped to think, "but I reckon his new family, they was like cool water to his fire, made him feel safe, like there wasn't nothing that was going to hurt him in the world, you see," her long brown hair flowed a little bit over her shoulders as the wind from outside came inside when the saloon door opened.

"So when you say he was angry, did he, what they say it now, did he act out, you know, do them bad things, be a bad boy, after his parents left this here world?"

"No," Charley shook her head. "Blue good. We'd have our share of high jinx, playing tricks on others in the village, but not nothing that no other boy his age not doing."

This didn't make sense. There had to be something wrong. Where was the turning point? But then I remembered from my talk with Blue, it all happened when he lost his Injun family in the Trail of Tears.

"But that changed, it all changed, right?" I asked.

"Yes, sir, it done changed when they took his Injun family away during that march, that death march that was just to torture and kill them people."

266

"They?"

"The feds, Mister Jasper, the feds," she leaned over and said "feds" with emphasis then sat back in her chair.

"And after that?"

"Blue was still a good boy, but he done become the bear I saw that one day, you know, them girls who were being the devil to me. He done a lot of bad things, but they was to bad people, you see."

She paused to think.

"Like what bad people you talking about?"

"I not saying nothing, Mister, cause I don't tell nothing bad about no friends of mine, but I do know that what this Hastert telling you is just not true."

"What not true?" I sipped some more beer.

"Him, Hastert, he like, what I gone to say now, he all church going, you know, all Christian crap saying, thinking he holy and shit, you know many of them politician types, saying one thing, doing another?"

I didn't comment because I knew that I was working for the mayor of San Francisco. Had to keep my mouth shut when I didn't want to keep my mouth shut. But Charley didn't give a damn.

She shrugged when I didn't say anything.

"What did this Hastert do that made him so bad?" I then asked.

She leaned over the table again, very calmly, and said in a quiet voice.

"Used our tax money, our God damn tax money, to pay to cover up his sins," she pointed to the table with her index finger.

"What you mean, Hastert covered up his lollipop stealing?"

She smiled and leaned back.

"Nope, cause Hastert done take little boys' innocence but then paying their families couldn't believe this shit, done take some taxpayer money to keep the boys' families quiet. So, yeah, cover up of him taking a boy's lollipop, you hear me mister Jasper?"

I couldn't believe this, Hastert, a child molester? The proper Republican man, the man I was speaking to just now?

"How you know this, how you know?" I asked Charley

"Mister Jasper, I may be just some waitress at some bar in the middle of Vandalia, but I hear these men talking to one another, and, sometimes, they talk to me, late at night, after I give them enough vodka or whiskey to get them to talk."

"I see," I said. I wrote in my book: "Hastert — don't trust?"

"So what about this killings that is going down here in town and Chicago for which Blue was convicted for, Hastert telling me about them 19 deaths that is going down, what about them? Wasn't Blue convicted for those killings?"

Honey Bear, the Injun bartender, came by with a new round of drinks, taking our old ones. He didn't look at me any more with mean eyes, but with softer ones.

"Thank you sweet heart," Charley said to the bear.

He smiled at her.

"Convictions?" She took more tequila and swished it around in her mouth. "What this lying Hastert saying now, convictions?"

"Yea," I opened my notes to the time I met with Hastert, "said Blue was convicted for doing some murders for hire, cutting 19 people in their stomachs and watching them die?"

"Blue not never been convicted of nothing, I tell you that much," she said.

"But what about him doing bad things to bad people?"

"You know who them dead people was, them 19 people Hastert talking about?" She asked.

"Don't know who the dead men were," I shook my head and sipped.

"They was honchos, presidents, of them 19 banks that Blue robbed, and them 19 banks was members of a company that was supposed to manage, what they call it, invest pension money, retirement money of teachers, horseshoe men, you name it," she swigged some tequila.

"But?" I asked.

"This company that them banks was members of, it invest the money with them investment bankers on Wall Street, in about 1846, and all the money lost in some bullshit finance crap, castles in the sky, which is why that there *Chicago Tribune* newspaper had articles and articles about this 1846 collapse and fraud. *But* you know who got rich off this collapse of castles on clouds?"

"Who?" I asked as I sipped my beer.

"The bankers, cause they got big commissions," Charley stuck out one finger, "the bank presidents, cause they got bonuses," another finger came out, "them Wall Street lawyers, cause they did all the work for them bankers," another finger, "the government, cause they collect them fines and shit."

"So everybody wins, no, everybody won?"

"No, sir, cause you got them folks who didn't get no more savings, life savings is gone, and now these folks, many of who don't got much more life to live, don't got no money."

She swigged some more tequila, an honorary Mexican the way she did it — slow, calm, like a fire could be outside, and she'd be ice queen inside.

"You see, mister lawman, this like a reverse bank robbery, cause it's the banks and Wall Street stealing from customers, but the sick part of it was that not one banker," she put her index finger up, "not one banker went to jail for this fraud," she put the finger down. "That cause all these lawmen down in Washington D.C. and up in Chicago for the government had just been working for the same law firms that working for these banks, so these lawmen not gone do nothing but slap their banker friend who done the fraud on the hand or wrist with some bullshit fine."

"But no jail time?" I asked.

"Right, mister, not nobody did no time cause they all in it, and that's why I hear the judges in here being sick to their stomachs about this, about the downright breaking down of this here government to do what's right — if they putting moonshiners in jail, they should putting them bankers in jail just the same."

She wiped her mouth of some tequila that was dripping on her mouth with the dirty top of her hand.

"Like what judges get sick to their stomachs?" I asked.

"Shit, all of them down here, but one I heard is Judge Neal, he actually was a family friend of Blue's poppa, and Judge Neal, who went to be a judge in a fancy court in Chicago, now live down here, cause he retired, but he in here a lot with his judge friends, and they downright disgusted about the fact that not nobody was prosecuted, went to jail, during the 1846, what they call it, financial meltdown bailouts of too fat to falls."

I understood that this Judge Neal would be testifying on behalf of Blue in the second half of the trial.

"Now, them 19 dead men, them dead banker executives not the ones . . ." She stopped to turn around and say hello to some new customers that came in through the front of the bar. "Hey y'all, what's going on there, come right on in," she said with tough eyes but a sincere smile.

"Not the ones?" I asked her as she turned back towards me.

"Yes, um, them dead men not like them other bankers, the good bankers, the great bankers, the ones who treat peoples like they was their own kind, like they would to their own family," she looked at me. I could tell people took her for a dummy, like she wasn't stable, just passing time doing the bar thing, but she had more of that knowledge, knowing about the world, than almost anybody I met in my life.

"Don't hear much about them good bankers, do you?" She took more tequila.

I shook my head, "not much in the papers, mostly the bad ones in the papers."

"That's right, mister lawman, cause good bankers, like my local bank man, Mr. Friedman, who treat people like me with respect, cause they want to make my money grow, not take it from me, and then hide behind lawyers, fancy contracts, and government officials that used to work for them, cause men like Mr. Friedman not too big for his britches, thinking, that he, what the word," she paused and then snapped her fingers, "untouchable. So not all them bank folks are bad apples, just the too fat to fall ones who getting government bonuses while investors done screwed."

"Them too fat to fall bankers were killed?" I asked.

"The ones who was killed in them bad ways, they had it coming," she nodded over to me, "cause they thieves with white collars, fancy houses, and degrees."

"So who was convicted of doing them things, them killings then?"

"Not nobody convicted, mister, cause that a bunch of bullshit. They thinking the killer this Satanic looking drifter with long sideburns passing through town and who need the money, so he done these things to these people for the people who paying him — the victims who done the paying, a few measly dollars a head, it was rumored, cause the God damn government not doing nothing."

"Feed the bear the food it needs, or it gets hungrier?"

"You got that right, mister," she said as she held up her tequila to me and sipped some more. I took a swig of my beer as she did.

"Wasn't there some fire," I said after I put my bottle on the table, "some fire to the record room, where they keep all of the court and conviction papers?"

"Reckon so, if I think back to it alright, but they wasn't no conviction of Blue for killing. He only *indicted* by a grand jury for the bank robbing, not any killing though. I'm telling you as God as my witness," she looked above, "that the word on the street is that this long side burned drifter or some drifters' friends is the one who done these killings."

"And the bad things that Blue did to the bad people that you mentioned before, what you mean?"

"Going to tell you something, and you not got it from me, but I guess it don't matter no now cause what they call it, that period where you can't go after somebody know more, for a crime, see?"

"Right, the statute of limitations."

"Right, lawman, you know what it called." She stopped to stare at her tequila for a moment. "So that limit done passed a long time ago on what I done going to tell you," she put her finger in the tequila and licked it.

"So Blue *did* rob those 19 banks with his crew."

Now Charley was looking at me with her Irish eyes that made me wonder — why was she telling me this? "Don't look a gift horse in the mouth," momma always told me. So I didn't ask Charley why. I just wrote "Blue — bank robber," in my notebook.

"And who was in his crew, this crew of his?" I asked.

"Don't nobody know that for sure, mister," she shrugged, "cause they use a different crew for each heist, and nobody know any of the other peoples' names. I do know that when they done do their bank robbing, they all making it look like they some hood niggers so nobody thinking it just some hood crackers that really doing it."

"Or maybe it's a little both?" I thought out loud. "Maybe them black city white and country hoods just some kissing cousins who doing their bank robbing pinky promises under the midnight moon when coppers can't see squat?"

She looked at me, broke a co-conspirator's smile, then said:

"One thing I do know, though, mister Jasper," as if she didn't know it all.

"What's that?"

"All them banks, keeping money for likes of Hastert, them 19 bank presidents who taking our money, saying they doing good things with it, and they just stealing from us hard working, what they call us, voters. They saying they caring, with them big smiles, then just going to have a cigar with their banking friends, who keeping their money in those tight knit circles."

"So they had it coming?" I asked.

"Shit, you bet they had it coming," she smiled satisfied. "But, you know, all of the banks had some type of insurance, so Blue and his crew, never stealing so much that it never not covered by this there insurance."

"How you know that Blue's crew trying to make it look like they just bunch of black hoods?"

"Cause I heard they found some of that black shoe polish cans they using on their faces in the last robbery on a country road just outside of Chicago, but not all in Blue's crew wearing that shoe polish on their faces, which means some men in that crew, I reckon, was black who did the last heist."

"How you know?"

"Witnesses say it was 8 black men who done this shit, but police only found 5 clothes with black shoe polish rubbed off on them outside of Chicago, which means . . ."

"Exactly three black hoods was in on the last heist," I said more than asked.

"Supposing you right, mister," Charley closed one of her eyes towards me, "and some different combination of hoods was in on the other heists, too, trust me on that one, smart, fast, big, scary hoods is the word from them bank tellers."

"Blue," I wrote in my notebook, "bank robbed in Illinois but didn't murder?"

"So they thinking Blue did all this, yea?" I asked.

"He was investigated, police found some money in some account that one of the Injuns having, someone he knew, linked the money to Blue."

"So he was only indicted for the robberies?"

"Yea, i . . . n . . . d . . . i . . . c . . . t . . . e . . . d, what the fuck ever the word is. But that the most of it, cause they couldn't find Blue. He gone before they go too far in their looking up his ass-hole, you see, cause he done do the craziest shit I ever done see."

"That is?"

"Joined the God damn American army to fight down in Mexico."

"Didn't they catch him, I mean, when he put his name down?"

"Mister, you think a man like that, with a brain like that, going to do something stupid without a reason for it? They didn't catch him cause word has it he used an alias to join the army."

"Right, well, do you know anything about a law man in Chicago by the name of Dick Holder?"

"Oh, that one, we call him Dick Hold Me, yea," Charley smirked. "I heard about him from what the judges down here and others saying about him. He will tell you a lot, but he in on it too, he with them Chicago fucks, the same ones that taking our shit, saying they keeping justice, meanwhile they just letting the real crooks, the real criminals, off the hook while they trying to lock up regular people who trying to get a taste of justice."

"Like Blue," I said.

"You got it, mister. There is that amendment, what they call it, about being able to tell your elected politician that he a piece of shit."

"The First Amendment?" I asked.

"Yea, whatever it is, thought this country about being able to tell the mayor, the president, he a lying piece of shit, and not going to jail for it . . . but this Hastert man, he done go after friends of mine, people who complaining about the 1846 financial meltdown bailouts, and they just, what they say, invested?"

"Investigated," I said.

"Right, investigated by the government under mayor Hastert cause they merely speaking their mind."

She took another dip in her tequila with her index finger and licked it. I could tell she liked talking to Jasper. I suppose was I fancying her, too.

"So what about Blue, what did he do in this Mexican-America war?"

"Shit, done fight with them dark people in some group, what they call it now, St. Patrick's Battalion, bunch of immigrants, Catholics I think mostly."

She smiled.

"So he joins the military to get out of Illinois, to get out of mayor Holder's hands, but then he fights with the Mexicans?"

She shrugged.

"Not fighting — nursing. Word has it he didn't kill one person during the war, but just nursed many an almost dead back to life down in Mexico, not wanting to lift no hand against an American or Mexican solider and all."

"But why he go with that St. Patrick's battalion in the first place?"

"Cause Blue done hear that we, the U.S. government, could have bought that Mexican land, California, all of that shit, from the Mexicans, but we done going on a blood spree, maybe cause the arms makers wanting to make more money, and they not going to make more money if there isn't a war of, what you call it, aggression?"

"Yea, that sounds right."

"Right, alright, aggression it is."

Felt like doing a high five with her, that we agreed on something.

"So these Americans," Charley went one, "was killing them Mexicans cause it making the money for, what, you know, them gun makers and shit like that."

"So that's why Blue did what he did, fight with the Mexicans, Blue done fight with them darkies, and then . . ."

"Two things happened," she looked at me. "First thing is this motherfucker the most infamous outlaw in Illinois history. Them Injuns can't not stop speaking about him, lovingly calling him 'morning star, planet Venus,' some shit like that."

In my notebook, I wrote down: "Blue — invisible, morning star, planet Venus." Mayor Hastert was right about that.

275

"And the second thing?"

"Shit, mister," she finished her tequila. "Second thing happened is that Blue become one of the biggest enemies of the state since Paul, what his name?"

"Revere."

Charley scratched her head, "didn't he done go through the streets saying them English is coming?"

"Yes, that's him," I nodded.

"And a lot of them English got their throats slit because of that man?"

"Yes," I said, "I guess that's true," I shrugged.

"Well, that's what the federal government was thinking about Blue. He like that Paul whatever man to them, and they is like the British soldiers — taxation without, what is it, r-e-p-r-e-s-e-n-t-a-t-i-o-n! So them feds in Chicago, they going to say anything but the truth about the war with the Mexicans to make it look like the war needed to be fought, to make Blue look like he was a traitor, not the patriot he was."

Wrote down in my booklet, "Blue — American terrorist or patriot?"

You might be surprised to hear this, but never did tell Jarboe about Charley. Shit, did tell Jarboe about the bank robberies, and what Hastert told me about Blue being this maniac murderer who seemed to get off on doing the bloody shit.

But I had my doubts, and they were growing, about Jarboe's version of the truth.

They came up after Charley told me how Blue stuck his neck out for her when they were youngsters. Why would a cold-blooded murderer, with no good qualities, go and do something like that? Was Jarboe not telling the jury something that they should know about Blue? Was there more about Blue that wasn't being told?

My interview of federal prosecutor Dick Holder, who was Jarboe's witness after Mayor Hastert, made the waters even murkier.

"We've been expecting you, sergeant," Holder, the mustached man of the law greeted me in his fancy federal office overlooking State Street. Behind his head on the wall was his undergraduate degree from Harvard and law degree from the University of Wisconsin. On the table behind him, pictures of his family, awards, and a jar full of candy.

"Please, please sit down," the lanky elegant forceful fed said as he offered me a chair in front of his large wooden desk with papers neatly piled.

After I exchanged some pleasantries with Holder we got down to it.

"Blue Hardin is a home grown terrorist, an absolute traitor to this country," Holder calmly said. "This white devil," he continued as he smoked his academic looking pipe, "joins the Army under an assumed name, Eden Taylor, so we don't see his record. Turns out this Eden Taylor fellow, when we looked into it further, was a wealthy Protestant fellow from the north side of Chicago who died many years go."

Dick Holder puffed his pipe as I asked.

"Did you check identification when people joined?"

"We did," Holder nodded, "but Blue had a fake identification card, a complete forgery."

"So Blue comes into the military, joins, and then?"

"This son-of-a-bitch," Holder says with some more force now, "goes and fights with the St. Patrick's Battalion, around 1847 or so, and they . . ."

"Who is they?" I asked.

"A group of 150 or so traitors, mostly immigrants, many Irish Catholic, who went to fight with . . . let me say that again . . . went to fight with the Mexicans, can you believe that?"

"Why?"

Holder shrugged.

"Don't know for sure, but some say that the Battalion felt more sympathy for the Catholic Mexicans, who they felt were the underdog in the war, which is complete nonsense," Holder said as he organized some files on his desk.

"And Hardin went to fight with them?"

"Yes, sergeant, we caught that son of a bitch, and he was court martialed, when was it," Holder pulled out a document from his desk to examine it, "about August 26, 1847, in San Angel, Mexico, that's it, and sentenced to death."

"I guess he missed that party," I said with some humor.

Holder just stared at me.

"Sorry, Mr. Holder."

He didn't respond and just looked at me with displeasure.

"So, moving on," I looked down at my notes to avoid his gaze, "what happened, I mean, sentenced to death and all, how did Blue survive?"

"He escaped from the brick and mortar prison we were holding him in, one of the best we ever constructed, I'm telling you," Holder leaned back and proudly spoke of the prison as if it was his growing son.

I wanted to say something like, "sounds like your prison has holes like Swiss cheese in it," but I bit my tongue. I knew that the machine of the federal government was putting a lot more people in prison for crimes ranging from smoking marijuana in public, to riding without a saddle in certain Illinois cities, and being too close to a place of worship without a shirt on. The machine needed to be fed, after all, and it got so busy that it was subcontracting out the prison construction and management to private companies. That was one of the biggest new money troughs to feed off of in California.

"How did he escape from that prison?" I asked.

"Nobody knows exactly how, but," he swiveled in his chair, "looks like one of his shitty Mexican friends dug a tunnel to the prison from a nearby bar called *Villa's*, made a hole underneath the brick wall, to get him out."

"How you know?"

"We found an empty tequila bottle in the dark tunnel and followed it to the *Villa's* bar."

"Creative," I said.

Holder looked at me with an annoyed look. I had seen his kind before in San Francisco. They come out of school with fancy degrees, work the right politics in their bureaucracy, and then get a lot of power in their hands. The power on paper, though, doesn't mean the person behind it has grit to get things done. It wasn't so much that I thought what Blue did was good. It wasn't. But the way he got out of that prison was just plain great survival stuff that I don't think Holder could do if his life depended on it, regardless of how many classes he took at Harvard.

Holder wasn't great — Blue was.

"Well, it doesn't matter how creative this Blue man is," Dick Holder continued, cause the long arm of the law will always win, always," he leaned over his desk to make the emphasis, his sharp dry elbows bursting from his rolled up sleeves as they rubbed his wooden desk top. "We get our man, sergeant, we always get him, and it seems like you all have got him right where you want him in San Francisco, isn't that right," Holder leaned back into his chair that creaked and which was comfortable.

But maybe Holder was so comfortable in his chair that he didn't ever have to think too much on his feet, outside of the box, cause he didn't need to.

"If the arm of the law wasn't long, I suppose I wouldn't be here, Mr. Holder," I closed my notebook. "I wanted to just confirm with you that you would be willing to testify at the murder trial of Mr. Hardin in San Francisco about him being a traitor and fighting with the Mexicans in the war?"

Knew from Charley that Blue didn't do one lick of fighting.

"I wouldn't miss that for anything, sergeant. Will bring some popcorn with me, cause I am going to love seeing that man hang for the things he has done," Holder punched the empty air between us.

All of my reasonable doubts about Blue made me do something that, if you told me I would do a few years ago, I would have said you were coo-coo. In a leap of faith, I sent an anonymous letter from Illinois to Benny Hyman's law office in San Francisco that read:

> *Charley Parkhurst — bar hand waitress, Vandalia, Illinois. She having the answers that going to help you in your case, mister. Address: 111 N. Race Street, Vandalia, IL 61801.*

However, I didn't have any doubts that Blue, Amber, and Shane celebrated with moonshine about the disappearance of those four church higher-ups priests from the Lenny's Fine Cuts butcher shop on Sunday, September 3, earlier that year.

During the next day of the trial, I questioned if Blue would have brought out the moonshine had he heard the screaming coming from Lenny's Fine Cuts that day.

Or maybe he brought out that moonshine *because* of that screaming?

CHAPTER ELEVEN

IT'S NOT WHAT YOU THINK

A man named Muddy Woodstock was responsible for the priests' disappearances.

Harvey Bronstein, the 54-year-old Archdiocese head accountant and secretary, testified about Woodstock, a beef salesman from Lenny's Fine Cuts who:

"Said something to me like, 'listen to me father, you chaps at the Archdiocese, they want to buy quality beef right? Well, this is a sample of the most lovely beef jerky you'll put in your mouth.'"

"Did the sales man use the word 'chaps'?" Jarboe asked his first witness during the next morning of the trial.

"Yes, the sales man's accent was foreign, East London sounding."

"And what makes you say that, sir?"
"Some of the worshippers in the San Francisco Archdiocese are Cockney, from East London, and they come into the offce sometimes, and I've heard their thick accents before."

"Now," Jarboe said as he looked down on his notes, "when did this Cockney sounding salesman come to your office at the Archdiocese?"

"Let me see," Bronstein started playing with his beard, "I think it was on August 4, must have been the morning of August 4," Bronstein said with his belly busting out of his dress shirt, and his tightly tied country black tie looked like it was strangling him, slowly. His hands rested softly on his belly like some Buddha man.

"And what was the name of the company Muddy Woodstock was doing the sales for?"

"Lenny's Fine Cuts!" Bronstein said with an almost appreciative smirk.

"Lenny's Fine Cuts being a butcher shop in town?"

"Yes," Bronstein said.

"Do you know of this shop?" Jarboe asked.

"Eh," Bronstein shrugged his shoulders as he looked over to the jury, "who wouldn't know of the shop," he looked back at Jarboe. "It's one of the top meat shops in San Francisco."

"Maybe you can describe Mr. Woodstock for me?" Jarboe asked.

"I think so," said the Santa Claus built Bronstein, "he had rotting teeth, but their canines was sharp like wolf's teeth, prune dry wrinkled ghost white skin, bouffant of snow white hair, crystal blue eyes, clean trimmed long sideburns went down to his cheek bone, and just remember staring at his super fancy suit, wondering where it was made."

"Did you ask him?"

"Yes, yes, sir."

"And what did he say?"

"Said it was hand made for him somewhere in London, remember cause he just staring down at his vest, little watch dangling on a chain from it."

"I see, so you would say it was an expensive suit?" Jarboe asked.

Could see Hyman just shaking his head, but he didn't object.

"Oh, yea sir, definitely fancy pants."

"So, Mr. Bronstein," Jarboe said as he played with the pocket watch in his three piece suit, something that I think he used more as a prop than to tell the time, "did you and the rest of the folks in that office taste Mr. Woodstock's beef jerky samples."

"Oh yes," Bronstein said as he clapped his hands in joy. "Muddy brought in these paper bags, they was labeled, what was they called, oh, yes, 'Jerky Time' up top, and they said something like, right below, that they was 'Sweet n' Spicy,' with, what was it, cause I never seen some packaging like this before, 'low fat, high protein,' with a little brown string on the top that made them close."

"And what did you all think of the samples?"

"Stupendous," Bronstein smiled, "the best beef jerky I had ever tasted in my life. The Archbishop said the same thing to me, plus the bishop and two other priests in the office."

"So what happened next?" Jarboe asked.

"Mr. Woodstock said he'd like to have the Archdiocese as a client, you know, supply all of our parishes with their beef needs, cause we need to feed all of those priests and nuns, you know," he said.

Bronstein paused.

"He pulled out a contract for us to sign, it was for a year, you know, installments of beef would be sent to us every Friday for distribution throughout the Archdiocese."

"And what did you do?" Jarboe asked.

"I told him that I would need the higher ups in the Archdiocese, like Cardinal Degollado and Archbishop Pilarczyk, to taste the jerky and review the contract, before we could proceed."

"And did you do that?" Jarboe asked.

"Yes, I gave the beef jerky samples to the Cardinal early on the following week, August 7 or 8, and he was very impressed, very impressed indeed. So he cleared the contract, cause we weren't too happy about our current beef vendor."

"Did you then have Mr. Woodstock come back into the Archdiocese?"

"Yes," Bronstein said.

"What date was that?"

"Let's see, it was about Friday, August 11."

"That's when the contract was finalized?"

""Yes, yes, sir."

"Mr. Bronstein," Jarboe said as he pulled out a piece of paper, "does this appear to be an accurate duplicate of the contract the Archdiocese signed with Lenny's Fine Cuts?"

Bronstein took the document and looked it over.

"Yes," this appears to be the contract. At which point Jarboe passed the contract to Hyman, and then to the judge.

"Your honor, I'd like to tender this document into evidence."

"Any objection, Mr. Hyman?" Parker asked.

"No, your honor," Hyman said.

"Now," Jarboe continued, "what is the company's name on this contract?"

"Lenny's Fine Cuts," Bronstein answered.

"And the purchaser is the Archdiocese of San Francisco?"

"Yes," Bronstein nodded.

"And the date on the contract?"

"August 11, 1876."

"Now, the Archbishop signed the contract, right?"

"Yes," Bronstein nodded.

"Did you ever see this man, this Muddy Woodstock sales-man, again?"

"Nope, never again."

"Now, Mr. Bronstein, I'd like to direct to your attention to August 31, 1876."

"Alright," Bronstein moved his sweaty elephant body around in the chair.

"Can you tell the jury what happened on the morning of that day?"

"Well, yes, um, let me see," Bronstein thought back, "we got an invitation to a day long client appreciation party at Lenny's Fine Cuts for Archbishop Pilarczyk, Cardinal Krol, Cardinal Bevilacqua, and Bishop O'Sullivan."

"And what was the date of the party, if you recall?"

"It was the weekend of September 2–3, if I remember right."

"The weekend after the invite?"

"Yes."

"Now, directing your attention to September 3," Jarboe said as he reviewed his notes.

"Alright," Bronstein said as he sipped his water slowly.

"Can you tell the jury what happened that day?"

"Well, yes," Bronstein said as he put the glass of water down, "that was the day of the party at Lenny's Fine Cuts, but Archbishop John Pilarczyk and Bishop Eugene O'Sullivan could only attend the event in the morning, so we had to arrange for their transport to Lenny's Fine Cuts."

"And did you personally arrange for that transport?"

"Yes," Bronstein said, "we use a livery service for that."

"The name of the service?"

"Big Sur Livery," he said.

"Alright, so this service comes along, picks up them up, and then drops the off at Lenny's Fine Cuts?"

"Yes."

"Did the service wait for the men, or did it leave?"

"Um, let me think back," Bronstein looked outside the court room window, "they were dropped off, cause it costs more for the Archdiocese to keep the livery waiting."

"And do you know the location of Lenny's Fine Cuts?"

"No."

"Is it listed here on the contract?"

"Yes," Bronstein said.

"Could you read that into the record please?"

"Yes," at which point Bronstein read the following address: "525 Harrison Street."

"So, the Archbishop John Pilarczyk and Bishop Eugene O'Sullivan are dropped off in the morning, and then did you have the two other priests, let's see," Jarboe reviewed his notes, "Cardinals John Krol and Justin Bevilacqua, transported to the Lenny's Fine Cuts party, too?"

"Yes, but they was dropped off there much later in the day, I think it was around 3:00 p.m."

"What time did the first two men get transported down there?"

"Around 10:00 a.m."

Jarboe just stood there for a minute. He pulled out his pocket watch to see how much time had passed since he started with this witness.

"Just to be clear, Mr. Bronstein," Jarboe looked at him, "what day of the week was this?"

"It was, um, it was a Sunday," he said.

"Are you aware that Lenny's Fine Cuts is closed on Sundays?"

Bronstein just stared at Jarboe.

"No, I am not aware of that.

"Were you aware of that fact on that day the Archbishop and the other priests shipped down there?"

"Well," Bronstein adjusted himself in his seat, visibly uncomfortable, "I was not."

Jarboe started pacing, the tiger moving around the cage thinking of his next move. Suddenly, he stopped after a few seconds of pacing, looked Bronstein in his chubby eyes, and then asked:

"Isn't it true, Mr. Bronstein, that September 3, 1876, was the last date that anybody had ever seen these four priests again?"

"Yes," Bronstein said.

Jarboe looked over his notes, making sure he crossed things off he needed to cross off, and then he looked up with a self-satisfied smile.

"Mr. Bronstein, thank you for your testimony today," Jarboe said as he closed his trial notebook, "that will be it for me with this witness, your honor," Jarboe said to judge Parker.

"Mr. Hyman, Mr. Hyman," Judge Parker repeated himself as he looked over to the defendant's table, trying to get Hyman's attention.

"Oh, oh, your honor," Hyman stopped himself in the middle of his sentence, as he made a stop sign to Blue, a stop talking sign, and then Blue backed off.

Hyman got up.

"Mr. Bronstein," Hyman said quickly before he even got close to the witness stand, "my name is Benny Hyman, and I represent the defendants sitting right behind me," he nodded over his shoulder to the defendant's table.

"Sitting here today, do you know who owns Big Sur Livery?"

"No, sir," Bronstein shook his head.

"Did the Archdiocese ever use the livery service before?"

Bronstein sat there for a moment.

"A few times, they were a new vendor for us," he said.

"Who did the archdiocese use before them?"

"I think we used a company, let me see, called Wet County Livery," he said.

"And when did you start using Big Sur?"

Bronstein shrugged.

"A few months before."

"A few months before the disappearances?"

"Yes," he nodded.

"Ever have any problems with them, Big Sur that is?"

"Never any problems, smooth sailing for us."

Hyman shuffled his shitty notes on the wooden fence around the witness stand.

"Why did you switch from Wet County Livery to Big Sur Livery?"

"They were a new outfit, Big Sur, and they were charging us much less than Wet County."

"So the Archdiocese switched to save?"

"Yes sir," Bronstein said.

"And you, as accountant and secretary for the Archdiocese, have responsibility for these type of financial decisions?"

"I make my recommendations to the Archbishop, and he has final say, but I just make my thoughts known to him."

"I see, I see," Hyman shuffled his paper shells to see what he would find underneath them, looking at one piece here, and then another over there.

"Never met the owner of Big Sur?"

"No, just the owner's wife, cause she came out to tell us about their product."

"And you remember her name?"

"I think it was Irma, something like Irma."

"Irma Thomas?"

"That sounds right, sounds right," Bronstein nodded.

"Is she a Negro woman?"

"Yes."

"So did you ever meet Mr. Huey Thomas, the owner of Big Sur Livery?"

"No," Bronstein said.

"Were you aware Mr. Thomas was a white man?"

"No."

"Did you know that Mr. Thomas was an outlaw from Louisiana?"

Bronstein just stared at Hyman.

"No, heavens no," Bronstein adjusted himself in an real uncomfortable way, you are camping or outside somewhere and you get these biting ants going up your ass, you try to get them off, moving any which way that would do it. Bronstein kept moving his ass like that a little bit before he settled back down.

"According to my research," Hyman said as he looked at one of his shitty notes, "he done used to be a law man, but became, let me see here," Hyman reviewed his note in more detail, "a gunslinger and outright outlaw."

Bronstein just stared at Hyman.

"Objection, hearsay evidence, your honor!" Jarboe shot up.

"Overruled, counsel," Parker patted Jarboe to sit down.

Hyman smiled a first date smile as he looked at Bronstein.

"Were you aware of this Mr. Thomas's criminal past when you hired Big Sur?"

"Oh my lord, heaven's no," Bronstein shook his head as his fat fingers tickled one another on this belly.

"Do you know, sitting here today, Mr. Bronstein, if those priests were ever delivered by Big Sur to the party at Lenny's Fine Cuts on September 3rd?"

"That was what they were hired for, it was what we paid them for," Bronstein said.

"Yes, sir, I understand that," Hyman shooed Bronstein away as you would a fl y in the summer coming too close to your face, "but do you know whether or not they, that is Big Sur, actually did their job that day?"

Bronstein sat there and didn't answer.

"Mr. Bronstein?"

"Yes, I'm thinking. And I suppose," he moved his fat fingers off his chubby knees, "I don't know for sure, Mr. Hyman."

"Very well," Hyman was now standing in front of the witness playing with some change in his pocket, "that day, did you see who from Big Sur came to pick up the priests?"

"I did not."

"Did you ever see the Big Sur carriage before?"

"Yes, yes sir."

"Usually one driver?"

"Sometimes one, sometimes more than one," Bronstein said.

"When would there be one, and when would there be more than one?"

"Usually only one when there was only one person they taking, more than one when there was more than one person they were taking."

"Did the driver, or the person coming with the driver, wear a firearm on previous occasions, to your knowledge?"

"Yes, they always had a pistol and a rifle inside the carriage for protection, cause they didn't only do the transportation, but the security, too."

"Were these Big Sur drivers you saw before, were they taller men, six feet or more?"

"Sometimes," Bronstein shrugged. "Sometimes it was a taller man who sat shotgun, and then the driver would be shorter."

"Under six feet?"

"Yes, yes sir," Bronstein nodded.

"Were you aware, when you hired Big Sur, whether any of the drivers had criminal records?"

"I was not, I was not," Bronstein asked more then said.

"Would it surprise you to know that all drivers with Big Sur had felony convictions, some for murder for hire, others for bank robbery?"

"Golly, you better bet it would surprise me," Bronstein said as he leaned forward with his eyes bulging, coming out of his head, it seemed.

"The evidence shows all of the Big Sur Livery drivers had such felony records."

Hyman produced a driver list for Big Sur, and copies of convictions he obtained, to the witness, judge Jarboe, and the jury.

"Now, do you know the owner of this San Francisco beef shop, Lenny's Fine Cuts?"

"No, I don't," Bronstein answered.

"He is a young man named Tommy Kelly," Hyman said looking at his notes. "Ring a bell?"

"No sir," Bronstein shook his head.

"Did you know this salesman, Muddy Woodstock, who said he was the salesman for Lenny's Fine Cuts, before he came to the Archdiocese?"

"I did not, never met him in my life," Bronstein said with confidence.

Hyman shuffled through his notes, making sure that he covered all he wanted to cover in his cross.

"Mr. Bronstein, I'm sure you'll be disappointed to know this, but I'm done with my questions for this witness, and you free to go now," Hyman gathered up his notes, "no more questions, your honor," Hyman walked back to defendants' table.

Jarboe called my boss, Police Commissioner Boyle, to the stand next.

"Mr. Boyle, when did your department fi rst become aware that, let me see," Jarboe looked into his trial notebook, "that Cardinal John Krol, Cardinal Justin Bevilacqua, Bishop Eugene O'Sullivan, and Archbishop John Pilarczyk were missing?"

The Commissioner tightened his black tie into the neck of his clean white shirt. Smart looking man, and he had the brains to match the look.

"It was," he said as his green Irish eyes closed, "it was on September 6, 1876, I think," he dropped his right hand off of is tie.

"And what happened on that date?"

"Mr. Bronstein came into headquarters to file a missing person report."

"And did you intake the report?" Jarboe asked, resting his elbow on this trial notebook.

"No sir," Boyle shook his head with his white haired comb over looking not so like he was some old man trying to cover up a bald spot, but a city slicker.

"Who took it in?"

"The sergeant on duty at the front desk at the time."

"But you received, you eventually received, the report?" Jarboe asked.

"Well," Boyle flicked off some dust from his black pants, "once the sergeant told me who was downstairs, cause he came right up after Bronstein came in, I came down to personally meet with Bronstein."

"About what time was this?"

"I'd say it was around lunch time on September 6, of this year."

"What did you, the police department, do after the missing person report was filed that date?"

"We do what we always do, we put up missing person posters all around the city of San Francisco, and even some on the outskirts of the city," he nodded proudly, "later that day and into the next."

"And the missing person poster, it was one of these," Jarboe went back over to his table, pulled out one of the posters, and showed it to Boyle.

"Yes, sir, that's it," Boyle said. Jarboe then passed the missing person sign to Hyman, the judge, and then to the jury. Th e sign had photos of the Archbishop and the missing priests, along with their names, and their last seen location, which was the address of Lenny's Fine Cuts.

"So you put these notices all around the city, and then what happened next?"

Looking up to the ceiling and thinking for a moment, the green-eyed police Commissioner said:

"It was about a week later, the following Wednesday . . ."

"That would be September 13, right?"

"Right, that sounds right," the Commissioner nodded. "So we had some people come in to the station to report about screaming they heard in or around the Lenny's Fine Cuts butcher shop on September 2–3, 1876."

"And that date is in or about the same date that the four men went missing, right?"

"Correct."

Hyman didn't do any cross of police Commissioner Boyle, and so Jarboe next called to testify some of the people from the community that had come into the police station to report the screaming.

"Just screaming, screaming, I head this screaming," Lila Khan testified as she covered her ears and tears started forming in her eyes.

"About what time was this, Mrs. Khan?" Jarboe asked.

Khan just sat at the witness stand and moved her body back in forth. Her hands were still on her ears.

"Mrs. Khan, could you please take your hands from your ears, you need to listen to my questions," Jarboe leaned over the wooden bannister separating him from her.

"I drop them, I drop them," she said with a thick Arab accent, tears still forming in her eyes.

"Bailiff, could you give me something I can give to her?" Jarboe nodded to Khan, at which point the bailiff brought over some paper to wipe away her tears, and Jarboe handed the papers to Khan.

"Thanks much," she said as she drenched the paper with her tears.

"Now, Mrs. Khan, about what time did you hear the screaming."

"It was something like, it was something like, 4:20 in the morning, cause my son, Imad, was crying when he hearing this noise."

"And where did you hear the screaming coming from?"

293

"It sounds like it was comes from the area across the street."

"Across the street from where?"

"From my apartment, the place I live with my husband, and two kids," she said as she wiped her tears.

"And what store is across the street from your apartment, Mrs. Khan?"

"The butcher place, is called, what is called," she looking down to do some thinking.

"Lenny's Fine Cuts?" Jarboe asked.

"Yes, this it," she nodded a yes.

"Were your windows open in your apartment?"

"Yes, this how we get the breeze, we get the winds coming from the bay this way."

"How long did the screaming last for?"

"Oh, oh . . . um . . . it was long time for us, it was not the quick screaming, not one scream, but many screams, of many difference mouths, it sounds like . . . oh . . . many different screams over this period, one begin, then stop, then another begin, that stop, then another begin," she started to have more tears again, "it was most evil sound I hear in my in my life," she then started crying in terror.

Jarboe leaned over to console her.

"It's alright, Mrs. Khan, please take your time, just take your time, and let me know when you are ready again," Jarboe stood there waiting patiently as he looked over his notes.

She wiped more of her tears away, stopped her crying, and then sat straight.

"What did your kids do when the screaming started?"

"They came into my bed where I sleep with husband, and the kids were crying on my chest, just crying, and so I holding them close to my chest when I hearing this screaming, when I hearing it."

"About how many people do you think was screaming?" Jarboe asked.

"Objection, your honor, calls for speculation," Hyman slowly got up.

"Overruled," Judge Parker quickly responded.

Hyman sat back down as slowly as he got up.

"Oh, it was more than . . . more than . . . more than one person screaming," Khan said with tremble in her voice.

"Two?" Jarboe asked.

"It sound to me like four or five men, cause they have different screaming, they all have difference in their yells."

After Jarboe finished up with Mrs. Khan, Hyman did a quick cross.

"Are you sure the screams came from across the street, Mrs. Khan?"

"I am quite sure, quite sure," she nodded.

"Do you know what an echo is?"

"I thinks so," she said.

"Reflection of sounds off material like brick and other hard surfaces, so that they come from one place but seem like they are from another place, understand that to be an echo?"

"Yes," she said.

"All around your apartment is brick, right, the walls of the stores across the street, the building you live in, the buildings next door, they are all made of brick and hard material, right?"

"Yes," she nodded.

"So these screams that you heard, the ones you said you thought were from across the street, they could have been echoes from somewhere else?"

She was tearing again, and said to herself, "those screams, those screams."

"Are you alright, Mrs. Khan?"

"Yes, just those screams, they make me . . . so . . . scared."

"I understand, I understand," Hyman said as he looked with sensitive eyes at her, shuffling his shit notes with his hands, a sly card dealer, "they would make me scared, too."

"Ok, ok," she said as she wiped more tears away from her eyes.

"So, back to my question, Mrs. Khan," Hyman kept going, a bull dog eating a piece of bone, "the screams you heard could have been echoes from sounds made somewhere else other than the butcher shop?"

"Yes, I thinks they could have," she nodded as she played with her wet tissue.

"And when you testified that you thought it was four to five screams, could have been one, echoed, through the crowded streets from around where you live, that industrial part of San Francisco, isn't that so?"

"It sounded like many screams of the many men," she said with worry.

"It sounded like that, but, remember, an echo makes one noise sound more like many, just as a rock drops in the calm water and makes many waves, you see?"

Khan sat there for a moment thinking.

"I guessing this can be what is happening, I guessing, thinking, this is the possible situation," she nodded. "It just the sounds of that noise, is up here," she pointed to her head, "and I can't get this things out, can't get out," she started crying again.

"Mrs. Khan," Hyman leaned over towards the witness and calmly said, "it's alright, we are done, you don't need to talk about this any more, you are free to go," at which point Judge Parker also said, in a sensitive voice to the crying woman, "thank you for your testimony, Mrs. Khan, you are free to go."

Then tear-soaked Khan got up from the witness stand, drying her eyes, and walked slowly towards the aisle as Jarboe called the next witness, an old Irish Catholic woman who had also made reports of hearing screams to the police. The audience watched the old lady walk to the witness stand, while I looked at Mrs. Khan walking down the aisle separating the courtroom into right and left.

Next thing I knew, I was wondering if I had some white lightning and didn't know it, cause I couldn't believe what I seen with my eyes.

Khan broke a small smile. One of those smiles a little child makes when he done something bad, but happy he done it, but don't want anybody to see. Kid keeps that smile between him and whoever else he doing the smile towards, while he sits and says how he is a "sinner," how he "repents," will do his confessions, needs the Lord in his life, and so on. I knew that smile that she made.

I knew it cause that little boy was me.

She cracked one of those smiles to me, I swear. Was over like a snap of a finger. Like those suds on the top of the Pacific Ocean, the smile was there, and then the smile was gone, before your eyes finish blinking. Then her dark mouth came back, the one of sad cloudy skies, before my brain was sure of what it had seen, my intuition leading the charge.

Couldn't control it, but when I think I saw what I saw, I pictured her and her husband, dressed in some fancy outfits, dancing on some wine grapes, drinking wine, and partying like it was some new years that they never thought they would see, laughing, kissing, dancing, drinking more wine, getting more wine juice on their bare feet, fancy clothes, but not caring. They would interlock their arms together, swing in a circle, laughing, and then interlock their other arms as they separate to do their own victory dance. That's because something just happened, that they were a part of, cause they heard it happen, which they had been dreaming of for a long time, and, finally, by golly, it happened: some Devilish priests finally partied with Lucifer!

Then I shook my head. It couldn't be.

But what if Khan's smile was real, and that dancing celebrating image my intuitive mind was real, too?

The old white haired Irish woman's crackling voice came in and took me out of my thoughts as she started testifying:

"I heard them, I heard them, I heard them screams,"

"And what did you do when you heard them, Mrs. Reynolds?" Jarboe asked.

"Oh, oh lord," she said pronounced "lord" like "lard." She started clutching the cross around her neck, rubbing the little Jesus hanging on the cross, like it was her lucky rabbit's foot. I supposed, in many ways, it was.

"I got up out of me bed, I went to the window, pulled the blinds up, and looked outside," she said as her white hair tussled off her small head, pretty like cotton blooming, her green eyes nicely placed deep in her wrinkled eye sockets.

"What, if anything, did you see outside, Mrs. Reynolds?"

"Didn't see nothing, mister," Reynolds finally took her hand off of her cross and put it underneath her behind. "Just saw an empty street, nothing on it but a little black cat that was doing his meowing, crawling around the night, but not seen nothing else other than that little black kitty, mister."

"About what time was this, Mrs. Reynolds?"

"It was let, me see," she took her hands out to put her pretty hair back in place, "about 4:20 or so, I thinks to me self."

"4:20 in the morning?" Jarboe asked as he leaned over the little wood separating him from the witness.

"Oh yes, oh yes, that was the time mister," she nodded.

"And how many screams did you hear?"

"Don't know, cause right after I looked outside, I didn't see nothing, and then I just closed the window, see, cause I don't want that type of racket making me not want to sleep," the 85 year old lady said as she tightened the bow on her Victorian dressed up white shirt.

"What did you do after you closed the window?"

"I took my black cat, Ace, back in my arms and we went to sleep."

"Could you tell from where the screaming was coming from, Mrs. Reynolds?" Jarboe asked.

"Well, it wasn't coming from my apartment building, I'll tell you that much. Must have been coming from outside, maybe across the street, maybe down the street, not too sure about that one."

"Did it sound like it was coming from across the street?" Jarboe asked.

"Objection, your honor, asked and answered," Hyman said.

"Sustained, counsel," Parker nodded. "Mr. Jarboe, she already answered your question, move on," Parker said with forceful voice.

"Yes, your honor," Jarboe said.

Jarboe finished and Hyman did a quick cross-examination of Mrs. Reynolds.

"Mrs. Reynolds," he said as he shuffled his notes, "it's Mrs. right?"

"Yes, sir, me husband just left this here world," she did a cross over her chest, "but I'll be a Mrs. until the day I die," she said with a firm eye and glance at Hyman.

He smiled and paused to take in her spirit.

"Thank you, Mrs. Reynolds," Hyman nodded and, said as he looked down on his notes, "you said you weren't sure about how many screams you heard, right?"

"That's what I said, mister," she said firmly.

"So it could have been one person screaming a few times?"

She sat for a second thinking, now with her hands clasped on her lap.

"Suppose that could be just what happened," she said calmly.

"Now, the screams," Hyman said now looking at her, "they were, what, how can I say this," he looked down at his ratty looking boots, "they were screams of pain?" He asked looking back at her.

She shrugged her shoulders.

"Could have been screams of pain, but, I reckon could also been screams of surprise, or maybe someone just having the time of their life on some white lightning," she smiled devilishly at Hyman.

He cracked a smile then asked:

"What do you mean when you say white lightening?"

"White lightening is what some of my family in Tennessee call moonshine, and I supposing I just taking the name with me west to here in California."

Hyman then said:

"Well, now, I'd want a taste of white lightening like that if it would make me scream with joy, too."

Th e audience chuckled, the judge stared, and Hyman moved on to his next question:

"So you are not sure, sitting her today, exactly what type of screaming it was, right, happy, sad, painful?"

"I'd be a fool to say I knew for sure, cause right aft er I heard those screams, and aft er I not see nothing outside, I just closed my window, then I don't hear nothing more aft er, see?"

"And then you reported the screaming to the police on about September 13th of this year, right?"

"Right," she said.

"Thank you, Mrs. Reynolds," Hyman said, "no more questions for this witness, your honor," Hyman moved waddled back to his table.

As Mr. Tommy Kelly, the 28 or 29-year-old owner of Lenny's Fine Cuts and Jarboe's next witness, walked to the witness stand, Mrs. Reynolds slowly walked down the middle of the courtroom. All eyes were on the boyish faced Tommy Kelly.

Who was classily dressed in white shirt, white tie, black suit, black vest, with his dark hair and tall, powerful, build.

Except for my eyes. They were on Mrs. Reynolds. Sometimes the fish go down stream — and I go up.

She was looking in front of her, walking, green eyes like they were behind blinders that horses have on their heads, so they don't look on either side. I was looking at her, cause I felt something, felt something like I did when I was the young man, speaking to the nun, saying one thing, thinking another, and she felt it.

Then it happened.

Her eyes strayed, the kid who goes to the right side of the tracks from the wrong side, or from the right side to the wrong side, or maybe just on the tracks. They caught mine looking at hers, two Christians maybe making a secret communion.

I felt a shiver in my body.

Reynolds's eyes were cold and mean. They reminded me of the cold and unforgiving San Francisco bay that Sergei the Siberian was swimming in when I met him that one day so many moons ago. Those green eyes looked at me, and I saw something deeper in them than I had originally thought. There was a mob of men standing behind Reynolds as she walked through that aisle. Some had green eyes just like hers, others had black eyes like the dark sky with no moon, no stars. Some had white skin like hers, others had dark skin like Vivaldi the Italian's, and still others had pitch-black skin. They had big hands, scarred bloodied faces, and they didn't flinch when they cut a man open to eat his fresh heart.

She looked away from me and then looked back in front her.

Then I heard Tommy Kelly testify:

"The store isn't open on Sundays."

"And so that would mean the store wasn't open on Sunday, September 3, right?"

"Yes, sir," Kelly nodded, his neatly parted hair fitting his put together thin framed I know how to cut meat look.

"Mr. Kelly, the police came to your shop after that date, right?"

"Yes."

"About when?"

"I think it was a Thursday, September 14th, I think was the date."

"And why did they come to your shop?"

301

"Well, they said that they had reports of screaming in the neighborhood on September 3, and that they were investigating those screams."

"Did they say why?" Jarboe asked as he tapped his fancy pen.

"Yes, sir."

"And what did they say?"

"That there was some missing men, missing priests from the Archdiocese of San Francisco, and that they were investigating their disappearance."

"Why did they want to inspect your butcher shop?"

Kelly shrugged his shoulders. They were tight shoulders, the type you get from cutting a lot of meat, leaning over and making sure there are no loose meat ends that will upset your customers. Could have seen him being a trapeze artist or gymnast in the Grizzly Adams circus that Amber partook in before her church going ways called her to duty.

"Said some folks had made reports that the last time that these men was seen was close to my butcher shop, on that Sunday when the shop was closed."

"Were you aware that there was a customer appreciation party held on that day, Sunday, September 3, in your shop?"

"No idea, sir. I was at home in Pacific Heights."

"Was anybody with you?"

"Yes, my butler, Winston Black."

"Alright sir," Jarboe said as he stopped tapping his pen, "so the police come to your butcher shop, and what happened next?"

"Said they wanted to take a look around the shop, and that I could either let them look around, or that they could come back with a warrant."

"And what did you say?"

"I welcomed them in, I didn't have anything to hide, so I welcomed them in, even offered them some water."

"So they come inside, the police that is," Jarboe said as he pulled out his pocket watch to check the time, closed it, then continued. "They come inside, was Mr. Boyle, the commissioner, with them?"

"Yes," Kelly nodded, "Boyle was the one asking the questions."

"What did Boyle and his men do next?"

"They started inspecting the doors to the shop, and searching around the sawdust floors."

"What, if anything, did they discover?"

Kelly had a sort of ashamed look on his face, cause when Jarboe asked the question, Kelly looked away for a moment, not really wanting to answer it:

"Commissioner Boyle told me that my shop, um, was broken into."

"And how did they know it was broken into?" Jarboe asked. "They checked the lock to the front door of the shop, and saw that there was someone who did some picking of it, cause there was some marks on it."

"You didn't notice those marks when you opened shop on Monday, September 4, did you?"

"No sir. Got there real early in the morning, and just went about my business."

"Now," Jarboe said as he looked through his neat, perfect, Ivy league looking trial notebook, "did your company, Lenny's Fine Cuts, employ a person by the name of Muddy Woodstock?"

"Never heard of that name before in my life, mister," Kelly said as he tightened his shoelaces.

"Are you aware that this Woodstock was meeting with the Archdiocese of San Francisco, representing himself as a sales person working on your behalf?"

"Today is the first time I became aware of that, mister, the first time." Jarboe took some notes in his notebook.

"So you have the front part of the store, right, where people come through the door, and then you have a counter inside where you take orders for meat?"

303

"That's right," Kelly agreed.

"And then, in the back of the store, is where you have your freezer, where you keep the meat that is shipped in?"

"Yes, sir," he nodded.

"Where do you get your meat from?"

"From farms in and about Northern California. We only carry local meat. Other places in San Francisco get meat from places in the Midwest, like from Chicago's meat yards, but we only carry the freshest items on the market."

"Alright, so how does this meat come into your shop?"

"Through the back door, behind that counter, behind the freezer, on the shipment deck, where our meat gets delivered by farmers, and where we ship meat out to our customers."

"Was the archdiocese of San Francisco ever one of your customers?"

"No sir, never," she shook his head.

"Going back to your store, sir, what else did the police discover when they did their inspection that day?"

"Boyle had is men look through the saw dust on the ground, all through the store, and they found little pieces of gold."

"Were you aware that this metal was there before?"

"No, sir, no idea."

"And these pieces of gold," Jarboe went back to his table, put his hand into a paper bag, and pulled out some items. "Do these pieces of gold look like what they found?" Jarboe walked close to Kelly and held the pieces out in his hand.

Tommy Kelly inspected the pieces.

"Yes, that looks like what they found," Kelly confirmed, at which point Jarboe passed the pieces to Hyman, the judge, and then, once there was no objections, to the jury for them to inspect.

"Did you know what these pieces of gold where when they found them?" Jarboe asked.

"I thought they were from customers who lost their necklaces, but I didn't know for sure."

"Afterwards, after the police did some more investigation?"

"Yes."

"And did they tell you what they discovered those pieces to be?"

Kelly sat there. He froze. His spit was going throughout his mouth, and he swallowed it. I could see him do it, cause his Adam's apple, went up and down a few times, working over time, in his shiny muscled neck.

"Mr. Kelly?" Jarboe leaned closer to the witness.

"Yes, sorry," Kelly was taken out of his minute trance.

"Did the police tell you what they discovered those gold pieces to be?"

"Yes."

"And what did they say?"

"They said that, um," Kelly played again with his shoelaces, the thin baby faced man, looking lost for his words. "They said that the pieces were from . . . were from . . . necklaces."

"Whose necklaces?" Jarboe asked.

"From some of those missing priests," Kelly said softly.

"Sorry, sir, please speak up so that the jury can hear you."

"Yes, I said the police told me that they thought that those pieces of gold they found on the floor in the store were from necklaces that the missing priests wore."

"And how did they know that, did they tell you?"

"Yes, they said that a nun at the Archdiocese inspected the pieces, and confirmed that, once she put them together with other pieces that were found, that they were the gold chain necklaces, and gold crosses, that the missing priests wore."

The nun testified at the trial and said the same thing that the cops told Mr. Kelly.

"Did you know the Archbishop?" Jarboe asked Kelly.

"No sir," Kelly said with certainty.

"Know any of the missing priests?"

"No sir, no I didn't."

"Mr. Kelly, are you Catholic?"

"Objection, relevance," Hyman objected as he sat, don't do any caring for the judge's previous order to stand. Judge didn't seem to care, or maybe he did care but was too tried of telling Hyman to stand up.

"Overruled," Parker said, "please continue, counsel."

"No sir, I'm not a Catholic," he answered.

"Are you a religious man?"

"Brought up Catholic, sir, but I have become more of a spiritual man," Kelly looked above, "than a church going man."

"I see. But were you disturbed when the police told you what they found in your store?"

"Mister, I couldn't stop crying for a few days, was up for a few nights, couldn't sleep, just tossing and turning in my bed."

"Because you were sad?" Jarboe asked.

"Damned upset that some things like that end up in my shop because of some thieves using my name, my place," Kelly pounded his fist on the wooden witness stand, "a place my family had built from nothing, and these damn thieves come in and use my family's good name to commit these crimes," he stopped pounding, satisfied his feelings were known.

Jarboe thought for a moment.

"Did it surprise you, Mr. Kelly, when you found out who the police suspected of doing these deeds in your shop?"

"Objection, relevance, your honor," Hyman shot up, "whether Mr. Kelly was surprised is irrelevant."

"Sustained, counsel," Parker quickly said, "please rephrase your question, Mr. Jarboe." Hyman sat down, taking a minute, it seemed, to do so.

"Sure," Jarboe said calmly.

"Did you know who broke into your store, Mr. Kelly, when the police told you it had been broken into?"

"No, I did not," he said.

"Eventually, did the police tell you who they suspected of doing these crimes in your store?"

"Yes," he said.

"And who did they tell you that they suspected?"

"Those people sitting right there," Kelly pointed over to the defendant's table.

"And do you know any of these people sitting at the defendant's table?"

"Never seen them in my life," he shook his head.

"Do you know of anybody who knows these people?"

"No sir, I do not," he shook his head.

"Did the police explain why they suspected these people sitting at the defendant's table for doing this?"

"Objection, hearsay," Hyman said as he sat drawing on a pad.

"The police commissioner testified already in this trial, counsel, why they suspected Amber, Blue, and Shane of committing the fourth set of murders at the butcher shop, so I am going to overrule your objection, please proceed Mr. Jarboe," Parker softly said.

Nonetheless, Hyman marked his objection, likely for appeal.

"I'll make my objection standing to the rest of this man's testimony, your honor, about what the commissioner told him, and on the further grounds that both Mr. Kelly's testimony, and that of the commissioner, assumes facts not in evidence and is overly prejudicial, cause the things I know he is going to testify about have never been proved, so . . ."

"That's enough," Parker shot at Hyman, who sat down. "Please continue, Mr. Kelly," Parker said.

"The police commissioner said that that man," Kelly pointed to Blue, "had a criminal record, which included breaking and entering into homes by picking their locks back in Illinois, and that the same things were done here."

"When you say that man, you mean Mr. Hardin, Mr. Blue Hardin, correct?"

"Yes, sir, that's right," he nodded.

"And the criminal record said what?"

"That this man, this Hardin man, knew how to pick locks, pick them good, without anybody hearing a thing, seeing a thing, cause he did the picking in the pitch black dark of the night," Kelly said as he remembered what the Commissioner told him.

"Any other reason why the police suspected those three defendants sitting over there?"

"Yes sir, the Commissioner said that that man," Kelly pointed towards Shane Egan.

"Let the record reflect that Mr. Kelly is pointing towards Defendant Shane Egan," Jarboe said.

"The record has been so noted," said Parker. "Please continue," he said to Kelly.

"Right, so, the Commissioner said that that man had a history of violence, too, and just, well," he looked outside the courtroom, not seeming to say what he wanted to say, "had done real horrible things to people, that his crime family done to people," Kelly said.

Hyman shook his head as he sat. "Ridiculous, this is all hearsay, what a joke," I could hear him say as he drew.

"One more like comment that, counsel, and I'll hold you in contempt," Parker shot at Hyman. Hyman nodded defiantly at Parker. "Please continue, Mr. Jarboe."

"Thank you, your honor," Jarboe said proudly as he looked over to Hyman.

"And what about Defendant Amber Francis, why did the police suspect her, too?"

Kelly shrugged.

"Commissioner said she had some of the same history, history of violence, that these others had hangings and what not, so I reckon that the police thought these three people were imposters in God's clothing doing the Devil's deeds," Kelly looked back up at Jarboe with anger, "all in my damn shop!"

"I understand your frustration, Mr. Kelly, I really do, but please refrain from using profanities in the courtroom," Parker looked down and said.

"Sorry, your honor," Kelly said with a sincere tone to his voice, "I guess I get carried away with what these people did to my, well, what is the pride and joy in my life."

"Please continue, Mr. Jarboe," Parker said. Jarboe was looking over his notes, and I could see Hyman leaning back saying something to Amber and Shane. They were making hand gestures, deaf people who speak to one another in their own code. I wondered what they said, maybe Shane was saying: "You going to cook us some Lenny's Fine Cuts steaks, Benny, when we get out of here?"

Jarboe then interrupted my rambling mind:

"Mr. Kelly, I don't have any more questions for you, I thank you for being such a great witness for us, and, your honor, I tender the witness."

"Mr. Hyman, Mr. Hyman?" Parker said to the defendants' table.

Hyman inched to the witness stand, dropping and picking up some notes along the way. After some nice small talk with Kelly, Hyman got to his punches.

"You say you were sitting pretty at home when this party was thrown by the burglars at your store, right?"

"Yes sir," Kelly said.

"And you said that your butler, Winston Black, was with you?"

"Yes," Kelly nodded.

"Did you know that Mr. Black cannot be found?"

"What do you mean he can't be found?"

"My investigator, Mr. Wu, tried to track him down, and it seems that he has left the state, without any forwarding address."

Kelly looked surprised, his face twitched, his eyes flickered.

"Well, I," he adjusted himself in his seat, "I don't know anything about that."

"Is he your full time butler?"

"No. He only works when I request his services."

"And, on that day, that is Sunday, September 3, you requested Mr. Black's services?"

"Yes, the night before he came, and he stayed over night."

"When is the last time you had seen Mr. Black?"

"Just this past weekend."

"Alright," Hyman shuffled some notes in his hands, going from a smaller to a bigger knife, "were you were aware that Mr. Black's cousin, Ms. Elizabeth Black, wasn't aware that her cousin had been to your home that weekend, that is, the date of September 2?"

"I was not, but I don't think that is out of the ordinary, since his cousin didn't live with him."

"Did you know if they are, or were, close, Mr. Black and his cousin Elizabeth?"

"I was not," Kelly shook his head.

"Were you were that one of Ms. Black's neighbors, namely one Eddie Carlin, a local comedian, said that he would see Mr. Black visit his cousin on an almost daily basis?"

"Objection, calls for hearsay, your honor!" Jarboe barked.

"Overruled, counselor," Parker shot back, a slap of the back of his hand. "Please continue, Mr. Hyman," Parker said.

"I was not aware of what Mr. Carlin saw, sir," Kelly said in response to Hyman's question about the butler's cousin's neighbor.

"Does that fact, that they saw each other almost every day, make it more or less likely that Winston's cousin, Elizabeth, would know about her cousin's whereabouts on September 3?"

Kelly looked uncomfortable now. He leaned forward when he adjusted himself in his seat, and looked away from Hyman, outside, into the California sun, to the trees, anywhere but at Hyman.

"Reckon it would make it more likely," Kelly looked back ay Hyman, "but I'm still telling you, sir, that I was at home on

310

September 3, and I can get some neighbors who saw me that day to tell you the same," Kelly pounded his hand on the wood.

"No need, Mr. Kelly, no need," Hyman used his midget like Jewish man's hand to waive the taut muscled Kelly off. "Now, have you ever been married?"

"Objection, relevance," Jarboe the white stallion shot up.

"Overruled," Parker said.

"No, I haven't," Kelly answered.

"Have any girlfriends in your life right now?"

"No sir, I don't," Kelly said.

"You get the *San Francisco Chronicle*, don't you?"

"Yes," Kelly nodded.

"So you were aware of the January 8, 1876 article in the Chronicle titled *Underbelly of the Catholic Church*, right?"

"Yes."

"How did that make you feel?"

Kelly stared at Hyman.

"Upset," the lien baby-faced young man said to the slightly overweight pothole faced lawyer with whiskers.

"You went to catholic school, didn't you, Mr. Kelly?"

"Yes," he nodded.

"But you aren't Catholic?"

"No."

"Your school was in St. Mary's Parish, right?"

"Yes," Kelly nodded.

"Did you know of any of the 19 dead priests?"

"No," Kelly said.

"Are you aware that Fathers Ricardo Aube, Roger MacRae, and Gordon Fortier, three of the dead priests, were priests at St. Mary's Parish?"

"I am not," Kelly shook his head.

Hyman shuffled through more of his notes.

"One more question, Mr. Kelly. Have you ever struck anybody violently?"

Kelly stared again at the mosquito that was Hyman.

"No," he shook his head finally.

"Do you remember a man named Adolf Peron?"

"No," he said.

"You don't recall being convicted for battering and assaulting Mr. Peron, almost to the point where he choked on his blood, after one of your men said he was the one who stole one of your horses."

Anger appeared in the young butcher's eyes. He just stared, and stared, and stared at Hyman.

"Mr. Kelly?" Hyman asked.

"He had it coming," Kelly finally said.

People in the audience started whispering.

Hyman smirked.

"Now," Hyman switched to another note, "you said you never knew Muddy Woodstock, the Cockney accented salesman, who said to the Archdiocese that he worked for Lenny's Fine Cuts, right?"

"I don't know that man, never met him," Kelly said.

"Did you know that, from August 11 to September 9, this fancy dressed Muddy Woodstock got the Archdiocese to buy beef, supposedly from your butcher shop?"

"No," he shook his head, now with his arms crossed, "I did not know that."

"Did you have any missing beef during that time period?"

"I did not."

"Were you aware that the beef which was delivered to the Archdiocese during this period was, according to Buck Owens, a meat purveyor from Salinas, California, the same as the type of meat that you all sell?"

Mr. Owens later testified that he tasted some of the meat which was delivered to the Archdiocese, compared it to some of the meat sold by Lenny's Fine Cuts, and found them to be the same grass fed beef. According to Mr. Owens, Lenny's Fine Cuts is the only shop in San Francisco that carries grass fed beef from local farms   312 around the Bay Area, whereas other ships in San Francisco only carry industrial corn fed beef from the Midwest.

"I am not aware of that," Kelly leaned forward and said, now with his arms crossed even more.

"No more questions, your honor," Hyman said as he walked back to the defendant's table.

A dirty blond haired twenty-one year old was Jarboe's next witness. As the stoned looking blond walked to the front of the room, the dang bad smell from his soiled white dress shirt, faded black country tie, black jeans, and dirty bare feet, which looked like they had stepped on cow shit, horse shit, and dog shit, crawled up and trespassed into my nose.

"What is your name, son?" Jarboe asked the dirty blond stoner.

"Yea, um, yea, my name is Willie . . . um . . . yea . . ." the boy said.

He didn't look like he knew why he was there. Judging from the scars on his face, and the deep scratches on his hands, maybe it was because he did too many daredevil moves — flips into a lake, jumping from horse to horse, getting thrown against the rocks under the ocean.

"Son, what's your last name son, your last name?" Jarboe leaned over and asked with his serious look.

The young buck looked down at his scarred up hands.

"Oh . . . yea . . . so . . . my last name is Kraus, yea, Kraus it is, mister lawyer," the long-haired Kraus nodded to the serious looking lawyer.

"Thank you, son, now I understand that you are the man who does the intake of all packages, shipments of food and the like, into the Archdiocese. Is that right?"

"Yes, mister lawyer," Kraus said as he caressed his dirty feet.

"Please just call me Mr. Jarboe, son."

"Yes, Mr. Jarboe," the young Kraus did a salute with his right hand to the lawyer.

313

"You working on the dock, in the back of the Archdiocese, right?"

"Yes, Mr. Jarboe," Kraus said like a parrot.

"So you worked on Fridays, right, at the in take dock, during the months of August and September of this year?"

"Which intake dock, I mean, um," Kraus said slow, "like the one over in the wharf, where the fisherman come in from the bay, cause, you know Mr. Jarboe, I work . . ."

"Son," Jarboe said with some frustration, "I mean that one at the Archdiocese.'"

"Oh, yea, yea, that one, that's right," Kraus said as he pushed his long hair back, showing more of his sandy-white Polish skin. "Th at was me, working the dock, yep, I was there Mr. Jarboe, was there that day," he said.

"Thank you, son," Jarboe looked down onto his notes. "Now, going back to Friday, September 8th of this year, did you recall receiving some boxes in from a company called Lenny's Fine Cuts?"

"Wait, let me . . . let me," Kraus said as he looked up and played with his blond hair with brown strains, "yah, yah Mr. Jarboe, yah, totally."

"Yah, what, son?" Jarboe leaned over, the dentist fighting the tooth who wants to stay in the mouth.

"Yah, I remember some boxes from Lenny's Fine Cuts, cool boxes, they had this, like, um . . ."

"Son," Jarboe put up his right hand, "you answered my question, thank you."

"Anytime, Mr. Jarboe, I really like your style," the boy said as he did some admiring of the old lawyer's fancy suit, looking up and down at Jarboe, "love the suit, Mr. Jarboe, just love it, where, um," he looked down at his feet to take some dirt off his toe, "where can I pick one up like that," he said looking the finely dressed lawyer up and down.

"Well, much obliged," Jarboe said as the audience did some of their giggling in the back.

"Now, son, what did you find, if anything, in those boxes from Lenny's Fine Cuts?"

"Oh, man, just the best beef in the world, man, I mean, don't tell nobody," he leaned over and whispered to Jarboe, "but I took off a little thing for me and my old lady, you know, so that we could cook it up when we go to the sea, man, epic, epic beef," Kraus leaned back with a proud look on his face.

Jarboe was downright angry looking at Kraus putting in answers to questions that Jarboe didn't ask.

"Son, I mean, did you find anything out of the ordinary that day, other than beef, in those boxes?"

"Oh, yea," Kraus snapped his fingers, "that's right, that stuff , totally, yea, um, so, I opened up the boxes, you know, in the morning, and, man, I was excited, cause that was like the best beef me and my old lady ever tasted," Kraus slapped his knee, "but, man, I saw something weird, and I had to look, you know, like, um, twice, cause it was like, so weird."

"What, son, what was so weird?" Jarboe asked eagerly.

"Saw these, um, what they called, yea, that's what they were, um, those things, what they called, yea, pieces of like a gold neck . . . lace . . . and what looked like . . . what the pope . . . that guy . . . you know . . . wears around his . . . neck . . . yea, that's it, like a piece of a gold cross or something, weird huh?"

Jarboe ignored Kraus.

"And those pieces of gold were in the shipment from Beefy Time on September 15th, right?"

"Yah, yah, that's right mister lawyer."

"Right son, right," Jarboe was now pushing his pen hard on his trial notebook, "so what did you do with those pieces of gold necklace that you found?"

"Gave them to what's his name, that fat . . . guy . . . yea, Bronstein . . . dude . . . Bronstein, gave them to him, that's what I did, right after I found them that morning."

"You mean the morning of Friday, September 15, right?"

315

"That sounds right to me, mister, yea," Kraus nodded slowly.

"Are these the pieces that you found that day," Jarboe held up some pieces of gold in front of Kraus.

"Yah, yah, that's them, that's totally them," Kraus said slowly as he pointed at the pieces, like he was seeing them for the first time, "how did you get those?" Kraus asked with wonder.

Jarboe introduced the necklaces into evidence at that point, passing the pieces to the judge, Hyman and jury, with no objection from Hyman.

At that point, Jarboe closed:

"Thank you, son, for your testimony. That's it for this witness, your honor," Jarboe said as he walked back to his table.

"Your honor, your honor," Kraus asked while Parker wrote some notes, "can I take off now, I mean my old lady is waiting for me," Kraus looked out into the audience and blew a kiss to a wild looking pretty blue eyed California bred blond girl around his age. She looked like she spent her time with Kraus at the beach, running in the mountains, partying.

"Not so fast, son," Parker looked down at Kraus. "Mr. Hyman, do you have any questions?"

There was silence as Hyman spoke to Blue.

"Mr. Hyman, Mr. Hyman," Parker slammed his judge hammer, "do I have to hold you in contempt?"

"Sorry, so sorry, your honor," Hyman gathered some more of the notes together, walked up to the witness stand, and started spreading them all along the wooden fence. He then asked:

"Mr. Kraus, isn't it true that you served time in, let's see," Hyman looked down at his notes, "juvenile hall for six months for selling moonshine in high school?"

"Objection, relevance, your honor!" Jarboe shot up.

"Overruled, may go to credibility," Parker said. "Please continue, Mr. Hyman," the judge said.

"Mister, mister," Kraus shook his head and put his hands over his eyes, "that was like, um," he started counting on his fingers when he took his hands off his eyes, "like three years ago."

"Thank you, Mr. Kraus," Hyman nodded. "Now, you had a bank account that the police seized," Hyman looked down, "with some $5,000.00 or so in it?"

"Man, I mean, this was like, total like, dinosaur history," he looked outside.

"So it's true?" Hyman asked.

"Yea, man, it's true, but so what?" He looked back at Hyman.

"Did the police not also confiscate, let me see," Hyman looked down at his notes, "six Colt .45 revolvers, sixteen twelve gauge shot guns, a hatchet, and, let me see here," Hyman was looking at the back side of his note, "40 sticks of dynamite?"

"Man," Kraus leaned over, "man," he leaned over further, "that was like, totally, like 100%, not 50%, or even 99%, but 100%, not my stash," Kraus then sat back in his chair. "That was like totally this guy's stash that I was just holding for him, cause he was on business, like, what was it," Kraus looked up, "like out of the country or something."

"But they found those weapons in a barn that you had paid for, right?"

"Yah, yah, man, but that stuff was like totally not mine," Kraus said.

This kid, in business like that, I couldn't believe it, to be honest. He didn't look like he could tie his own shoes, and storing a bunch of hard-core firepower was, for me, just a fantasy, the way he looking and smelling.

"Right, right, kid," Hyman waived his hand, as you would to your grandmother when you don't want to listen to her, "now," Hyman looked down at his wrinkled note. "You mentioned an old lady earlier, right?"

"Yes," Kraus said, now sitting low in his chair.

"Is her name Rose, what is it," Hyman looked again, "Rose Burns?"

"Yah, man, yea, but, like," he Kraus leaned over, "how did you know that?"

"I have my sources," Hyman smiled. "So, about Ms. Burns, do you know where she went to high school?"

Kraus just looked at Hyman for a moment, a boy who doesn't want to leave the ocean.

"No," Kraus said.

"How old is Ms. Burns?"

"Let me see . . . I think she is like, well, like 19."

"How long have you been with her?" Hyman came back.

"Man, um, let me see," Kraus counted on his fingers, "like three years."

"And, for that amount of time, you have no idea where she went to high school?"

"No, mister, no clue."

I looked over to Rose and her chiseled jaw was chewing on some nuts she brought in a leather satchel that was at her side. She could have passed for Amber's cousin. Rose and Kraus must have spent time dazed and confused at the park, but she still looked like a white stallion racehorse, tall and powerful, and lengthy Kraus was quietly muscled the same way.

"Rose went to," Hyman now looked down at his notes, "St. Patrick's Parish elementary school, right?" Hyman pulled a longer piece of paper out of his bag of tricks. "Here is the graduation record for Ms. Burns," Hyman pushed the paper in front of Kraus's face, and then passed it around for Jarboe, the judge, and jury to see.

"Okay, alright, so what?" Kraus asked.

"Were you aware, Mr. Kraus, that Cardinal John Krol, who is one of the men who went missing on September 3, taught at that school for some time before becoming cardinal?"

Kraus was just staring outside, not listening to the doctor who was telling him things he didn't want to hear.

"Mr. Kraus, do you hear me?"

"Yea, yea, man, I heard you," Kraus looked back at Hyman with some surprising fire in his eyes.

"But I don't know who that father Krol man is," Kraus said, "never met him before, so I don't know nothing about no school he teaching at," he waved his long hair back, and pulled up his shirt sleeves exposing Japanese tattoos all over his upper wrist. It looked like they went up his whole arm cause I could see some peeking out from underneath his shirt around his neck.

Hyman just stood smiling at Kraus.

"No more questions for this witness, your honor," Hyman gathered his notes and did his penguin walk back to his table.

And then it was my turn on the witness stand.

CHAPTER TWELVE

TRUTH OR DARE?

"**S**ergeant Jasper Amos, do you know if any of the defendants personally knew Mr. Tommy Kelly, the owner of the Lenny's Fine Cuts butcher shop?" Jarboe asked.

Blue, Amber, and Shane all just stared at me as I sat in the witness stand. You don't need to choose a team when you sit in the bleachers and watch the game. You can be a critic, an analyzer, but not when you are in the hot seat, as I was.

Of course, Jarboe's question came only after the regular ones.

"Jasper Amos, Sergeant, San Francisco Police Department," I said when Jarboe asked me my title.

"In that capacity, Sergeant Amos, what were your responsibilities as they pertain to the allegations against the defendants?"

"I was sent to the Mission Delores as an undercover officer, wearing this priest outfit I'm wearing today, and my responsibility was to investigate who was responsible for doing these murders."

"And why did the police department send you to the Mission Dolores as opposed to another church?" Jarboe asked, leaning over his trial notebook, looking intensely at me.

"Cause we received a tip," I said.

"And that was the note, let me see here," Jarboe pulled out and read the original note that was left at the police station: '***Dolores*** is her name, and she kills with no shame, cause she thinks she is on a ***Mission***, but she is just a killer, and you had better get her.' Correct?"

"I reckon that is what the tip said," I nodded.

"Do you remember when that note came in?"

"It was a few days after the fifteenth priest was found dead."

"That was in or about of May 24 of this year?"

"Sounds right, yes."

"And when was it that you went undercover?"

"It was about June 8, 1876."

"Now, for these defendants sitting over there," Jarboe looked behind him, "when did you first meet them?"

"Didn't meet all of them at the same time, mister Jarboe, cause the first I met was Mr. Hardin, and that was not long after I got to the Mission."

"Alright, and who did you meet next?"

"Ms. Francis, and then Mr. Egan."

"And, after you first met these defendants, how often did you spend time with them after?"

"Well, let me see," I said out loud, thinking to myself, "I suppose almost every day, it was about every day that I saw them, cause we were in the same mission and all," I said.

"From morning to the evening, you mean, every day, all, day?"

"No sir, I don't mean that. What I was trying to say was that, you know, um," I nervously started to look over at the defendant's table.

"Sergeant Amos?" Jarboe caught my attention.

"Sorry, sir, sorry," I said. "What I was trying to say was that we didn't sleep far from another, and, when we were awake, we usually had food in the mess hall and all, then made plans for the day."

"So you didn't spend all day, every day, with them, but enough time to get to know them over the six months you spent undercover, right?"

"Oh, yes sir, no doubt," I said.

"And did they ever suspect you of being an undercover police officer?"

"No sir," I said.

"Very good work, Sergeant Amos," Jarboe looked at me with approval in his eyes. "Now, let's go to September 9th of this year, which is the date on which there was an article in the San Francisco Chronicle about the suspicious disappearances of the four priests, including Archbishop John Pilarczyk, from the Lenny's Fine Cuts butcher shop"

"Alright," I said.

"On the morning of September 9th, where were you?"

"Early in the morning, I was in the Mission."

"So, when the paper came, cause I understand it was delivered to you all, where were you?"

"Was outside in the courtyard next to the mess hall, cause I was the one who would go and fetch the paper, and bring it back into the mission," I said. "Remember it was a pretty day out, and we usually ate outside, you know, breakfast outside on the bench in the courtyard when we had having nice weather and all."

"And who read that paper?"

"Usually me or Mr. Egan," I nodded over to Shane, who was staring at me with his green eyes.

"Would you read the paper out loud, or to yourself?"

"Usually read it to myself, but, when they were around, and when there was some article that either me or Mr. Egan thought the others would fancy, we'd read it out loud."

"So, on that day, Sergeant Amos, did either you or Mr. Egan read any articles out loud from the news paper?"

"Yes, yes, sir."

"And what article was that?"

"If I remembering right, it was the headline article."

"What was that headline, if you recall?"

"The headline was something like *Four Church Higher Ups Reported Missing*, and the byline was something like, 'San Francisco Archbishop and three priests mysteriously disappear — foul play suspected.'"

Jarboe went back to the defendant's table, went into his satchel, and pulled out a newspaper.

"Is this the article you are referring to?"

He held a copy of the *Four Church Higher Ups Reported Missing* article, dated September 9, 1876, in front of me.

"Yes, yes sir," I said as I reviewed the article in his hand. He passed the copies of the paper to Hyman, then to the judge, and then to jury.

"So, you are sitting on the bench outside the mess hall, and are the rest of the defendants sitting with you, too?"

"Yes."

"When you started to read the article, what, if anything, did they do?"

"They just kept eating."

"But, as you kept reading, what, if anything, did they start doing differently?"

"Yea, um, I was reading, and looked on over, and I saw, as they were sitting, eating, they were, well, they were doing some small smiling, like those smiles little kids make in the class room, you see, when they want to smile at something, and laugh at it, but the teacher doesn't let them."

"So the defendants seemed happy about the news?"

"Yes, yes sir, they seemed so."

"Now, Sergeant Amos, were the defendants looking at one another when they were smiling?"

"Not initially, sir, not initially, they were not," I shook my head.

"But then?"

"Well, as I read, I could see Mr. Hardin eating his eggs, you know, but then I saw him look over to Ms. Francis, and that's when I saw them smiling at one another, just smiling for a moment, but then they looked back at their food again.'"

"Did they do the smile again to one another?"

"Oh, yes, yes sir, they did it a few times to one another as I read the article."

"Okay," Jarboe made a note in his book, "and what about Mr. Egan, did he smile?"

"Yes, yes sir," I said, "he was eating some of his oatmeal, eating it like he did every morning and, as I kept reading on, I looked up, and seen him look at Ms. Francis and Mr. Hardin as they were looking at one another, and then that's when he, I mean Father Wolf or, uh, Blue, oh, um, Defendant Hardin, that's when he and Mr. Egan caught each other's eyes, and they smiled at one another."

"Did Mr. Egan also smile in the direction of Ms. Francis?"

"Yes, sir, yes," I nodded.

"As you read through the article, did you see any other behavior from the defendants?"

"Yes, yes, sir."

"What was that?"

"When I got to the part of the article about how these priests, and the Archbishop, was rumored to have these abusive histories with children, you know, I mean, what it is saying there in the article, Ms. Francis started to cry as she ate."

"Did the other defendants see this?"

"Not initially, but, then I saw Mr. Hardin moving his hand over and he just started to touch her arm, you know, rubbing her arm softly."

"Soft like you would sooth a baby?"

"You could say that, it was a nice touch."

"So Mr. Hardin is doing this, and what is Mr. Egan doing?"

"He stopped eating, could see he had some concern in his eyes for Ms. Francis."

"She kept crying?"

"Yes, sir, but the tears got worse, you know, she started to cry heavily, I mean outright crying, after the first tears came."

"And what, if anything, did Mr. Hardin do?" Jarboe asked me.

"He got up, wiped his face clean of the food, and walked over next to Ms. Francis, grabbed her arm, pulled her up to him so that she was now standing, and he put her arms around him."

"And did he hug her back?"

"Yes, sir."

"She cried to him?"

"More like cried on him, Mister Jarboe, cause her head was on his shoulder and, you know, by this point, she was just full out sobbing, making them noises you make when you cry."

"What did Mr. Hardin say, if anything?"

"Didn't say nothing, didn't say nothing, initially. Just stood there, holding her head, holding her head as she cried on his shoulder.

"What did Mr. Egan do or say, if anything?"

"First, he didn't do anything, just stopped eating and was looking over at them doing their hugging, but then . . ."

I paused.

I thought back to grade school in Virginia. I remember seeing the priests that I looked up to, the ones who would cheer me up when I was down on myself, the ones who were amazing baseball players but didn't flaunt it with us, the ones who helped local poor folks, the ones who told us dirty funny jokes, the ones I saw console widows and widowers when all their faith seemed to be lost. I knew great priests existed, because I knew the ones in my school were great. I wondered if these 19 dead priests in the *San Francisco Chronicle* articles, like *Underbelly of the Church*, were great like the ones I had seen, or if they were rotten like Hyman says they were.

"But then, Sergeant Amos?" Jarboe interrupted my thoughts.

"Oh, um, yea, so Mr. Egan, he was looking over at Mr. Hardin and Ms. Francis hugging, and, after we heard Ms. Francis sobbing for some time, Mr. Egan said the most, how should I say it, yea, p-e-c-u-l-i-a-r thing?"

"And what was that?"

"If I remembering right, it was something like, 'sister Amber, it is over, it is finally over.'"

"'Sister Amber, it is over, it is finally over,' is that right, that's what Mr. Egan said to her?"

"Yes, that's right," I answered.

Jarboe wrote down something in his notes, and then he looked up to me:

"And what, if anything, did either Ms. Francis or Mr. Hardin say?"

"She didn't say anything, cause she was just crying, but I heard Mr. Hardin, he said something like, as he softly touched her shoulder, 'he right, he right, it's all over, it's all over, sister, they done never coming back,' he said as he kept caressing her hair in a soothing way."

"Was she still crying?"

"Yes, sir, yes, sir."

"Did you keep reading?"

"No, when she started crying, I just sat there staring with the newspaper in my hand, and didn't know what to do, so I just . . ."

"Stared?"

"Yes, yes sir."

"What, if anything, did Mr. Egan do next?"

"He got up from his chair, dropped his eating spoon on the table, and, when he got to his feet, he said to Ms. Francis, in a soft voice, but it was a firm one, like when you trying to, um, let me see, how I gone to put this, when you trying to make someone you love, someone you caring about, feel better, let them know they aren't alone, cause sometimes words are like that soft comforting hand on your shoulder, and then Mr. Egan said something like, "sister, the lads are minced meat, and they never coming back again.""

The audience made the same noises of disgust to these words as when Jarboe used them in his opening statement.

"Did you take that to mean that Mr. Egan knew they were mince meat?"

"Objection, calls for speculation," Hyman said as he doodled.

"Overruled," Parker said. "Please answer, son," he said to me.

"Well, sir," I hesitated. "I suppose Defendant Egan was just trying to make her feel better."

"Why, in your opinion, was she so upset?"

"Objection, your honor, calls for speculation," Hyman said as he played with his pencil in his fingers, between the index and the middle, not bothering to stand up.

"Overruled," Parker quickly said, "he can give his impression."

"Not really sure," I shrugged, "I guess she had some down-right scared in her, mister, from what I was reading, just the terror of it all, you know, important powerful men going missing like that and all."

"Or scared that she would get caught?"

"Objection," Hyman got up the quickest I seen him get up the whole trial. "Assumes facts in his question that are inflammatory, prejudicial, and could be grounds for a mistrial!"

"Sustained, counsel," Parker said with what looked like some pause. "I suggest you refrain from asking such loaded questions for now on," he looked sternly at Jarboe, who made a snarky face towards Hyman.

"Understood, your honor," Jarboe finally said looking at the judge with some fake I'm sorry in his voice.

Judge Parker looked over to the jury.

"Ladies and gentlemen of the jury, I am going to instruct you to disregard Mr. Jarboe's last question, and his statement therein concerning the guilt of Ms. Francis, which, of course, you must assume is not proven unless and until the prosecution satisfies their burden."

The jurors sat and spoke to one another for a moment.

Jarboe looked over his notes, and, after he made some marks, started again:

"What, if anything, happened next, Sergeant Amos?"

"Mr. Hardin just kept hugging Ms. Francis and started rocking her a little bit from side to side, like you do to a baby when you trying to get it to sleep. And then her crying started to go down."

"What did Mr. Hardin do next, if anything?"

"As he was hugging Ms. Francis, he said in a quiet voice, 'Shane is right, sister, they is minced meat, good riddance,' and then he spit on the ground."

"What happened next, if anything?" Jarboe asked.

"Mr. Hardin said to her, with a quiet voice, like a whisper, 'spit like I done, spit like I done, it going to make you feel better sister Amber, going to make you feel better, going to make you feel better, going to make you feel better,' he said a few times as he closed his eyes and kept her head close to his chest."

"Did she spit?" Jarboe leaned over with his right eyebrow up, the man who wants to know things nobody else knows.

Didn't say anything cause I was thinking to myself: am I going to tell everything I know to Jarboe? Was there any reason for me to hold back, to not tell all the truth, not tell him everything

I have seen since I was planted in the Mission Dolores? But what if Hyman's side of the story was right?

"Yes, sir, she did spit on the ground," I finally said.

Hyman may be right, but maybe he was wrong. Even if he was right, how right was he? I'd have my chances now, with this direct, and even later in the trial, to spill the beans I saw that I should spill, to nobly dare what parts of me greatly thought. I just had to make sure my thinking was great — and that meant sifting the kernels of truth from the miles and miles of lies.

"So Defendant Francis spits on ground, she spits, right?"

"Yes, sir."

"Still crying?"

"Yes, sir, she was still crying."

"As hard?"

"A little less, I suppose."

"And then what did she do next, if anything?"

"She did the darn oddest thing," I thought back, "she actually broke, I couldn't believe this now, Mr. Jarboe, but she broke a damn smile, tears coming over her mouth, dripping down, and she broke a smile as she was still in Mr. Hardin's arms, looking over at me, and then putting her head back on his shoulder, crying slowing down."

I paused, closed my eyes, thinking back to what happened, and then, when I opened them, I said to Jarboe:

"Then she moved her head off Mr. Hardin's chest again, and she moved her boot, her dirty boot, over the spit like she was smothering a cigarette, not with a smile on her face this time, but an intense aggressive one, like she was killing the cigarette."

"What was Mr. Egan doing now?"

"He was just standing, looking concerned, with his arms crossed, but I could see he was breaking a smile, too, as he saw sister Amber smother the spit with her cowboy boot."

"And Mr. Hardin?"

"He just watched over Ms. Francis."

"What did Ms. Francis do after she smothered her spit on the ground?"

"She looked at Mr. Hardin, smiled the biggest smile, and then she just put her head back on his shoulder and started screaming. It was the screaming you scream when you make it big, like, um, gambling in Lake Tahoe, or something?"

"What did they do then, if anything, her and Mr. Hardin, after she did her joyous scream?"

"They went from hugging to dancing with each other. There wasn't any music, but they were dancing anyway."

"And Mr. Egan? What was he doing, if anything, when Mr. Hardin and Ms. Francis were dancing?"

"He started clapping, like we was at some state fair or something, first slow, cause they was dancing slow, but then, as they started to lock arms and do a celebration dance, Mr. Egan started to clap even faster now," I said as I pictured them in my head, remembering back, just as I pictured Mr. and Mrs. Khan dancing in their apartment that night when they heard the screams coming from the butcher shop across the street.

"Please tell the jurors, Sergeant Amos, what happened next?"

"Well, they were dancing, Mr. Egan was clapping, and I started clapping along, cause I didn't want them to think anything funny about me, and that's when Mr. Hardin stopped and said: 'this cause for a god damn celebration, I done going to get something to celebrate with.'"

"And did he?"

"Yes, sir. Brought back a bottle of white lightning, some moonshine he getting from I don't know where, and some glasses, pouring them for us."

"How did you know it was moonshine?"

"Cause the county I'm from in Virginia was the headquarters for moonshine, and I remember seeing my poppa with his friends sometimes drinking it out back while they smoked."

"Did you all drink this liquor together?"

"Yes, sir, we all stood, and did a toast."

"And what was that toast?"

"'No more suffering,' Amber said with a smile and a little bit of those tears still in her eyes."

Jarboe was now looking at his notes, making sure, I thought to myself as I sat there, that he was getting all he needed.

"Just a few more questions, Sergeant Amos, and then we are done," he said.

Jarboe looked up at me, with his eyes focused, and asked me the question I told you about earlier:

"Do you know if any of the defendants knew the owner of Lenny's Fine Cuts, that is Mr. Tommy Kelly?"

In just that moment, I remembered that I **had** seen this Tommy Kelly, the baby faced owner of the butcher shop, before. Didn't hit me when I saw him testifying earlier in the trial. But when Jarboe asked me the question, it was like one of those things, whether it is a whiskey, a cold wind, or a jump in the ocean, that makes you remember something you didn't remember before.

This is what I remembered:

The man whose head Shane was kissing in those photos that I found underneath his bed that day, you know, the day when I was searching for the shoe polish and also opened up that fancy Tiffany box full of photos, was this man, the butcher, Tommy Kelly.

As I sat in that steamy Mariposa County courthouse outside of San Francisco, I asked myself: So what do I say, oh great Lord of this world? Or is it Mother Nature? Or maybe Mother Nature and the Lord are together, and gave birth to this twisted world of Lucifer, where, according to what Hyman says, these dead men, of high priestly powers, these ordained for life kings, were doing Devilish things in God's clothes? **All** of it can't be made up. Maybe some of it was made up — but all of it?

Couldn't be so.

I didn't know for sure, but something inside said some of it could be true.

So I did what most of you would do, unsure of which way to go, which fork in the road to take, I did that hedge, like when you want to keep your dang options open. Didn't want to put the screw too tight into the coffin of the defendants sitting over there, cause, maybe, just maybe, when I heard Hyman's side of things, and his witnesses, I'd want to open the coffin back up — but if I screwed it too tight, I'd be unable to.

So I fudged my answers.

"Sergeant Amos, did you hear my question?"

"Yes, yes sir, I was trying to think, and the answer is that I don't think I recall ever seeing Mr. Kelly with any of the defendants."

Didn't bother me much that I fudged. That cause I'd seen Hyman's witness line up before the trial started. Knew that I'd have my chances to feed Jarboe everything I knew about them, make them look like liars. Plus, I could eventually tell all to Jarboe about Blue's cigar smoking that day in church, and Shane's under the covers relationship with Tommy Kelly, for the Jarboe's cross examination in the second half of the trial.

After Jarboe asked me some more follow up questions, it was Hyman's turn.

He didn't wear gloves.

"How could you see the defendants and their little smiles when you were reading that *San Francisco Chronicle* article?" Hyman asked as he held the lengthy article in front of me.

"Cause I was looking out of the corner of my eye," I said, "plus, I suppose that I stopped reading when I looked over to see them after Ms. Francis started crying."

Hyman looked at me without believing a word I said.

"Did you know, at the time that the newspaper article came out, whether the Devilish things they were saying about the

Archbishop and the three priests who went missing on September 3rd was true?"

"I did not."

"What about the evil things that the papers said these other priests did," Hyman made quotation marks with his index and middle finger for the word "priests." "Did you believe these evil things to be true?"

"I didn't."

"So you disapproved of the defendants' celebration?"

"Yes, whole heatedly, found it disgusting."

"Well now," Hyman pushed some of his ratty looking notes into a pile, cause they were the ones he went over already, then asked, "assume you believed that all of these evil things they say about the priests in here were true," Hyman pointed to the *Four Church Higher Ups Reported Missing* article. "Would you have disapproved of the defendants' celebration?"

"Objection, relevance," Jarboe shot up. "That's just completely irrelevant!"

"Overruled, counsel," Parker looked over to Jarboe. "Please answer the question, Sergeant Amos."

"Well, Mr. Hyman," I said as I changed my position on my seat, you know, pulling up my cowboy boots and just getting more comfortable on the hot seat, "I must admit, I reckon . . . I reckon . . . I would."

As the words came out of my mouth, some of the Catholic priests and nuns I'd seen during my stay at Mission Dolores, the ones who were "true believers" and thought all of the ungodly allegations against the church were made up, started yelling at me in my head:

"You going to hell, boy, thou shall not kill!"

"Remember the words of the Bible — why you forgetting those lessons!"

"Sinner, sinner, you approve of the work of the Devil!"

"Confession, confession, confession for you!"

But I didn't pay them as much mind. I had responses for them all from the Catholic priests and nuns who I came across that secretly celebrated the murders. Sick and tired of their faith being ruined by apparent priest transfers by some of those in the Vatican more concerned with form over substance, these insiders said:

"Look at what they have been doing, why shouldn't they be killed?"

"We aren't forgetting the Bible — these men are the ones who forget the Bible!"

"I approve of the Devil's dark work when it is God whispering in his ear."

"He has nothing to confess to you, cause if Jesus were alive, he would have been the pirate in the closet that did this slaughtering!"

Hyman then looked into my eyes, his pieces of paper, tigers, lions, and wolves, sitting at his side, ready to strike at me, when he asked: "So there is difference between celebrating an event that you approve of, and causing it, isn't that right, Sergeant Amos?"

"Yes, sir, that sounds right to me, I nodded."

"The defendants could very well have been celebrating the disappearances without having caused them, right?" Hyman asked, moving closer to his checkmate.

"Yes, that sounds right," I nodded.

"And that means, Sergeant, that by merely celebrating the disappearances," Hyman looked outside the courtroom window, like he wanted to be somewhere else, maybe with his son, and was just sort of cruising down hill during the trial, "that the defendants didn't necessarily cause them, isn't that right?"

He quickly moved his head to stare at me. Caught me off guard cause I actually was looking outside with him.

"Well, um," I adjusted myself in my seat.

I dared to fudge again.

"Mister, I don't see how they couldn't have been on this, when they said things like 'minced meat,' and why she would have been crying that way. Those facts wouldn't make sense if they weren't in on it."

Hyman just looked at me. I don't think he really cared that I fudged, cause he had more tricks up his sleeve for when it was his turn to present evidence to the jury.

"So," Hyman paused to think, like he was winding up his pitch, "are you saying Sergeant Amos, that you've never used the words 'minced meat' before without being involved in a murder?"

"What do you mean?" I asked.

"Son, haven't you ever heard someone saying, when they are asked if one baseball team is going to cream the other, say 'they don't have a chance, they are going to be minced meat.' Never heard that before?"

I sat thinking for a moment.

"I reckon I have," I nodded.

"Well, then, did the folks who used 'minced meat,' did they actually play in the game, did they actually do the mincing?"

"I reckon not," I said.

"So it's possible," he smiled that smart ass New York smile I'd seen him smile many times during the trial, "that Mr. Egan," he looked back at Shane, "was just describing to Ms. Francis what he thought happened to these men?"

"Objection," Jarboe shot up, "calls for speculation, your honor, and the question has been asked and answered already," he said with the pen in his hand.

"Overruled," Parker said quickly. "Please proceed with your answer, Sergeant Amos."

"I'm thinking, now that I am thinking about it, I suppose that it is possible, but this is just not likely mister, cause it was the way that they said it, you see, was, what they call it . . ."

"The circumstances?" Hyman asked in his smart ass way.

"Yes, sir, them things, the circumstances."

"That's fine son, but you have stated on the record that it is possible that Mr. Egan was just saying what he thought happened, not that he actually caused it, correct?"

"Yes, mister."

"Thank you," Hyman looked down onto his crumbs on the table notes.

He looked up at me.

"Sergeant Amos, you initially went undercover at the Mission Dolores on June 8 of this year, 1876, right?"

"Yes, sir, that sounds about right."

"And up until today, did any of the defendants know that you were a police officer?"

"No sir, absolutely not," I moved uncomfortably around in my chair.

"Now, son," Hyman paused for a moment, "did any of the defendants ever talk about any of these murders or disappearances in front of you between June 8, 1876, and now?"

I had to think about that one, going through all of the files in my mind.

"I reckon they didn't."

"From June 8, 1876 until now, did you actually see any of the defendants commit any of the crimes they are alleged to have committed?"

"What do you mean, mister, like did I see them hanging, cutting, bleeding, making mince meat of these poor men?"

"Yes, son, that's exactly what I mean. Let's be absolutely clear with each other," Hyman was leaning over:

"Did you ever see Ms. Francis hang any of the priests that she is alleged to have hung?"

"No sir."

"Did you ever see Mr. Egan cut up any of these priests he is alleged to have cut up, hang their parts up, and put their bodies in the San Francisco bay?"

"No sir."

"Did you ever see Mr. Hardin abduct the priests he is charged with abducting, cutting their bellies up like they say, and watching them, like some sick soul, as they suffered while he fed them?"

"No sir, I did not."

"And did you ever see any of these defendants," Hyman looked back to the defendants, "torture those four men in the Lenny's Fine Cuts butcher shop?"

"No sir, I did not."

"Did you see any of those four defendants smoke a cigar like the ones they found at these murder scenes?"

I paused to remember how to weasel out of a question while leaving the door open to answer it right later, and that is to use "I don't recall."

"I don't recall of seeing any of them smoke any cigars."

"Did you see any of them smoke cigarettes?"

I paused, acting like I had a hard time thinking about all those months.

"Not to my recollection," I said scratching my head.

"Sergeant, I thank you for your testimony today and as always, your honor," Hyman looked up at the judge, "I reserve my right to call the witness back to the stand should other evidence present itself that has not, up until now, either been produced by counsel for the prosecution, or which wasn't discovered as of yet."

"Duly noted, counsel," Parker, the white haired judge, said.

"Can I leave now?" I asked.

"Yes, Sergeant Amos, thank you."

"Your honor, the prosecution rests its case. Of course, we also reserve the right to call witnesses back to the stand if there is any new evidence that comes to light, but, as of now, we shall rest."

"Very well," I heard Parker say as I almost got to my seat on the bench behind the prosecutor's table, "ladies and gentlemen, this court shall be adjourned until Monday, at which point we shall reconvene at 9:00 a.m. for the case to be presented by counsel for the defense."

After I sat down, I felt something under my ass.

It wasn't my finger.

I pulled out a little white torn piece of paper that was on the bench under my right ass cheek. Written on it, in childish writing, like a five year old wrote it, was:

We knew, who you was, all along.

End of Volume I